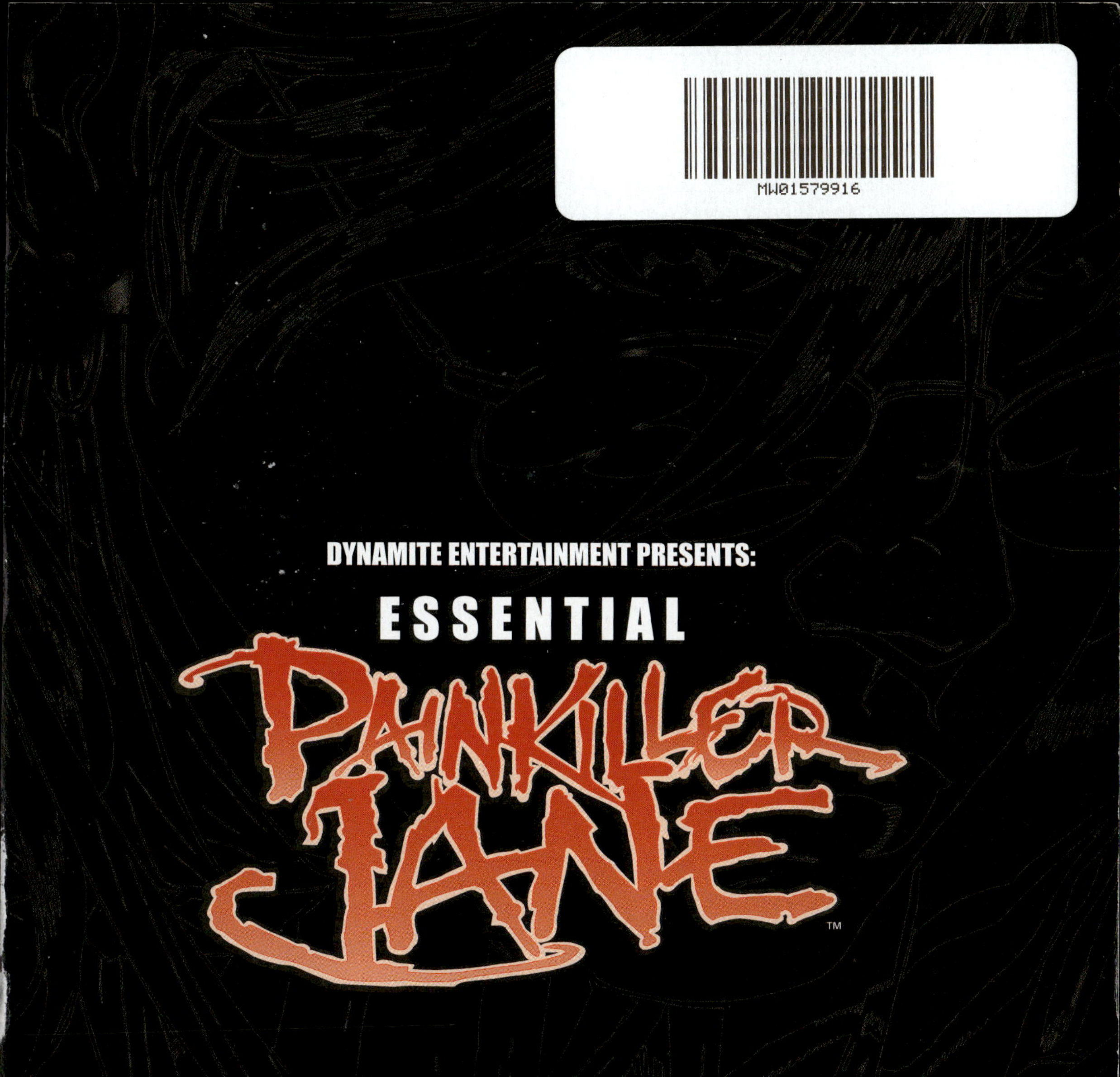

DYNAMITE ENTERTAINMENT PRESENTS:

ESSENTIAL PAINKILLER JANE™

STORY BY
**JOE QUESADA & JIMMY PALMIOTTI
BRIAN AUGUSTYN & MARK WAID**

PENCILS
AMANDA CONNER (Issue #0)
RICK LEONARDI (Issues #1-5)
ERIC BATTLE (Issue #5)

INKS
JIMMY PALMIOTTI (Issues #0-6)
KEN BRANCH (Issue #5)

COLORS
ELIZABETH LEWIS (issue #0)
BEN PRENEVOST (Issue #0)
ATOMIC PAINTBRUSH (Issues #1-5)
WILL QUINTANA (Issue #1)

LETTERING
**RICHARD STARKINGS
& COMICRAFT**

ORIGINAL STORY EDITORS
NANCI DAKESIAN (issue #0)
JUSTIN GRAY (Assistant Editor Issue #0)
LAURIE BRADACH (Isues #1-5)

PAINKILLER JANE CREATED BY
JIMMY PALMIOTTI & JOE QUESADA

DYNAMITE ENTERTAINMENT
NICK BARRUCCI — PRESIDENT
JUAN COLLADO — CHIEF OPERATING OFFICER
JOSEPH RYBANDT — DIRECTOR OF MARKETING
JOSH JOHNSON — CREATIVE DIRECTOR
JASON ULLMEYER — GRAPHIC DESIGNER

ESSENTIAL PAINKILLER JANE™ Volume #1. Contains material originally published by Event Comics as PAINKILLER JANE #0-5. First printing. Published by Dynamite Entertainment, 155 Ninth Avenue, Suite B, Runnemede, NJ 08078. Painkiller Jane ™ and © 2007 Joe Quesada and Jimmy Palmiotti. All Rights Reserved. "Dynamite," "Dynamite Entertainment" and its logo are ™ and © 2007 of DFI. All names, characters, events, and locales in this publication are entirely fictional. Any resemblance to actual persons (living, dead or undead), events or places, without satiric intent, is coincidental. No portion of this book may be reproduced by any means (digital or print) without the written permission of Dynamite Entertainment, except for review purposes.
For information regarding promotions, licensing and advertising please
e-mail: marketing@dynamiteentertainment.com
Printed in Canada.

First Printing
ISBN-10: 1-933305-97-5   ISBN-13: 1-781933-305974
10 9 8 7 6 5 4 3 2 1

To find a comic shop in your area, call the comic shop locator service toll-free 1-888-266-4226

INTRODUCTIONS

JOE QUESADA

With the production of a project like *Painkiller Jane*, there are so many people to thank. Lucky for me, Jimmy has already done the heavy lifting for both of us, so I'm going to take this opportunity to give thanks simply to two people.

First and foremost, the fans.

Thank you for all you've done for us over these wild and crazy years. Thanks for your support, love, hate mail, chocolates, handshakes, e-mails, bloggings, fan art, porn, beer, winks, wiggles, jiggles and kindness. You have all changed and enriched my life beyond anything I ever imagined.

Secondly, and most importantly, I want to thank Jimmy. Thank you for propping me up when I was about to collapse, for watching my back and covering my tracks and thank you for your undying friendship, that alone is a debt I will never be able to repay. Without doubt, our early collaborative partnership, to this day, remains the single most important and formative event of my entire professional career. Those early days were incredibly exciting, we both went through a lot and made most of it up as we went along, heck, that's what made it fun. Like the day Jimmy called me with a name for a character. He said, "Painkiller." I said, "add Jane at the end." Jimmy said, "cool!" I immediately put pencil to paper and within fifteen minutes, Jane lived.

That story's absolutely true, but it wasn't unique for us, that's just how stuff happened every day.

Jimmy says "Painkiller," I say "Jane."

Ain't that somthin'!

See ya in the funnybooks,
Joe Quesada
Somewhere in New York City

JIMMY PALMIOTTI

Some of the best ideas come out of frustration.

I just came back from the set of the *Painkiller Jane* TV series being shot in Vancouver and proofed the very book you have in your hands. What a trip it is looking back on all these issues…a trip back to a simpler time in my life. By simpler, I don't mean better, just less hectic, but let me explain.

It all started with Event Comics: a company born on the idea that Joe Quesada and I can do it better than the big boys. Better than DC, better than Marvel…even better than those west coast clowns [it's an east coast vs. west coast thing, lol] that formed Image. Better stories, better art, better production and eventually, better sales. The trick was that we believed in each other's talent and in each other and collectively, we could do anything we set our minds to do.

We did well for a while…*Ash*, our primary creation about a down to earth fireman superhero did great, made the covers of the trades and sold like hotcakes. Sure, we might have been ripped a new hole here and there by the non-believers or the guys who actually knew how to tell a story, but we didn't care…nope, not us. We were brilliant and would launch some more titles because we could. Hell, we got a million character ideas. Let's launch a book about a bratty kid and his robot dinosaur called Kid Death and Fluffy! Here's another one, let's launch a series about a gang of girls running the New York underground and base one of the lead characters on my ex girlfriend and call it *22 Brides*. Hell, let's go against the grain and create a female character that isn't sporting a double "d" figure, with so much attitude she literally doesn't understand the phrase "quit while you are ahead" and for the fun of it, let's name her *Painkiller Jane*.

Yeah, so there we are…two guys from New York, creating what we felt were the beginnings of an empire. Things were going well…we hired help for the publishing end, got some guest creators involved and even got a call from Hollywood interested in one of our characters. Looking back, that was the beginning of the end for Event Comics in a lot of ways. Once we took the bait and sold Ash to DreamWorks [yes, they still own it and we have heard there is something once again inthe works] things changed. Production schedules were broken, people who committed to publishing with us flaked out and it got worse from there. It was a case of too much too soon…but we learned a boatload…really.

continued

It was a great and fun time for us both. Take a good look where Joe and I are now and you can see every mistake and success put into play in our day to day careers. Hell, Joe is the Editor in Chief of Marvel Comics for Pete's sake!

Ok, now here we are, simpler times...a collection of all those Event PKJ books being put out by Dynamite Comics. It was an easy deal to make since Dynamite Comics is owned by a personal friend of ours, Nick Barrucci. We have known Nick for so long that he actually was a cast member in our books, along with a lot of our other close friends along the way. You will also notice the credits page inside gives credit to a whole bunch of talented people. Most important I feel are Brian Augustyn and Mark Waid...the only people we trusted with Jane other than ourselves to write...something that is really hard for any creator to do with something so personal. Special thanks go out to the ever vigilant Laurie Bradach, our editor and gate keeper who kept just about every person in line for the years she was with us...not an easy job for anyone, trust me, and more props for Nanci Dakesian [now Nanci Quesada] and assistant editor Justin Gray on the *Painkiller Jane* #0 issue.

We got really lucky with the artists on this series...Amanda Conner, Rick Leonardi and Eric Battle...three dynamic storytellers that have made a career way beyond their work on Jane, and the list goes on...all super talented people that believed in the character. Give that credit page a read, we couldn't have asked for a finer crew. You might also note that there seems to be two origins of Jane in the book as well. Trust us, the *Painkiller Jane* #0 is the right one...the one we actually put a lot more thought into once we figured we didn't want to tie the titles too closely together.

So here we are today, collection in hand, two hour movie on the Sci-Fi channel and an hour long, 22 episode series on the way staring the super talented Kristanna Loken and a supporting cast of future stars, and a new series of books on the way. All in all, Jane has come a long, amazing way and the only thing more thrilling for me is what the future holds for our gun toting creation. Thanks again for everyone's support.

Jimmy Palmiotti
Safety Harbor, Florida

This book is dedicated to Lillian Palmiotti, the most wonderful, loving mother any son could ever wish for. Until we see each other again, you will stay in my heart forever.

NICK BARRUCCI

I first met Joe Quesada and Jimmy Palmiotti at one of the very first San Diego Comic-Con's I attended. Joe was working on *Azrael* and if memory serves, Jimmy was inking quite a few high profile Marvel books. The pair of them, individually, were vibrant and exciting creators, but when you put them together, you had a true Event (A little bit of foreshowing there). The three of us found common ground in the comics we loved and from that point forward, through it all, have remained friends through the years.

And from there you know the story, how Joey and Jimmy started their own publishing company - Event Comics - after success after success at DC and Marvel (and a few other publishers as well); From Event they started Marvel Knights, a renaissance at Marvel Comics, which helped raise the bar in terms of quality at the House of Ideas. There they revived *Daredevil*, the *Punisher*, the *Inhumans* - turning out an Eisner Award winning title, quite a feat for Marvel at the time - and more. Together they blazed a trail, and working together they created magic.

And now you're saying, "thanks for the history lesson, Nick, but what about *Painkiller Jane*? What does any of that have to do with this massive and definitive edition I hold in my hands?"

Well, what these guys did for Marvel and for DC, and for every book they worked on, they also did for themselves - created strong and lasting characters. While at Event, Jimmy and Joe created *Painkiller Jane:* one of the most compelling, independent comic characters ever. Now, Jane is truly a unique character with a foundation so strong that she's survived not only the ups and downs of two decades in the comics market, but re-emerged and stars in her own TV show on the Sci Fi Channel.

When Jimmy and Joe were looking for a publisher for their creations, we set aside friendship and got down to business. We made a play for the collections of the older material as well as new comics starring Painkiller Jane, and we got lucky. Out of all of their options, friendships aside, Jimmy and Joey chose to make theirs Dynamite.

And now, in many ways, Dynamite has become the Godfather of *Painkiller Jane* -- one of the most exciting characters in comics. But enough of the history lesson, take a look and see for yourself, because it's here that Jane's story begins.

Nick Barrucci
President and Publisher,
Dynamite Entertainment

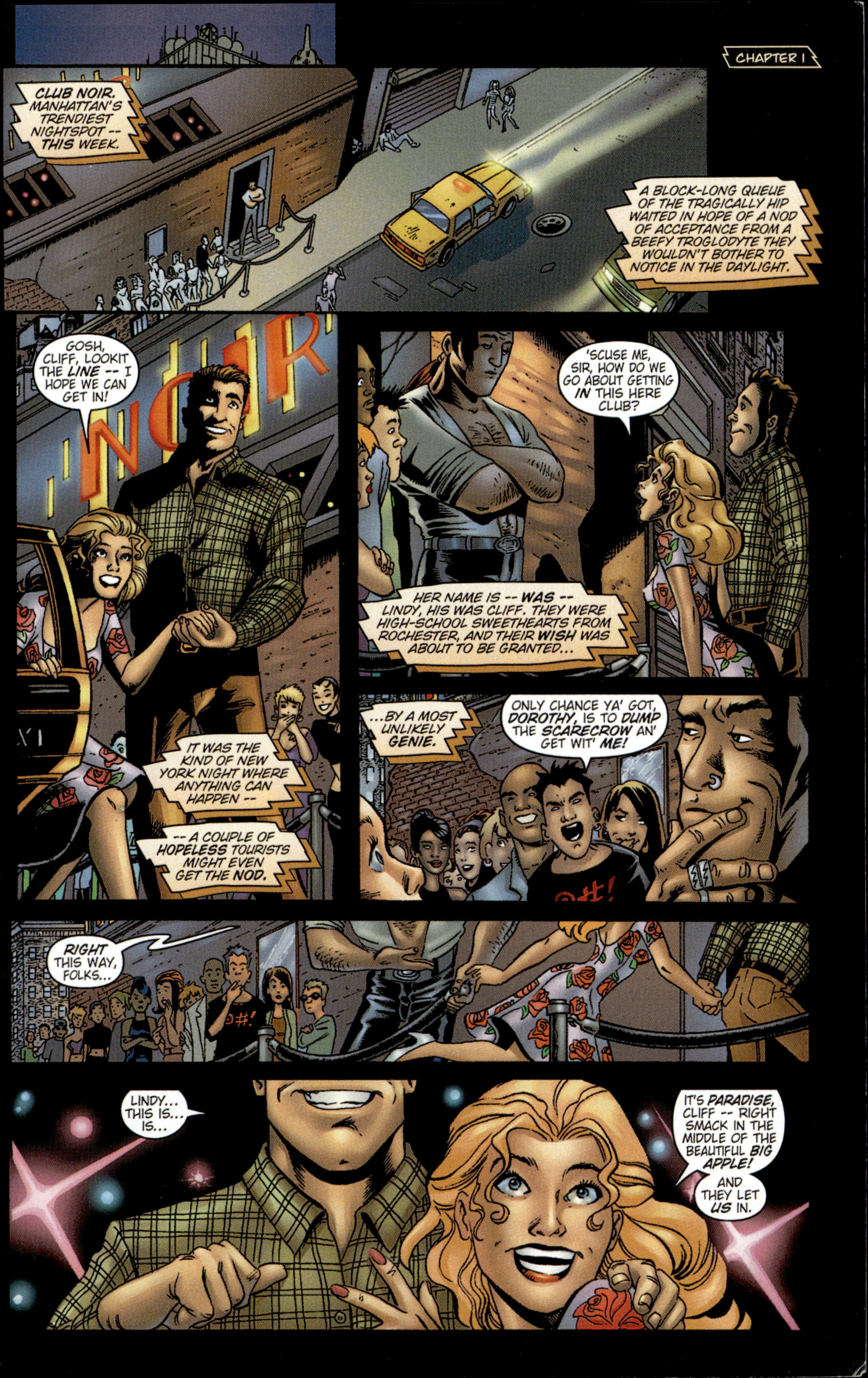

CHAPTER I
CLUB NOIR. MANHATTAN'S TRENDIEST NIGHTSPOT -- THIS WEEK.
A BLOCK-LONG QUEUE OF THE TRAGICALLY HIP WAITED IN HOPE OF A NOD OF ACCEPTANCE FROM A BEEFY TROGLODYTE THEY WOULDN'T BOTHER TO NOTICE IN THE DAYLIGHT.
NOIR
GOSH, CLIFF, LOOKIT THE LINE -- I HOPE WE CAN GET IN!
IT WAS THE KIND OF NEW YORK NIGHT WHERE ANYTHING CAN HAPPEN --
-- A COUPLE OF HOPELESS TOURISTS MIGHT EVEN GET THE NOD.
'SCUSE ME, SIR, HOW DO WE GO ABOUT GETTING IN THIS HERE CLUB?
HER NAME IS -- WAS -- LINDY, HIS WAS CLIFF. THEY WERE HIGH-SCHOOL SWEETHEARTS FROM ROCHESTER, AND THEIR WISH WAS ABOUT TO BE GRANTED...
...BY A MOST UNLIKELY GENIE.
ONLY CHANCE YA' GOT, DOROTHY, IS TO DUMP THE SCARECROW AN' GET WIT' ME!
RIGHT THIS WAY, FOLKS...
LINDY... THIS IS... IS...
IT'S PARADISE, CLIFF -- RIGHT SMACK IN THE MIDDLE OF THE BEAUTIFUL BIG APPLE!
AND THEY LET US IN.

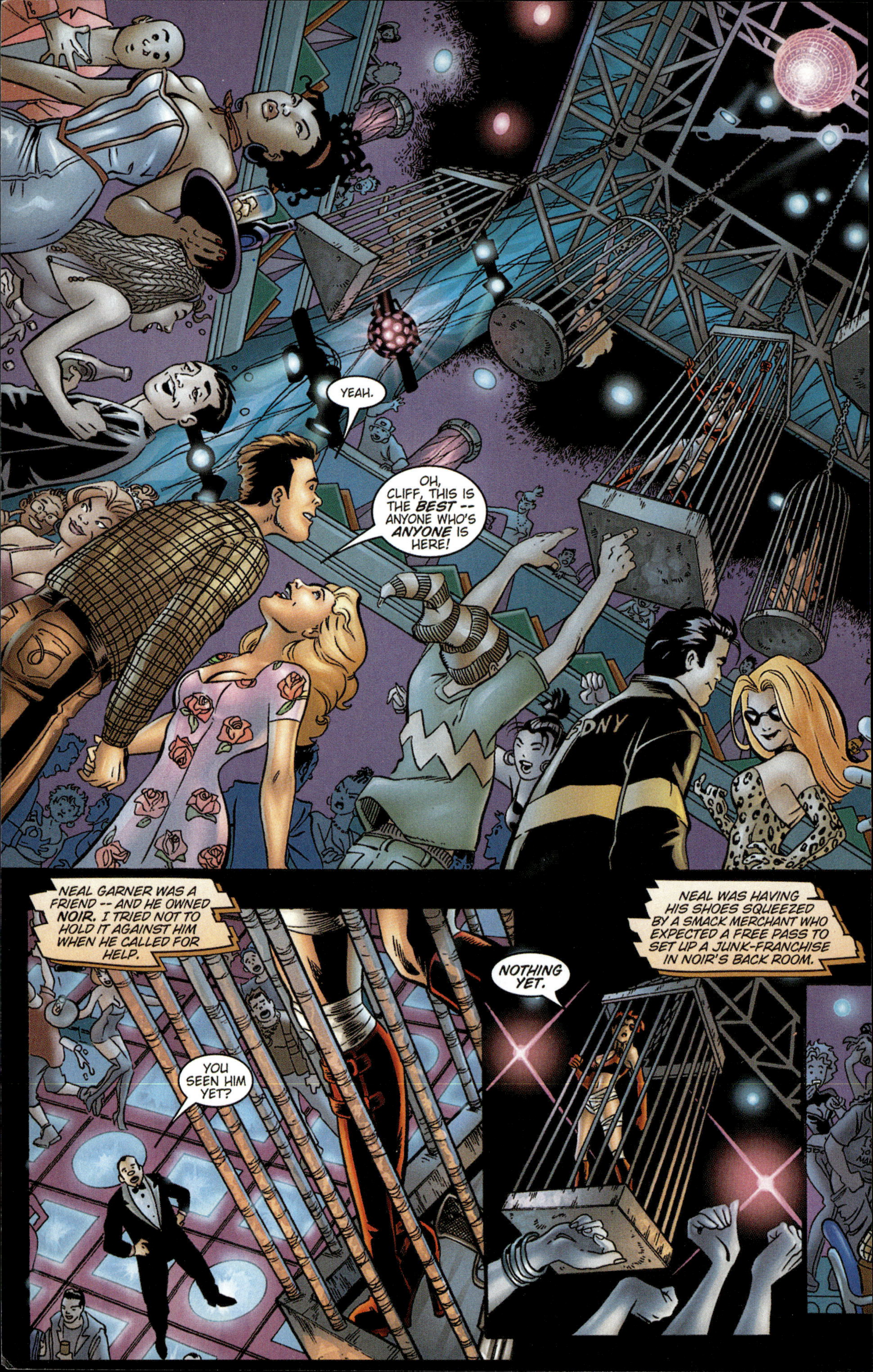
YEAH.
OH, CLIFF, THIS IS THE BEST -- ANYONE WHO'S ANYONE IS HERE!
NEAL GARNER WAS A FRIEND -- AND HE OWNED NOIR. I TRIED NOT TO HOLD IT AGAINST HIM WHEN HE CALLED FOR HELP.
YOU SEEN HIM YET?
NOTHING YET.
NEAL WAS HAVING HIS SHOES SQUEEZED BY A SMACK MERCHANT WHO EXPECTED A FREE PASS TO SET UP A JUNK-FRANCHISE IN NOIR'S BACK ROOM.

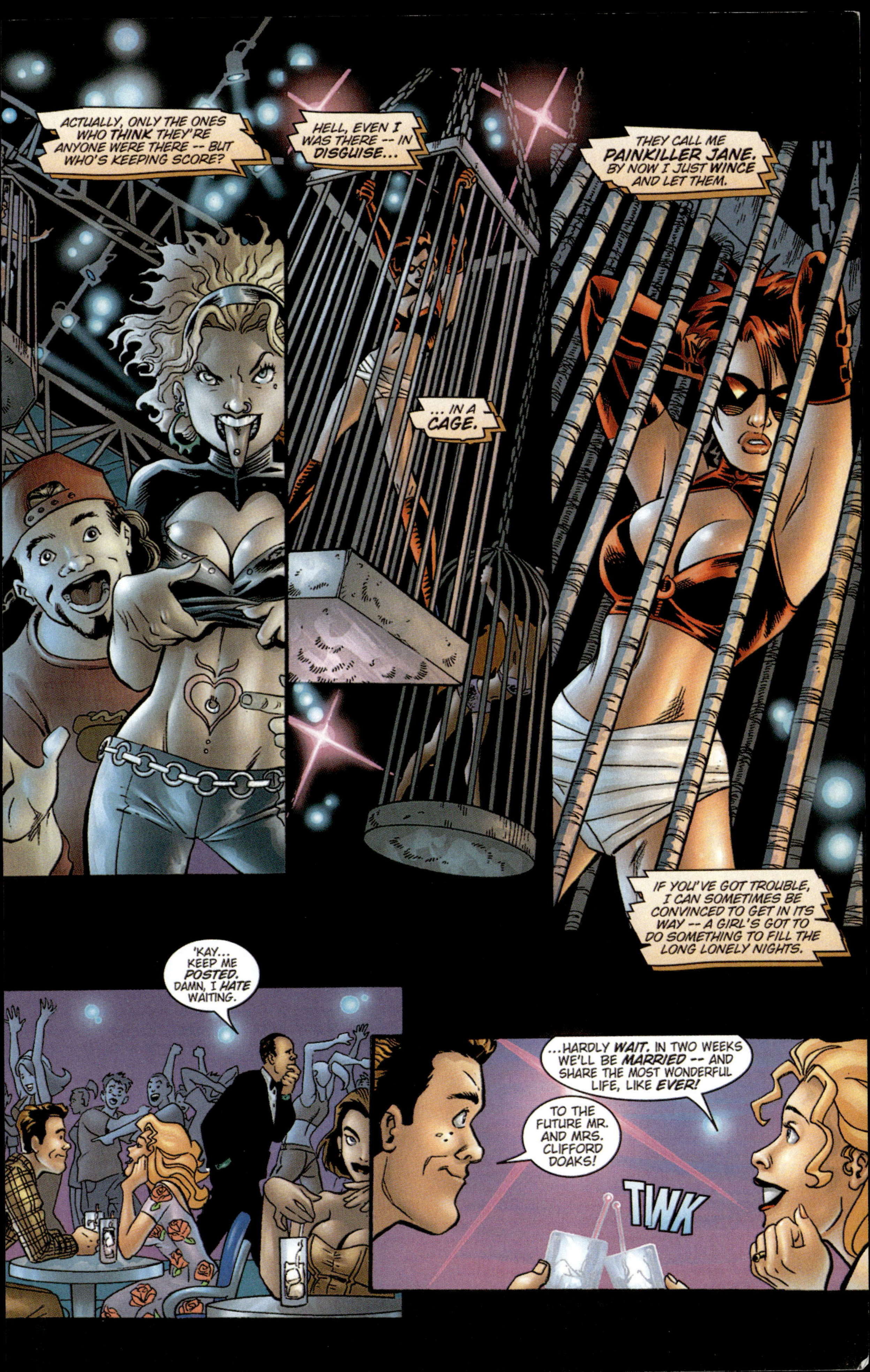

ACTUALLY, ONLY THE ONES WHO THINK THEY'RE ANYONE WERE THERE -- BUT WHO'S KEEPING SCORE?
HELL, EVEN I WAS THERE -- IN DISGUISE...
...IN A CAGE.
THEY CALL ME PAINKILLER JANE. BY NOW I JUST WINCE AND LET THEM.
IF YOU'VE GOT TROUBLE, I CAN SOMETIMES BE CONVINCED TO GET IN ITS WAY -- A GIRL'S GOT TO DO SOMETHING TO FILL THE LONG LONELY NIGHTS.
'KAY... KEEP ME POSTED. DAMN, I HATE WAITING.
...HARDLY WAIT. IN TWO WEEKS WE'LL BE MARRIED -- AND SHARE THE MOST WONDERFUL LIFE, LIKE EVER!
TO THE FUTURE MR. AND MRS. CLIFFORD DOAKS!
TWK

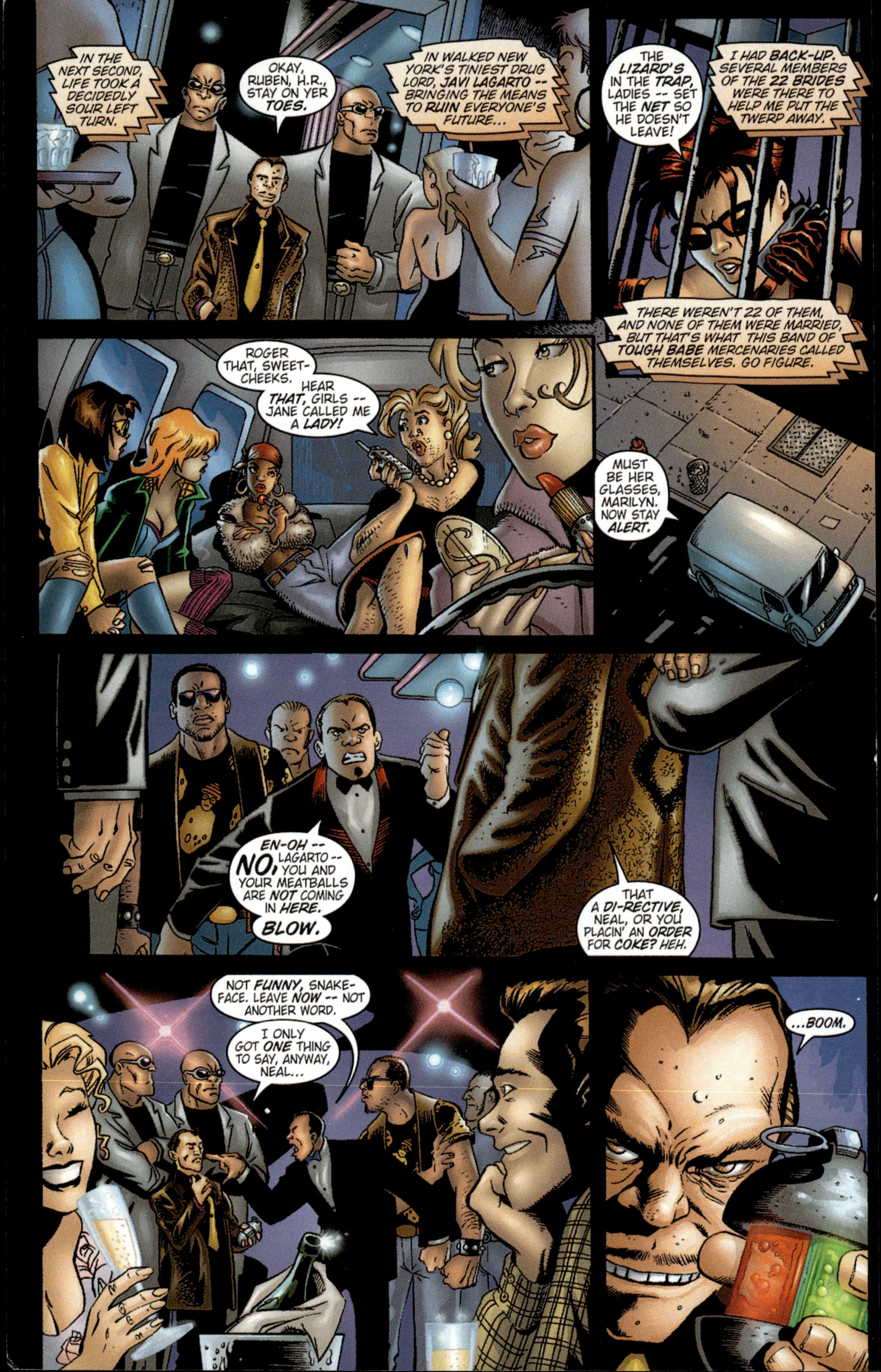
IN THE NEXT SECOND, LIFE TOOK A DECIDEDLY SOUR LEFT TURN.
OKAY, RUBEN, H.R., STAY ON YER TOES.
IN WALKED NEW YORK'S TINIEST DRUG LORD, JAVI LAGARTO -- BRINGING THE MEANS TO RUIN EVERYONE'S FUTURE...
THE LIZARD'S IN THE TRAP, LADIES -- SET THE NET SO HE DOESN'T LEAVE!
I HAD BACK-UP. SEVERAL MEMBERS OF THE 22 BRIDES WERE THERE TO HELP ME PUT THE TWERP AWAY.
THERE WEREN'T 22 OF THEM, AND NONE OF THEM WERE MARRIED, BUT THAT'S WHAT THIS BAND OF TOUGH BABE MERCENARIES CALLED THEMSELVES. GO FIGURE.
ROGER THAT, SWEET-CHEEKS.
HEAR THAT, GIRLS -- JANE CALLED ME A LADY!
MUST BE HER GLASSES, MARILYN. NOW STAY ALERT.
EN-OH -- NO, LAGARTO -- YOU AND YOUR MEATBALLS ARE NOT COMING IN HERE. BLOW.
THAT A DI-RECTIVE, NEAL, OR YOU PLACIN' AN ORDER FOR COKE? HEH.
NOT FUNNY, SNAKE-FACE. LEAVE NOW -- NOT ANOTHER WORD.
I ONLY GOT ONE THING TO SAY, ANYWAY, NEAL...
...BOOM.

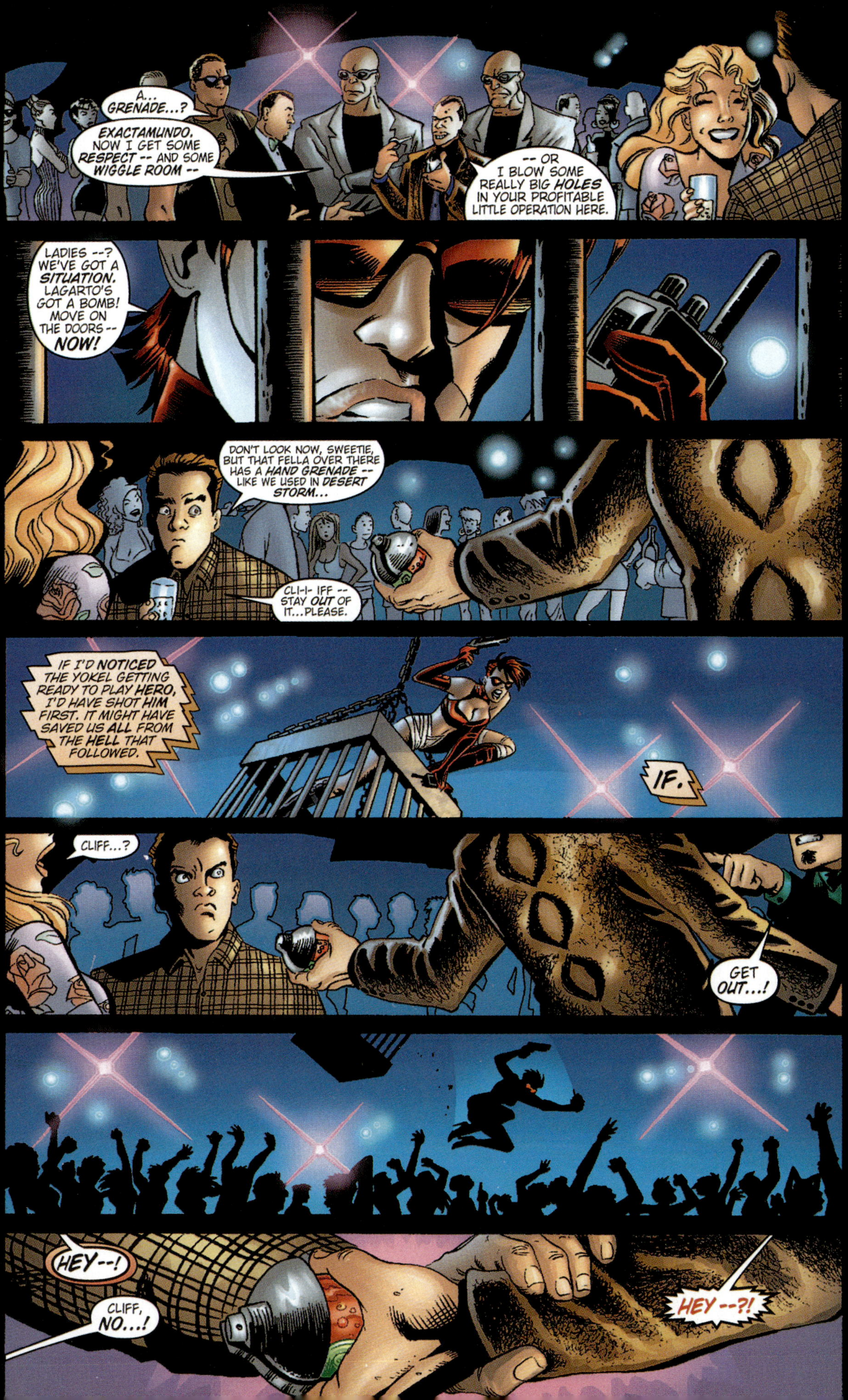

A... GRENADE...?
EXACTAMUNDO. NOW I GET SOME RESPECT -- AND SOME WIGGLE ROOM --
-- OR I BLOW SOME REALLY BIG HOLES IN YOUR PROFITABLE LITTLE OPERATION HERE.
LADIES --? WE'VE GOT A SITUATION. LAGARTO'S GOT A BOMB! MOVE ON THE DOORS -- NOW!
DON'T LOOK NOW, SWEETIE, BUT THAT FELLA OVER THERE HAS A HAND GRENADE -- LIKE WE USED IN DESERT STORM...
CLI-I- IFF -- STAY OUT OF IT... PLEASE.
IF I'D NOTICED THE YOKEL GETTING READY TO PLAY HERO, I'D HAVE SHOT HIM FIRST. IT MIGHT HAVE SAVED US ALL FROM THE HELL THAT FOLLOWED.
IF.
CLIFF...?
GET OUT...!
HEY --!
CLIFF, NO...!
HEY --?!

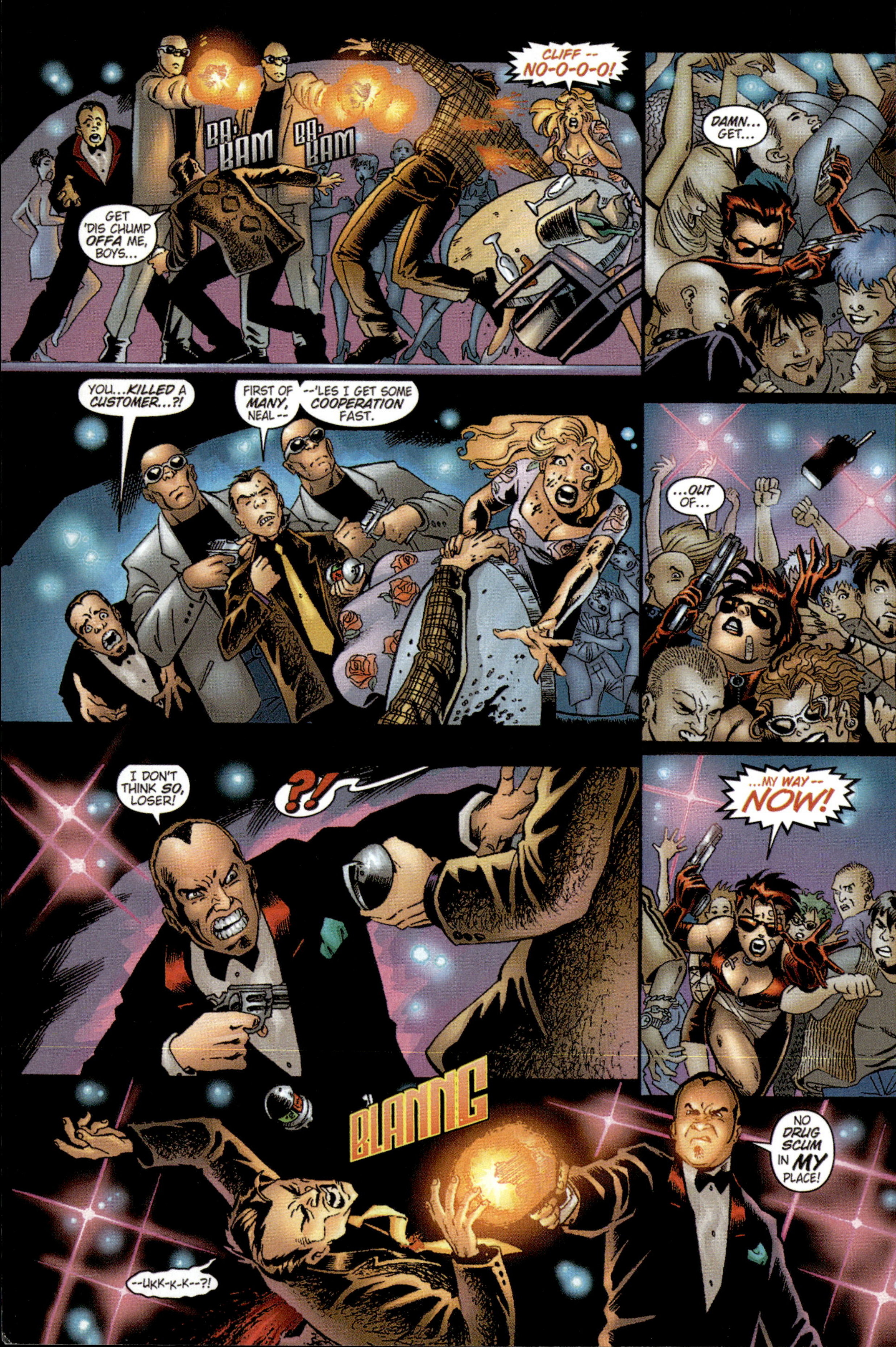
BA-BAM BA-BAM
CLIFF -- NO-O-O-O!
GET 'DIS CHUMP OFFA ME, BOYS...
DAMN... GET...
YOU...KILLED A CUSTOMER...?!
FIRST OF MANY, NEAL --
--'LES I GET SOME COOPERATION FAST.
...OUT OF...
I DON'T THINK SO, LOSER!
?!
...MY WAY -- NOW!
BLANNG
NO DRUG SCUM IN MY PLACE!
--UKK-K-K--?!

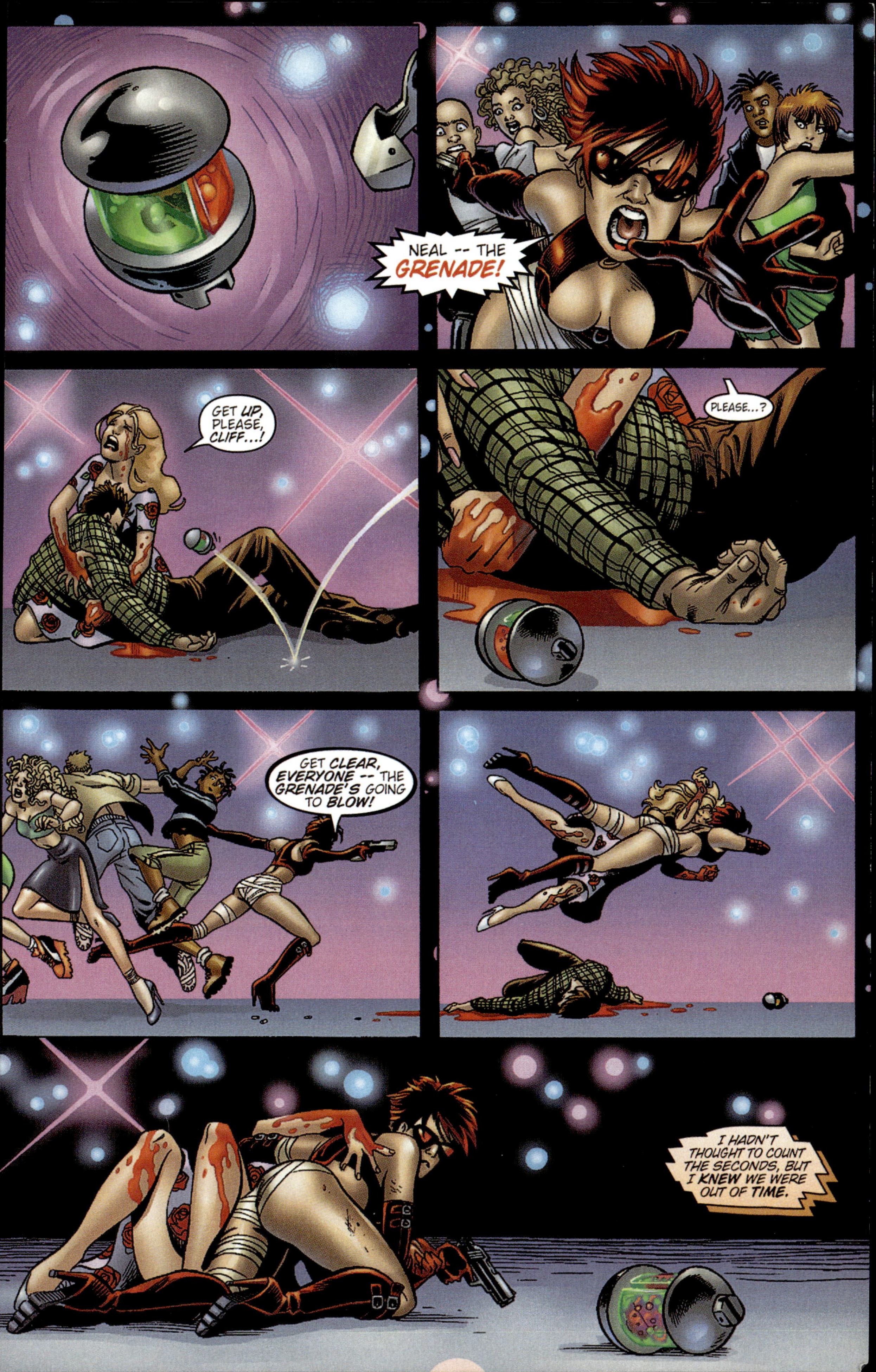
NEAL -- THE GRENADE!
GET UP, PLEASE, CLIFF...!
PLEASE...?
GET CLEAR, EVERYONE -- THE GRENADE'S GOING TO BLOW!
I HADN'T THOUGHT TO COUNT THE SECONDS, BUT I KNEW WE WERE OUT OF TIME.

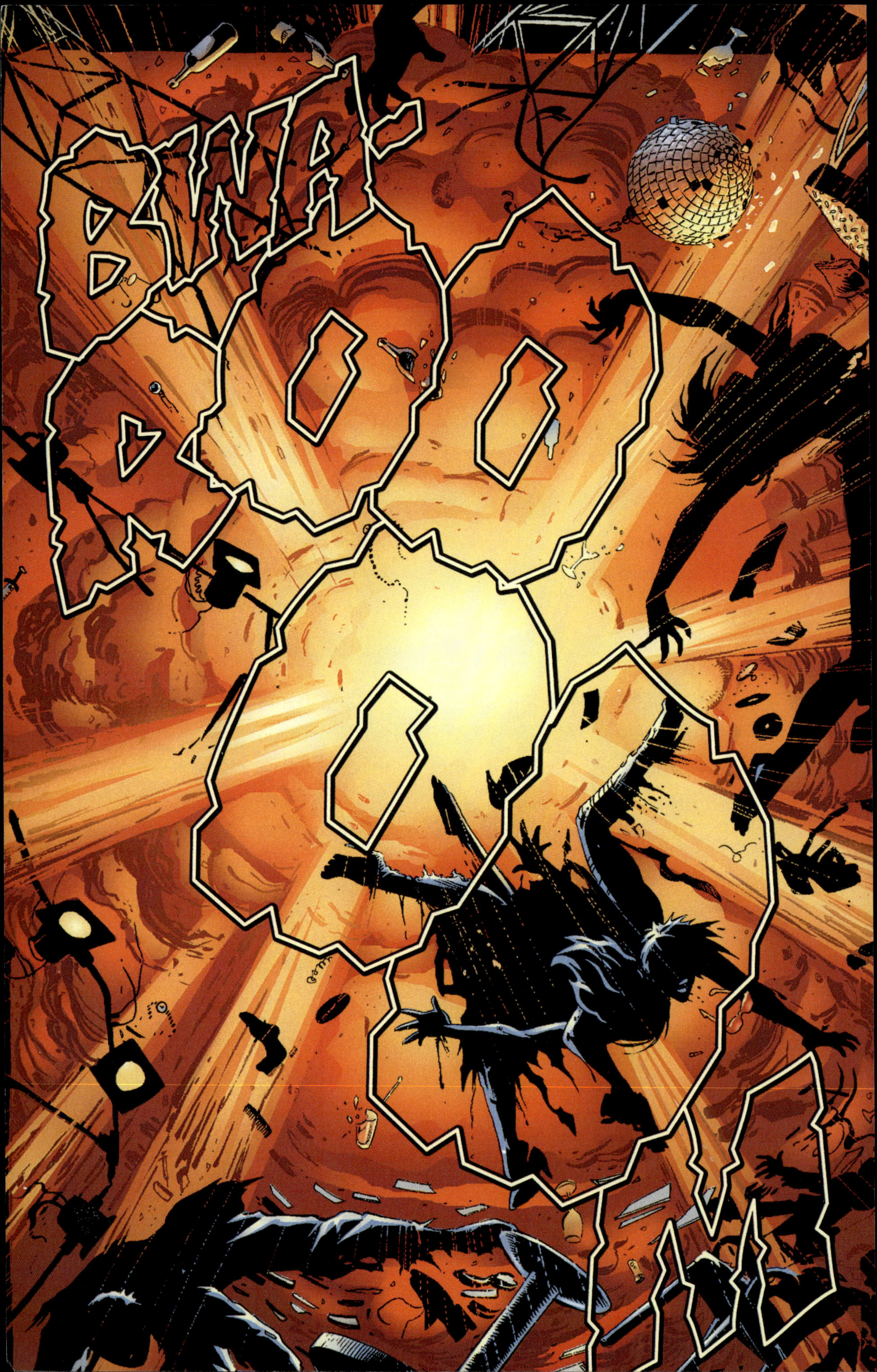
BWA-BOOOOM

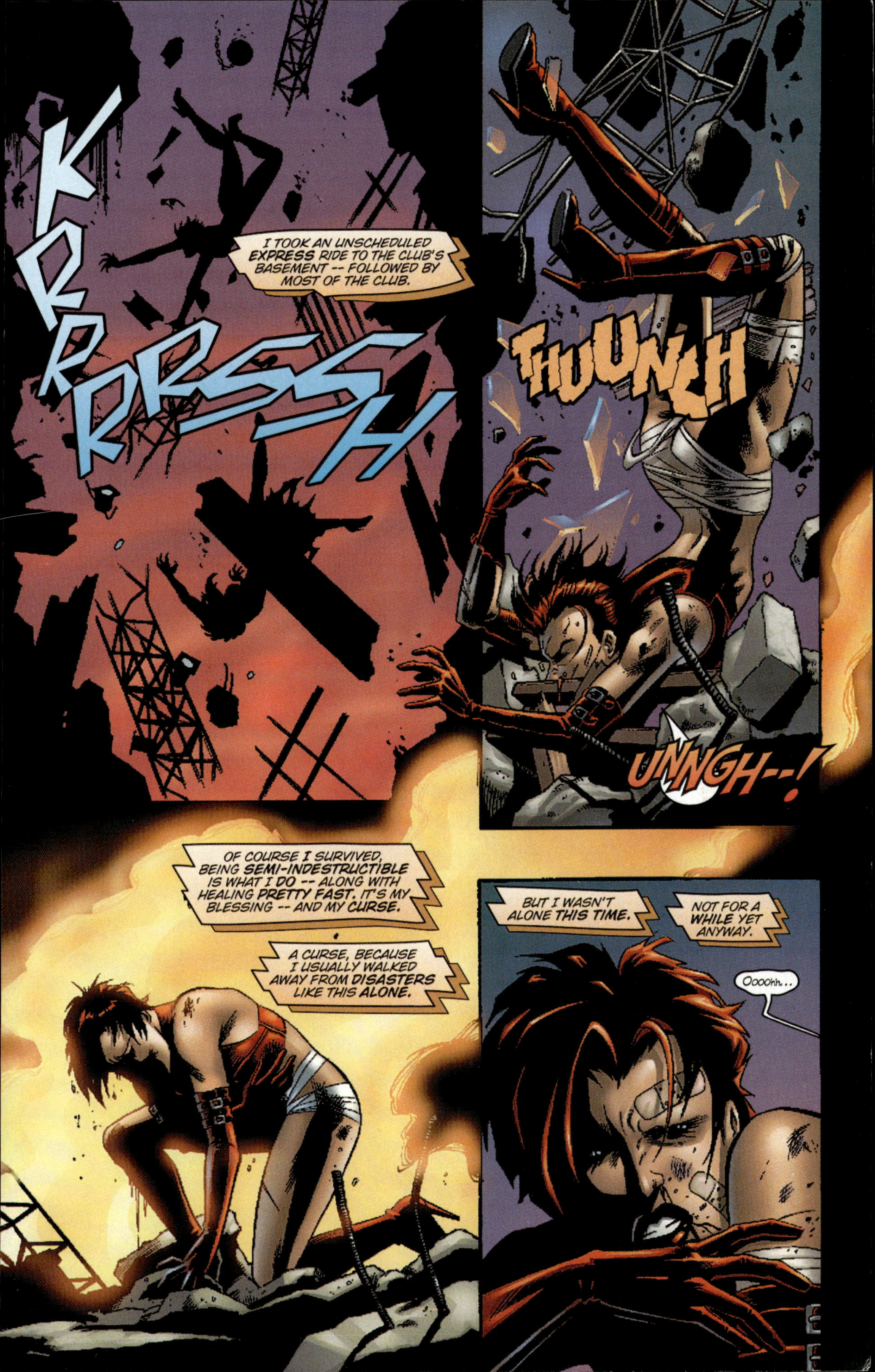
KRRRRSSSH
I TOOK AN UNSCHEDULED EXPRESS RIDE TO THE CLUB'S BASEMENT -- FOLLOWED BY MOST OF THE CLUB.
THUUNCH
UNNGH--!
OF COURSE I SURVIVED. BEING SEMI-INDESTRUCTIBLE IS WHAT I DO -- ALONG WITH HEALING PRETTY FAST. IT'S MY BLESSING -- AND MY CURSE.
A CURSE, BECAUSE I USUALLY WALKED AWAY FROM DISASTERS LIKE THIS ALONE.
BUT I WASN'T ALONE THIS TIME.
NOT FOR A WHILE YET ANYWAY.
Oooohh...

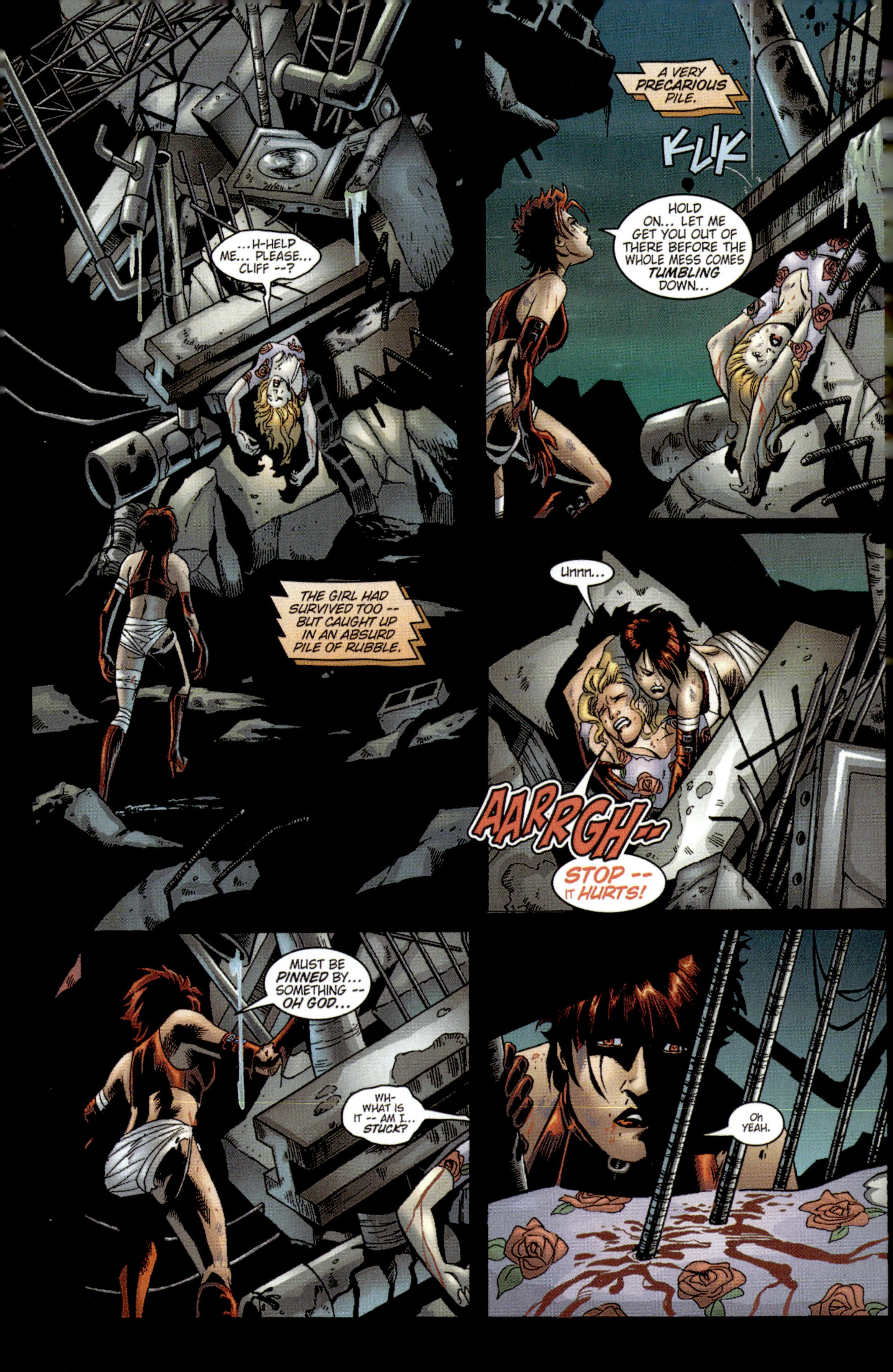
...H-HELP ME... PLEASE... CLIFF --?
A VERY PRECARIOUS PILE.
KLIK
HOLD ON... LET ME GET YOU OUT OF THERE BEFORE THE WHOLE MESS COMES TUMBLING DOWN...
THE GIRL HAD SURVIVED TOO -- BUT CAUGHT UP IN AN ABSURD PILE OF RUBBLE.
Unnn...
AARRGH--
STOP -- IT HURTS!
MUST BE PINNED BY... SOMETHING -- OH GOD...
WH-WHAT IS IT -- AM I... STUCK?
Oh YEAH.

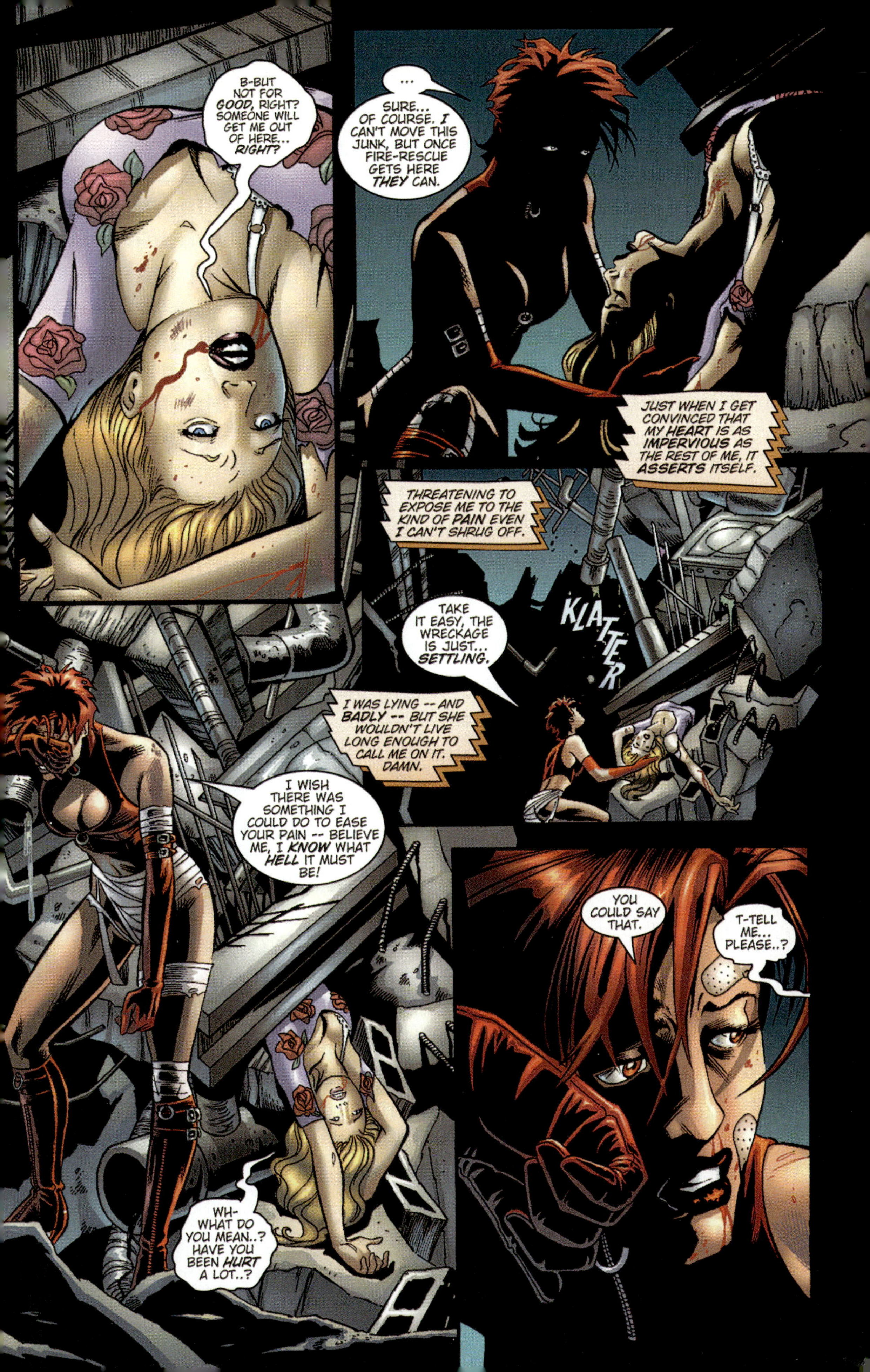
B-BUT NOT FOR GOOD, RIGHT? SOMEONE WILL GET ME OUT OF HERE... RIGHT?
...
SURE... OF COURSE. I CAN'T MOVE THIS JUNK, BUT ONCE FIRE-RESCUE GETS HERE THEY CAN.
JUST WHEN I GET CONVINCED THAT MY HEART IS AS IMPERVIOUS AS THE REST OF ME, IT ASSERTS ITSELF.
THREATENING TO EXPOSE ME TO THE KIND OF PAIN EVEN I CAN'T SHRUG OFF.
KLATTER
TAKE IT EASY, THE WRECKAGE IS JUST... SETTLING.
I WAS LYING -- AND BADLY -- BUT SHE WOULDN'T LIVE LONG ENOUGH TO CALL ME ON IT. DAMN.
I WISH THERE WAS SOMETHING I COULD DO TO EASE YOUR PAIN -- BELIEVE ME, I KNOW WHAT HELL IT MUST BE!
WH-WHAT DO YOU MEAN..? HAVE YOU BEEN HURT A LOT..?
YOU COULD SAY THAT.
T-TELL ME... PLEASE..?

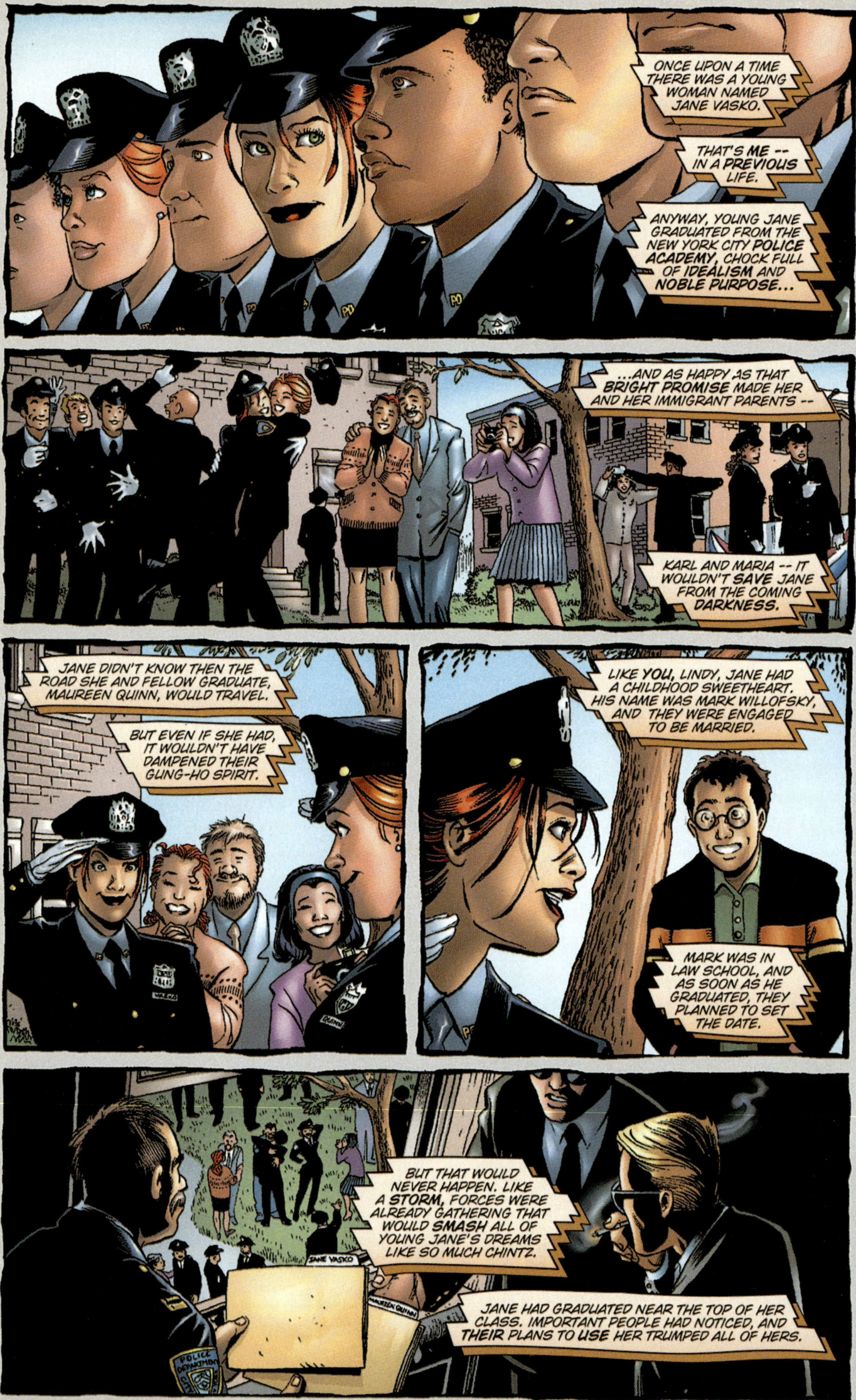
ONCE UPON A TIME THERE WAS A YOUNG WOMAN NAMED JANE VASKO.
THAT'S ME -- IN A PREVIOUS LIFE.
ANYWAY, YOUNG JANE GRADUATED FROM THE NEW YORK CITY POLICE ACADEMY, CHOCK FULL OF IDEALISM AND NOBLE PURPOSE...
...AND AS HAPPY AS THAT BRIGHT PROMISE MADE HER AND HER IMMIGRANT PARENTS --
KARL AND MARIA -- IT WOULDN'T SAVE JANE FROM THE COMING DARKNESS.
JANE DIDN'T KNOW THEN THE ROAD SHE AND FELLOW GRADUATE, MAUREEN QUINN, WOULD TRAVEL.
BUT EVEN IF SHE HAD, IT WOULDN'T HAVE DAMPENED THEIR GUNG-HO SPIRIT.
LIKE YOU, LINDY, JANE HAD A CHILDHOOD SWEETHEART. HIS NAME WAS MARK WILLOFSKY, AND THEY WERE ENGAGED TO BE MARRIED.
MARK WAS IN LAW SCHOOL, AND AS SOON AS HE GRADUATED, THEY PLANNED TO SET THE DATE.
BUT THAT WOULD NEVER HAPPEN. LIKE A STORM, FORCES WERE ALREADY GATHERING THAT WOULD SMASH ALL OF YOUNG JANE'S DREAMS LIKE SO MUCH CHINTZ.
JANE VASKO
MAUREEN QUINN
JANE HAD GRADUATED NEAR THE TOP OF HER CLASS. IMPORTANT PEOPLE HAD NOTICED, AND THEIR PLANS TO USE HER TRUMPED ALL OF HERS.

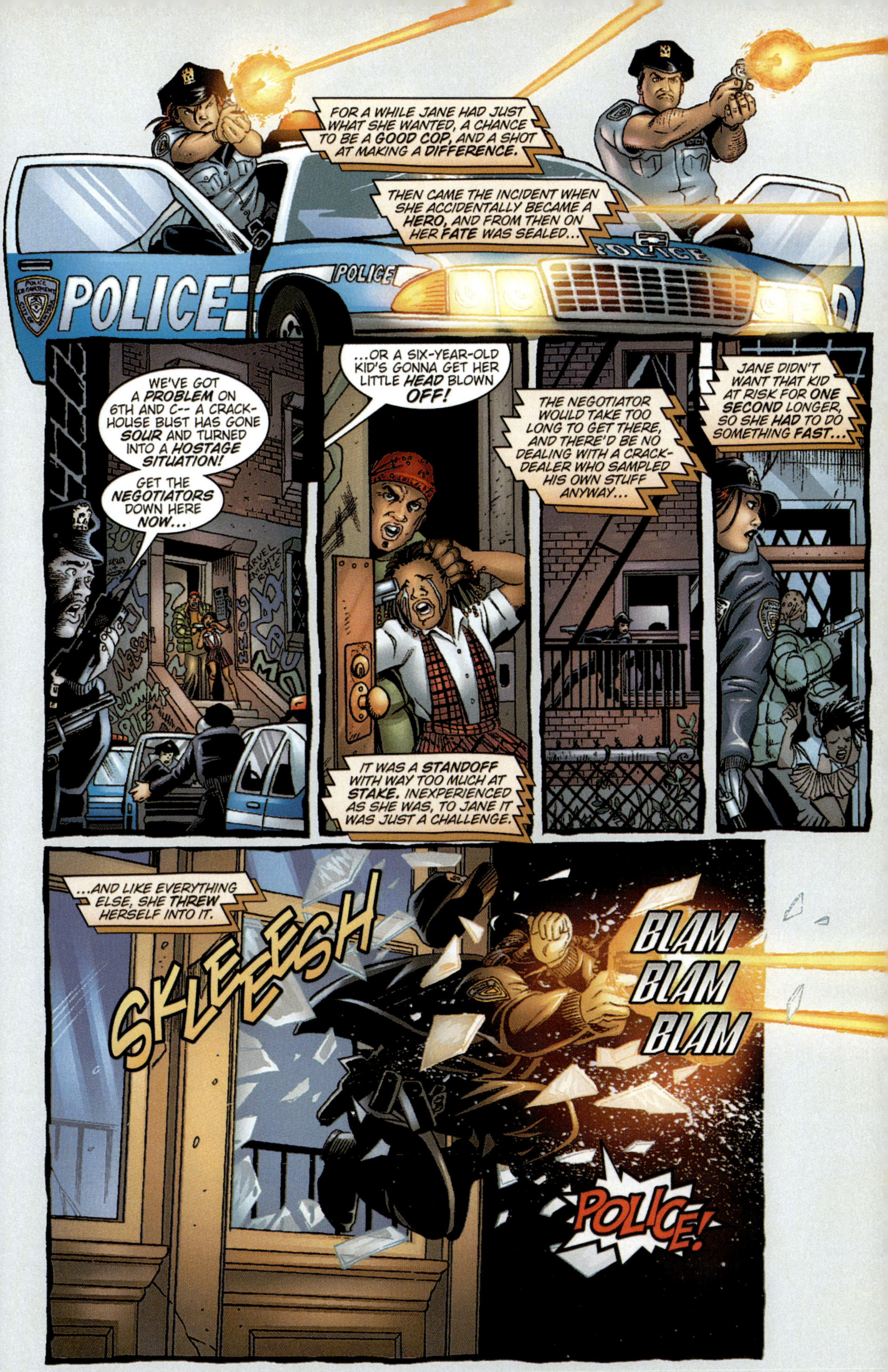
FOR A WHILE JANE HAD JUST WHAT SHE WANTED, A CHANCE TO BE A GOOD COP, AND A SHOT AT MAKING A DIFFERENCE.
THEN CAME THE INCIDENT WHEN SHE ACCIDENTALLY BECAME A HERO, AND FROM THEN ON HER FATE WAS SEALED...
POLICE
WE'VE GOT A PROBLEM ON 6TH AND C-- A CRACK-HOUSE BUST HAS GONE SOUR AND TURNED INTO A HOSTAGE SITUATION!
GET THE NEGOTIATORS DOWN HERE NOW...
...OR A SIX-YEAR-OLD KID'S GONNA GET HER LITTLE HEAD BLOWN OFF!
IT WAS A STANDOFF WITH WAY TOO MUCH AT STAKE. INEXPERIENCED AS SHE WAS, TO JANE IT WAS JUST A CHALLENGE.
THE NEGOTIATOR WOULD TAKE TOO LONG TO GET THERE, AND THERE'D BE NO DEALING WITH A CRACK-DEALER WHO SAMPLED HIS OWN STUFF ANYWAY...
JANE DIDN'T WANT THAT KID AT RISK FOR ONE SECOND LONGER, SO SHE HAD TO DO SOMETHING FAST...
...AND LIKE EVERYTHING ELSE, SHE THREW HERSELF INTO IT.
SKLEEESH
BLAM
BLAM
BLAM
POLICE!

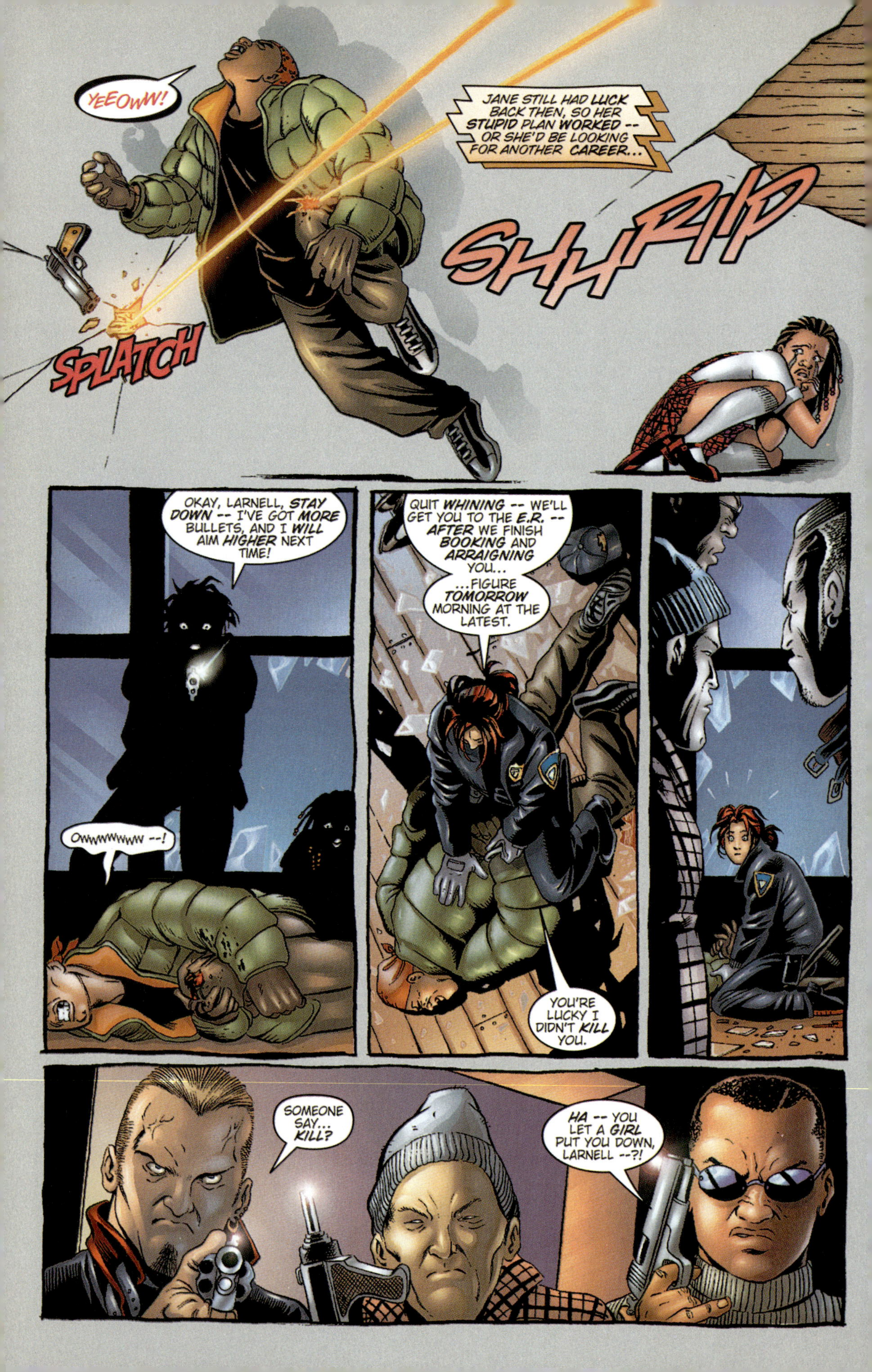
YEEOWW!
JANE STILL HAD LUCK BACK THEN, SO HER STUPID PLAN WORKED -- OR SHE'D BE LOOKING FOR ANOTHER CAREER...
SHHRIP
SPLATCH
OKAY, LARNELL, STAY DOWN -- I'VE GOT MORE BULLETS, AND I WILL AIM HIGHER NEXT TIME!
OWWWWWWW --!
QUIT WHINING -- WE'LL GET YOU TO THE E.R. -- AFTER WE FINISH BOOKING AND ARRAIGNING YOU...
...FIGURE TOMORROW MORNING AT THE LATEST.
YOU'RE LUCKY I DIDN'T KILL YOU.
SOMEONE SAY... KILL?
HA -- YOU LET A GIRL PUT YOU DOWN, LARNELL --?!

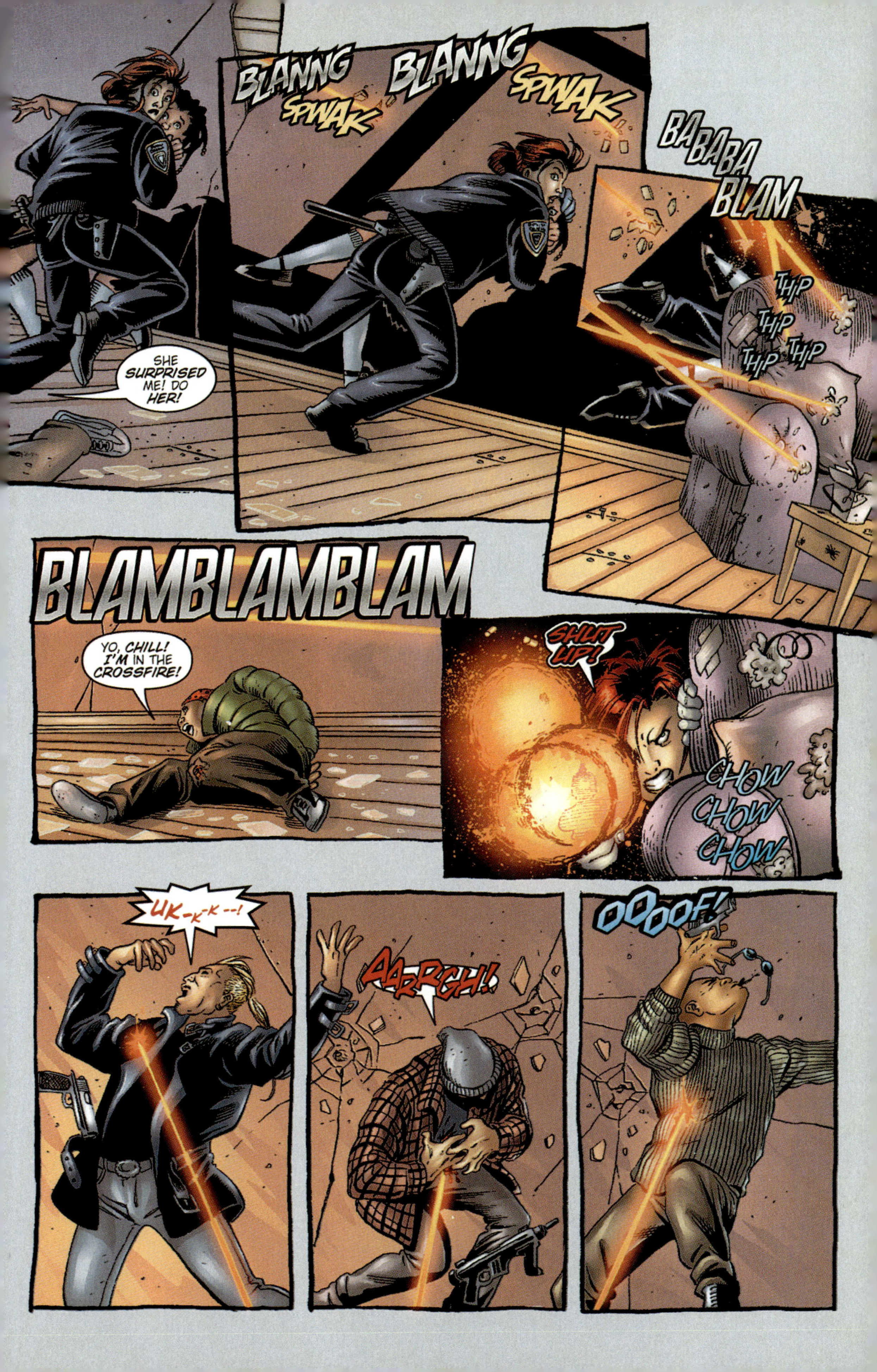
BLANNG
SPWAK
BLANNG
SPWAK
BABABA BLAM
THIP THIP THIP THIP
SHE SURPRISED ME! DO HER!
BLAMBLAMBLAM
YO, CHILL! I'M IN THE CROSSFIRE!
SHUT UP!
CHOW CHOW CHOW
UK-K-K--!
AARRGH!
OOOOF!

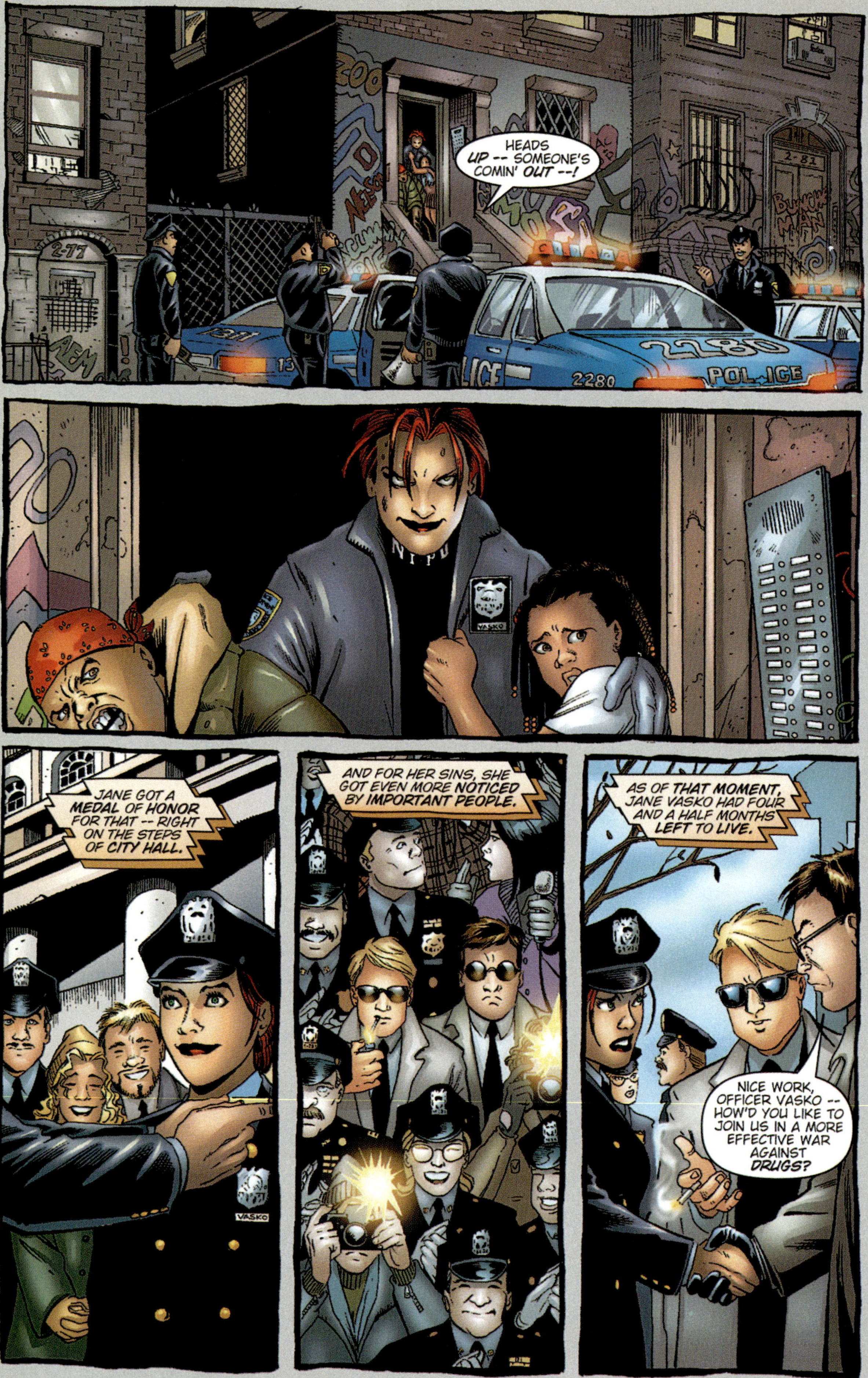
HEADS UP -- SOMEONE'S COMIN' OUT --!
JANE GOT A MEDAL OF HONOR FOR THAT -- RIGHT ON THE STEPS OF CITY HALL.
AND FOR HER SINS, SHE GOT EVEN MORE NOTICED BY IMPORTANT PEOPLE.
AS OF THAT MOMENT, JANE VASKO HAD FOUR AND A HALF MONTHS LEFT TO LIVE.
NICE WORK, OFFICER VASKO -- HOW'D YOU LIKE TO JOIN US IN A MORE EFFECTIVE WAR AGAINST DRUGS?

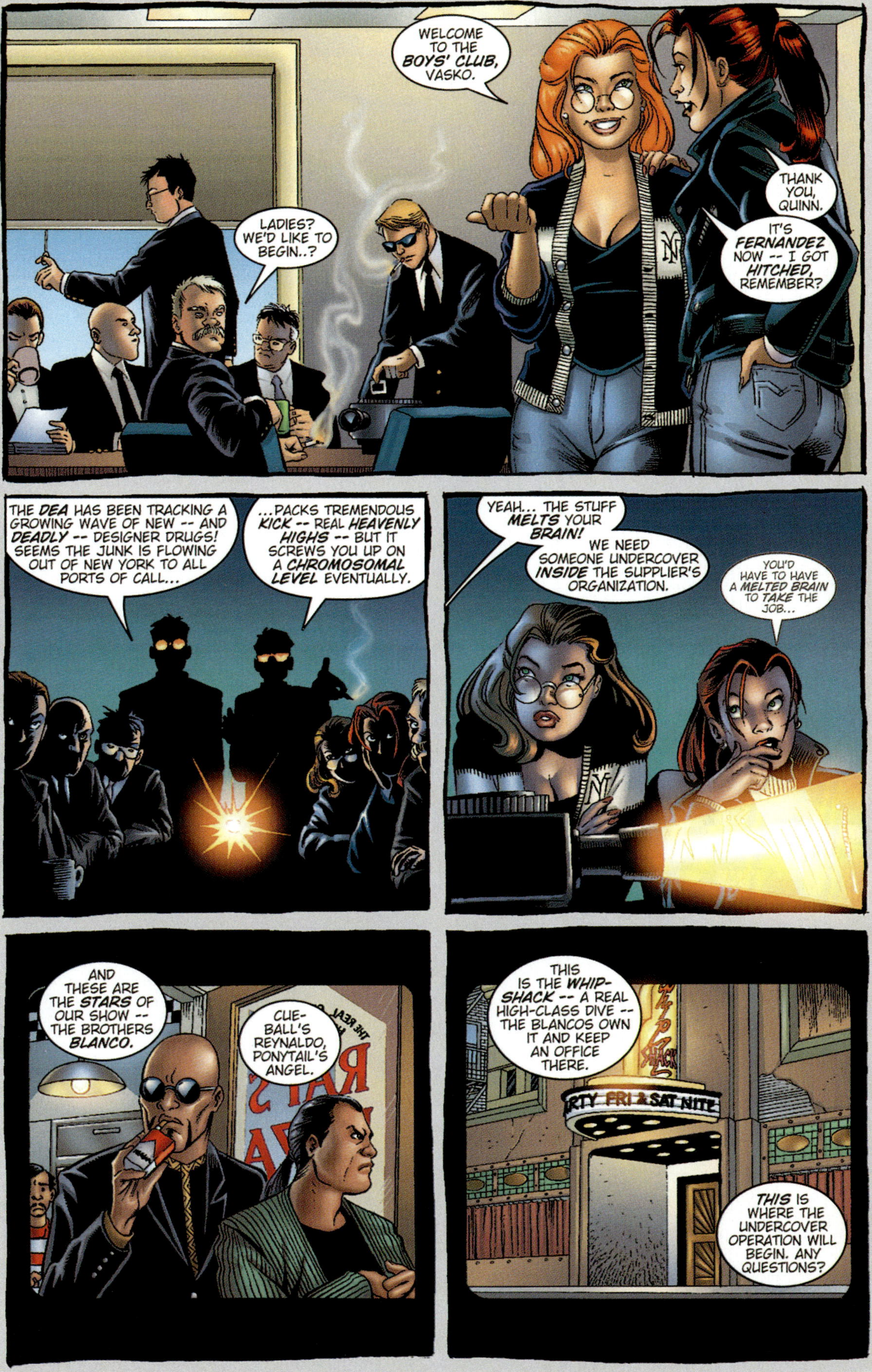

WELCOME TO THE BOYS' CLUB, VASKO.
LADIES? WE'D LIKE TO BEGIN..?
THANK YOU, QUINN.
IT'S FERNANDEZ NOW -- I GOT HITCHED, REMEMBER?
THE DEA HAS BEEN TRACKING A GROWING WAVE OF NEW -- AND DEADLY -- DESIGNER DRUGS! SEEMS THE JUNK IS FLOWING OUT OF NEW YORK TO ALL PORTS OF CALL...
...PACKS TREMENDOUS KICK -- REAL HEAVENLY HIGHS -- BUT IT SCREWS YOU UP ON A CHROMOSOMAL LEVEL EVENTUALLY.
YEAH... THE STUFF MELTS YOUR BRAIN!
WE NEED SOMEONE UNDERCOVER INSIDE THE SUPPLIER'S ORGANIZATION.
YOU'D HAVE TO HAVE A MELTED BRAIN TO TAKE THE JOB...
AND THESE ARE THE STARS OF OUR SHOW -- THE BROTHERS BLANCO.
CUE-BALL'S REYNALDO, PONYTAIL'S ANGEL.
THIS IS THE WHIP-SHACK -- A REAL HIGH-CLASS DIVE -- THE BLANCOS OWN IT AND KEEP AN OFFICE THERE.
PARTY FRI & SAT NITE
THIS IS WHERE THE UNDERCOVER OPERATION WILL BEGIN. ANY QUESTIONS?

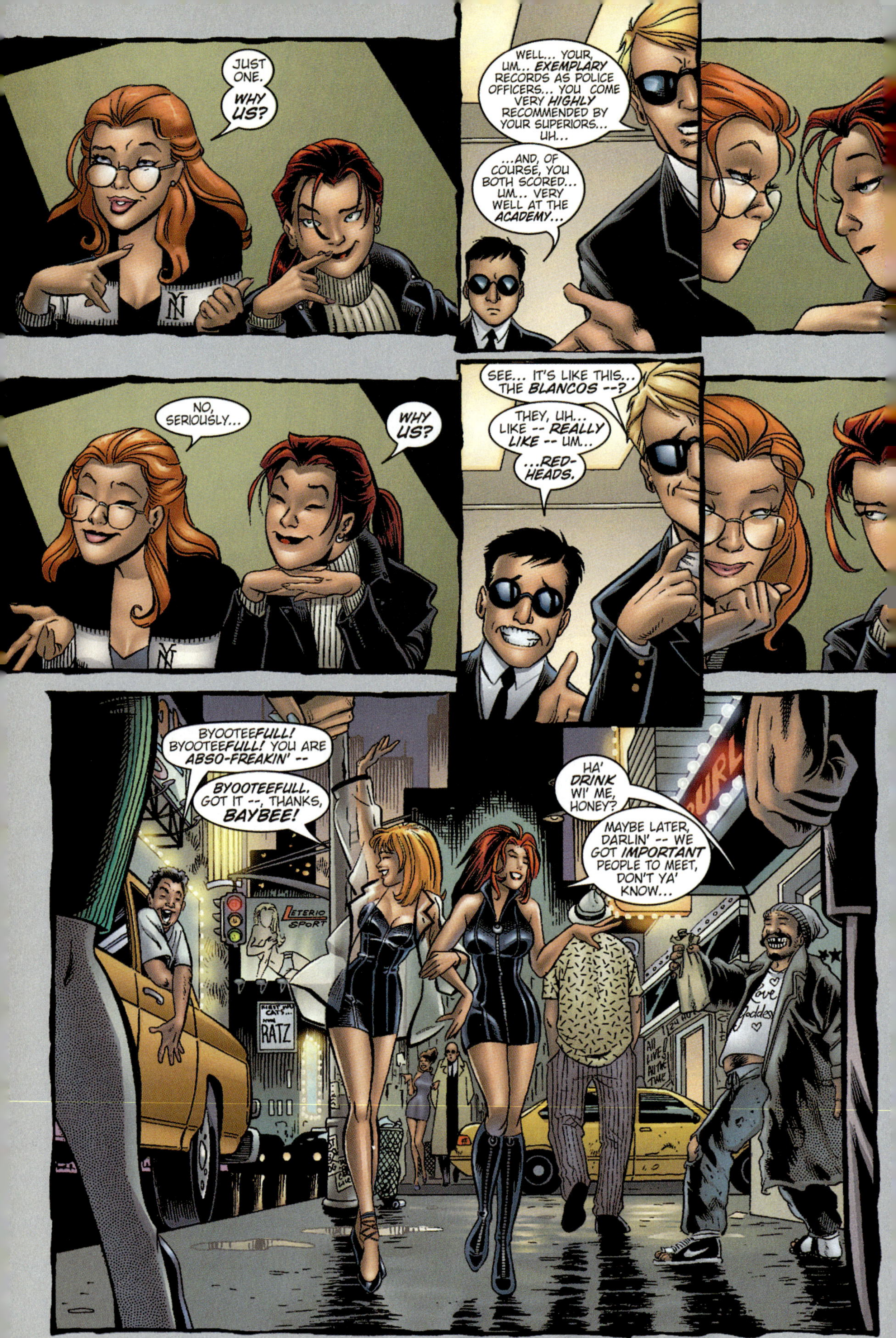
JUST ONE. WHY US?
WELL... YOUR, UM... EXEMPLARY RECORDS AS POLICE OFFICERS... YOU COME VERY HIGHLY RECOMMENDED BY YOUR SUPERIORS... UH...
...AND, OF COURSE, YOU BOTH SCORED... UM... VERY WELL AT THE ACADEMY...
NO, SERIOUSLY...
WHY US?
SEE... IT'S LIKE THIS... THE BLANCOS --?
THEY, UH... LIKE -- REALLY LIKE -- UM...
...RED-HEADS.
BYOOTEEFULL! BYOOTEEFULL! YOU ARE ABSO-FREAKIN' --
BYOOTEEFULL. GOT IT --, THANKS, BAYBEE!
HA' DRINK WI' ME, HONEY?
MAYBE LATER, DARLIN' -- WE GOT IMPORTANT PEOPLE TO MEET, DON'T YA' KNOW...
LETERIO SPORT
RATZ

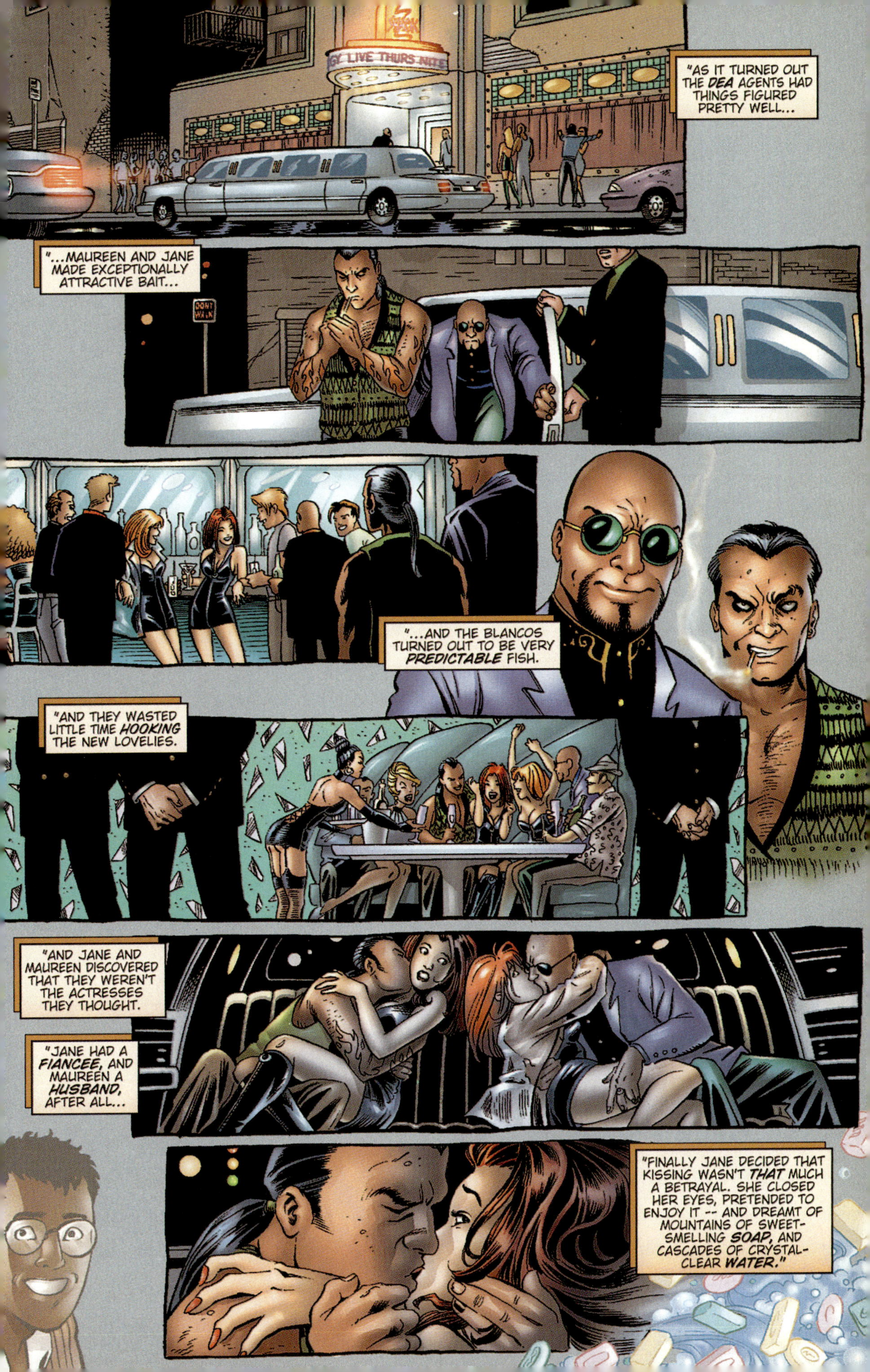
LIVE THURS NITE
"AS IT TURNED OUT THE DEA AGENTS HAD THINGS FIGURED PRETTY WELL...
"...MAUREEN AND JANE MADE EXCEPTIONALLY ATTRACTIVE BAIT...
DON'T WALK
"...AND THE BLANCOS TURNED OUT TO BE VERY PREDICTABLE FISH.
"AND THEY WASTED LITTLE TIME HOOKING THE NEW LOVELIES.
"AND JANE AND MAUREEN DISCOVERED THAT THEY WEREN'T THE ACTRESSES THEY THOUGHT.
"JANE HAD A FIANCEE, AND MAUREEN A HUSBAND, AFTER ALL...
"FINALLY JANE DECIDED THAT KISSING WASN'T THAT MUCH A BETRAYAL. SHE CLOSED HER EYES, PRETENDED TO ENJOY IT -- AND DREAMT OF MOUNTAINS OF SWEET-SMELLING SOAP, AND CASCADES OF CRYSTAL-CLEAR WATER."

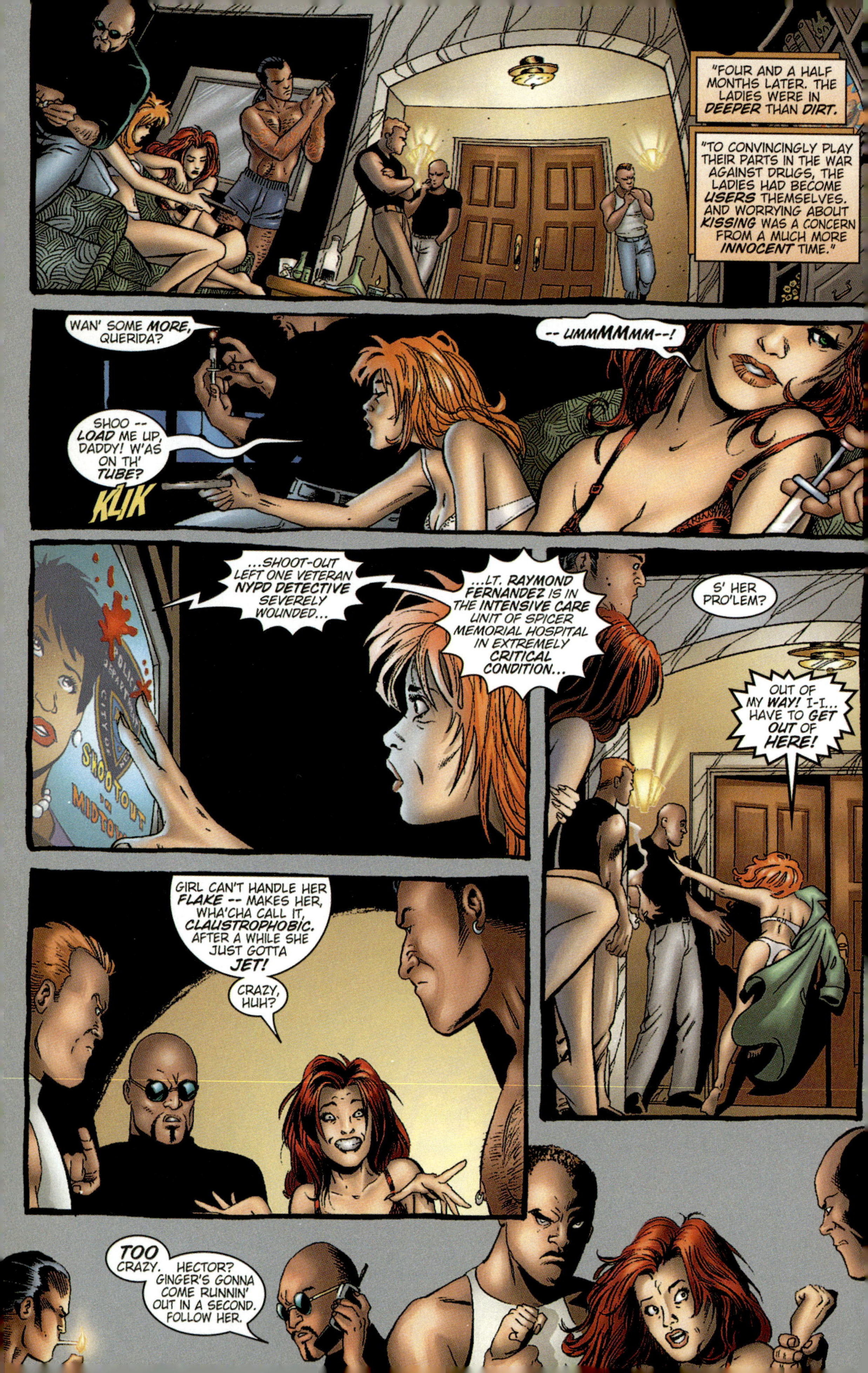
"FOUR AND A HALF MONTHS LATER. THE LADIES WERE IN DEEPER THAN DIRT.
"TO CONVINCINGLY PLAY THEIR PARTS IN THE WAR AGAINST DRUGS, THE LADIES HAD BECOME USERS THEMSELVES. AND WORRYING ABOUT KISSING WAS A CONCERN FROM A MUCH MORE INNOCENT TIME."
WAN' SOME MORE, QUERIDA?
-- UMMMMMM--!
SHOO -- LOAD ME UP, DADDY! W'AS ON TH' TUBE?
KLIK
...SHOOT-OUT LEFT ONE VETERAN NYPD DETECTIVE SEVERELY WOUNDED...
...LT. RAYMOND FERNANDEZ IS IN THE INTENSIVE CARE UNIT OF SPICER MEMORIAL HOSPITAL IN EXTREMELY CRITICAL CONDITION...
SHOOTOUT IN MIDTOW
S' HER PRO'LEM?
OUT OF MY WAY! I-I... HAVE TO GET OUT OF HERE!
GIRL CAN'T HANDLE HER FLAKE -- MAKES HER, WHA'CHA CALL IT, CLAUSTROPHOBIC. AFTER A WHILE SHE JUST GOTTA JET!
CRAZY, HUH?
TOO CRAZY. HECTOR? GINGER'S GONNA COME RUNNIN' OUT IN A SECOND. FOLLOW HER.

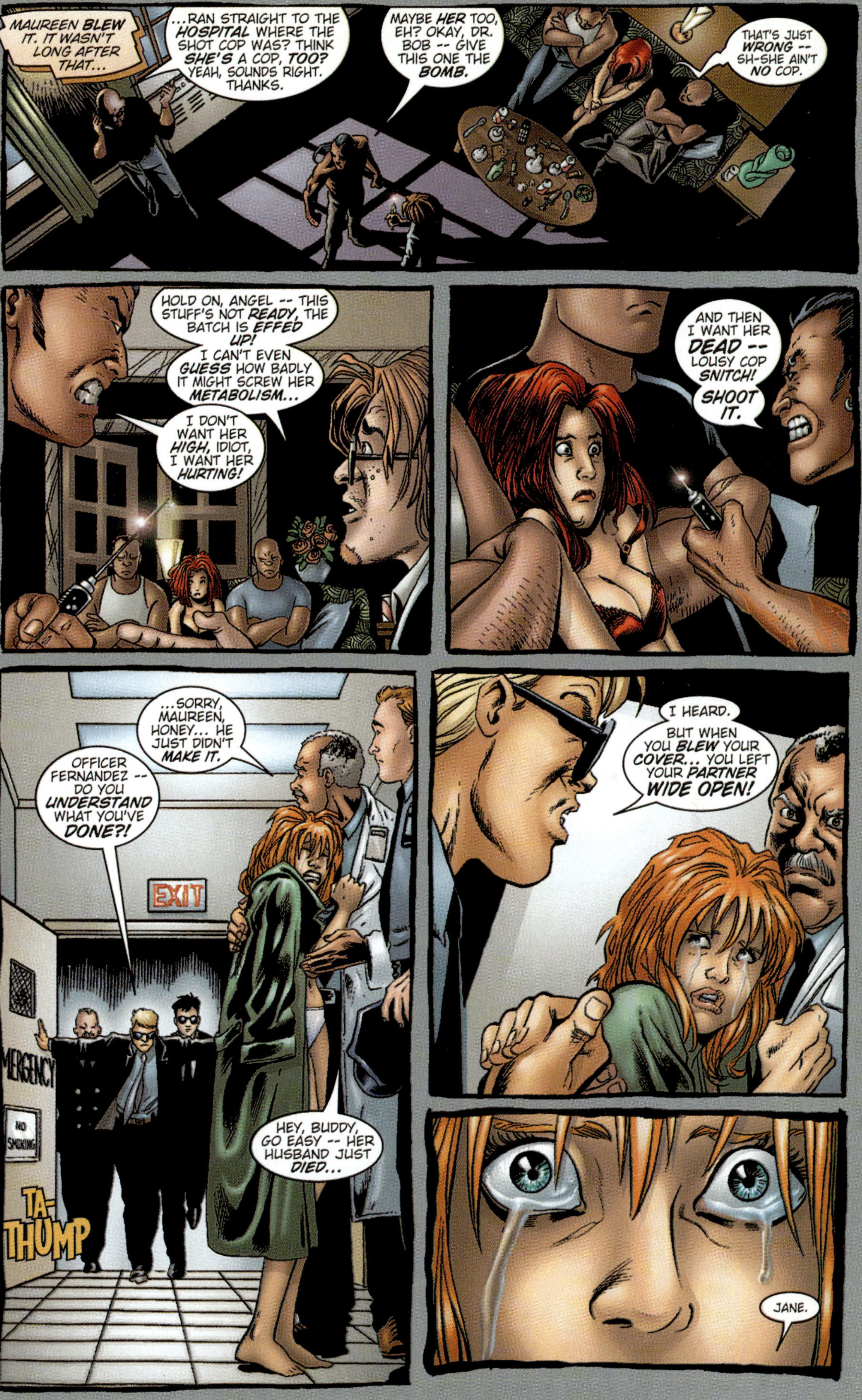
MAUREEN BLEW IT. IT WASN'T LONG AFTER THAT...
...RAN STRAIGHT TO THE HOSPITAL WHERE THE SHOT COP WAS? THINK SHE'S A COP, TOO? YEAH, SOUNDS RIGHT. THANKS.
MAYBE HER TOO, EH? OKAY, DR. BOB -- GIVE THIS ONE THE BOMB.
THAT'S JUST WRONG -- SH-SHE AIN'T NO COP.
HOLD ON, ANGEL -- THIS STUFF'S NOT READY, THE BATCH IS EFFED UP!
I CAN'T EVEN GUESS HOW BADLY IT MIGHT SCREW HER METABOLISM...
I DON'T WANT HER HIGH, IDIOT, I WANT HER HURTING!
AND THEN I WANT HER DEAD -- LOUSY COP SNITCH!
SHOOT IT.
...SORRY, MAUREEN, HONEY... HE JUST DIDN'T MAKE IT.
OFFICER FERNANDEZ -- DO YOU UNDERSTAND WHAT YOU'VE DONE?!
EXIT
MERGENCY
NO SMOKING
TA-THUMP
HEY, BUDDY, GO EASY -- HER HUSBAND JUST DIED...
I HEARD.
BUT WHEN YOU BLEW YOUR COVER... YOU LEFT YOUR PARTNER WIDE OPEN!
JANE.

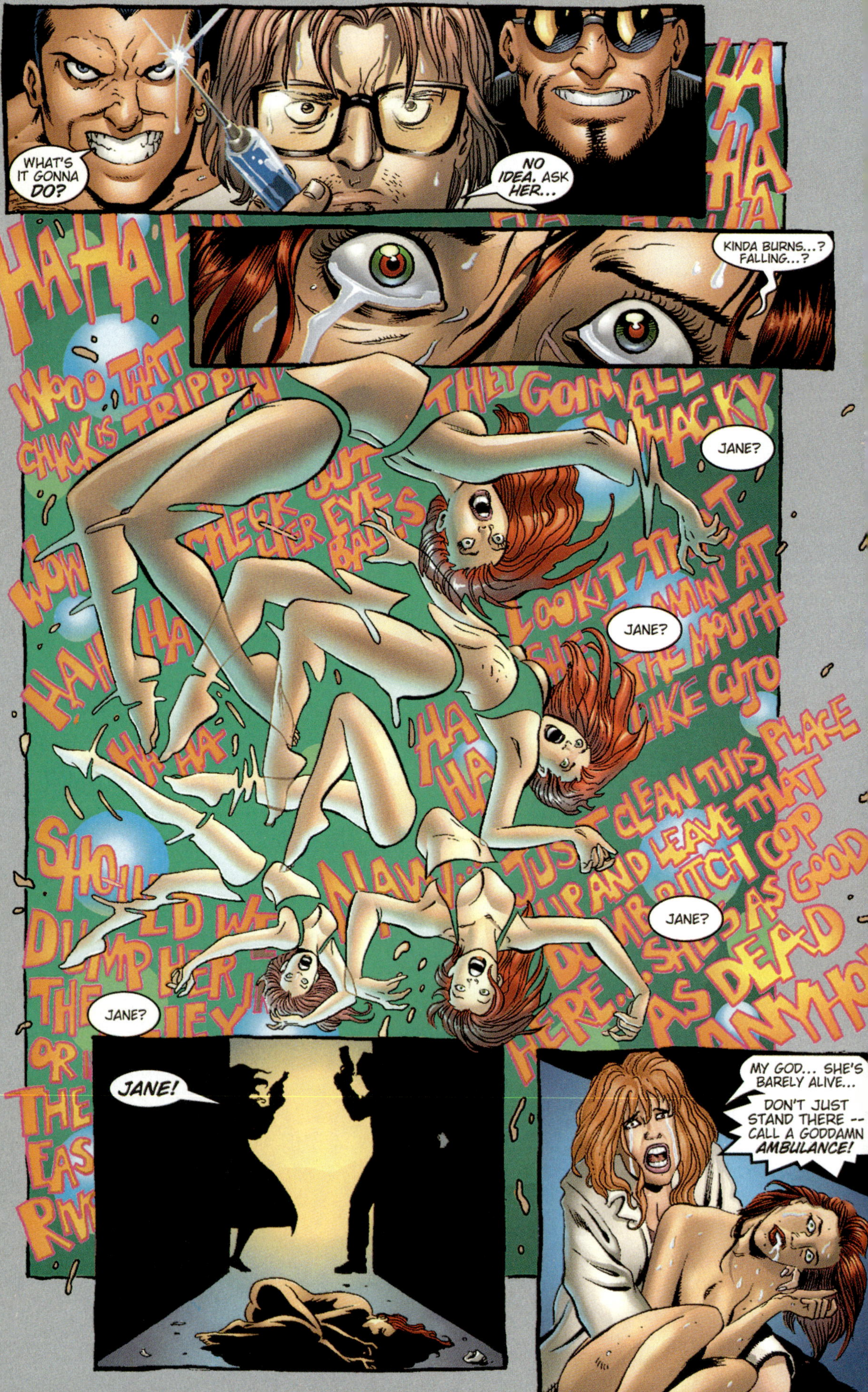

WHAT'S IT GONNA DO?
NO IDEA. ASK HER...
HA HA HA
KINDA BURNS...? FALLING...?
WOOO THAT CHICK IS TRIPPIN'
JANE?
CHECK OUT HER EYE BALLS
JANE?
JANE?
JANE?
JANE!
MY GOD... SHE'S BARELY ALIVE...
DON'T JUST STAND THERE -- CALL A GODDAMN AMBULANCE!

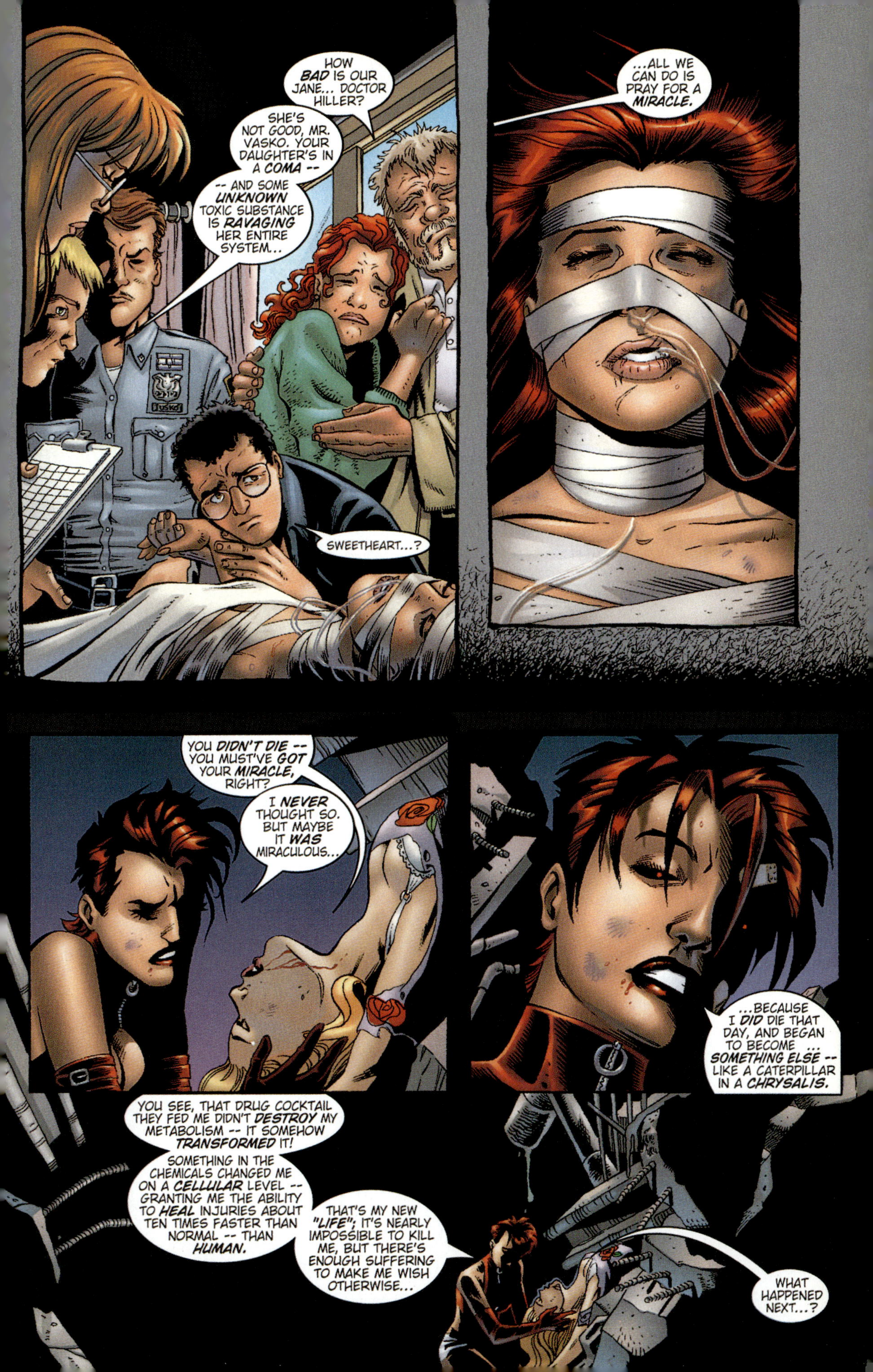
HOW BAD IS OUR JANE... DOCTOR HILLER?
SHE'S NOT GOOD, MR. VASKO. YOUR DAUGHTER'S IN A COMA --
-- AND SOME UNKNOWN TOXIC SUBSTANCE IS RAVAGING HER ENTIRE SYSTEM...
SWEETHEART...?
...ALL WE CAN DO IS PRAY FOR A MIRACLE.
YOU DIDN'T DIE -- YOU MUST'VE GOT YOUR MIRACLE, RIGHT?
I NEVER THOUGHT SO. BUT MAYBE IT WAS MIRACULOUS...
...BECAUSE I DID DIE THAT DAY, AND BEGAN TO BECOME ... SOMETHING ELSE -- LIKE A CATERPILLAR IN A CHRYSALIS.
YOU SEE, THAT DRUG COCKTAIL THEY FED ME DIDN'T DESTROY MY METABOLISM -- IT SOMEHOW TRANSFORMED IT!
SOMETHING IN THE CHEMICALS CHANGED ME ON A CELLULAR LEVEL -- GRANTING ME THE ABILITY TO HEAL INJURIES ABOUT TEN TIMES FASTER THAN NORMAL -- THAN HUMAN.
THAT'S MY NEW "LIFE"; IT'S NEARLY IMPOSSIBLE TO KILL ME, BUT THERE'S ENOUGH SUFFERING TO MAKE ME WISH OTHERWISE...
WHAT HAPPENED NEXT...?

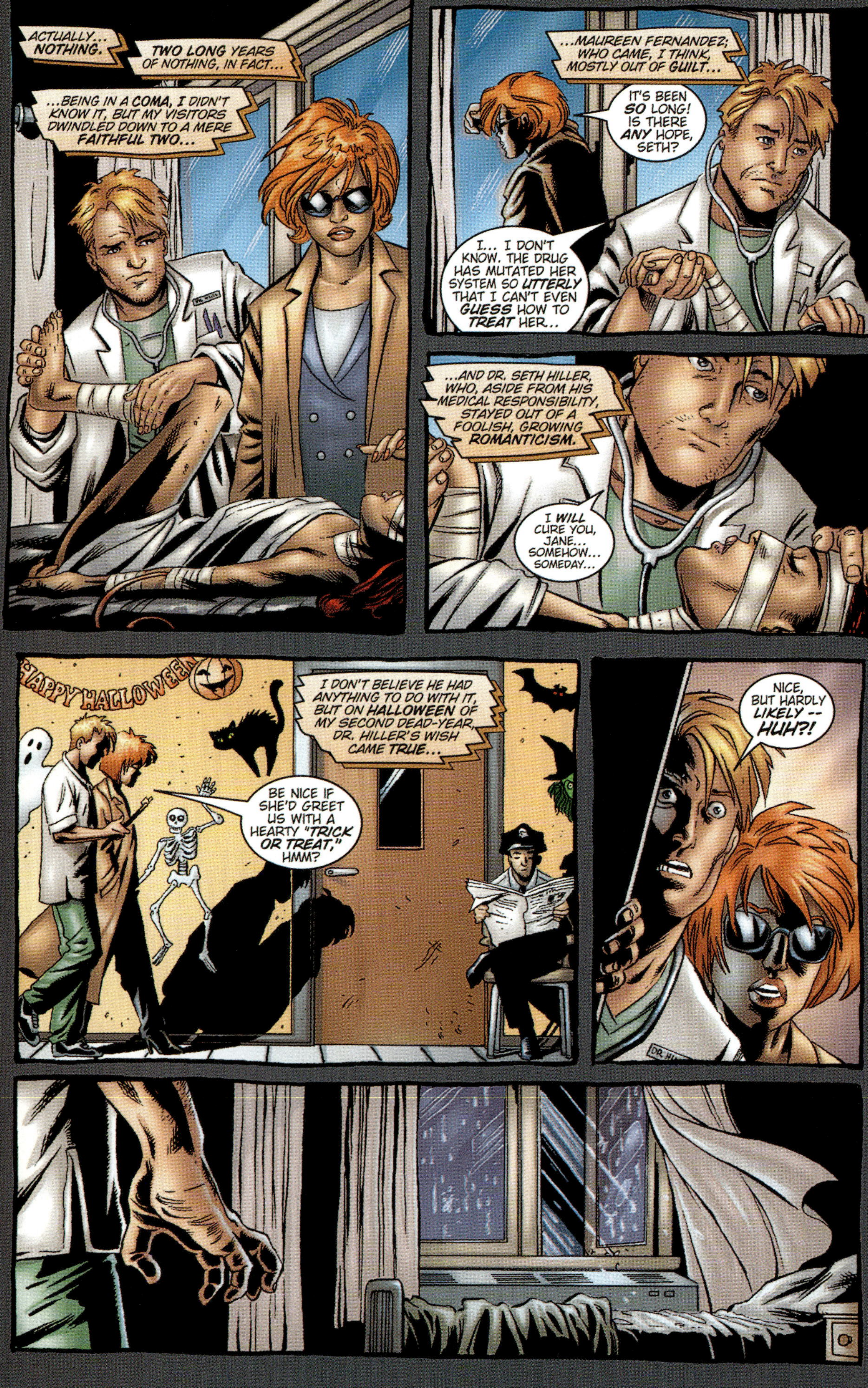

ACTUALLY... NOTHING.
TWO LONG YEARS OF NOTHING, IN FACT...
...BEING IN A COMA, I DIDN'T KNOW IT, BUT MY VISITORS DWINDLED DOWN TO A MERE FAITHFUL TWO...
...MAUREEN FERNANDEZ; WHO CAME, I THINK, MOSTLY OUT OF GUILT...
IT'S BEEN SO LONG! IS THERE ANY HOPE, SETH?
I... I DON'T KNOW. THE DRUG HAS MUTATED HER SYSTEM SO UTTERLY THAT I CAN'T EVEN GUESS HOW TO TREAT HER...
...AND DR. SETH HILLER, WHO, ASIDE FROM HIS MEDICAL RESPONSIBILITY, STAYED OUT OF A FOOLISH, GROWING ROMANTICISM.
I WILL CURE YOU, JANE... SOMEHOW... SOMEDAY...
HAPPY HALLOWEEN
I DON'T BELIEVE HE HAD ANYTHING TO DO WITH IT, BUT ON HALLOWEEN OF MY SECOND DEAD-YEAR, DR. HILLER'S WISH CAME TRUE...
BE NICE IF SHE'D GREET US WITH A HEARTY "TRICK OR TREAT," HMM?
NICE, BUT HARDLY LIKELY -- HUH?!

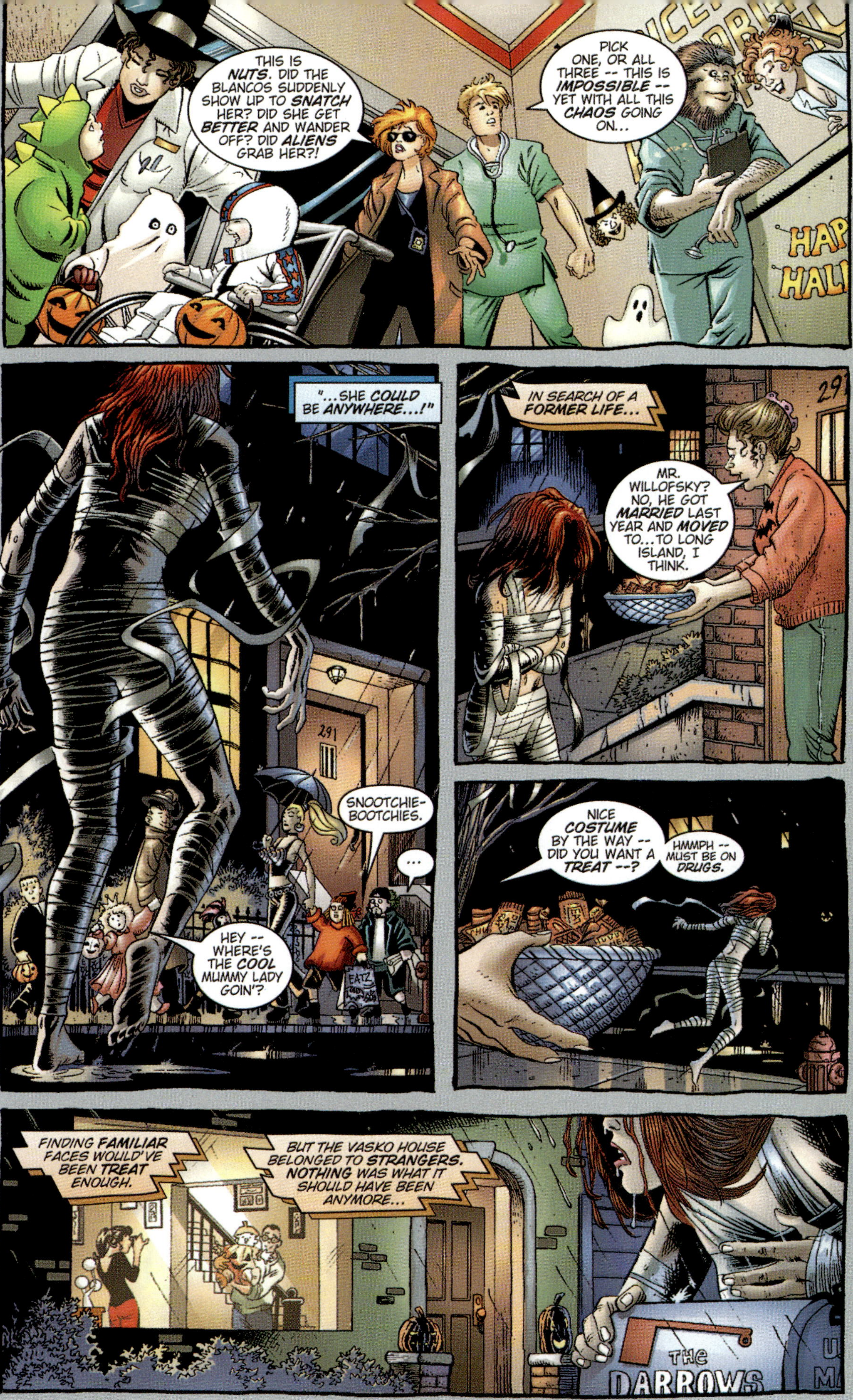
THIS IS NUTS. DID THE BLANCOS SUDDENLY SHOW UP TO SNATCH HER? DID SHE GET BETTER AND WANDER OFF? DID ALIENS GRAB HER?!
PICK ONE, OR ALL THREE -- THIS IS IMPOSSIBLE -- YET WITH ALL THIS CHAOS GOING ON...
"...SHE COULD BE ANYWHERE...!"
291
SNOOTCHIE-BOOTCHIES.
...
HEY -- WHERE'S THE COOL MUMMY LADY GOIN'?
IN SEARCH OF A FORMER LIFE...
MR. WILLOFSKY? NO, HE GOT MARRIED LAST YEAR AND MOVED TO...TO LONG ISLAND, I THINK.
NICE COSTUME BY THE WAY -- DID YOU WANT A TREAT --?
HMMPH -- MUST BE ON DRUGS.
FINDING FAMILIAR FACES WOULD'VE BEEN TREAT ENOUGH.
BUT THE VASKO HOUSE BELONGED TO STRANGERS. NOTHING WAS WHAT IT SHOULD HAVE BEEN ANYMORE...
THE DARROWS

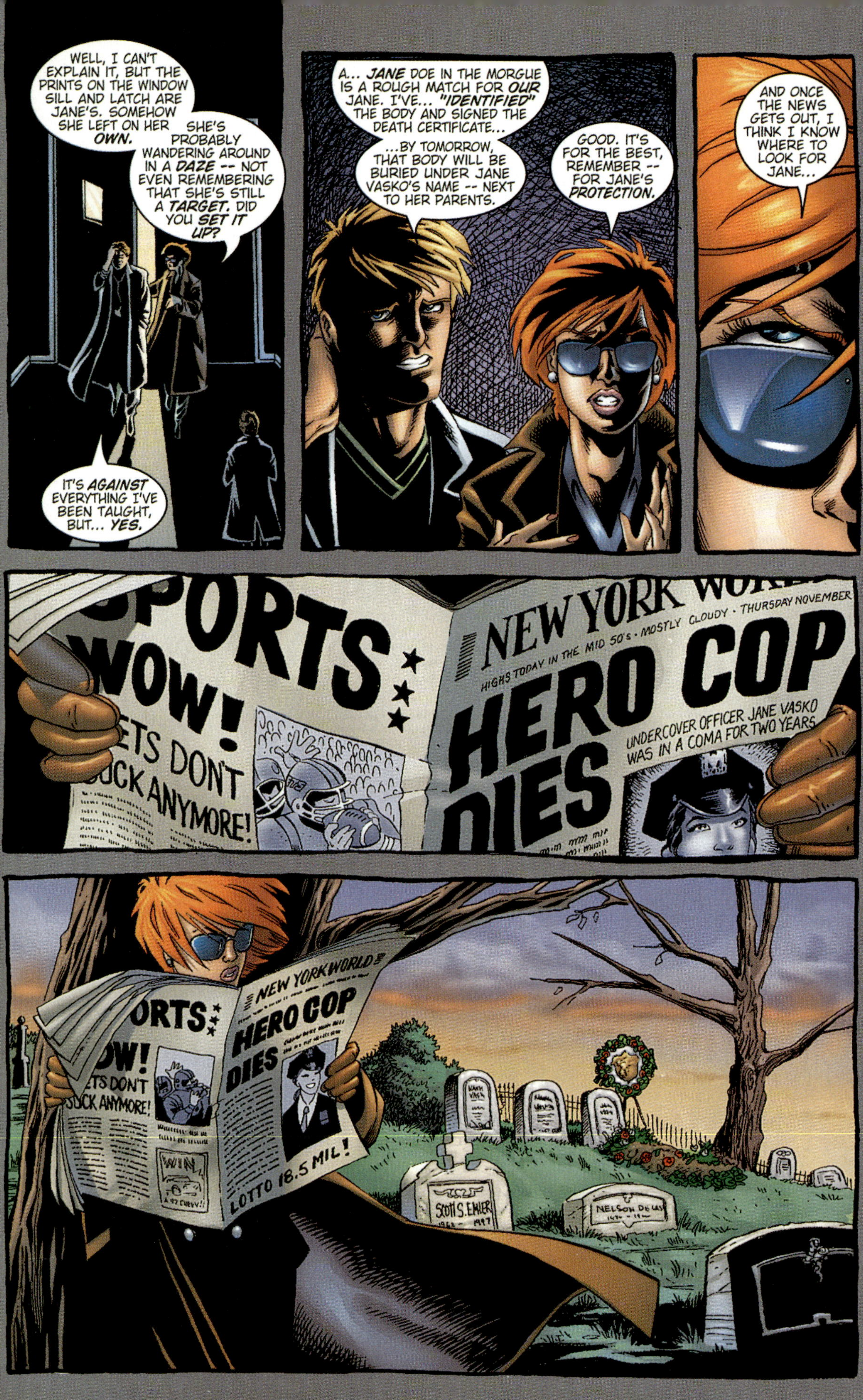
WELL, I CAN'T EXPLAIN IT, BUT THE PRINTS ON THE WINDOW SILL AND LATCH ARE JANE'S. SOMEHOW SHE LEFT ON HER OWN.
SHE'S PROBABLY WANDERING AROUND IN A DAZE -- NOT EVEN REMEMBERING THAT SHE'S STILL A TARGET. DID YOU SET IT UP?
IT'S AGAINST EVERYTHING I'VE BEEN TAUGHT, BUT... YES.
A... JANE DOE IN THE MORGUE IS A ROUGH MATCH FOR OUR JANE. I'VE... "IDENTIFIED" THE BODY AND SIGNED THE DEATH CERTIFICATE...
...BY TOMORROW, THAT BODY WILL BE BURIED UNDER JANE VASKO'S NAME -- NEXT TO HER PARENTS.
GOOD. IT'S FOR THE BEST, REMEMBER -- FOR JANE'S PROTECTION.
AND ONCE THE NEWS GETS OUT, I THINK I KNOW WHERE TO LOOK FOR JANE...
SPORTS
WOW!
ETS DON'T UCK ANYMORE!
NEW YORK WOR
HIGHS TODAY IN THE MID 50'S · MOSTLY CLOUDY · THURSDAY NOVEMBER
HERO COP DIES
UNDERCOVER OFFICER JANE VASKO WAS IN A COMA FOR TWO YEARS
NEW YORK WORLD
HERO COP DIES
ORTS
OW!
ETS DON'T SUCK ANYMORE!
WIN
LOTTO 18.5 MIL!
SCOTT S. EMLER
NELSON DE

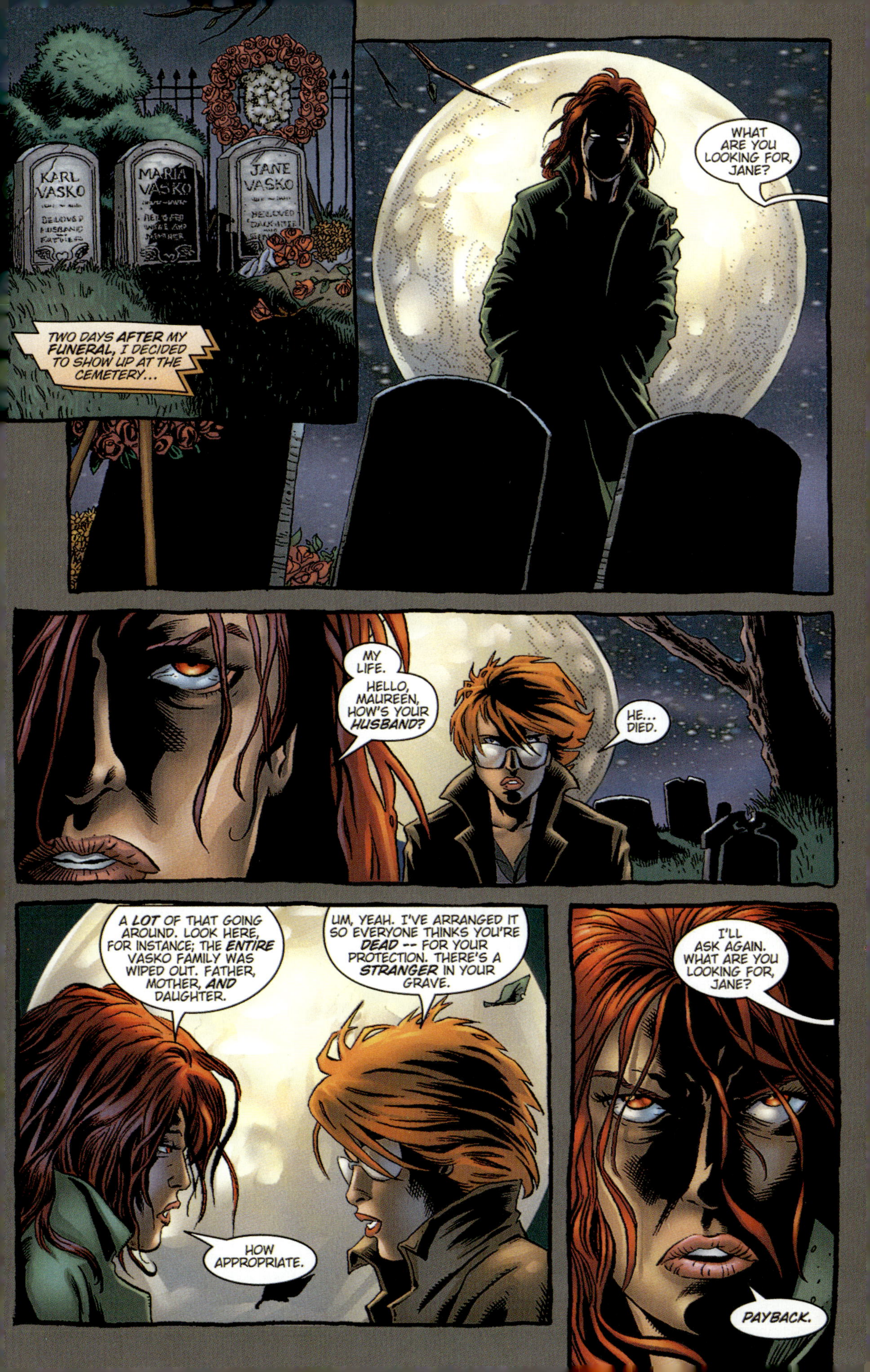
KARL VASKO
BELOVED HUSBAND FATHER
MARIA VASKO
BELOVED WIFE AND MOTHER
JANE VASKO
BELOVED DAUGHTER
TWO DAYS AFTER MY FUNERAL, I DECIDED TO SHOW UP AT THE CEMETERY...
WHAT ARE YOU LOOKING FOR, JANE?
MY LIFE.
HELLO, MAUREEN, HOW'S YOUR HUSBAND?
HE... DIED.
A LOT OF THAT GOING AROUND. LOOK HERE, FOR INSTANCE; THE ENTIRE VASKO FAMILY WAS WIPED OUT. FATHER, MOTHER, AND DAUGHTER.
UM, YEAH. I'VE ARRANGED IT SO EVERYONE THINKS YOU'RE DEAD -- FOR YOUR PROTECTION. THERE'S A STRANGER IN YOUR GRAVE.
HOW APPROPRIATE.
I'LL ASK AGAIN. WHAT ARE YOU LOOKING FOR, JANE?
PAYBACK.

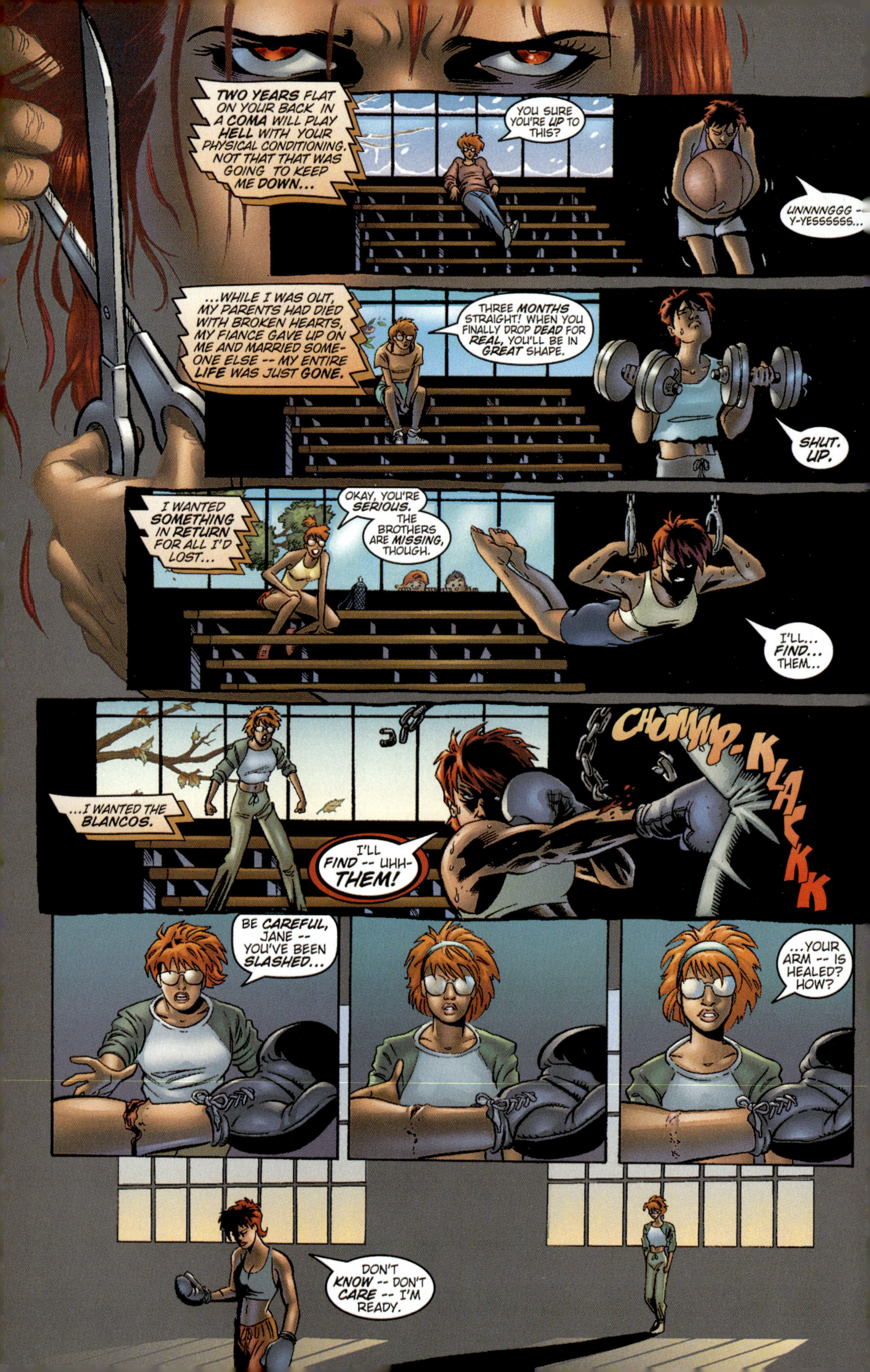

TWO YEARS FLAT ON YOUR BACK IN A COMA WILL PLAY HELL WITH YOUR PHYSICAL CONDITIONING. NOT THAT THAT WAS GOING TO KEEP ME DOWN...
YOU SURE YOU'RE UP TO THIS?
UNNNNGGG -- Y-YESSSSSS...
...WHILE I WAS OUT, MY PARENTS HAD DIED WITH BROKEN HEARTS, MY FIANCE GAVE UP ON ME AND MARRIED SOMEONE ELSE -- MY ENTIRE LIFE WAS JUST GONE.
THREE MONTHS STRAIGHT! WHEN YOU FINALLY DROP DEAD FOR REAL, YOU'LL BE IN GREAT SHAPE.
SHUT. UP.
I WANTED SOMETHING IN RETURN FOR ALL I'D LOST...
OKAY, YOU'RE SERIOUS. THE BROTHERS ARE MISSING, THOUGH.
I'LL... FIND... THEM...
...I WANTED THE BLANCOS.
I'LL FIND -- UHH- THEM!
CHOMMP-KLACKK
BE CAREFUL, JANE -- YOU'VE BEEN SLASHED...
...YOUR ARM -- IS HEALED? HOW?
DON'T KNOW -- DON'T CARE -- I'M READY.

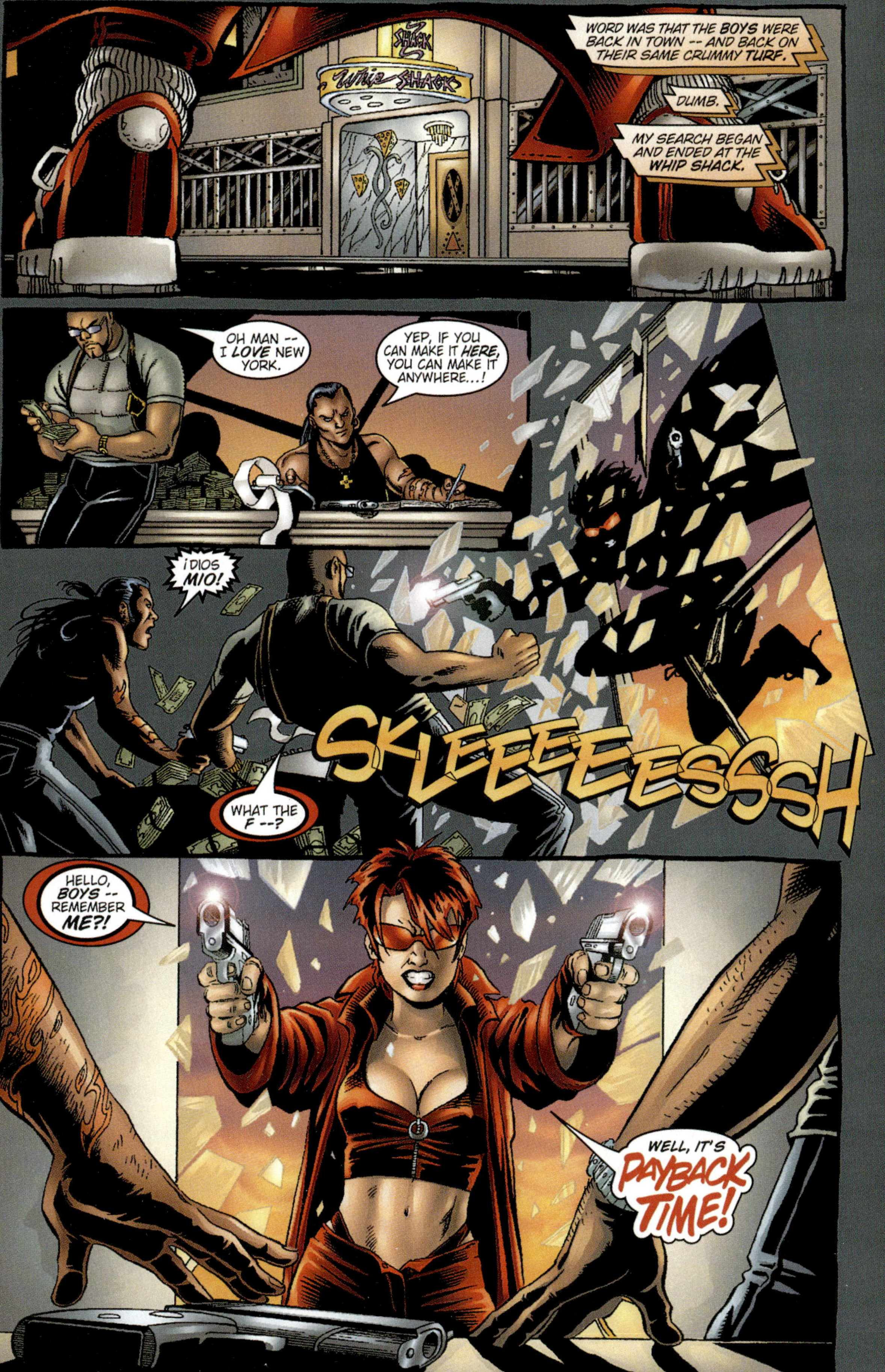
WORD WAS THAT THE BOYS WERE BACK IN TOWN -- AND BACK ON THEIR SAME CRUMMY TURF.
DUMB.
MY SEARCH BEGAN AND ENDED AT THE WHIP SHACK.
OH MAN -- I LOVE NEW YORK.
YEP, IF YOU CAN MAKE IT HERE, YOU CAN MAKE IT ANYWHERE...!
¡DIOS MIO!
SKLEEEEEESSSSH
WHAT THE F --?
HELLO, BOYS -- REMEMBER ME?!
WELL, IT'S PAYBACK TIME!

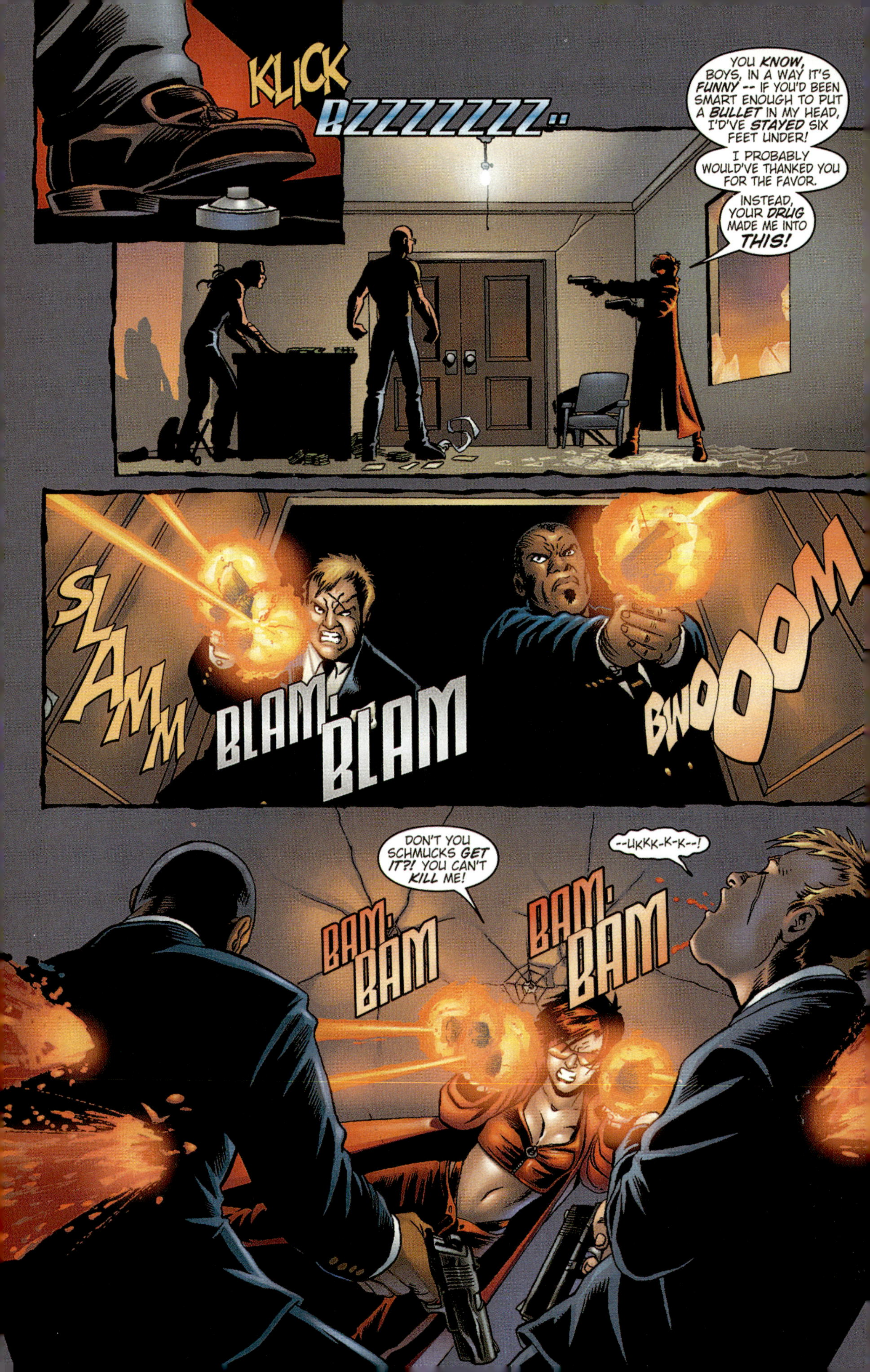
KLICK
BZZZZZZZZ..
YOU KNOW, BOYS, IN A WAY IT'S FUNNY -- IF YOU'D BEEN SMART ENOUGH TO PUT A BULLET IN MY HEAD, I'D'VE STAYED SIX FEET UNDER!
I PROBABLY WOULD'VE THANKED YOU FOR THE FAVOR.
INSTEAD, YOUR DRUG MADE ME INTO THIS!
SLAMM
BLAM BLAM
BWOOOOM
DON'T YOU SCHMUCKS GET IT?! YOU CAN'T KILL ME!
--UKKK-K-K--!
BAM BAM
BAM BAM

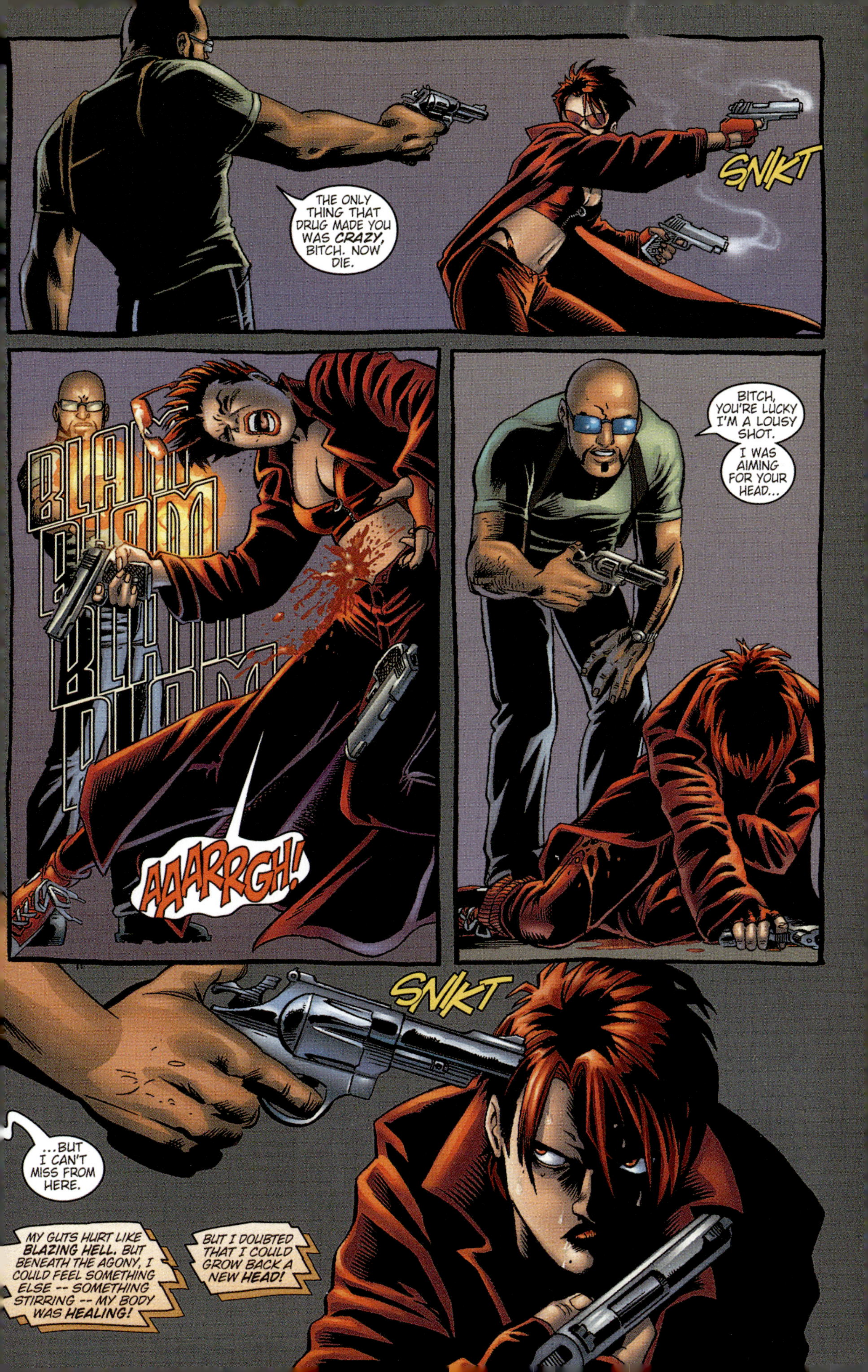
SNIKT
THE ONLY THING THAT DRUG MADE YOU WAS CRAZY, BITCH. NOW DIE.
BLAM BLAM BLAM BLAM
AAARRGH!
BITCH, YOU'RE LUCKY I'M A LOUSY SHOT.
I WAS AIMING FOR YOUR HEAD...
SNIKT
...BUT I CAN'T MISS FROM HERE.
MY GUTS HURT LIKE BLAZING HELL. BUT BENEATH THE AGONY, I COULD FEEL SOMETHING ELSE -- SOMETHING STIRRING -- MY BODY WAS HEALING!
BUT I DOUBTED THAT I COULD GROW BACK A NEW HEAD!

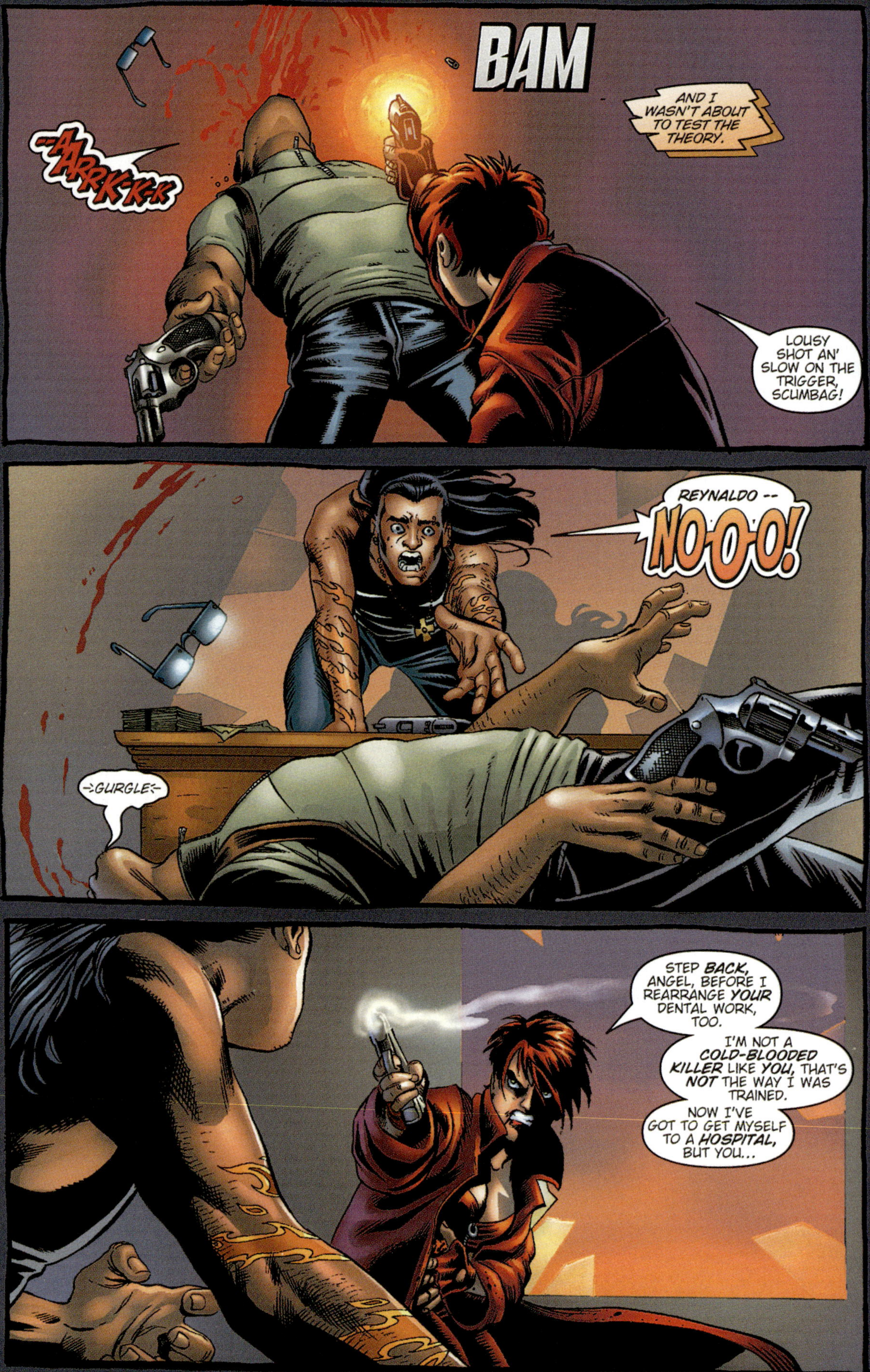
BAM
AND I WASN'T ABOUT TO TEST THE THEORY.
-AARRK-K-K
LOUSY SHOT AN' SLOW ON THE TRIGGER, SCUMBAG!
REYNALDO -- NO-O-O!
-GURGLE-
STEP BACK, ANGEL, BEFORE I REARRANGE YOUR DENTAL WORK, TOO.
I'M NOT A COLD-BLOODED KILLER LIKE YOU, THAT'S NOT THE WAY I WAS TRAINED.
NOW I'VE GOT TO GET MYSELF TO A HOSPITAL, BUT YOU...

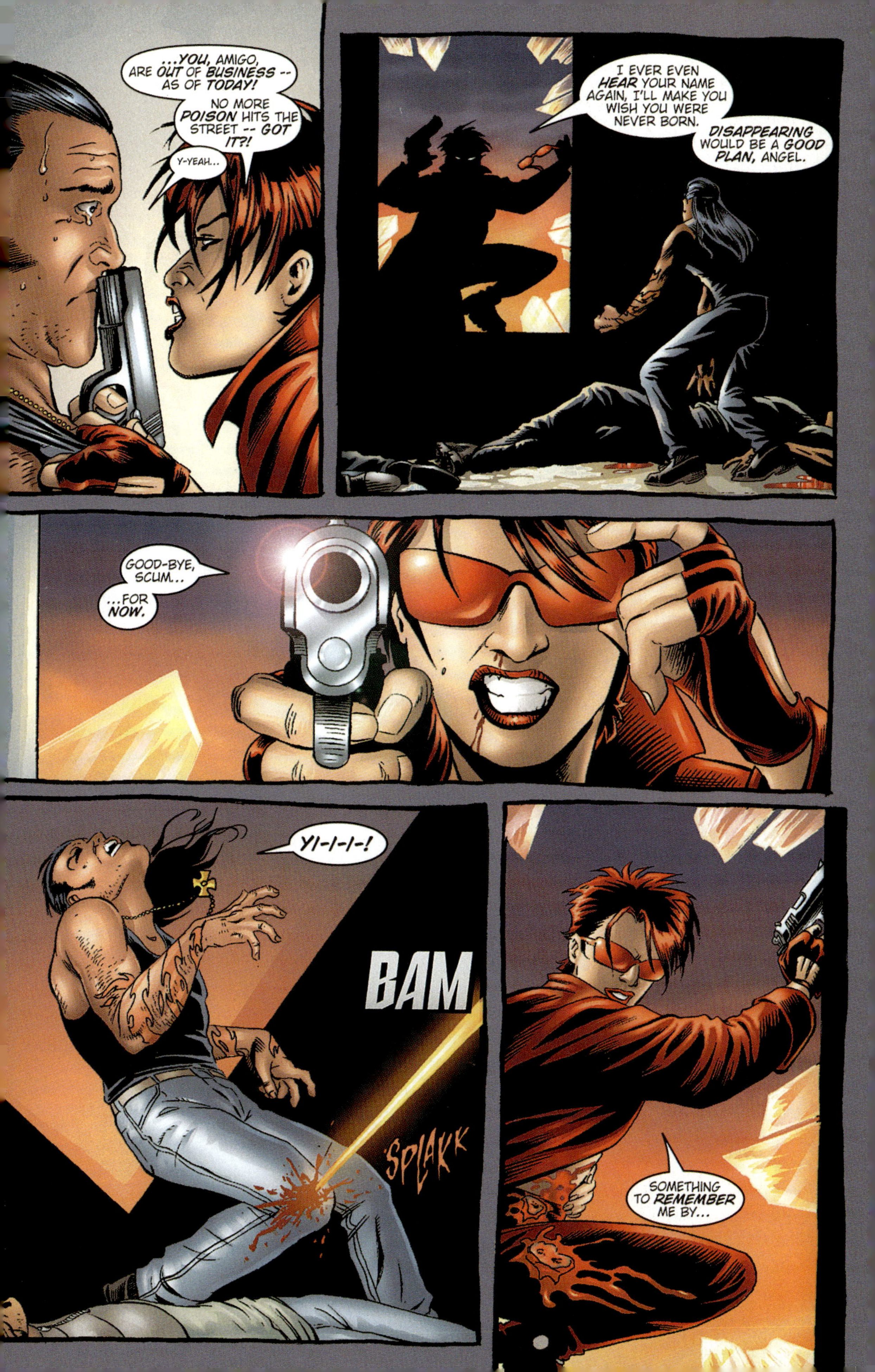
...YOU, AMIGO, ARE OUT OF BUSINESS -- AS OF TODAY!
NO MORE POISON HITS THE STREET -- GOT IT?!
Y-YEAH...
I EVER EVEN HEAR YOUR NAME AGAIN, I'LL MAKE YOU WISH YOU WERE NEVER BORN.
DISAPPEARING WOULD BE A GOOD PLAN, ANGEL.
GOOD-BYE, SCUM...
...FOR NOW.
YI-I-I-!
BAM
SPLAKK
SOMETHING TO REMEMBER ME BY...

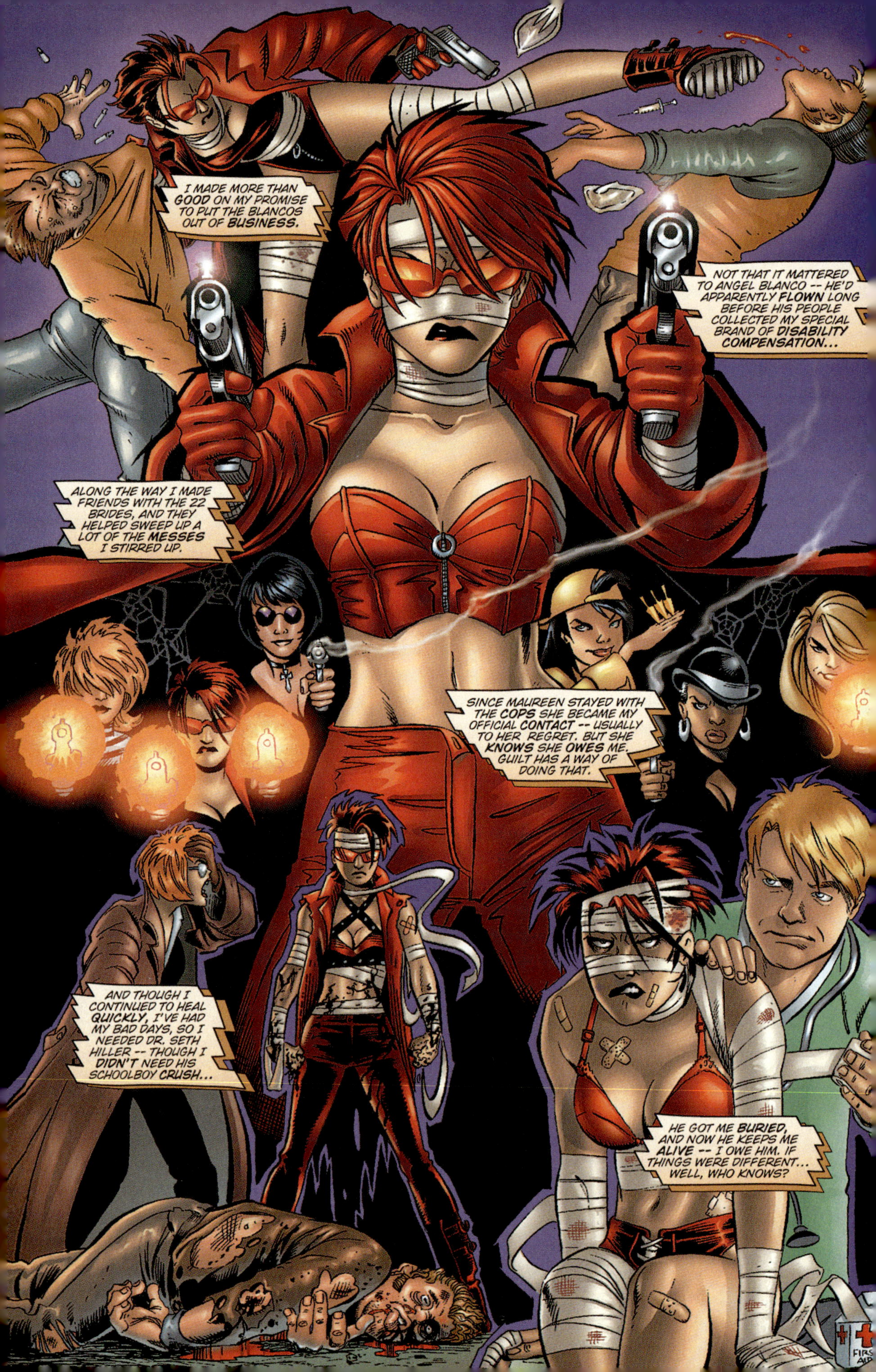

I MADE MORE THAN GOOD ON MY PROMISE TO PUT THE BLANCOS OUT OF BUSINESS.
NOT THAT IT MATTERED TO ANGEL BLANCO -- HE'D APPARENTLY FLOWN LONG BEFORE HIS PEOPLE COLLECTED MY SPECIAL BRAND OF DISABILITY COMPENSATION...
ALONG THE WAY I MADE FRIENDS WITH THE 22 BRIDES, AND THEY HELPED SWEEP UP A LOT OF THE MESSES I STIRRED UP.
SINCE MAUREEN STAYED WITH THE COPS SHE BECAME MY OFFICIAL CONTACT -- USUALLY TO HER REGRET. BUT SHE KNOWS SHE OWES ME. GUILT HAS A WAY OF DOING THAT.
AND THOUGH I CONTINUED TO HEAL QUICKLY, I'VE HAD MY BAD DAYS, SO I NEEDED DR. SETH HILLER -- THOUGH I DIDN'T NEED HIS SCHOOLBOY CRUSH...
HE GOT ME BURIED, AND NOW HE KEEPS ME ALIVE -- I OWE HIM. IF THINGS WERE DIFFERENT... WELL, WHO KNOWS?

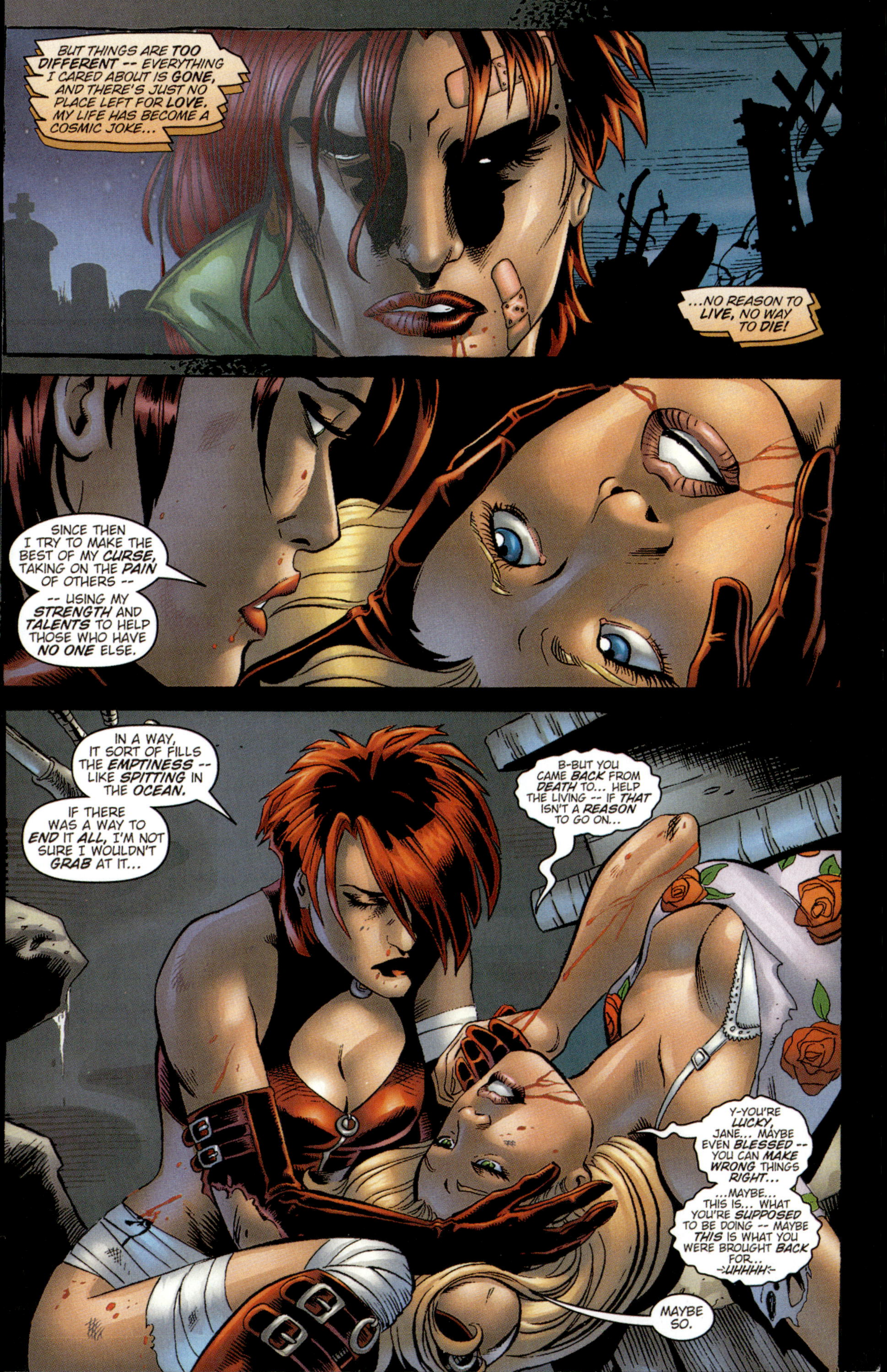
BUT THINGS ARE TOO DIFFERENT -- EVERYTHING I CARED ABOUT IS GONE, AND THERE'S JUST NO PLACE LEFT FOR LOVE. MY LIFE HAS BECOME A COSMIC JOKE...
...NO REASON TO LIVE, NO WAY TO DIE!
SINCE THEN I TRY TO MAKE THE BEST OF MY CURSE, TAKING ON THE PAIN OF OTHERS --
-- USING MY STRENGTH AND TALENTS TO HELP THOSE WHO HAVE NO ONE ELSE.
IN A WAY, IT SORT OF FILLS THE EMPTINESS -- LIKE SPITTING IN THE OCEAN.
IF THERE WAS A WAY TO END IT ALL, I'M NOT SURE I WOULDN'T GRAB AT IT...
B-BUT YOU CAME BACK FROM DEATH TO... HELP THE LIVING -- IF THAT ISN'T A REASON TO GO ON...
Y-YOU'RE LUCKY, JANE... MAYBE EVEN BLESSED -- YOU CAN MAKE WRONG THINGS RIGHT...
...MAYBE... THIS IS... WHAT YOU'RE SUPPOSED TO BE DOING -- MAYBE THIS IS WHAT YOU WERE BROUGHT BACK FOR... -UHHHH-
MAYBE SO.

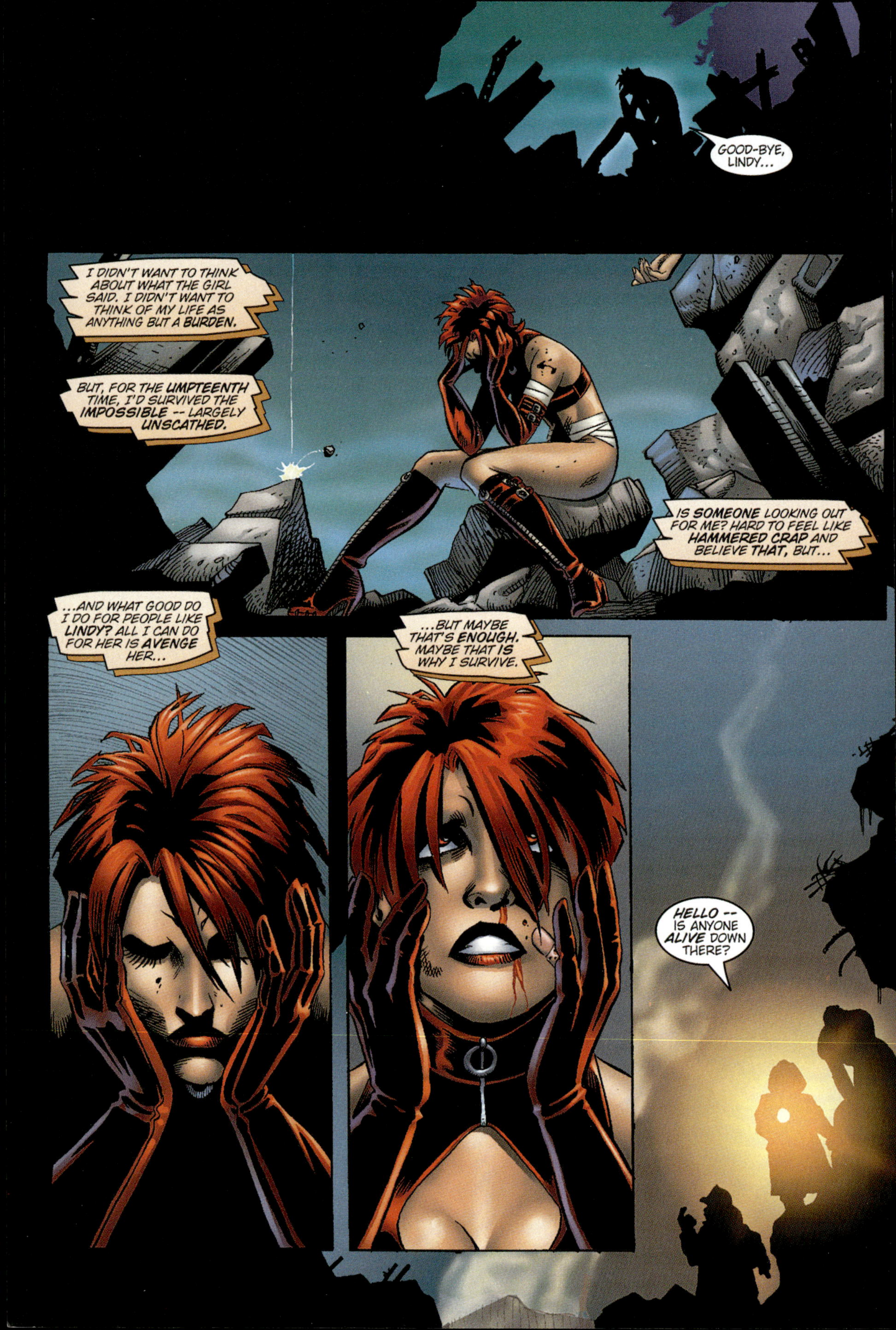
GOOD-BYE, LINDY...
I DIDN'T WANT TO THINK ABOUT WHAT THE GIRL SAID. I DIDN'T WANT TO THINK OF MY LIFE AS ANYTHING BUT A BURDEN.
BUT, FOR THE UMPTEENTH TIME, I'D SURVIVED THE IMPOSSIBLE -- LARGELY UNSCATHED.
IS SOMEONE LOOKING OUT FOR ME? HARD TO FEEL LIKE HAMMERED CRAP AND BELIEVE THAT, BUT...
...AND WHAT GOOD DO I DO FOR PEOPLE LIKE LINDY? ALL I CAN DO FOR HER IS AVENGE HER...
...BUT MAYBE THAT'S ENOUGH. MAYBE THAT IS WHY I SURVIVE.
HELLO -- IS ANYONE ALIVE DOWN THERE?

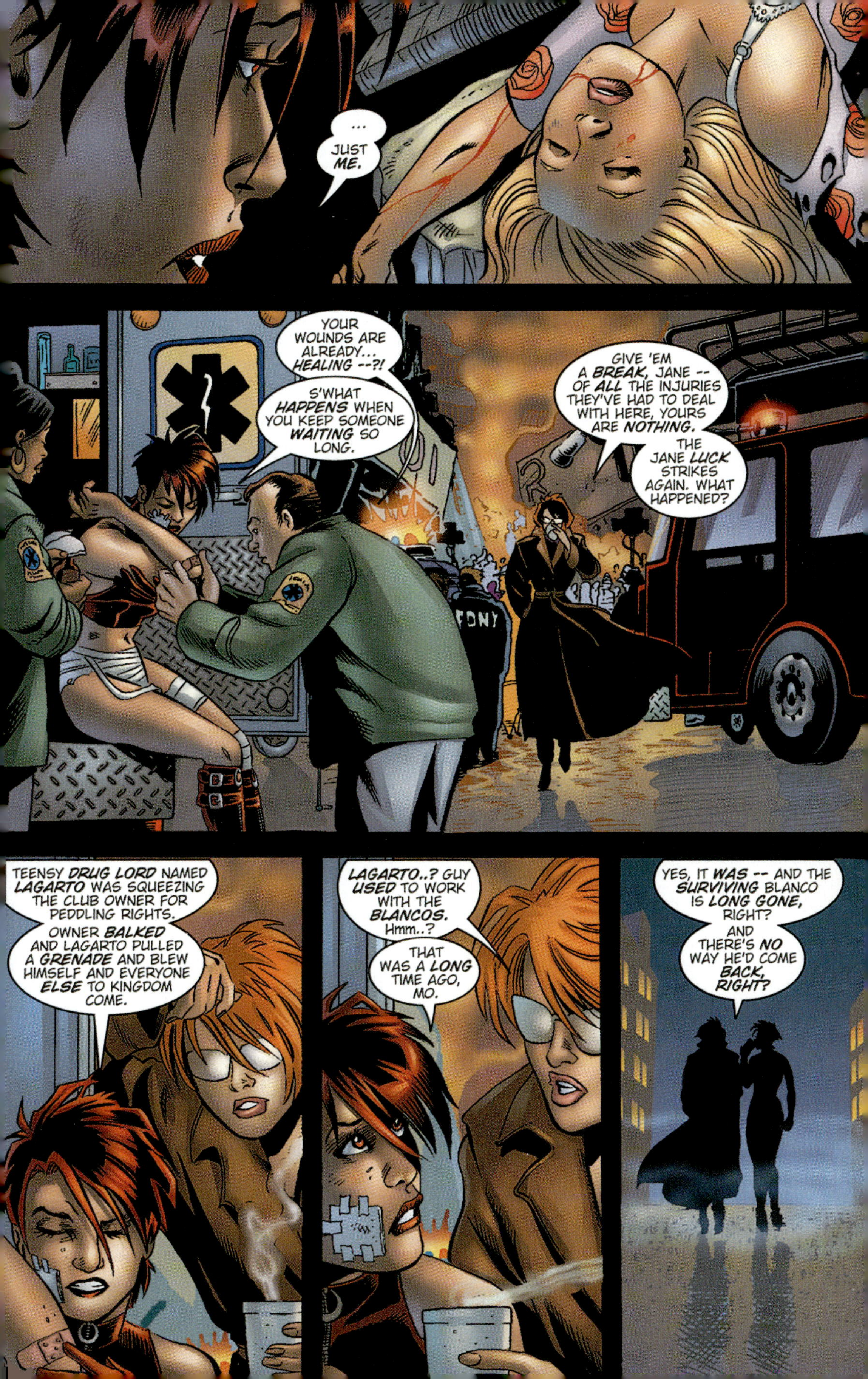
... JUST ME.
YOUR WOUNDS ARE ALREADY... HEALING --?!
S'WHAT HAPPENS WHEN YOU KEEP SOMEONE WAITING SO LONG.
GIVE 'EM A BREAK, JANE -- OF ALL THE INJURIES THEY'VE HAD TO DEAL WITH HERE, YOURS ARE NOTHING.
THE JANE LUCK STRIKES AGAIN. WHAT HAPPENED?
FDNY
TEENSY DRUG LORD NAMED LAGARTO WAS SQUEEZING THE CLUB OWNER FOR PEDDLING RIGHTS.
OWNER BALKED AND LAGARTO PULLED A GRENADE AND BLEW HIMSELF AND EVERYONE ELSE TO KINGDOM COME.
LAGARTO..? GUY USED TO WORK WITH THE BLANCOS. Hmm..?
THAT WAS A LONG TIME AGO, MO.
YES, IT WAS -- AND THE SURVIVING BLANCO IS LONG GONE, RIGHT?
AND THERE'S NO WAY HE'D COME BACK, RIGHT?

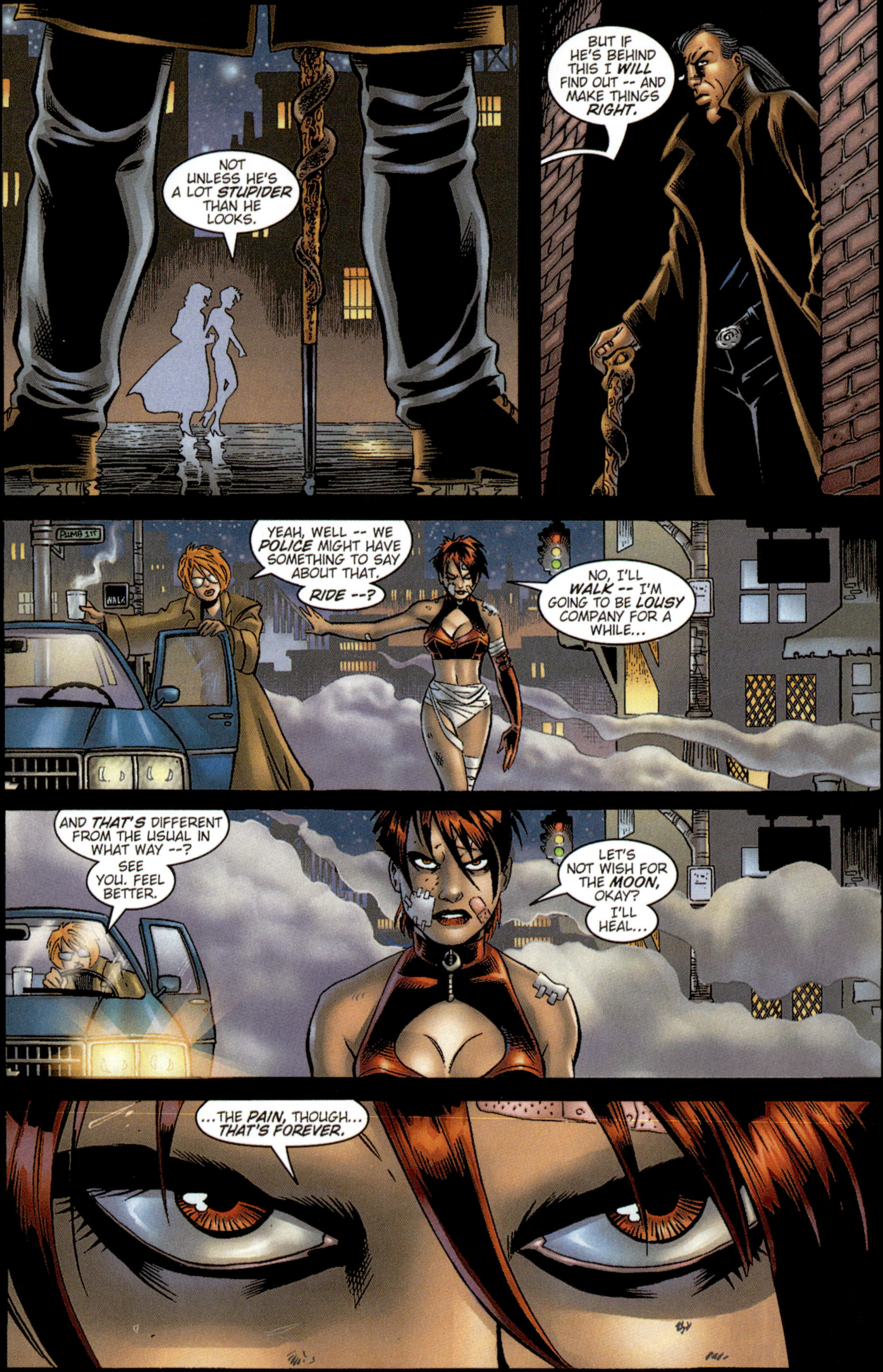
NOT UNLESS HE'S A LOT STUPIDER THAN HE LOOKS.
BUT IF HE'S BEHIND THIS I WILL FIND OUT -- AND MAKE THINGS RIGHT.
PLUMB ST
WALK
YEAH, WELL -- WE POLICE MIGHT HAVE SOMETHING TO SAY ABOUT THAT. RIDE --?
NO, I'LL WALK -- I'M GOING TO BE LOUSY COMPANY FOR A WHILE...
AND THAT'S DIFFERENT FROM THE USUAL IN WHAT WAY --? SEE YOU. FEEL BETTER.
LET'S NOT WISH FOR THE MOON, OKAY? I'LL HEAL...
...THE PAIN, THOUGH... THAT'S FOREVER.

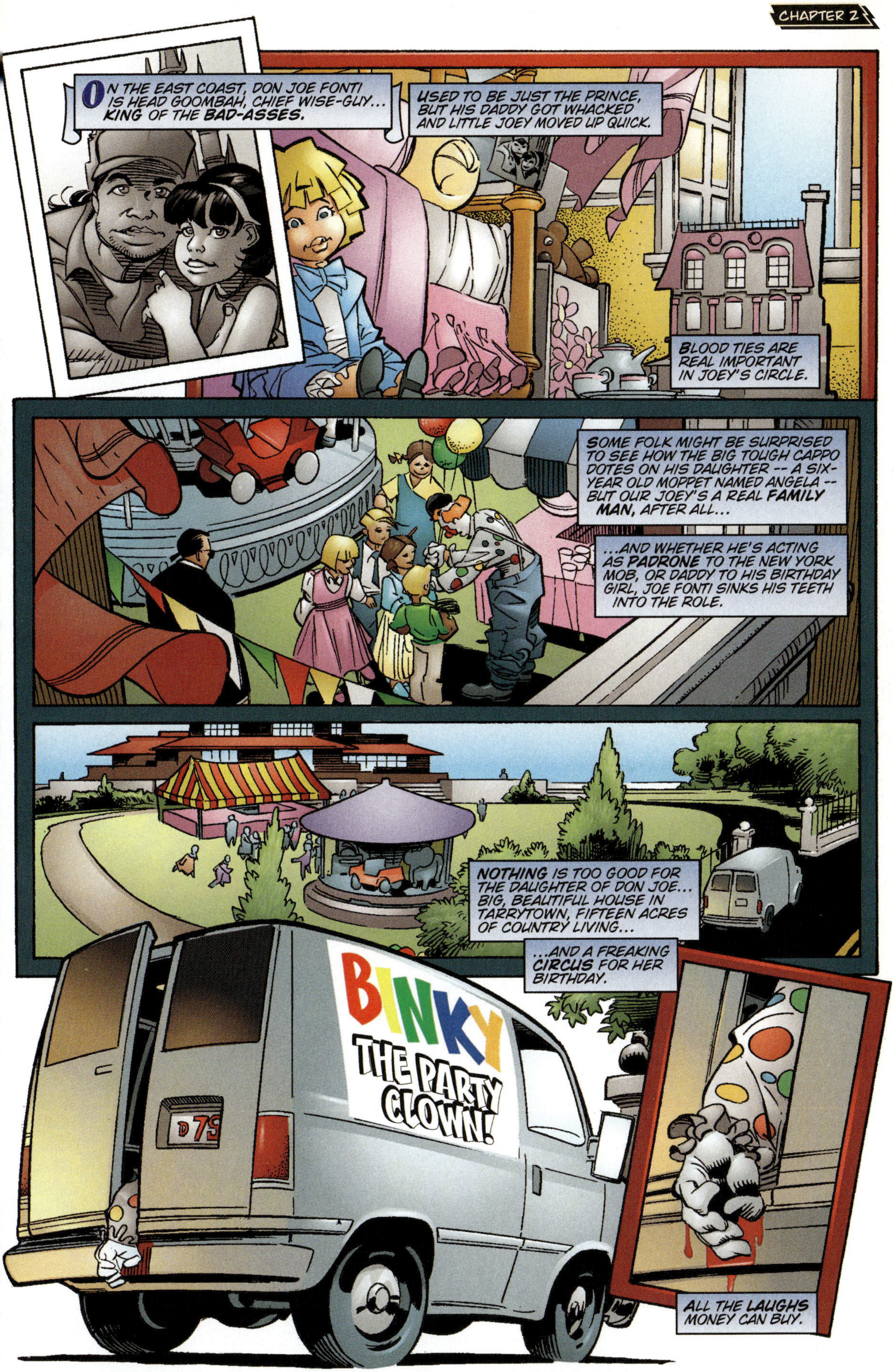
ON THE EAST COAST, DON JOE FONTI IS HEAD GOOMBAH, CHIEF WISE-GUY... KING OF THE BAD-ASSES.
USED TO BE JUST THE PRINCE, BUT HIS DADDY GOT WHACKED AND LITTLE JOEY MOVED UP QUICK.
BLOOD TIES ARE REAL IMPORTANT IN JOEY'S CIRCLE.
SOME FOLK MIGHT BE SURPRISED TO SEE HOW THE BIG TOUGH CAPPO DOTES ON HIS DAUGHTER -- A SIX-YEAR OLD MOPPET NAMED ANGELA -- BUT OUR JOEY'S A REAL FAMILY MAN, AFTER ALL...
...AND WHETHER HE'S ACTING AS PADRONE TO THE NEW YORK MOB, OR DADDY TO HIS BIRTHDAY GIRL, JOE FONTI SINKS HIS TEETH INTO THE ROLE.
NOTHING IS TOO GOOD FOR THE DAUGHTER OF DON JOE... BIG, BEAUTIFUL HOUSE IN TARRYTOWN, FIFTEEN ACRES OF COUNTRY LIVING...
...AND A FREAKING CIRCUS FOR HER BIRTHDAY.
BINKY THE PARTY CLOWN!
D79
ALL THE LAUGHS MONEY CAN BUY.

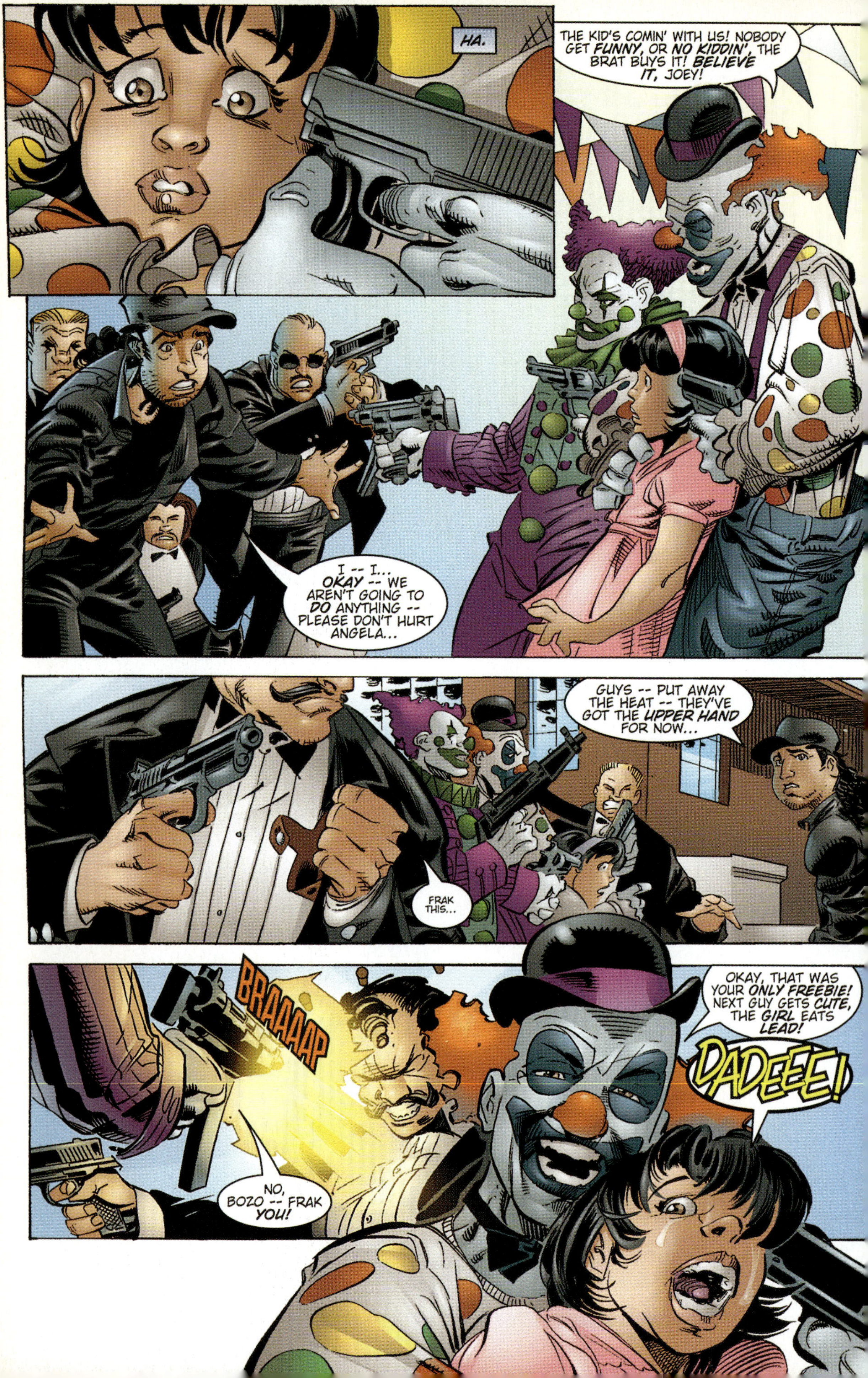
HA.
THE KID'S COMIN' WITH US! NOBODY GET FUNNY, OR NO KIDDIN', THE BRAT BUYS IT! BELIEVE IT, JOEY!
I -- I... OKAY -- WE AREN'T GOING TO DO ANYTHING -- PLEASE DON'T HURT ANGELA...
GUYS -- PUT AWAY THE HEAT -- THEY'VE GOT THE UPPER HAND FOR NOW...
FRAK THIS...
BRAAAAP
NO, BOZO -- FRAK YOU!
OKAY, THAT WAS YOUR ONLY FREEBIE! NEXT GUY GETS CUTE, THE GIRL EATS LEAD!
DADEEE!

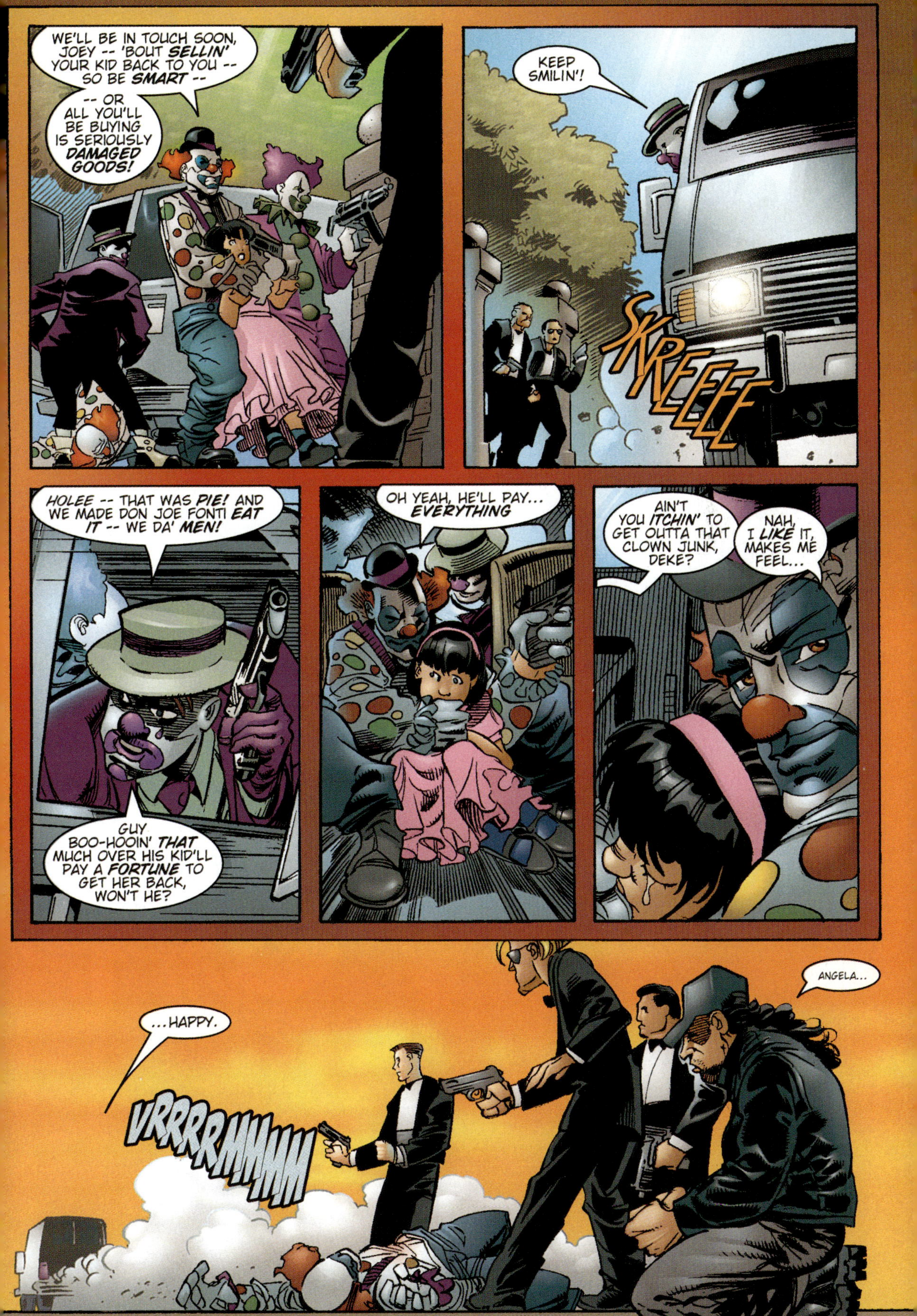
WE'LL BE IN TOUCH SOON, JOEY -- 'BOUT SELLIN' YOUR KID BACK TO YOU -- SO BE SMART --
-- OR ALL YOU'LL BE BUYING IS SERIOUSLY DAMAGED GOODS!
KEEP SMILIN'!
SKREEEE
HOLEE -- THAT WAS PIE! AND WE MADE DON JOE FONTI EAT IT -- WE DA' MEN!
GUY BOO-HOOIN' THAT MUCH OVER HIS KID'LL PAY A FORTUNE TO GET HER BACK, WON'T HE?
OH YEAH, HE'LL PAY... EVERYTHING
AIN'T YOU ITCHIN' TO GET OUTTA THAT CLOWN JUNK, DEKE?
NAH, I LIKE IT, MAKES ME FEEL...
...HAPPY.
VRRRRMMMM
ANGELA...

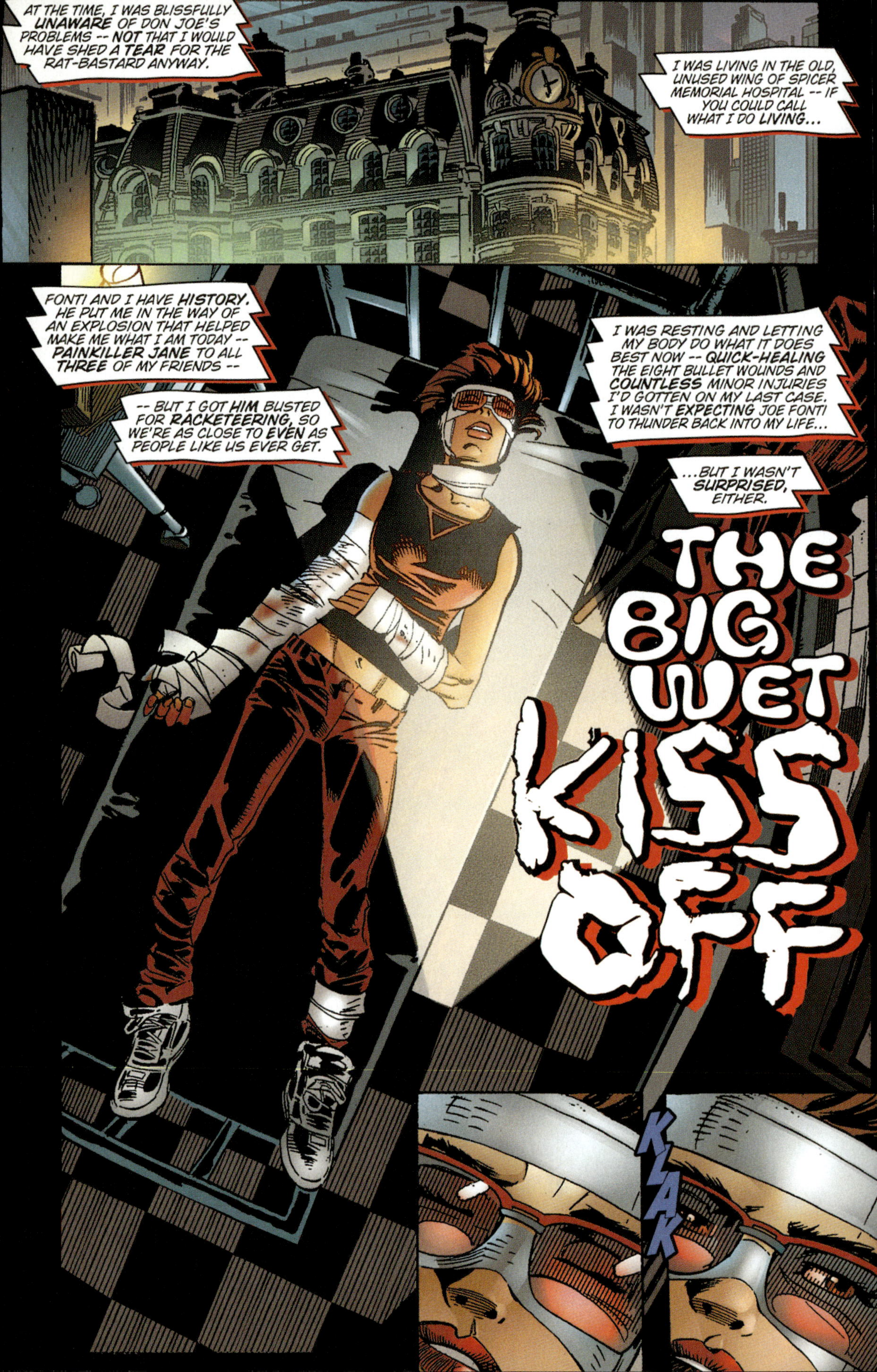
AT THE TIME, I WAS BLISSFULLY UNAWARE OF DON JOE'S PROBLEMS -- NOT THAT I WOULD HAVE SHED A TEAR FOR THE RAT-BASTARD ANYWAY.
I WAS LIVING IN THE OLD, UNUSED WING OF SPICER MEMORIAL HOSPITAL -- IF YOU COULD CALL WHAT I DO LIVING...
FONTI AND I HAVE HISTORY. HE PUT ME IN THE WAY OF AN EXPLOSION THAT HELPED MAKE ME WHAT I AM TODAY -- PAINKILLER JANE TO ALL THREE OF MY FRIENDS --
-- BUT I GOT HIM BUSTED FOR RACKETEERING, SO WE'RE AS CLOSE TO EVEN AS PEOPLE LIKE US EVER GET.
I WAS RESTING AND LETTING MY BODY DO WHAT IT DOES BEST NOW -- QUICK-HEALING THE EIGHT BULLET WOUNDS AND COUNTLESS MINOR INJURIES I'D GOTTEN ON MY LAST CASE. I WASN'T EXPECTING JOE FONTI TO THUNDER BACK INTO MY LIFE...
...BUT I WASN'T SURPRISED, EITHER.
THE BIG WET KISS OFF
KLAK

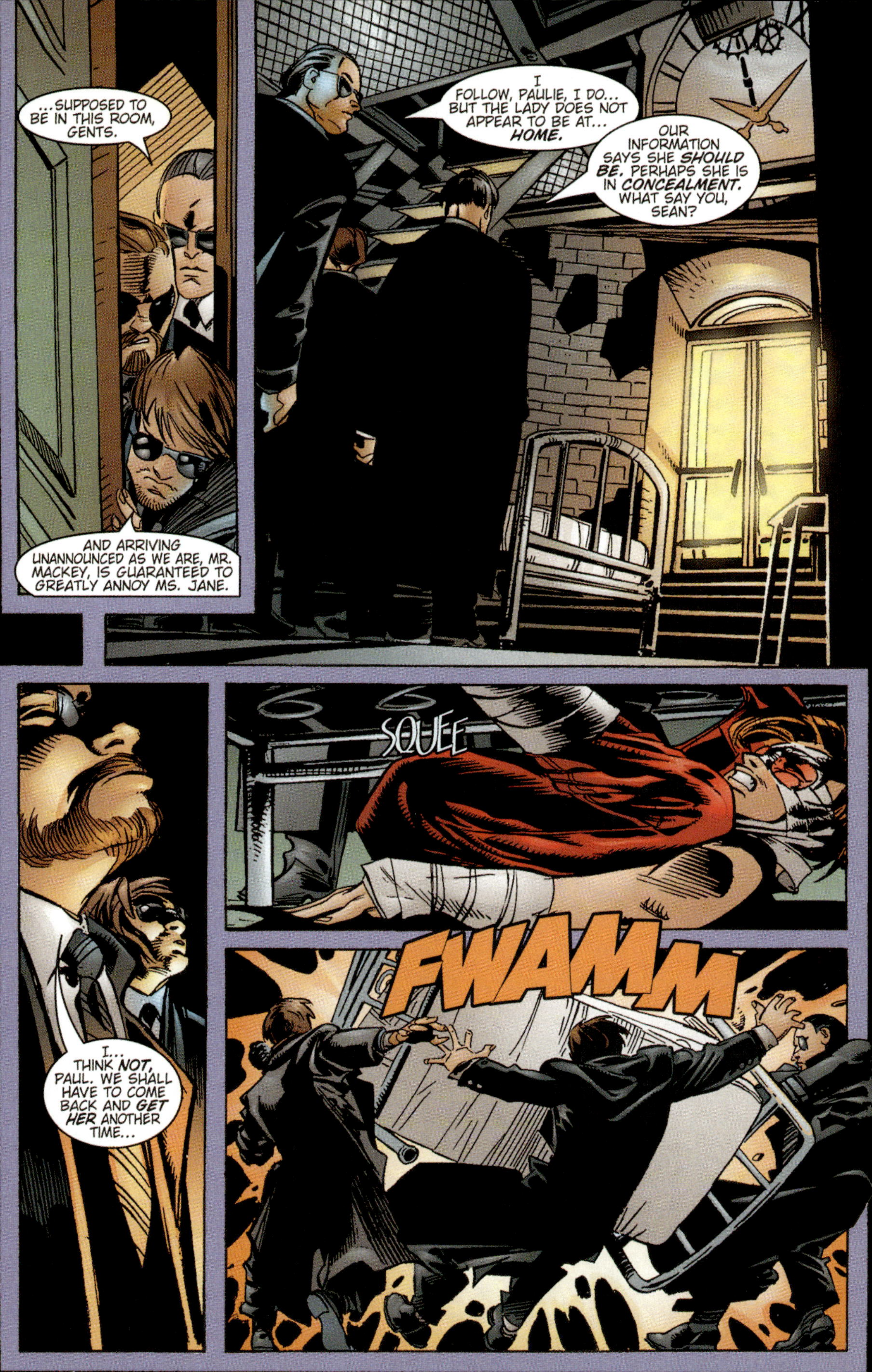
...SUPPOSED TO BE IN THIS ROOM, GENTS.
AND ARRIVING UNANNOUNCED AS WE ARE, MR. MACKEY, IS GUARANTEED TO GREATLY ANNOY MS. JANE.
I FOLLOW, PAULIE, I DO... BUT THE LADY DOES NOT APPEAR TO BE AT... **HOME.**
OUR INFORMATION SAYS SHE **SHOULD BE.** PERHAPS SHE IS IN **CONCEALMENT.** WHAT SAY YOU, SEAN?
I... THINK **NOT,** PAUL. WE SHALL HAVE TO COME BACK AND **GET HER** ANOTHER TIME...
SQUEE
FWAMM

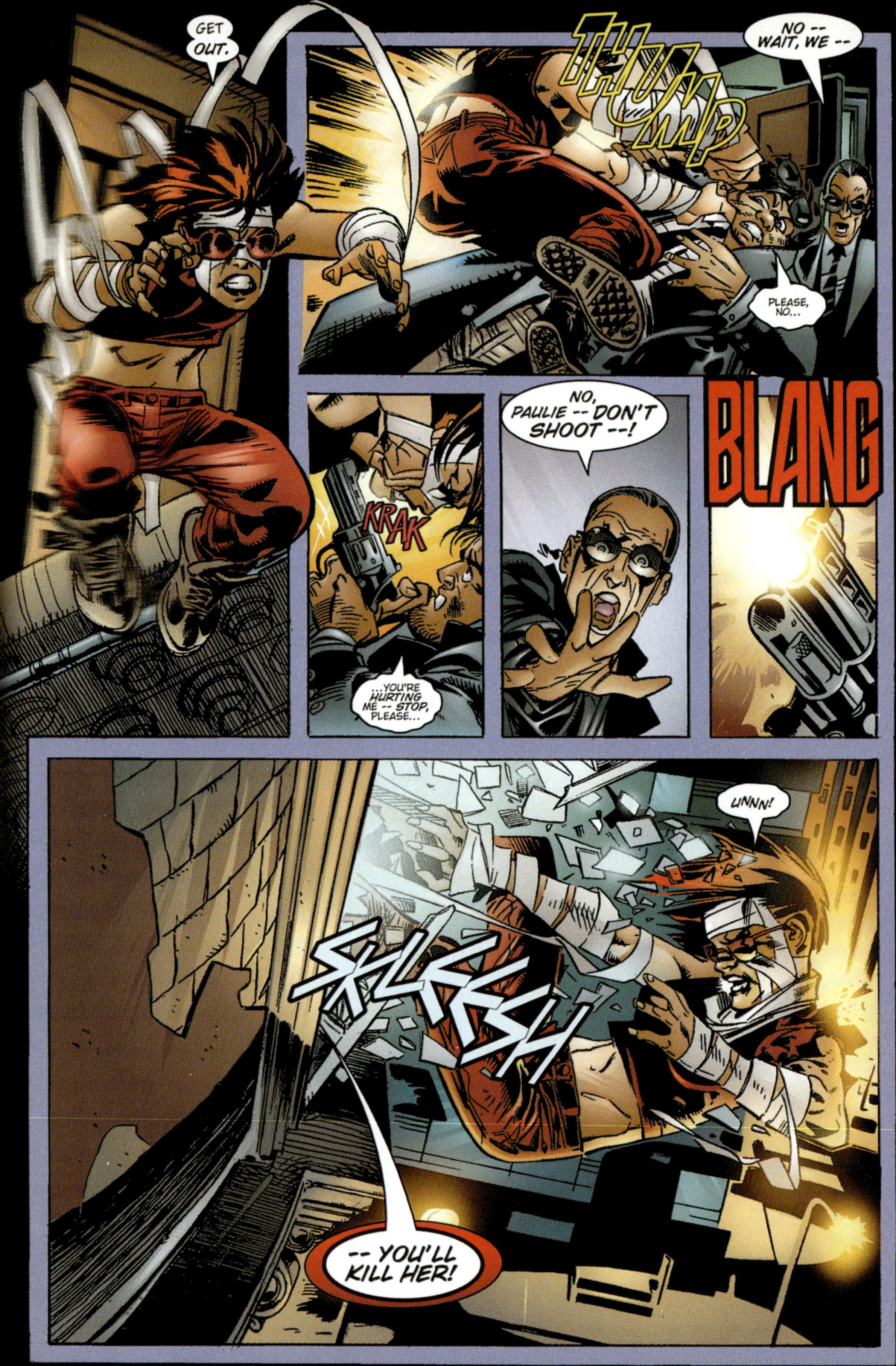
GET OUT.
THUMP
NO -- WAIT, WE --
PLEASE, NO...
KRAK
...YOU'RE HURTING ME -- STOP, PLEASE...
NO, PAULIE -- DON'T SHOOT --!
BLANG
UNNN!
SKLKESH
-- YOU'LL KILL HER!

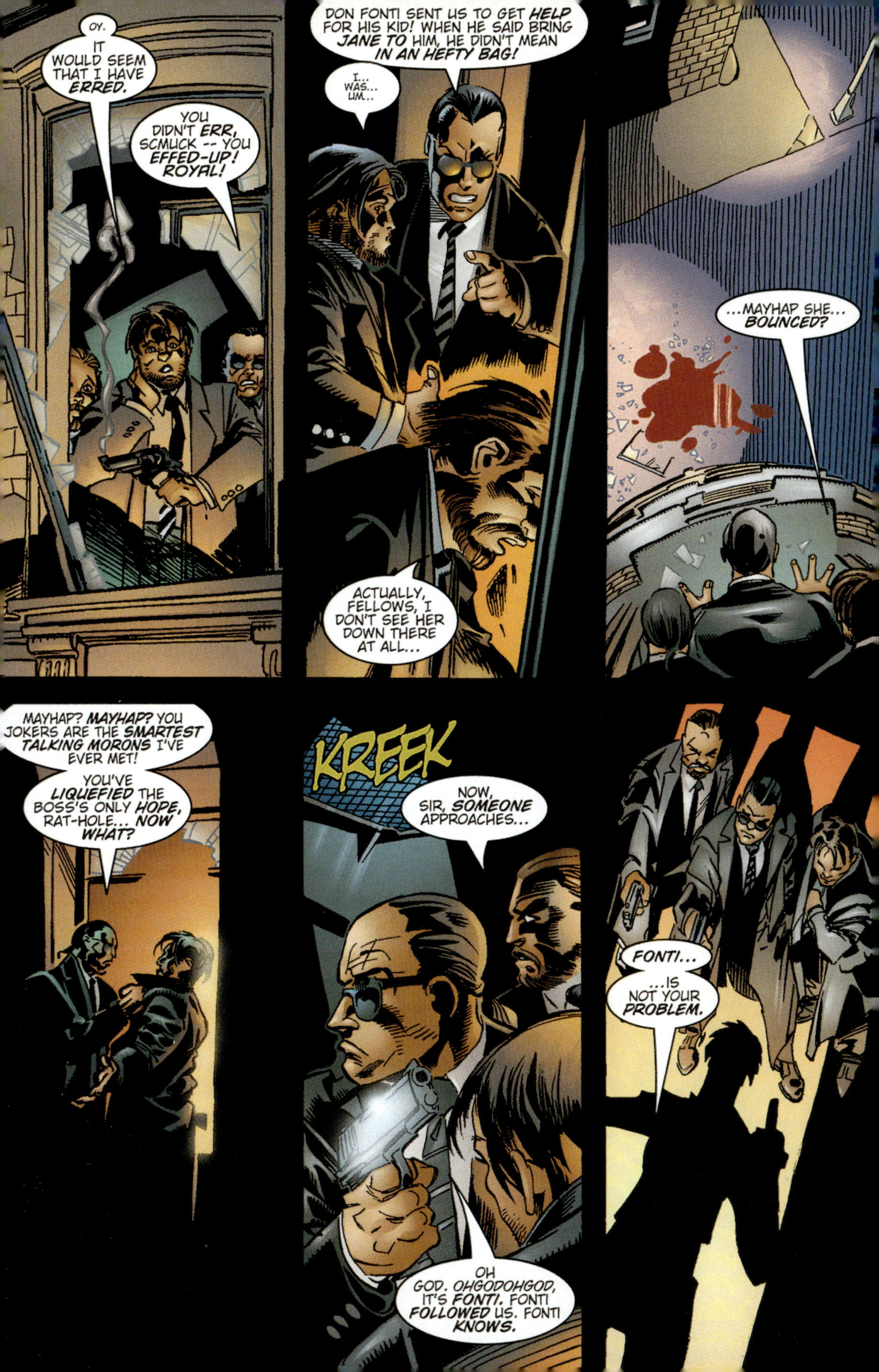
OY.
IT WOULD SEEM THAT I HAVE ERRED.
YOU DIDN'T ERR, SCMUCK -- YOU EFFED-UP! ROYAL!
DON FONTI SENT US TO GET HELP FOR HIS KID! WHEN HE SAID BRING JANE TO HIM, HE DIDN'T MEAN IN AN HEFTY BAG!
I... WAS... UM...
ACTUALLY, FELLOWS, I DON'T SEE HER DOWN THERE AT ALL...
...MAYHAP SHE... BOUNCED?
MAYHAP? MAYHAP? YOU JOKERS ARE THE SMARTEST TALKING MORONS I'VE EVER MET!
YOU'VE LIQUEFIED THE BOSS'S ONLY HOPE, RAT-HOLE... NOW WHAT?
KREEK
NOW, SIR, SOMEONE APPROACHES...
OH GOD. OHGODOHGOD, IT'S FONTI. FONTI FOLLOWED US. FONTI KNOWS.
FONTI...
...IS NOT YOUR PROBLEM.

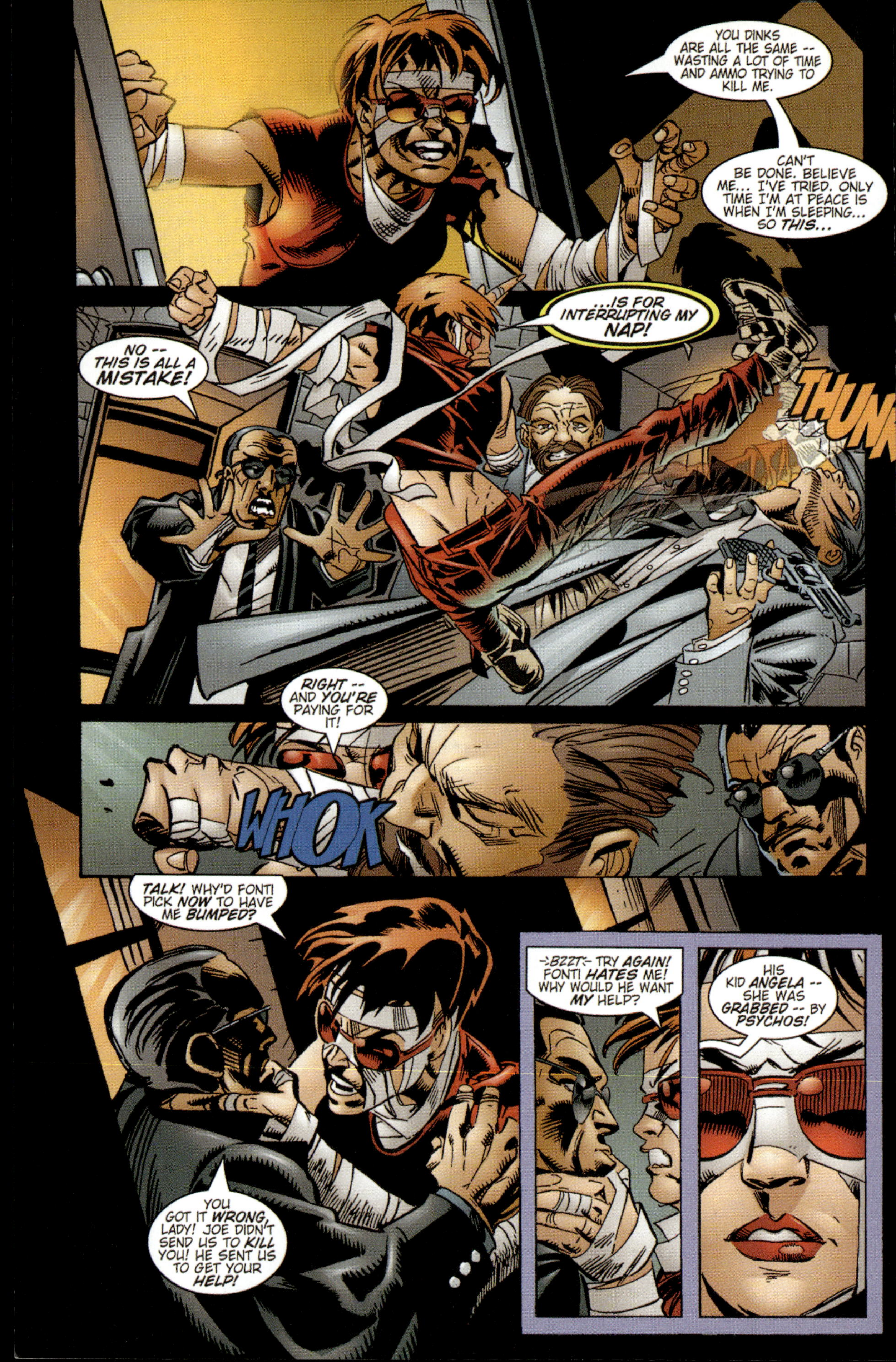
YOU DINKS ARE ALL THE SAME -- WASTING A LOT OF TIME AND AMMO TRYING TO KILL ME.
CAN'T BE DONE. BELIEVE ME... I'VE TRIED. ONLY TIME I'M AT PEACE IS WHEN I'M SLEEPING... SO THIS...
...IS FOR INTERRUPTING MY NAP!
NO -- THIS IS ALL A MISTAKE!
THUNK
RIGHT -- AND YOU'RE PAYING FOR IT!
WHOK
TALK! WHY'D FONTI PICK NOW TO HAVE ME BUMPED?
YOU GOT IT WRONG, LADY! JOE DIDN'T SEND US TO KILL YOU! HE SENT US TO GET YOUR HELP!
-BZZT- TRY AGAIN! FONTI HATES ME! WHY WOULD HE WANT MY HELP?
HIS KID ANGELA -- SHE WAS GRABBED -- BY PSYCHOS!

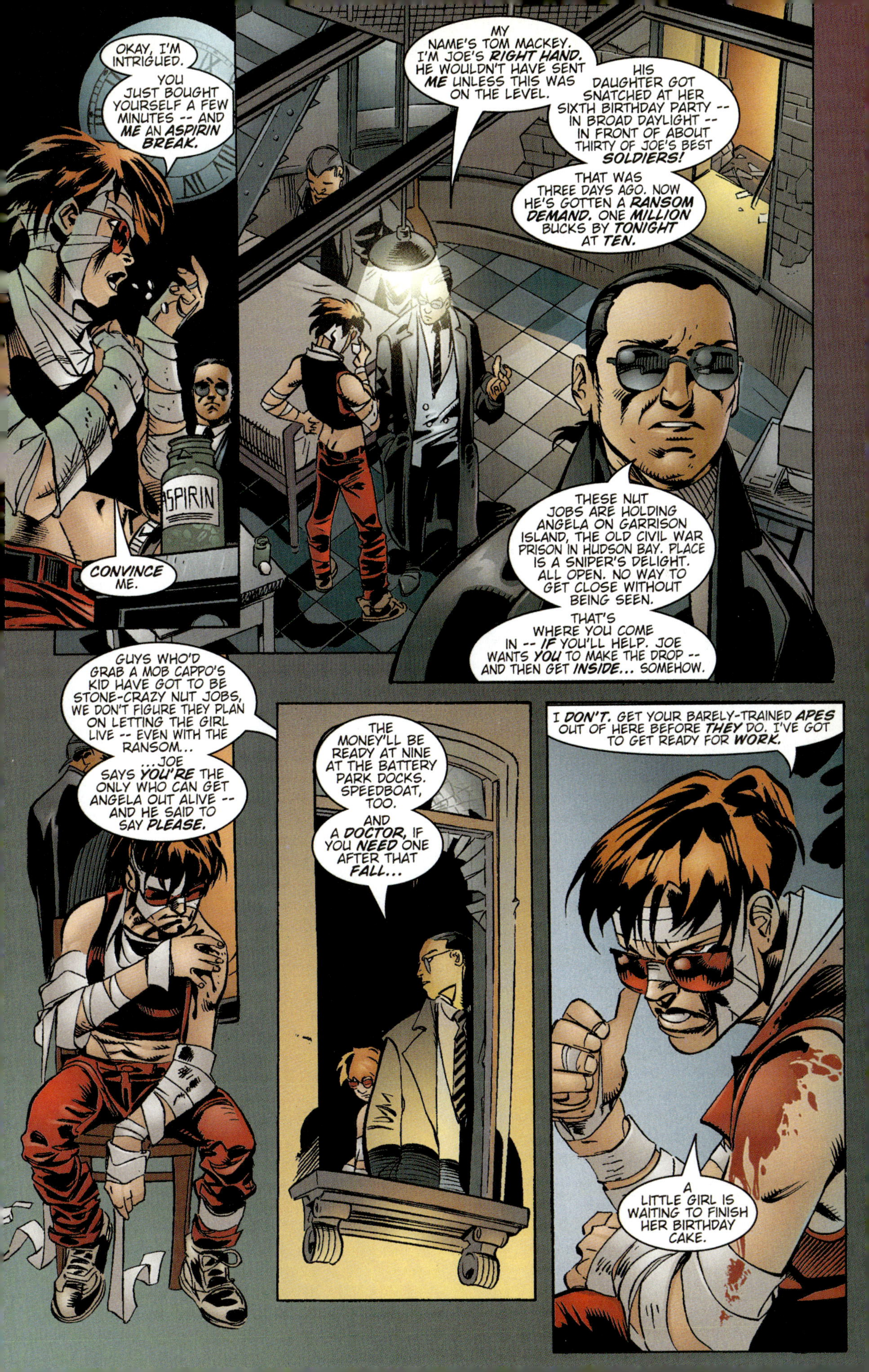
OKAY, I'M INTRIGUED.
YOU JUST BOUGHT YOURSELF A FEW MINUTES -- AND ME AN ASPIRIN BREAK.
ASPIRIN
CONVINCE ME.
MY NAME'S TOM MACKEY. I'M JOE'S RIGHT HAND. HE WOULDN'T HAVE SENT ME UNLESS THIS WAS ON THE LEVEL.
HIS DAUGHTER GOT SNATCHED AT HER SIXTH BIRTHDAY PARTY -- IN BROAD DAYLIGHT -- IN FRONT OF ABOUT THIRTY OF JOE'S BEST SOLDIERS!
THAT WAS THREE DAYS AGO. NOW HE'S GOTTEN A RANSOM DEMAND. ONE MILLION BUCKS BY TONIGHT AT TEN.
THESE NUT JOBS ARE HOLDING ANGELA ON GARRISON ISLAND, THE OLD CIVIL WAR PRISON IN HUDSON BAY. PLACE IS A SNIPER'S DELIGHT. ALL OPEN. NO WAY TO GET CLOSE WITHOUT BEING SEEN.
THAT'S WHERE YOU COME IN -- IF YOU'LL HELP. JOE WANTS YOU TO MAKE THE DROP -- AND THEN GET INSIDE... SOMEHOW.
GUYS WHO'D GRAB A MOB CAPPO'S KID HAVE GOT TO BE STONE-CRAZY NUT JOBS, WE DON'T FIGURE THEY PLAN ON LETTING THE GIRL LIVE -- EVEN WITH THE RANSOM...
...JOE SAYS YOU'RE THE ONLY WHO CAN GET ANGELA OUT ALIVE -- AND HE SAID TO SAY PLEASE.
THE MONEY'LL BE READY AT NINE AT THE BATTERY PARK DOCKS. SPEEDBOAT, TOO.
AND A DOCTOR, IF YOU NEED ONE AFTER THAT FALL...
I DON'T. GET YOUR BARELY-TRAINED APES OUT OF HERE BEFORE THEY DO. I'VE GOT TO GET READY FOR WORK.
A LITTLE GIRL IS WAITING TO FINISH HER BIRTHDAY CAKE.

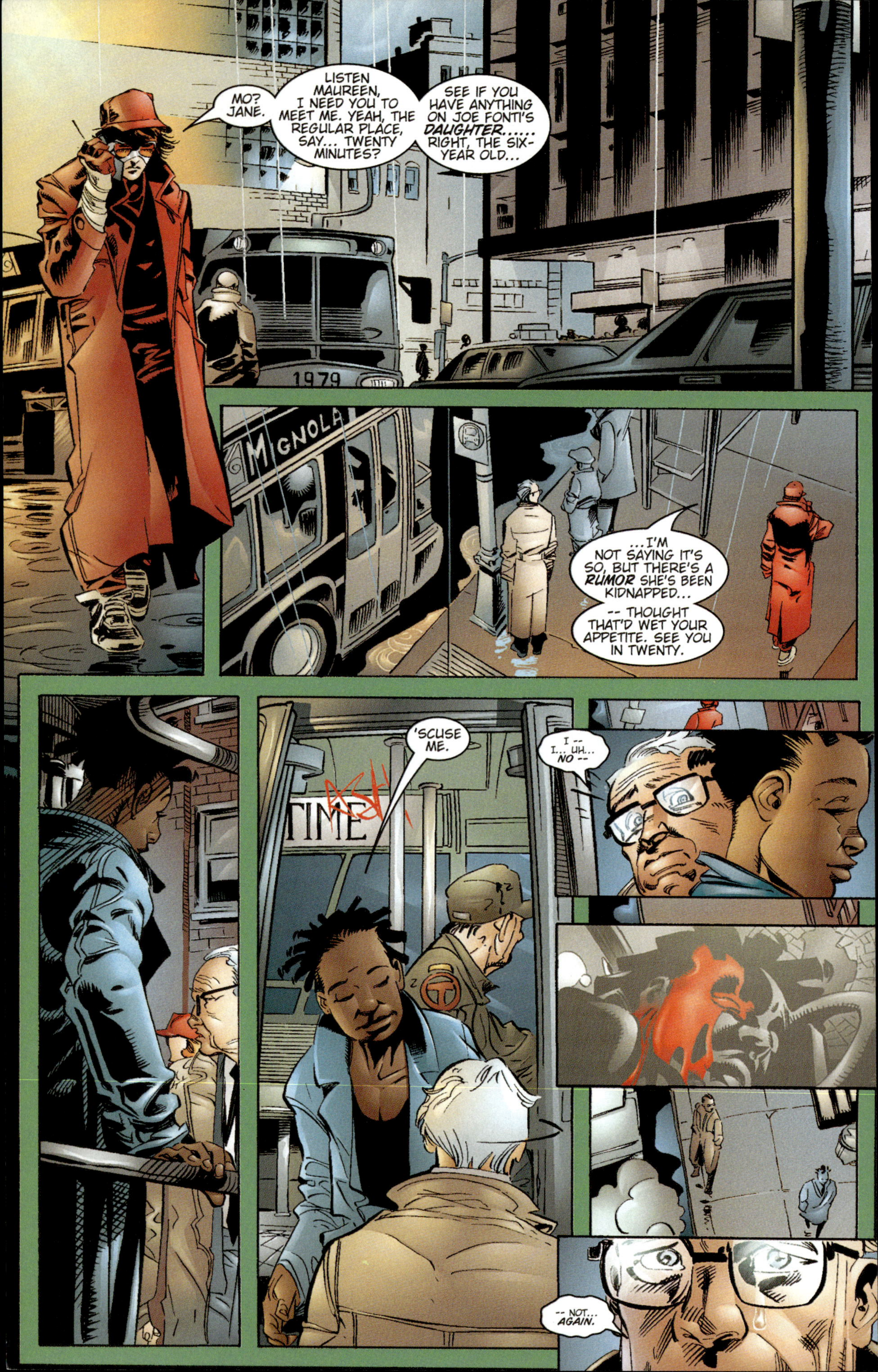
MO? JANE.
LISTEN MAUREEN, I NEED YOU TO MEET ME. YEAH, THE REGULAR PLACE, SAY... TWENTY MINUTES?
SEE IF YOU HAVE ANYTHING ON JOE FONTI'S DAUGHTER...... RIGHT, THE SIX-YEAR OLD...
1979
MIGNOLA
...I'M NOT SAYING IT'S SO, BUT THERE'S A RUMOR SHE'S BEEN KIDNAPPED...
-- THOUGHT THAT'D WET YOUR APPETITE. SEE YOU IN TWENTY.
'SCUSE ME.
TIME
I -- I... UH... NO --
-- NOT... AGAIN.

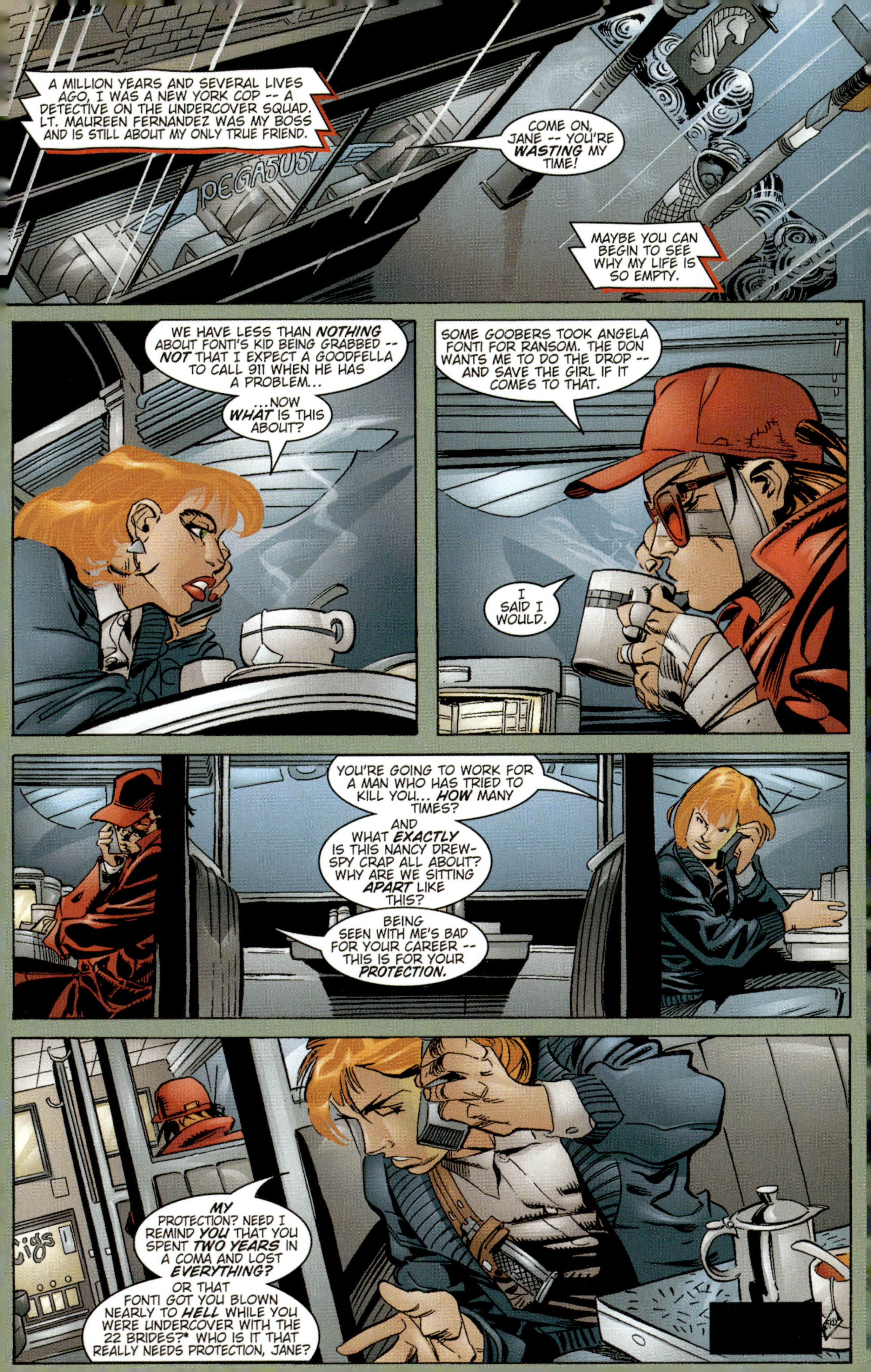
A MILLION YEARS AND SEVERAL LIVES AGO, I WAS A NEW YORK COP -- A DETECTIVE ON THE UNDERCOVER SQUAD. LT. MAUREEN FERNANDEZ WAS MY BOSS AND IS STILL ABOUT MY ONLY TRUE FRIEND.
COME ON, JANE -- YOU'RE WASTING MY TIME!
MAYBE YOU CAN BEGIN TO SEE WHY MY LIFE IS SO EMPTY.
PEGASUS
WE HAVE LESS THAN NOTHING ABOUT FONTI'S KID BEING GRABBED -- NOT THAT I EXPECT A GOODFELLA TO CALL 911 WHEN HE HAS A PROBLEM...
...NOW WHAT IS THIS ABOUT?
SOME GOOBERS TOOK ANGELA FONTI FOR RANSOM. THE DON WANTS ME TO DO THE DROP -- AND SAVE THE GIRL IF IT COMES TO THAT.
I SAID I WOULD.
YOU'RE GOING TO WORK FOR A MAN WHO HAS TRIED TO KILL YOU... HOW MANY TIMES?
AND WHAT EXACTLY IS THIS NANCY DREW-SPY CRAP ALL ABOUT? WHY ARE WE SITTING APART LIKE THIS?
BEING SEEN WITH ME'S BAD FOR YOUR CAREER -- THIS IS FOR YOUR PROTECTION.
MY PROTECTION? NEED I REMIND YOU THAT YOU SPENT TWO YEARS IN A COMA AND LOST EVERYTHING?
OR THAT FONTI GOT YOU BLOWN NEARLY TO HELL WHILE YOU WERE UNDERCOVER WITH THE 22 BRIDES?* WHO IS IT THAT REALLY NEEDS PROTECTION, JANE?
Cigs
[redacted]

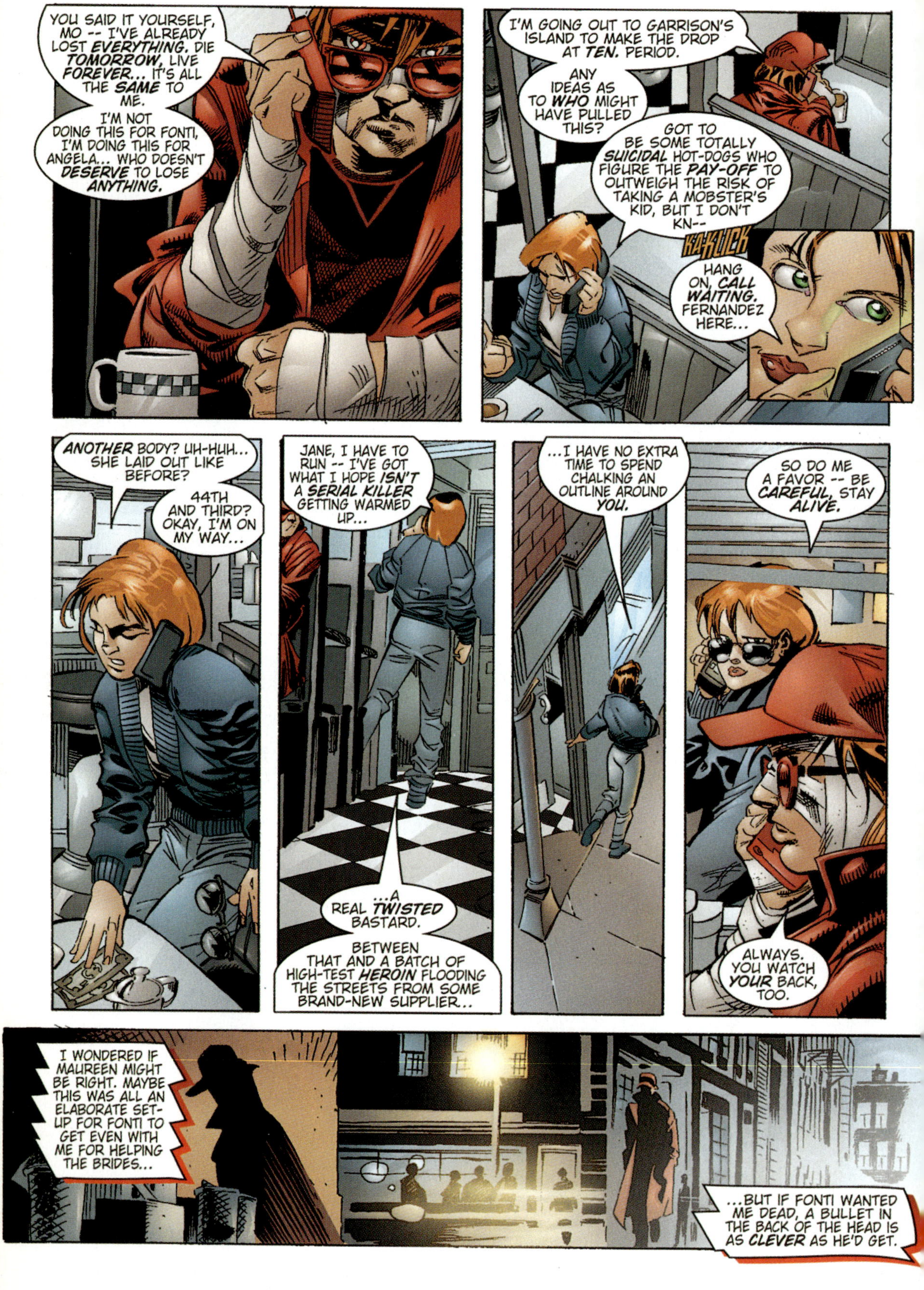
YOU SAID IT YOURSELF, MO -- I'VE ALREADY LOST EVERYTHING. DIE TOMORROW, LIVE FOREVER... IT'S ALL THE SAME TO ME.
I'M NOT DOING THIS FOR FONTI, I'M DOING THIS FOR ANGELA... WHO DOESN'T DESERVE TO LOSE ANYTHING.
I'M GOING OUT TO GARRISON'S ISLAND TO MAKE THE DROP AT TEN. PERIOD.
ANY IDEAS AS TO WHO MIGHT HAVE PULLED THIS?
GOT TO BE SOME TOTALLY SUICIDAL HOT-DOGS WHO FIGURE THE PAY-OFF TO OUTWEIGH THE RISK OF TAKING A MOBSTER'S KID, BUT I DON'T KN--
KA-KLICK
HANG ON, CALL WAITING. FERNANDEZ HERE...
ANOTHER BODY? UH-HUH... SHE LAID OUT LIKE BEFORE?
44TH AND THIRD? OKAY, I'M ON MY WAY...
JANE, I HAVE TO RUN -- I'VE GOT WHAT I HOPE ISN'T A SERIAL KILLER GETTING WARMED UP...
...A REAL TWISTED BASTARD.
BETWEEN THAT AND A BATCH OF HIGH-TEST HEROIN FLOODING THE STREETS FROM SOME BRAND-NEW SUPPLIER...
...I HAVE NO EXTRA TIME TO SPEND CHALKING AN OUTLINE AROUND YOU.
SO DO ME A FAVOR -- BE CAREFUL. STAY ALIVE.
ALWAYS. YOU WATCH YOUR BACK, TOO.
I WONDERED IF MAUREEN MIGHT BE RIGHT. MAYBE THIS WAS ALL AN ELABORATE SET-UP FOR FONTI TO GET EVEN WITH ME FOR HELPING THE BRIDES...
...BUT IF FONTI WANTED ME DEAD, A BULLET IN THE BACK OF THE HEAD IS AS CLEVER AS HE'D GET.

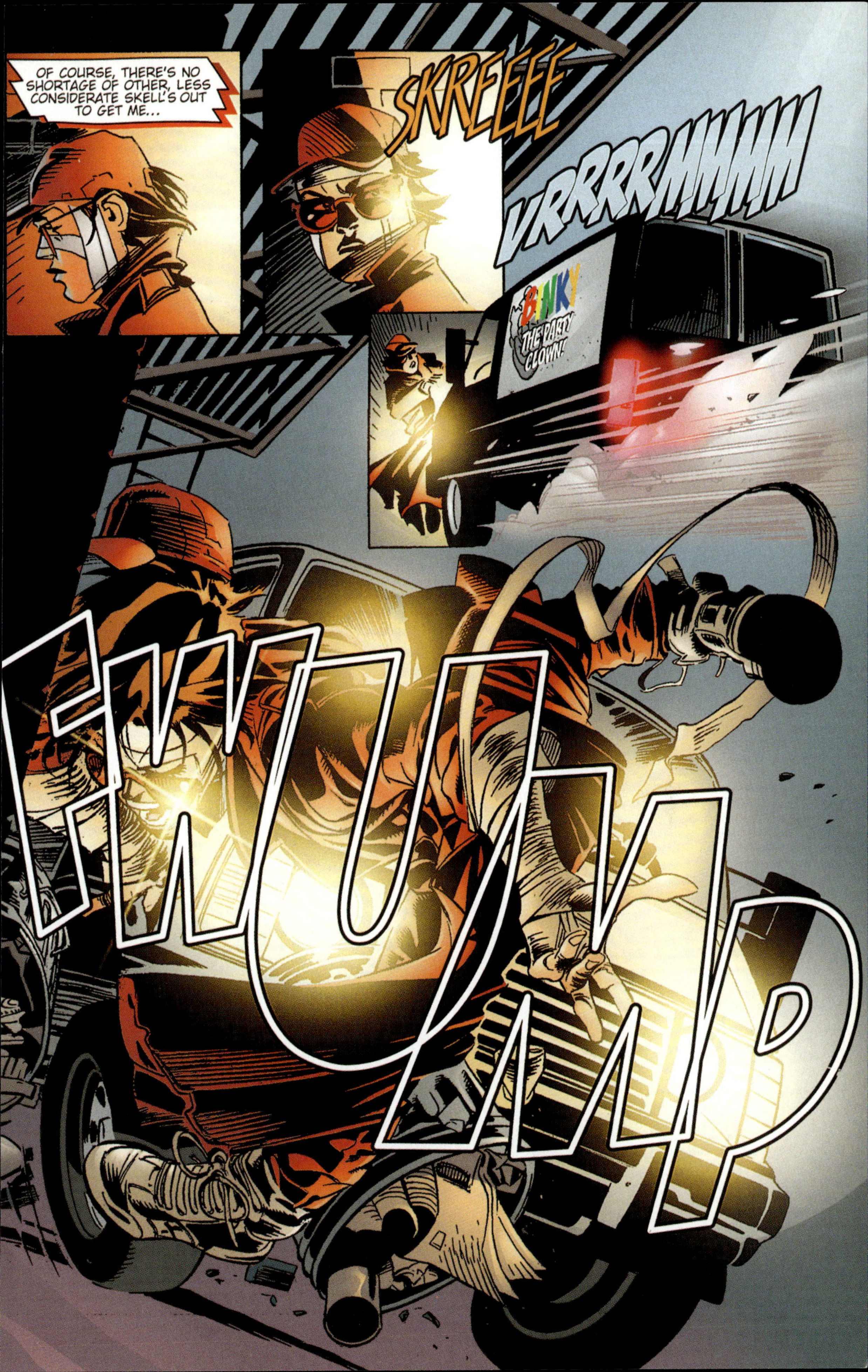
OF COURSE, THERE'S NO SHORTAGE OF OTHER, LESS CONSIDERATE SKELL'S OUT TO GET ME...
SKREEEE
VRRRRMMMMM
BINKY THE PARTY CLOWN!
FWUMP

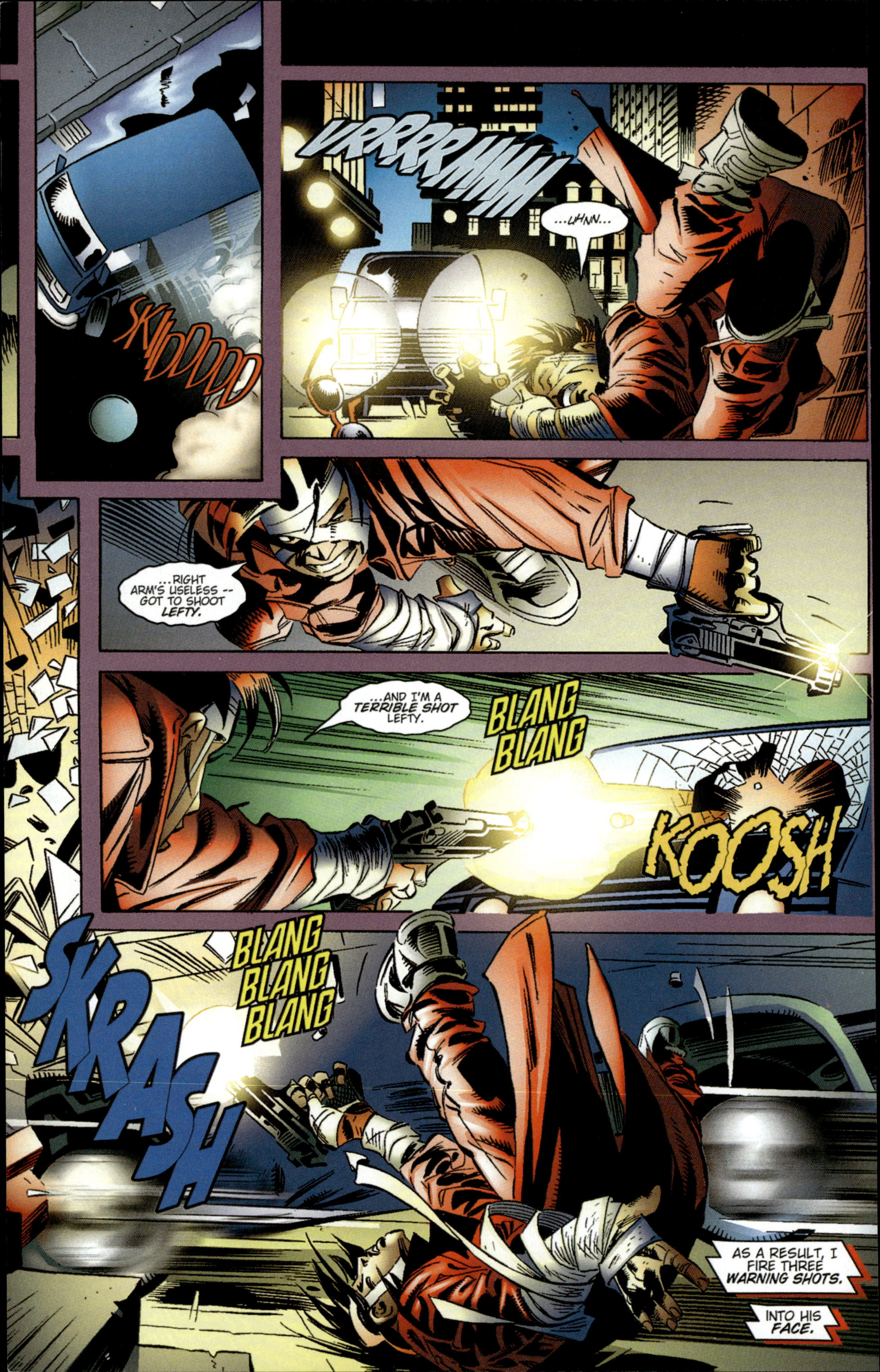

SKIDDDDDD
URRRRMMM
...UHNN...
...RIGHT ARM'S USELESS -- GOT TO SHOOT LEFTY.
...AND I'M A TERRIBLE SHOT LEFTY.
BLANG BLANG
KOOSH
SKRASH
BLANG BLANG BLANG
AS A RESULT, I FIRE THREE WARNING SHOTS.
INTO HIS FACE.

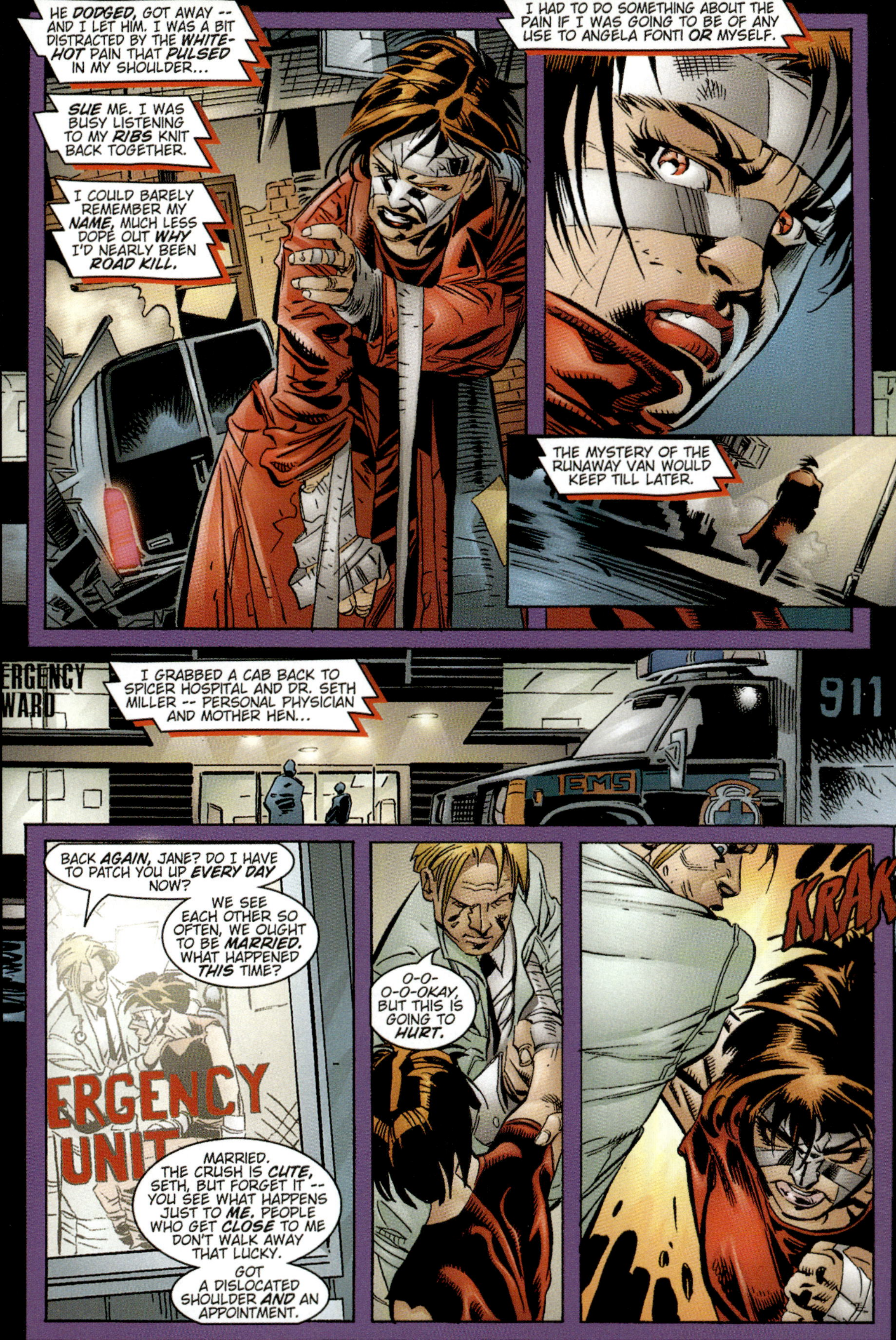
HE DODGED, GOT AWAY -- AND I LET HIM. I WAS A BIT DISTRACTED BY THE WHITE-HOT PAIN THAT PULSED IN MY SHOULDER...
SUE ME. I WAS BUSY LISTENING TO MY RIBS KNIT BACK TOGETHER.
I COULD BARELY REMEMBER MY NAME, MUCH LESS DOPE OUT WHY I'D NEARLY BEEN ROAD KILL.
I HAD TO DO SOMETHING ABOUT THE PAIN IF I WAS GOING TO BE OF ANY USE TO ANGELA FONTI OR MYSELF.
THE MYSTERY OF THE RUNAWAY VAN WOULD KEEP TILL LATER.
ERGENCY
WARD
I GRABBED A CAB BACK TO SPICER HOSPITAL AND DR. SETH MILLER -- PERSONAL PHYSICIAN AND MOTHER HEN...
911
EMS
BACK AGAIN, JANE? DO I HAVE TO PATCH YOU UP EVERY DAY NOW?
WE SEE EACH OTHER SO OFTEN, WE OUGHT TO BE MARRIED. WHAT HAPPENED THIS TIME?
ERGENCY
UNIT
MARRIED. THE CRUSH IS CUTE, SETH, BUT FORGET IT -- YOU SEE WHAT HAPPENS JUST TO ME. PEOPLE WHO GET CLOSE TO ME DON'T WALK AWAY THAT LUCKY.
GOT A DISLOCATED SHOULDER AND AN APPOINTMENT.
O-O-O-O-OKAY, BUT THIS IS GOING TO HURT.
KRAK

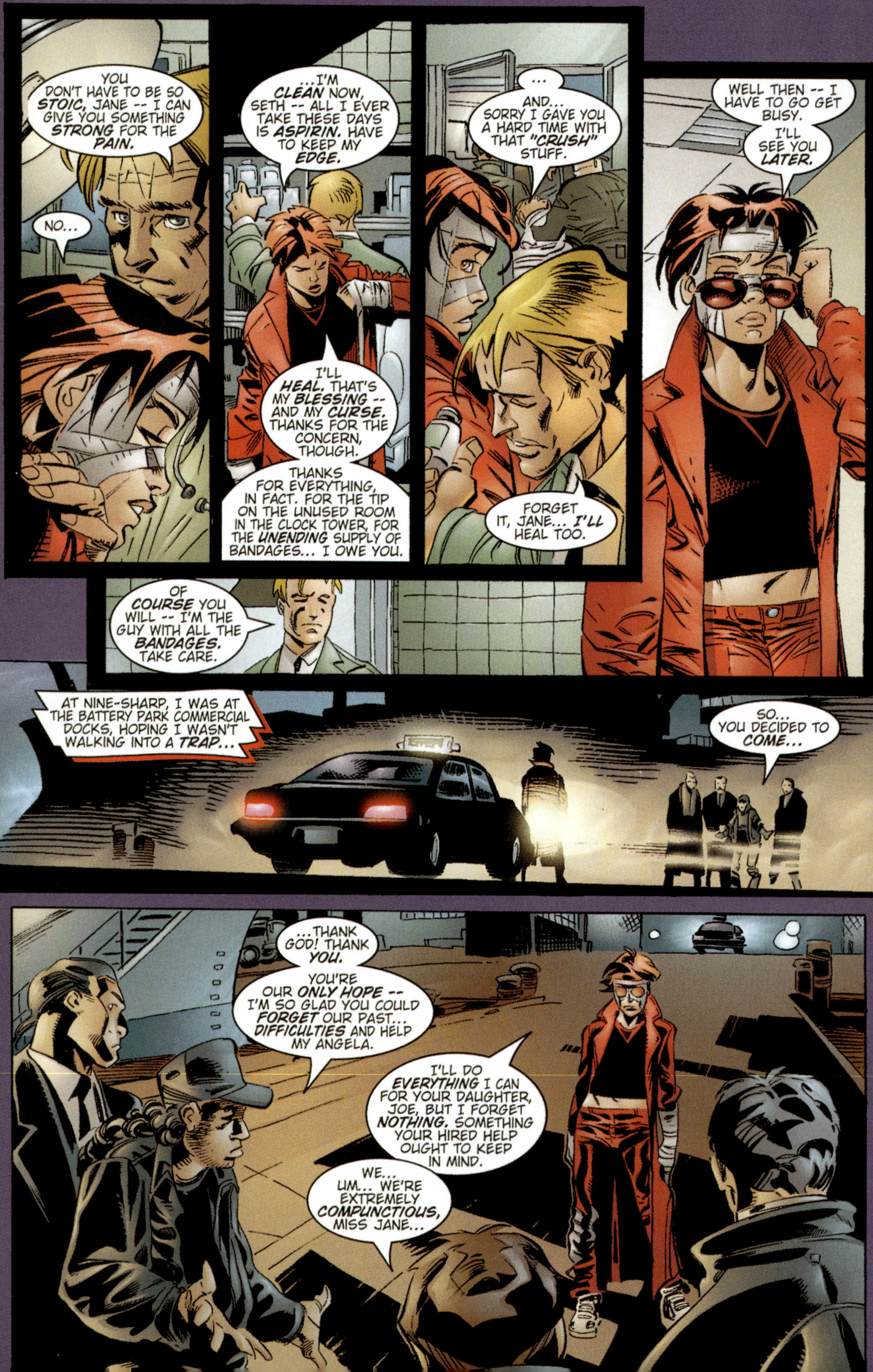
YOU DON'T HAVE TO BE SO STOIC, JANE -- I CAN GIVE YOU SOMETHING STRONG FOR THE PAIN.
NO...
...I'M CLEAN NOW, SETH -- ALL I EVER TAKE THESE DAYS IS ASPIRIN. HAVE TO KEEP MY EDGE.
I'LL HEAL. THAT'S MY BLESSING -- AND MY CURSE. THANKS FOR THE CONCERN, THOUGH.
THANKS FOR EVERYTHING, IN FACT. FOR THE TIP ON THE UNUSED ROOM IN THE CLOCK TOWER, FOR THE UNENDING SUPPLY OF BANDAGES... I OWE YOU.
...
AND... SORRY I GAVE YOU A HARD TIME WITH THAT "CRUSH" STUFF.
FORGET IT, JANE... I'LL HEAL TOO.
WELL THEN -- I HAVE TO GO GET BUSY.
I'LL SEE YOU LATER.
OF COURSE YOU WILL -- I'M THE GUY WITH ALL THE BANDAGES. TAKE CARE.
AT NINE-SHARP, I WAS AT THE BATTERY PARK COMMERCIAL DOCKS, HOPING I WASN'T WALKING INTO A TRAP...
SO... YOU DECIDED TO COME...
...THANK GOD! THANK YOU.
YOU'RE OUR ONLY HOPE -- I'M SO GLAD YOU COULD FORGET OUR PAST... DIFFICULTIES AND HELP MY ANGELA.
I'LL DO EVERYTHING I CAN FOR YOUR DAUGHTER, JOE, BUT I FORGET NOTHING. SOMETHING YOUR HIRED HELP OUGHT TO KEEP IN MIND.
WE... UM... WE'RE EXTREMELY COMPUNCTIOUS, MISS JANE...

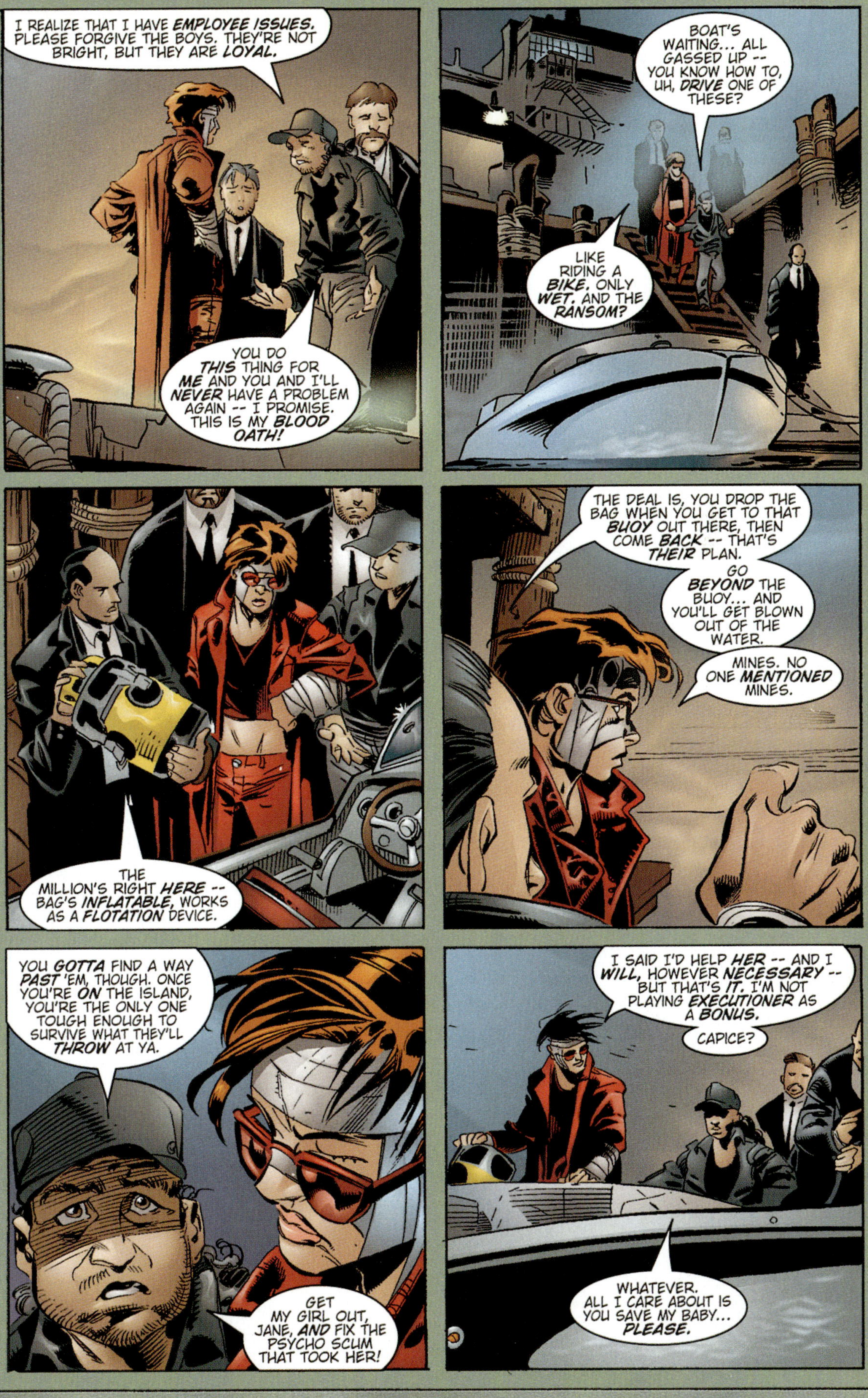
I REALIZE THAT I HAVE EMPLOYEE ISSUES. PLEASE FORGIVE THE BOYS. THEY'RE NOT BRIGHT, BUT THEY ARE LOYAL.
YOU DO THIS THING FOR ME AND YOU AND I'LL NEVER HAVE A PROBLEM AGAIN -- I PROMISE. THIS IS MY BLOOD OATH!
BOAT'S WAITING... ALL GASSED UP -- YOU KNOW HOW TO, UH, DRIVE ONE OF THESE?
LIKE RIDING A BIKE. ONLY WET. AND THE RANSOM?
THE MILLION'S RIGHT HERE -- BAG'S INFLATABLE, WORKS AS A FLOTATION DEVICE.
THE DEAL IS, YOU DROP THE BAG WHEN YOU GET TO THAT BUOY OUT THERE, THEN COME BACK -- THAT'S THEIR PLAN.
GO BEYOND THE BUOY... AND YOU'LL GET BLOWN OUT OF THE WATER.
MINES. NO ONE MENTIONED MINES.
YOU GOTTA FIND A WAY PAST 'EM, THOUGH. ONCE YOU'RE ON THE ISLAND, YOU'RE THE ONLY ONE TOUGH ENOUGH TO SURVIVE WHAT THEY'LL THROW AT YA.
GET MY GIRL OUT, JANE, AND FIX THE PSYCHO SCUM THAT TOOK HER!
I SAID I'D HELP HER -- AND I WILL, HOWEVER NECESSARY -- BUT THAT'S IT. I'M NOT PLAYING EXECUTIONER AS A BONUS.
CAPICE?
WHATEVER. ALL I CARE ABOUT IS YOU SAVE MY BABY... PLEASE.

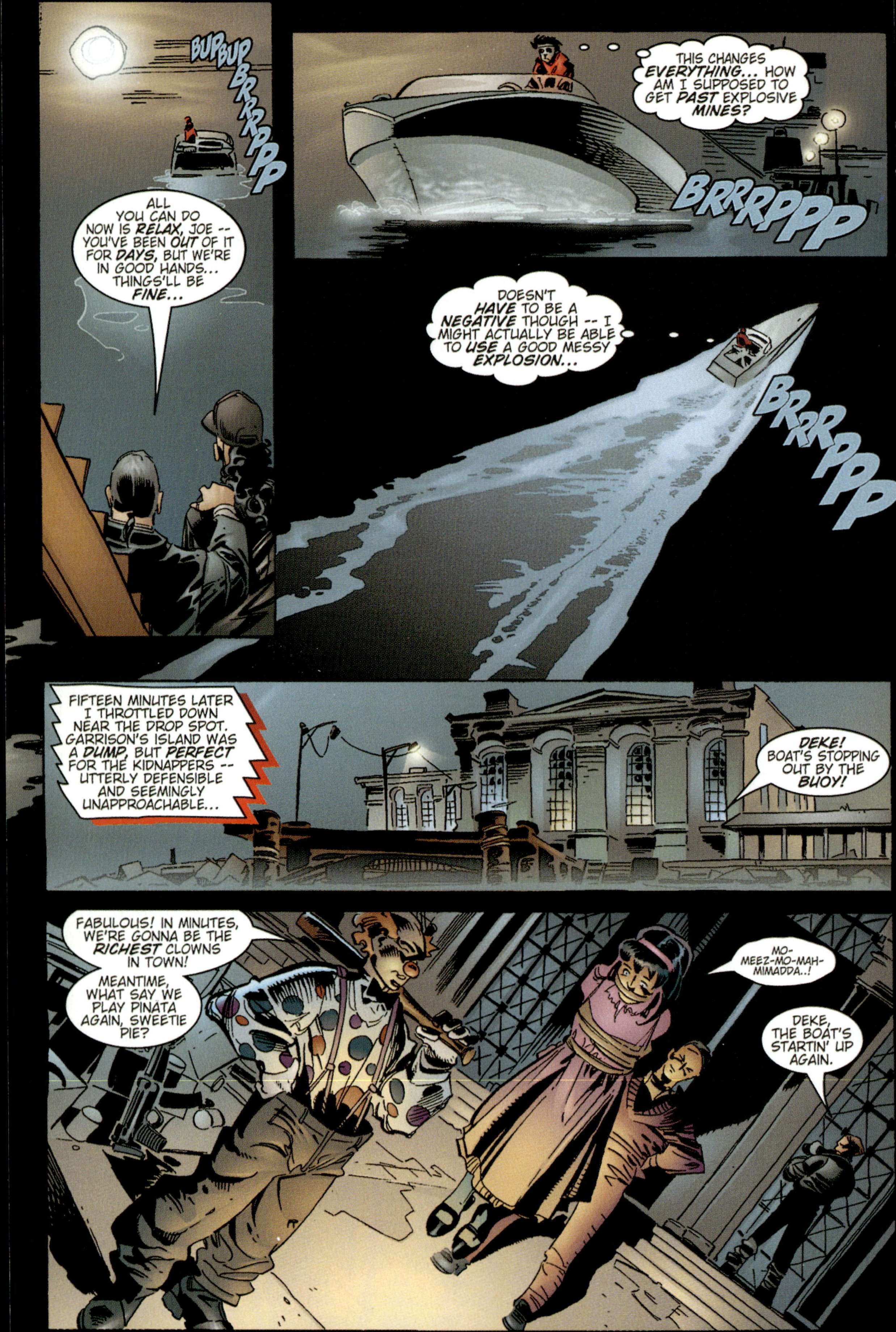
BUPBUP BRRRPPP
THIS CHANGES EVERYTHING... HOW AM I SUPPOSED TO GET PAST EXPLOSIVE MINES?
BRRRPPP
ALL YOU CAN DO NOW IS RELAX, JOE -- YOU'VE BEEN OUT OF IT FOR DAYS, BUT WE'RE IN GOOD HANDS... THINGS'LL BE FINE...
DOESN'T HAVE TO BE A NEGATIVE THOUGH -- I MIGHT ACTUALLY BE ABLE TO USE A GOOD MESSY EXPLOSION...
BRRRPPP
FIFTEEN MINUTES LATER I THROTTLED DOWN NEAR THE DROP SPOT. GARRISON'S ISLAND WAS A DUMP, BUT PERFECT FOR THE KIDNAPPERS -- UTTERLY DEFENSIBLE AND SEEMINGLY UNAPPROACHABLE...
DEKE! BOAT'S STOPPING OUT BY THE BUOY!
FABULOUS! IN MINUTES, WE'RE GONNA BE THE RICHEST CLOWNS IN TOWN!
MEANTIME, WHAT SAY WE PLAY PINATA AGAIN, SWEETIE PIE?
MO-MEEZ-MO-MAH-MIMADDA..!
DEKE, THE BOAT'S STARTIN' UP AGAIN.

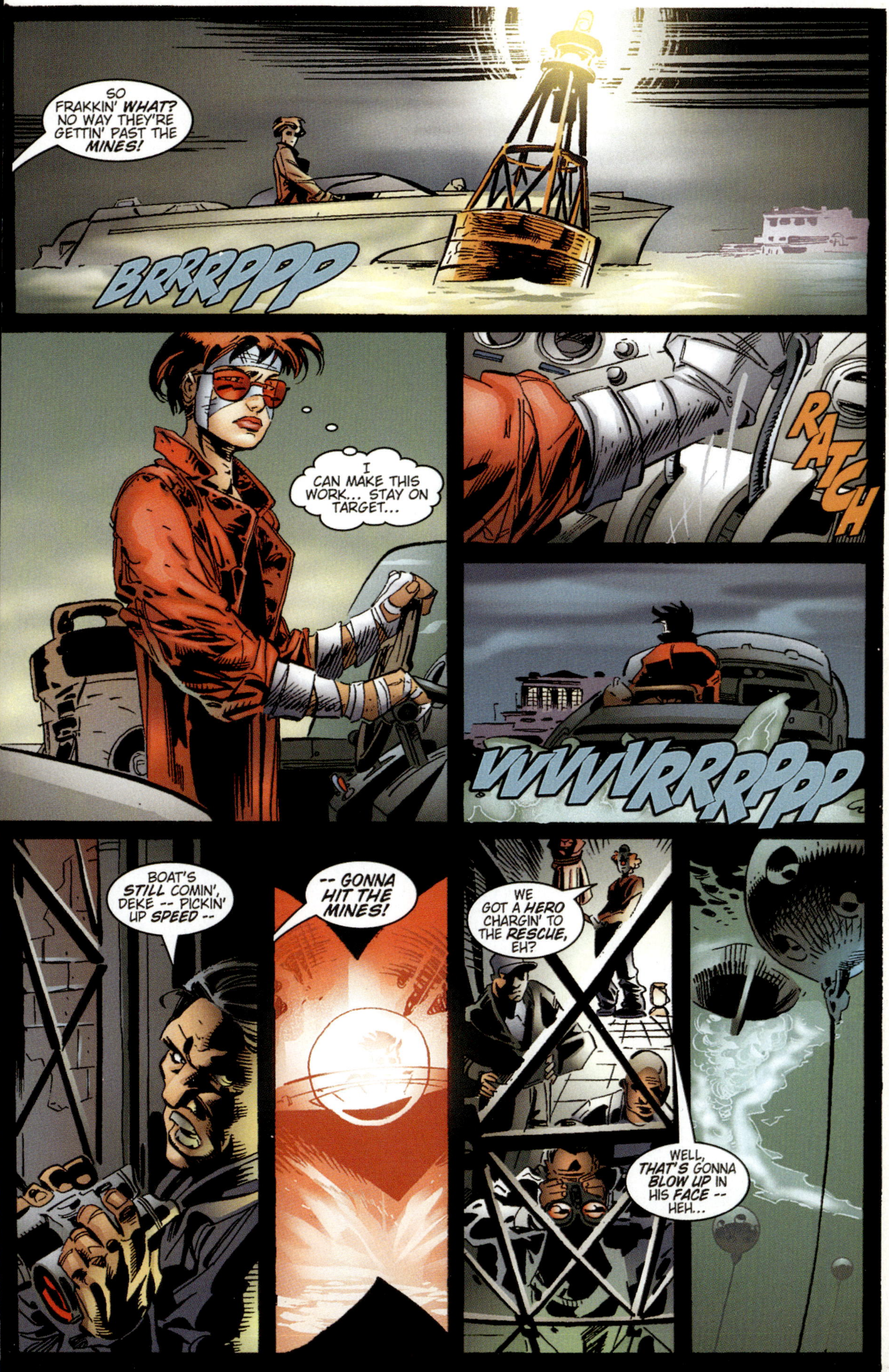
SO FRAKKIN' WHAT? NO WAY THEY'RE GETTIN' PAST THE MINES!
BRRRPPP
I CAN MAKE THIS WORK... STAY ON TARGET...
RATCH
VVVVRRRPPP
BOAT'S STILL COMIN', DEKE -- PICKIN' UP SPEED --
-- GONNA HIT THE MINES!
WE GOT A HERO CHARGIN' TO THE RESCUE, EH?
WELL, THAT'S GONNA BLOW UP IN HIS FACE -- HEH...

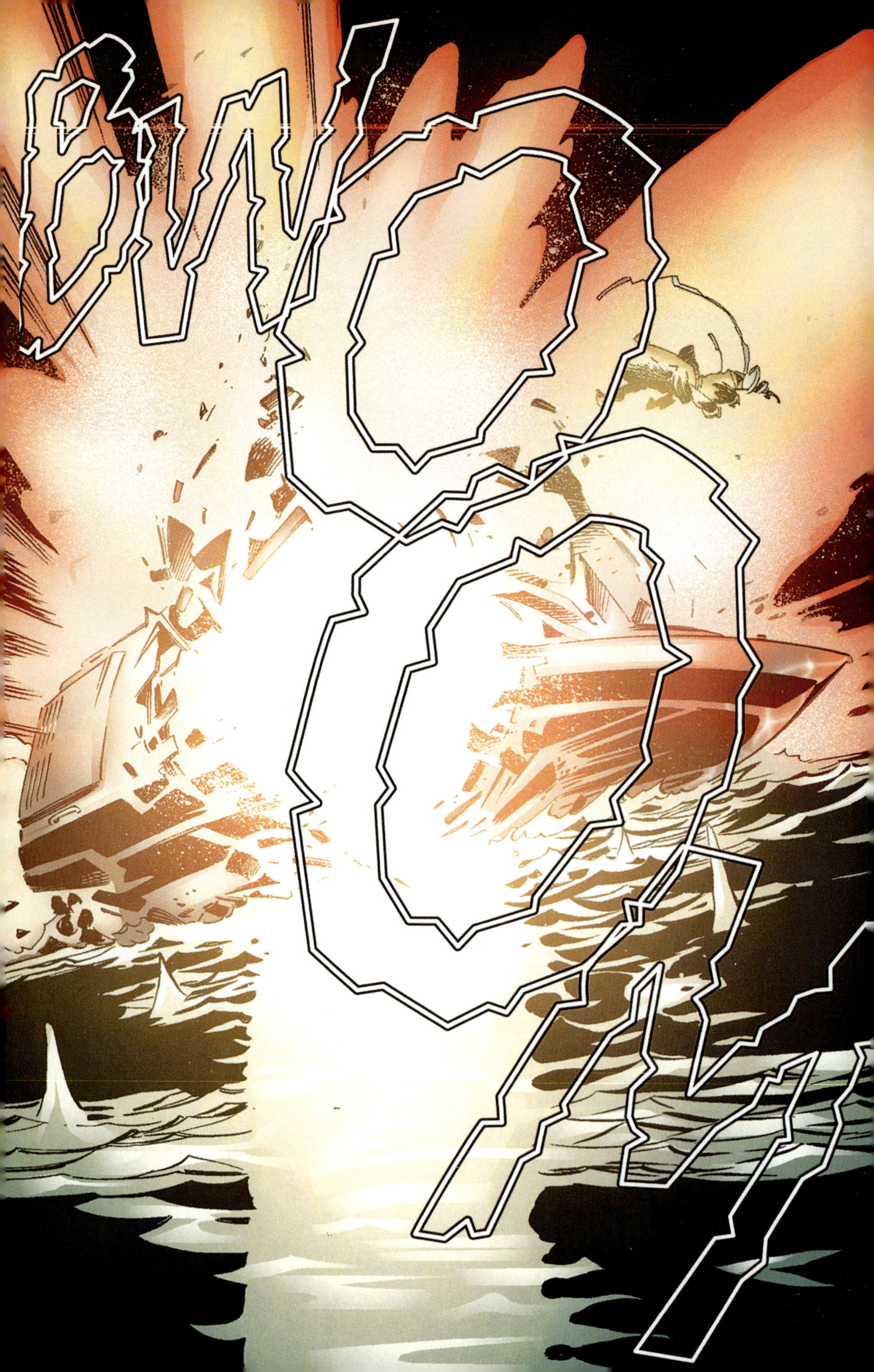
BWOOM!

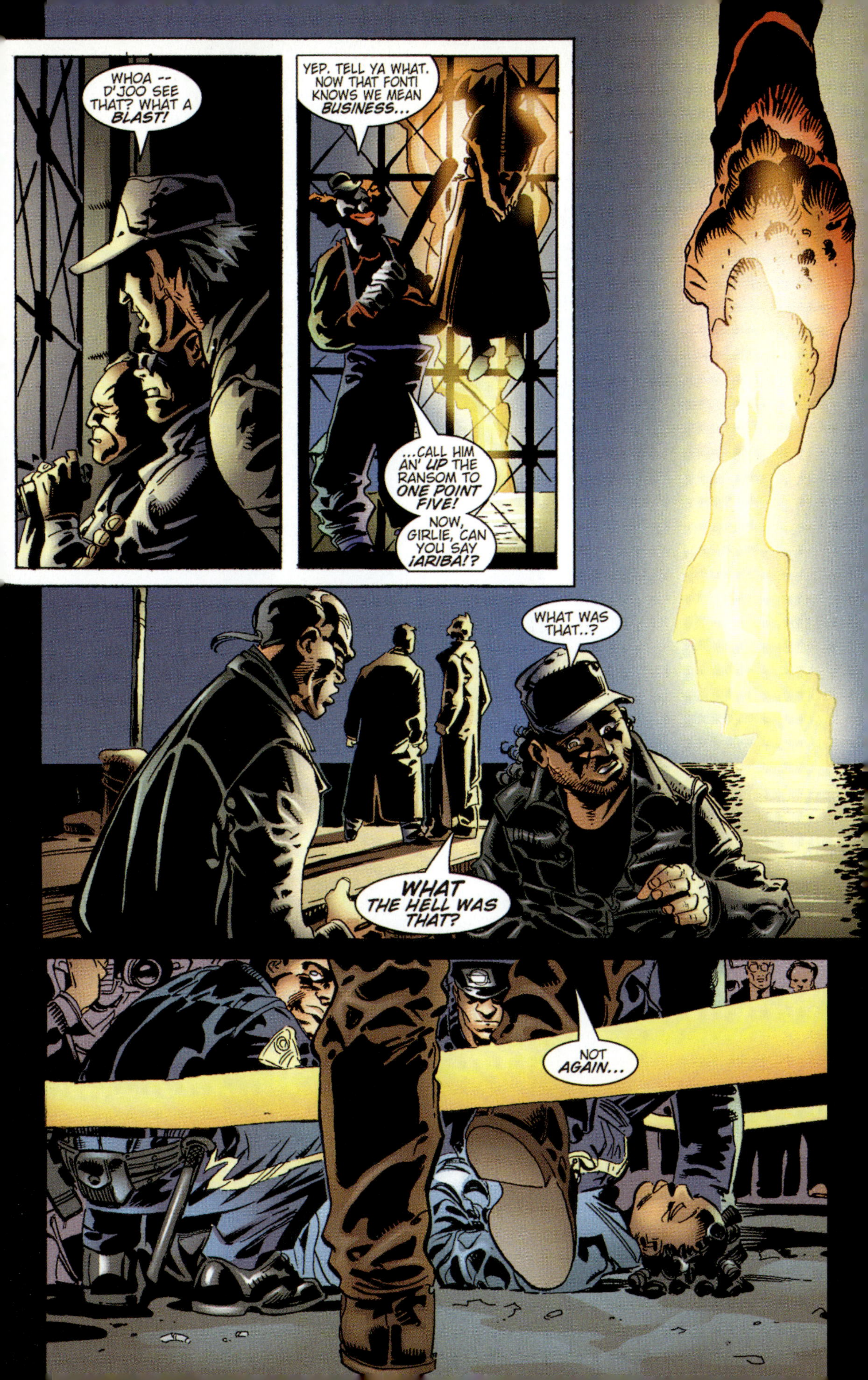
WHOA -- D'JOO SEE THAT? WHAT A BLAST!
YEP. TELL YA WHAT. NOW THAT FONTI KNOWS WE MEAN BUSINESS...
...CALL HIM AN' UP THE RANSOM TO ONE POINT FIVE!
NOW, GIRLIE, CAN YOU SAY ¡ARIBA!?
WHAT WAS THAT..?
WHAT THE HELL WAS THAT?
NOT AGAIN...

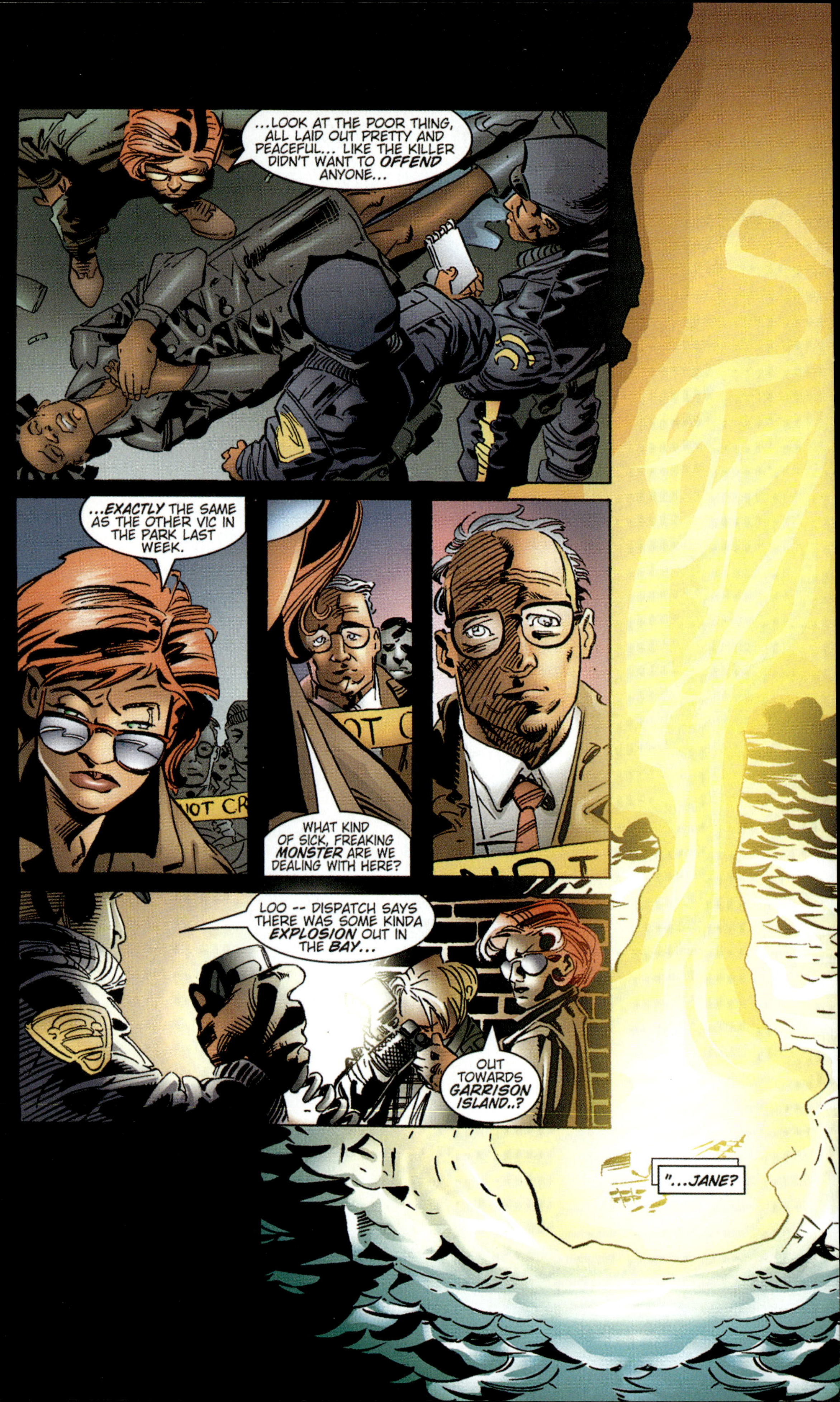
...LOOK AT THE POOR THING, ALL LAID OUT PRETTY AND PEACEFUL... LIKE THE KILLER DIDN'T WANT TO OFFEND ANYONE...
...EXACTLY THE SAME AS THE OTHER VIC IN THE PARK LAST WEEK.
WHAT KIND OF SICK, FREAKING MONSTER ARE WE DEALING WITH HERE?
LOO -- DISPATCH SAYS THERE WAS SOME KINDA EXPLOSION OUT IN THE BAY...
OUT TOWARDS GARRISON ISLAND..?
"...JANE?

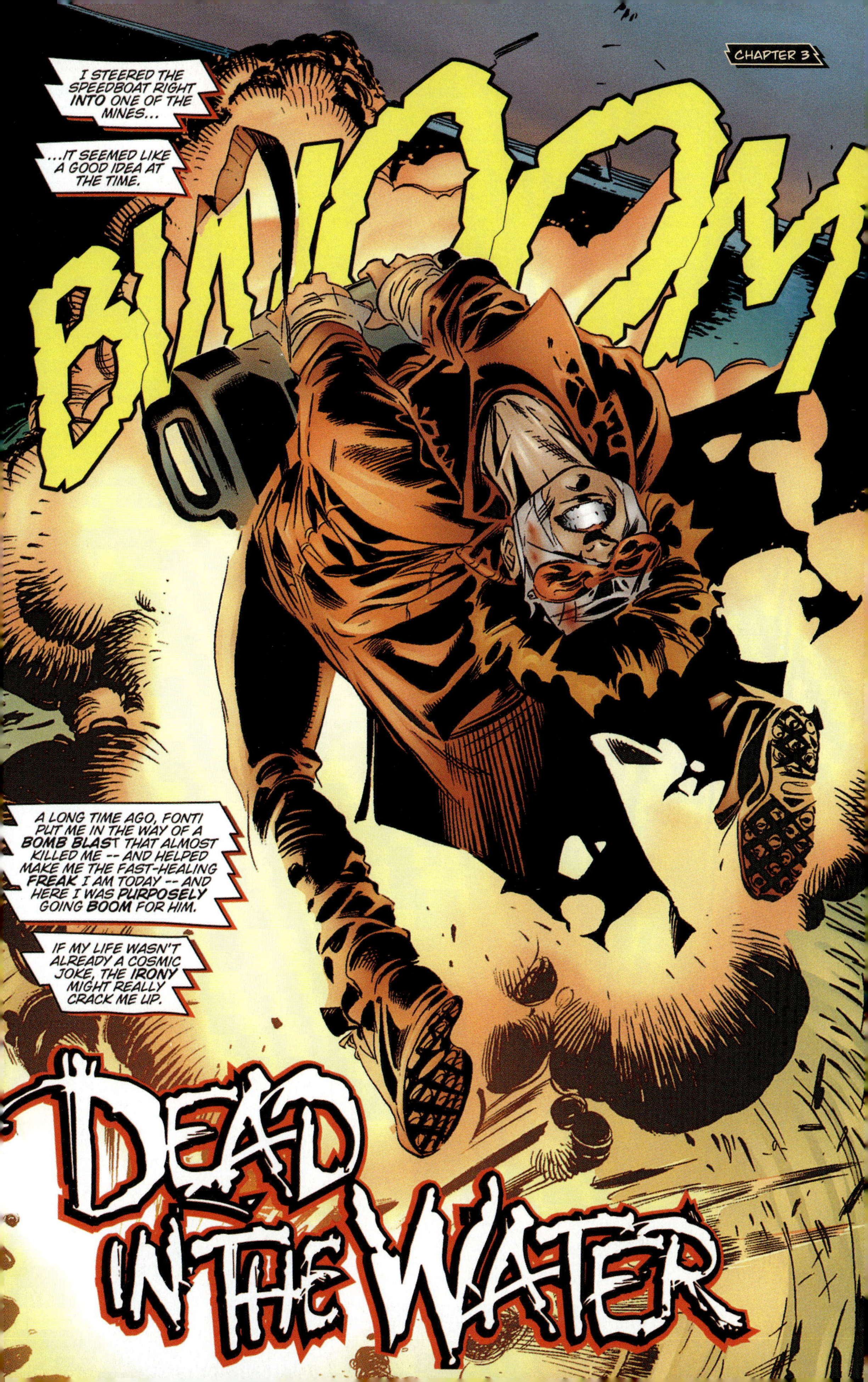
CHAPTER 3
I STEERED THE SPEEDBOAT RIGHT INTO ONE OF THE MINES...
...IT SEEMED LIKE A GOOD IDEA AT THE TIME.
BWOOOM
A LONG TIME AGO, FONTI PUT ME IN THE WAY OF A BOMB BLAST THAT ALMOST KILLED ME -- AND HELPED MAKE ME THE FAST-HEALING FREAK I AM TODAY -- AND HERE I WAS PURPOSELY GOING BOOM FOR HIM.
IF MY LIFE WASN'T ALREADY A COSMIC JOKE, THE IRONY MIGHT REALLY CRACK ME UP.
DEAD IN THE WATER

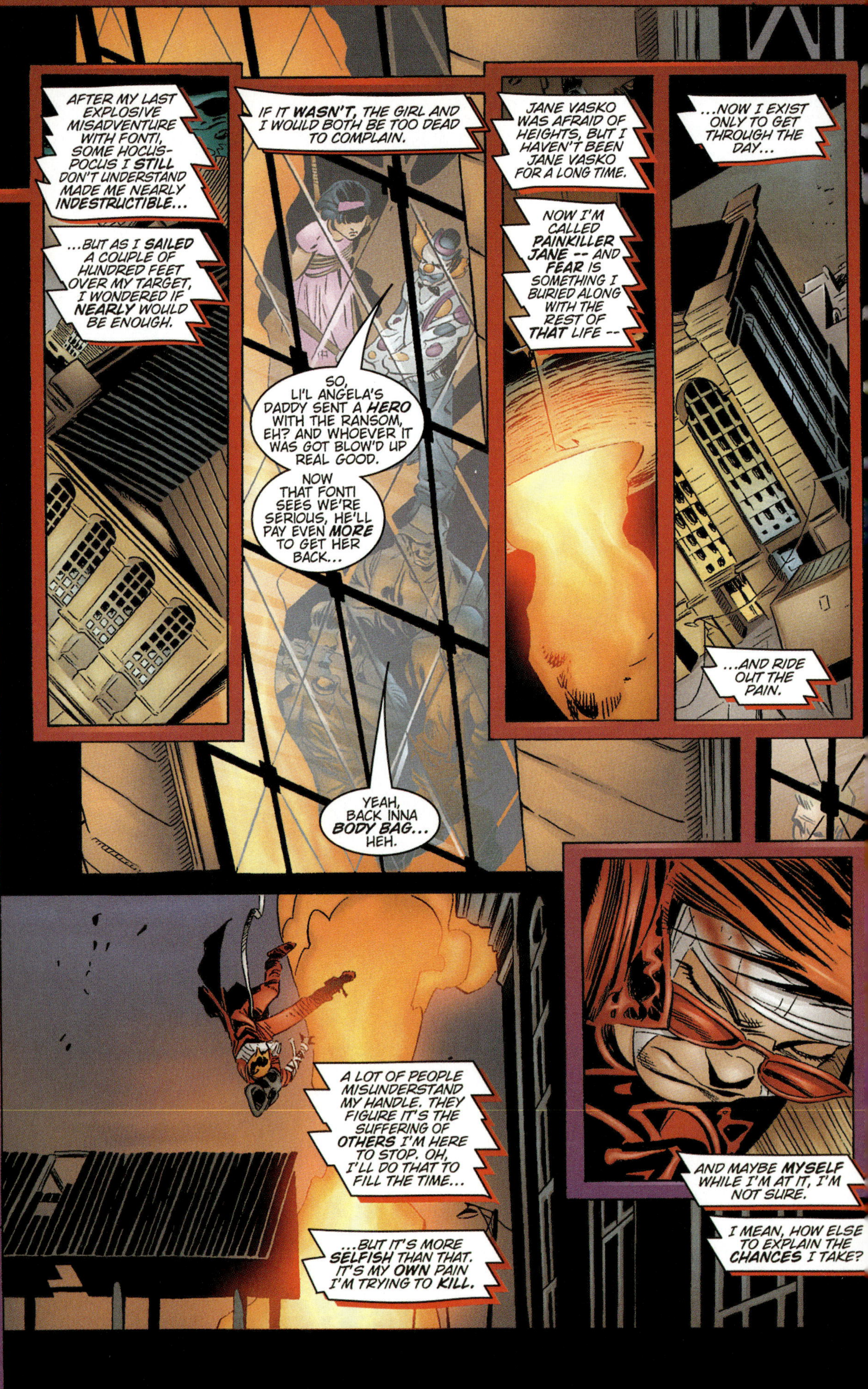
AFTER MY LAST EXPLOSIVE MISADVENTURE WITH FONTI, SOME HOCUS-POCUS I STILL DON'T UNDERSTAND MADE ME NEARLY INDESTRUCTIBLE...
...BUT AS I SAILED A COUPLE OF HUNDRED FEET OVER MY TARGET, I WONDERED IF NEARLY WOULD BE ENOUGH.
IF IT WASN'T, THE GIRL AND I WOULD BOTH BE TOO DEAD TO COMPLAIN.
SO, LI'L ANGELA'S DADDY SENT A HERO WITH THE RANSOM, EH? AND WHOEVER IT WAS GOT BLOW'D UP REAL GOOD.
NOW THAT FONTI SEES WE'RE SERIOUS, HE'LL PAY EVEN MORE TO GET HER BACK...
YEAH, BACK INNA BODY BAG... HEH.
JANE VASKO WAS AFRAID OF HEIGHTS, BUT I HAVEN'T BEEN JANE VASKO FOR A LONG TIME.
NOW I'M CALLED PAINKILLER JANE -- AND FEAR IS SOMETHING I BURIED ALONG WITH THE REST OF THAT LIFE --
...NOW I EXIST ONLY TO GET THROUGH THE DAY...
...AND RIDE OUT THE PAIN.
A LOT OF PEOPLE MISUNDERSTAND MY HANDLE. THEY FIGURE IT'S THE SUFFERING OF OTHERS I'M HERE TO STOP. OH, I'LL DO THAT TO FILL THE TIME...
...BUT IT'S MORE SELFISH THAN THAT. IT'S MY OWN PAIN I'M TRYING TO KILL.
AND MAYBE MYSELF WHILE I'M AT IT, I'M NOT SURE.
I MEAN, HOW ELSE TO EXPLAIN THE CHANCES I TAKE?

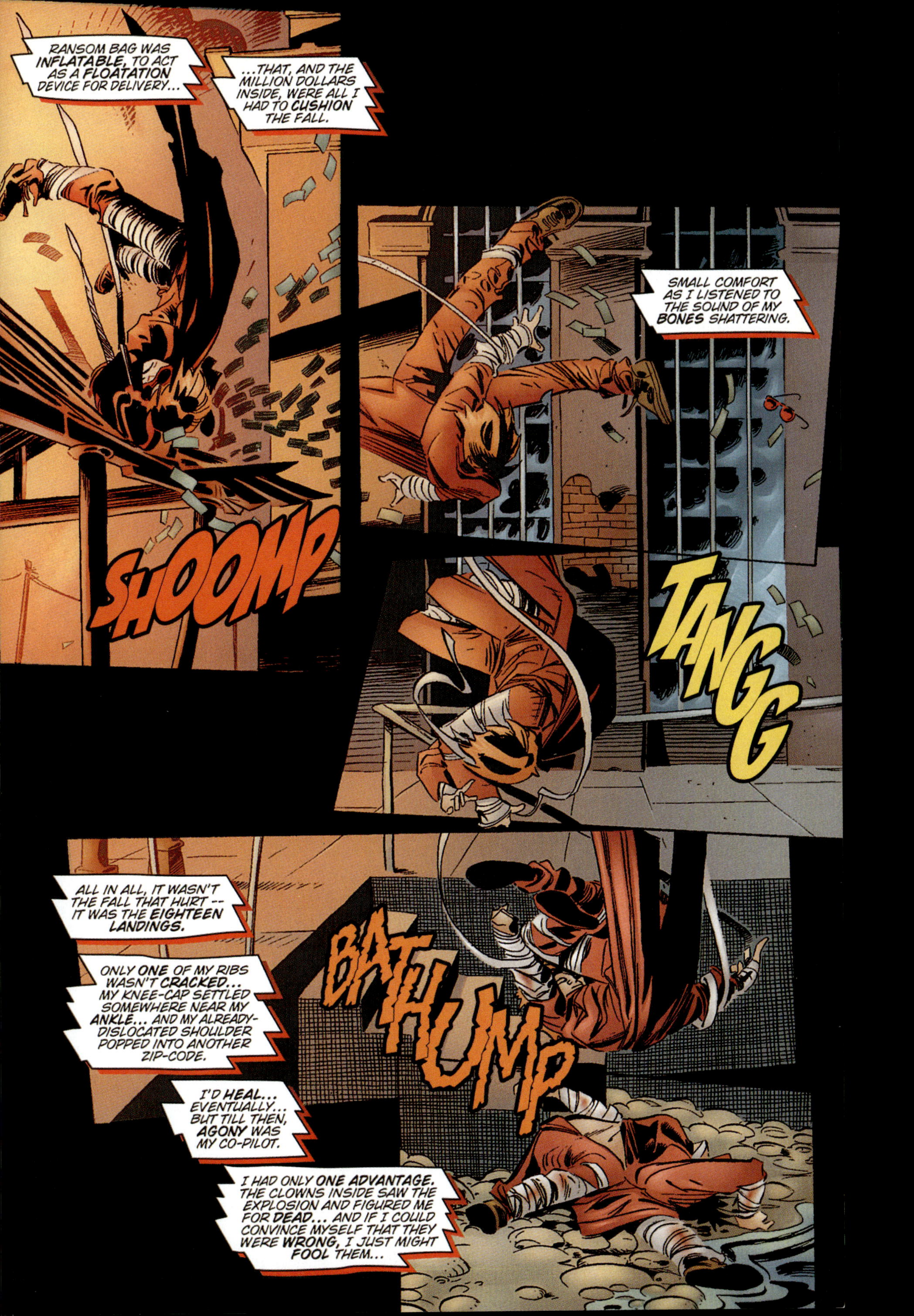
RANSOM BAG WAS INFLATABLE, TO ACT AS A FLOATATION DEVICE FOR DELIVERY...
...THAT, AND THE MILLION DOLLARS INSIDE, WERE ALL I HAD TO CUSHION THE FALL.
SHOOMP
SMALL COMFORT AS I LISTENED TO THE SOUND OF MY BONES SHATTERING.
TANGG
ALL IN ALL, IT WASN'T THE FALL THAT HURT -- IT WAS THE EIGHTEEN LANDINGS.
ONLY ONE OF MY RIBS WASN'T CRACKED... MY KNEE-CAP SETTLED SOMEWHERE NEAR MY ANKLE... AND MY ALREADY-DISLOCATED SHOULDER POPPED INTO ANOTHER ZIP-CODE.
BATHUMP
I'D HEAL... EVENTUALLY... BUT TILL THEN, AGONY WAS MY CO-PILOT.
I HAD ONLY ONE ADVANTAGE. THE CLOWNS INSIDE SAW THE EXPLOSION AND FIGURED ME FOR DEAD... AND IF I COULD CONVINCE MYSELF THAT THEY WERE WRONG, I JUST MIGHT FOOL THEM...

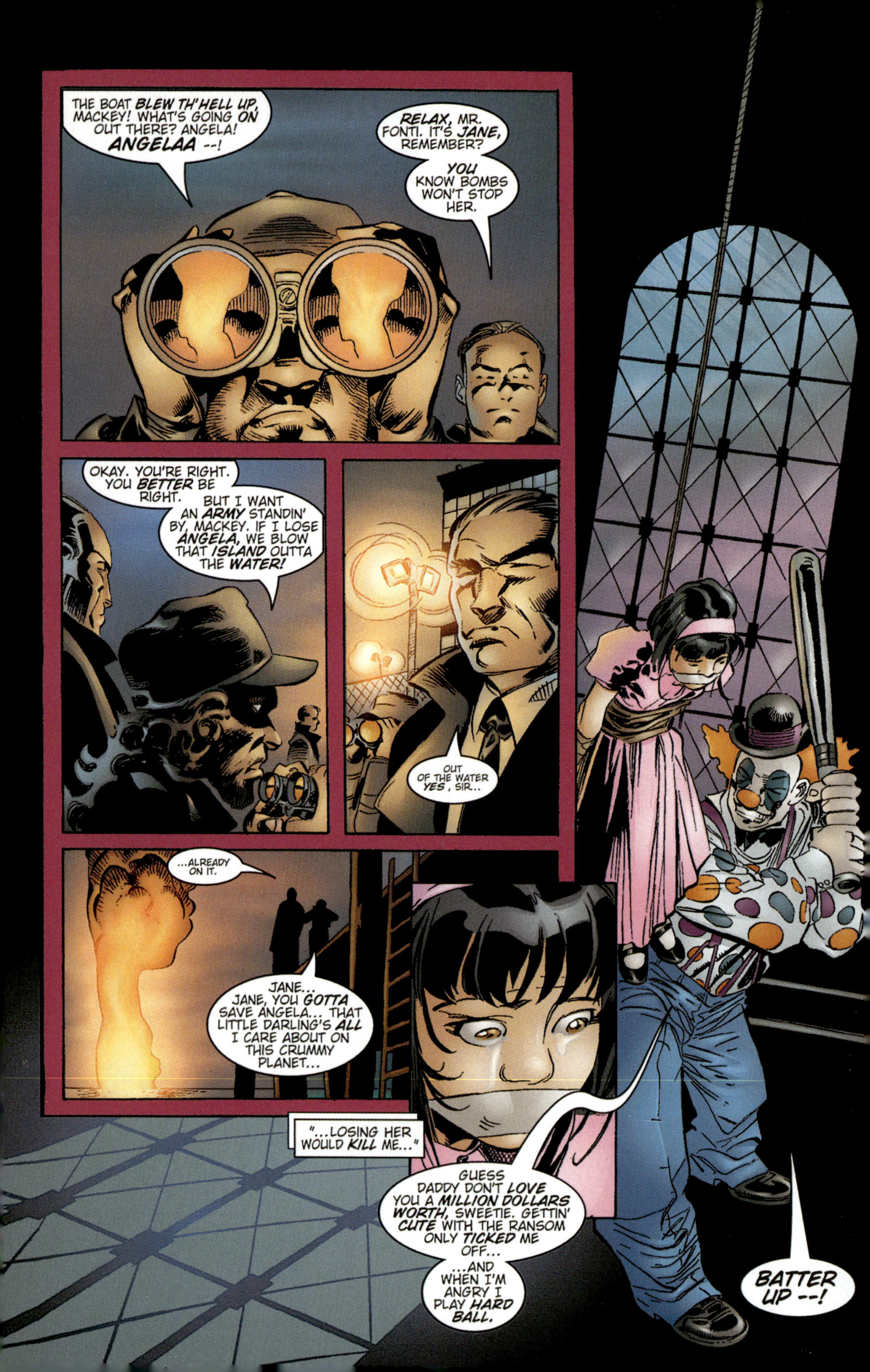
THE BOAT BLEW TH' HELL UP, MACKEY! WHAT'S GOING ON OUT THERE? ANGELA! ANGELAA --!
RELAX, MR. FONTI. IT'S JANE, REMEMBER?
YOU KNOW BOMBS WON'T STOP HER.
OKAY. YOU'RE RIGHT. YOU BETTER BE RIGHT.
BUT I WANT AN ARMY STANDIN' BY, MACKEY. IF I LOSE ANGELA, WE BLOW THAT ISLAND OUTTA THE WATER!
OUT OF THE WATER YES, SIR...
...ALREADY ON IT.
JANE... JANE, YOU GOTTA SAVE ANGELA... THAT LITTLE DARLING'S ALL I CARE ABOUT ON THIS CRUMMY PLANET...
"...LOSING HER WOULD KILL ME..."
GUESS DADDY DON'T LOVE YOU A MILLION DOLLARS WORTH, SWEETIE. GETTIN' CUTE WITH THE RANSOM ONLY TICKED ME OFF...
...AND WHEN I'M ANGRY I PLAY HARD BALL.
BATTER UP --!

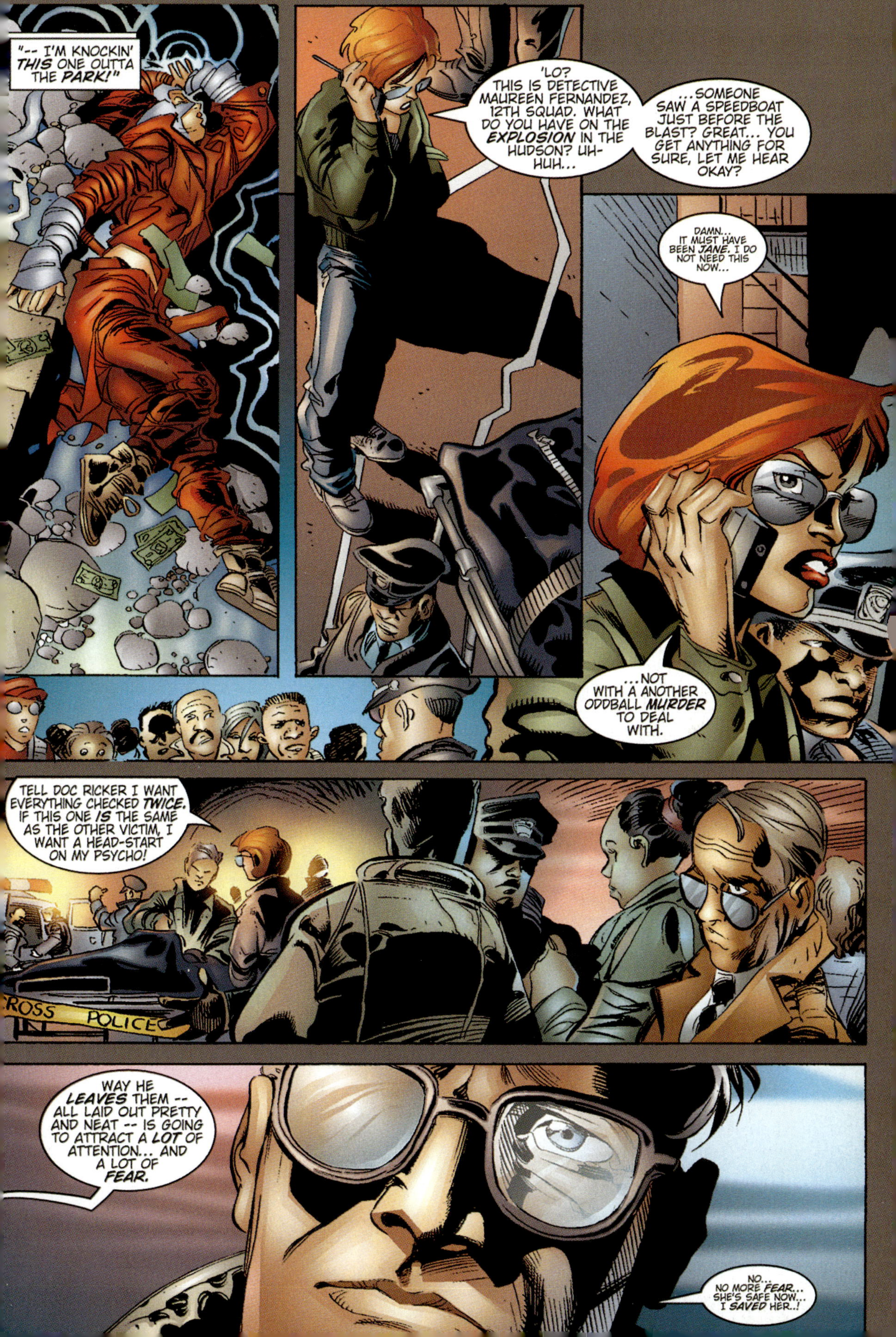
"-- I'M KNOCKIN' THIS ONE OUTTA THE PARK!"
'LO? THIS IS DETECTIVE MAUREEN FERNANDEZ, 12TH SQUAD. WHAT DO YOU HAVE ON THE EXPLOSION IN THE HUDSON? UH-HUH...
...SOMEONE SAW A SPEEDBOAT JUST BEFORE THE BLAST? GREAT... YOU GET ANYTHING FOR SURE, LET ME HEAR OKAY?
DAMN... IT MUST HAVE BEEN JANE. I DO NOT NEED THIS NOW...
...NOT WITH A ANOTHER ODDBALL MURDER TO DEAL WITH.
TELL DOC RICKER I WANT EVERYTHING CHECKED TWICE. IF THIS ONE IS THE SAME AS THE OTHER VICTIM, I WANT A HEAD-START ON MY PSYCHO!
ROSS POLICE
WAY HE LEAVES THEM -- ALL LAID OUT PRETTY AND NEAT -- IS GOING TO ATTRACT A LOT OF ATTENTION... AND A LOT OF FEAR.
NO... NO MORE FEAR... SHE'S SAFE NOW... I SAVED HER...!

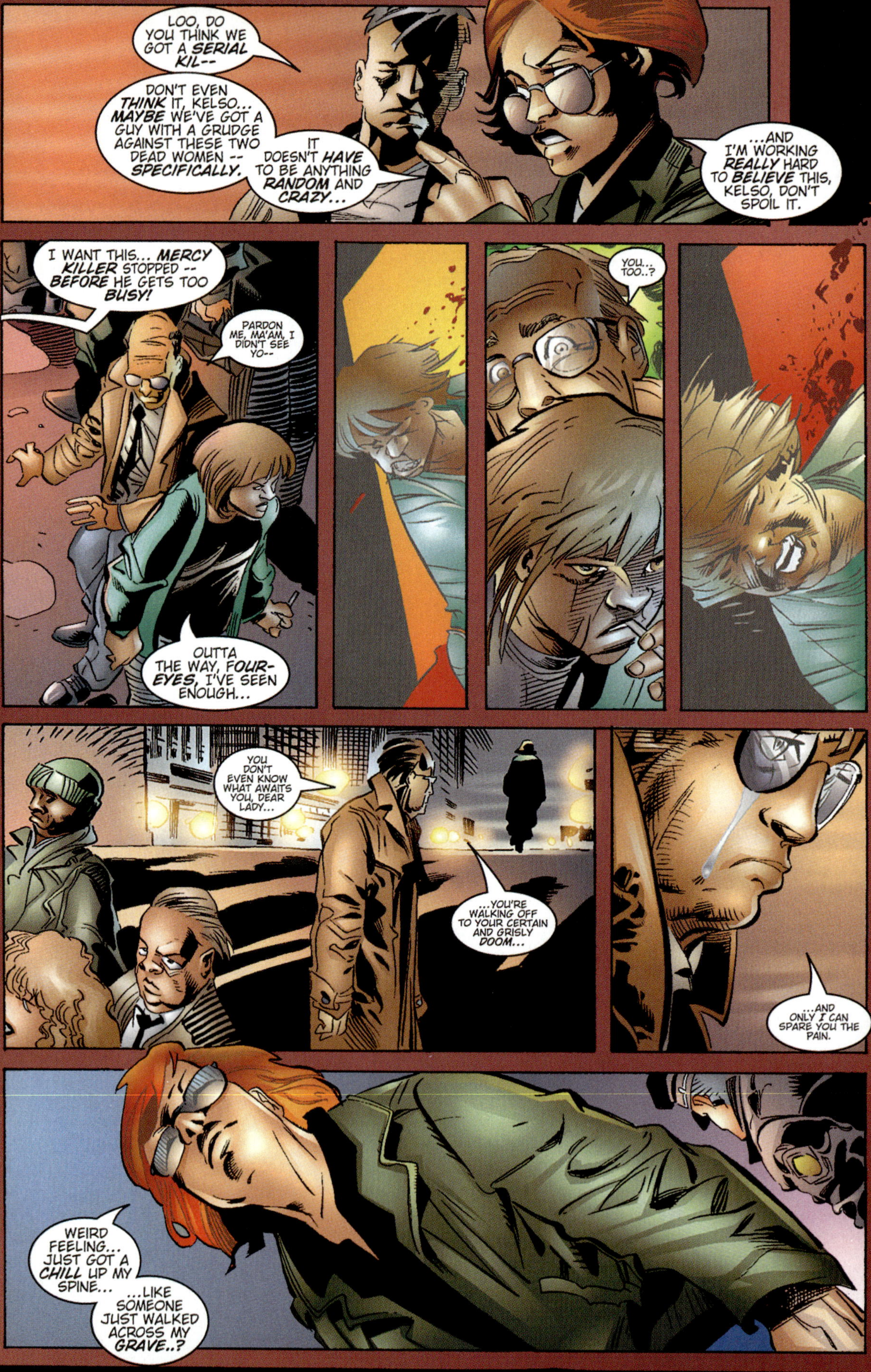
LOO, DO YOU THINK WE GOT A SERIAL KIL--
DON'T EVEN THINK IT, KELSO... MAYBE WE'VE GOT A GUY WITH A GRUDGE AGAINST THESE TWO DEAD WOMEN -- SPECIFICALLY.
IT DOESN'T HAVE TO BE ANYTHING RANDOM AND CRAZY...
...AND I'M WORKING REALLY HARD TO BELIEVE THIS, KELSO, DON'T SPOIL IT.
I WANT THIS... MERCY KILLER STOPPED -- BEFORE HE GETS TOO BUSY!
PARDON ME, MA'AM, I DIDN'T SEE YO--
OUTTA THE WAY, FOUR-EYES, I'VE SEEN ENOUGH...
YOU... TOO..?
YOU DON'T EVEN KNOW WHAT AWAITS YOU, DEAR LADY...
...YOU'RE WALKING OFF TO YOUR CERTAIN AND GRISLY DOOM...
...AND ONLY I CAN SPARE YOU THE PAIN.
WEIRD FEELING... JUST GOT A CHILL UP MY SPINE...
...LIKE SOMEONE JUST WALKED ACROSS MY GRAVE..?

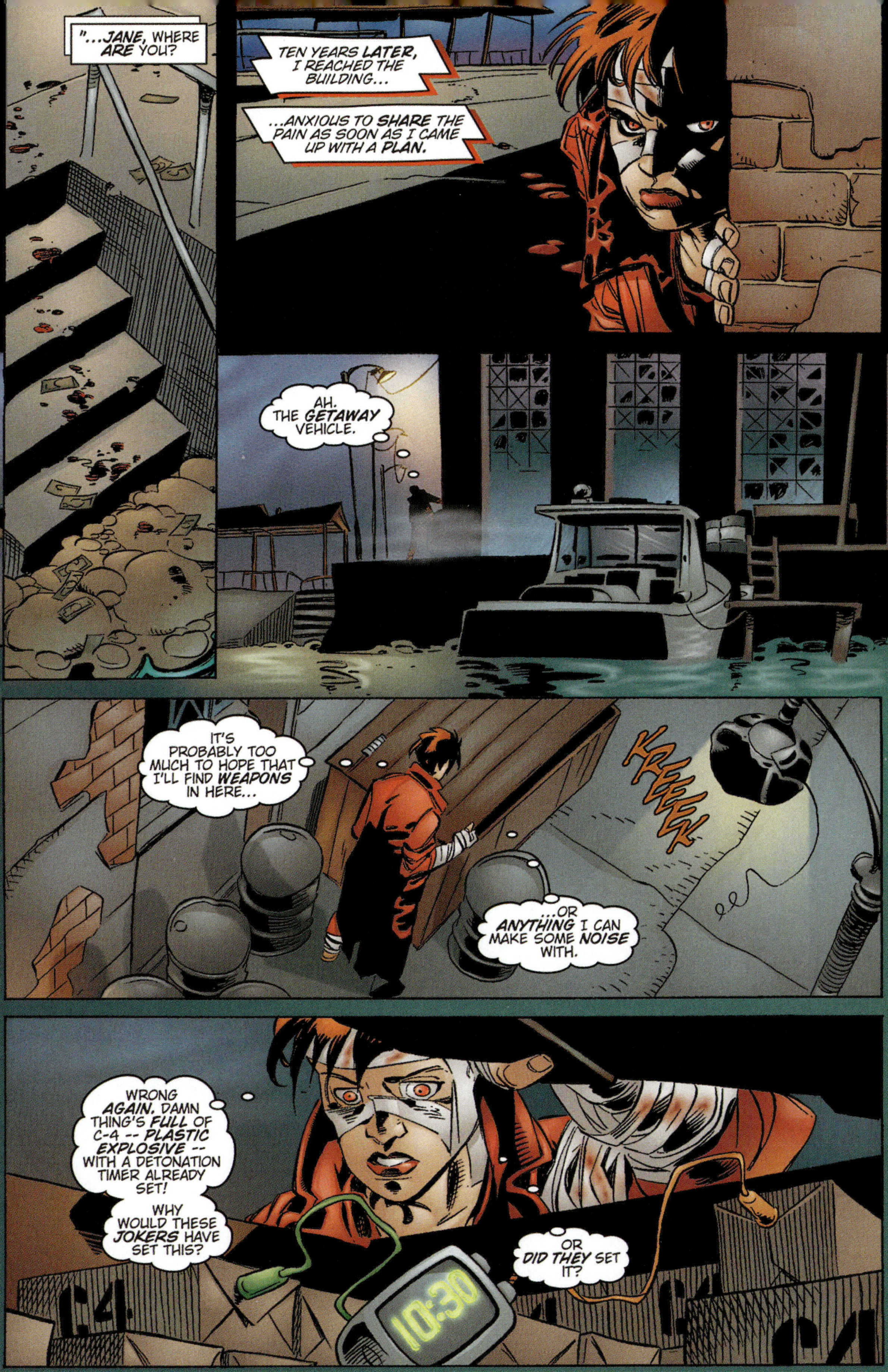
"...JANE, WHERE ARE YOU?
TEN YEARS LATER, I REACHED THE BUILDING...
...ANXIOUS TO SHARE THE PAIN AS SOON AS I CAME UP WITH A PLAN.
AH. THE GETAWAY VEHICLE.
IT'S PROBABLY TOO MUCH TO HOPE THAT I'LL FIND WEAPONS IN HERE...
KREEEK
...OR ANYTHING I CAN MAKE SOME NOISE WITH.
WRONG AGAIN. DAMN THING'S FULL OF C-4 -- PLASTIC EXPLOSIVE -- WITH A DETONATION TIMER ALREADY SET!
WHY WOULD THESE JOKERS HAVE SET THIS?
OR DID THEY SET IT?
10:30

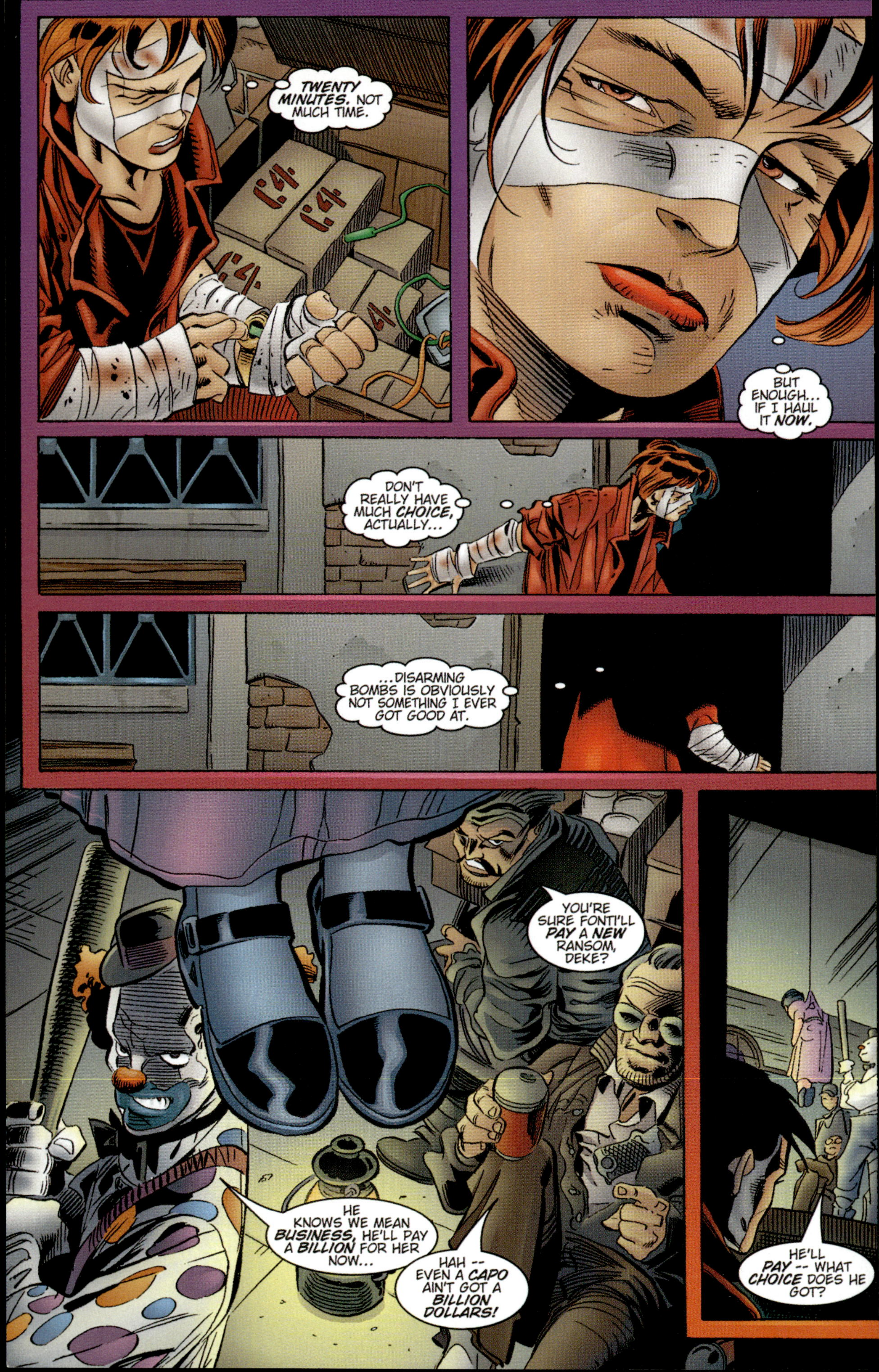
TWENTY MINUTES. NOT MUCH TIME.
BUT ENOUGH... IF I HAUL IT NOW.
DON'T REALLY HAVE MUCH CHOICE, ACTUALLY...
...DISARMING BOMBS IS OBVIOUSLY NOT SOMETHING I EVER GOT GOOD AT.
YOU'RE SURE FONTI'LL PAY A NEW RANSOM, DEKE?
HE KNOWS WE MEAN BUSINESS, HE'LL PAY A BILLION FOR HER NOW...
HAH -- EVEN A CAPO AIN'T GOT A BILLION DOLLARS!
HE'LL PAY -- WHAT CHOICE DOES HE GOT?

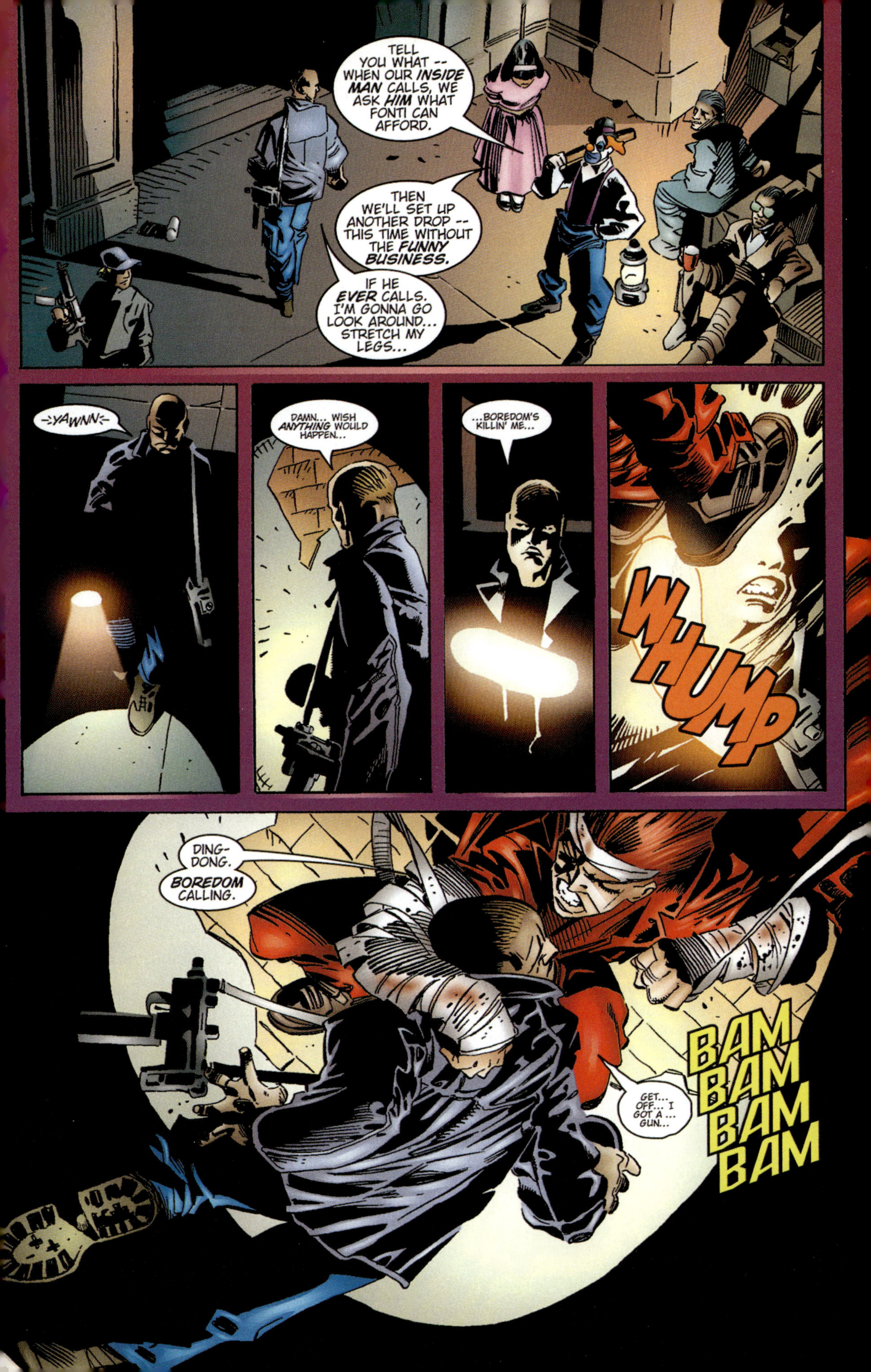
TELL YOU WHAT -- WHEN OUR *INSIDE MAN* CALLS, WE ASK *HIM* WHAT FONTI CAN AFFORD.
THEN WE'LL SET UP ANOTHER DROP -- THIS TIME WITHOUT THE *FUNNY BUSINESS.*
IF HE *EVER* CALLS. I'M GONNA GO LOOK AROUND... STRETCH MY LEGS...
-YAWNN-
DAMN... WISH *ANYTHING* WOULD HAPPEN...
...BOREDOM'S KILLIN' ME...
WHUMP
DING-DONG. *BOREDOM* CALLING.
GET... OFF... I GOT A... GUN...
BAM BAM BAM BAM

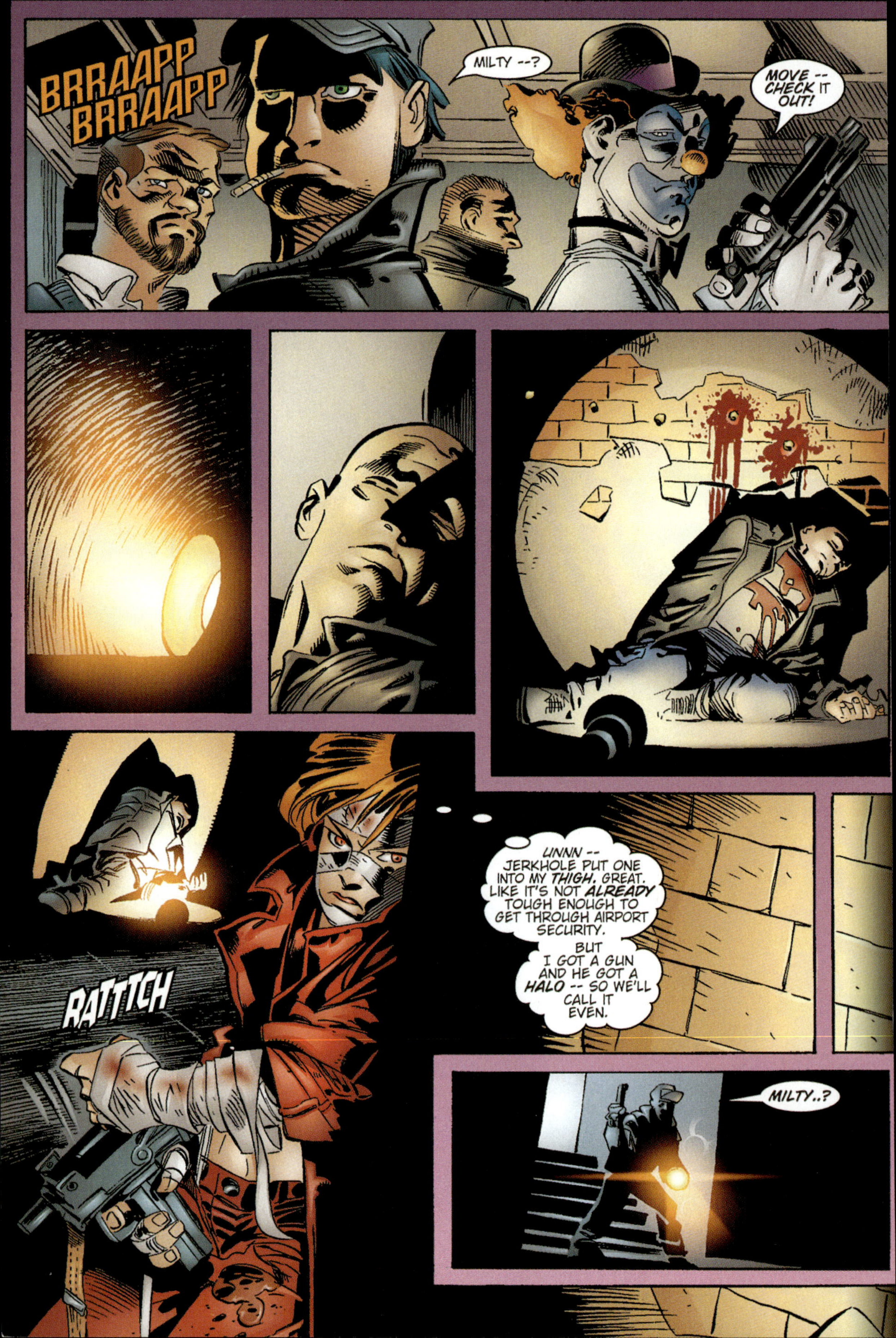
BRRAAPP BRRAAPP
MILTY --?
MOVE -- CHECK IT OUT!
UNNN -- JERKHOLE PUT ONE INTO MY THIGH. GREAT. LIKE IT'S NOT ALREADY TOUGH ENOUGH TO GET THROUGH AIRPORT SECURITY.
BUT I GOT A GUN AND HE GOT A HALO -- SO WE'LL CALL IT EVEN.
RATTTCH
MILTY..?

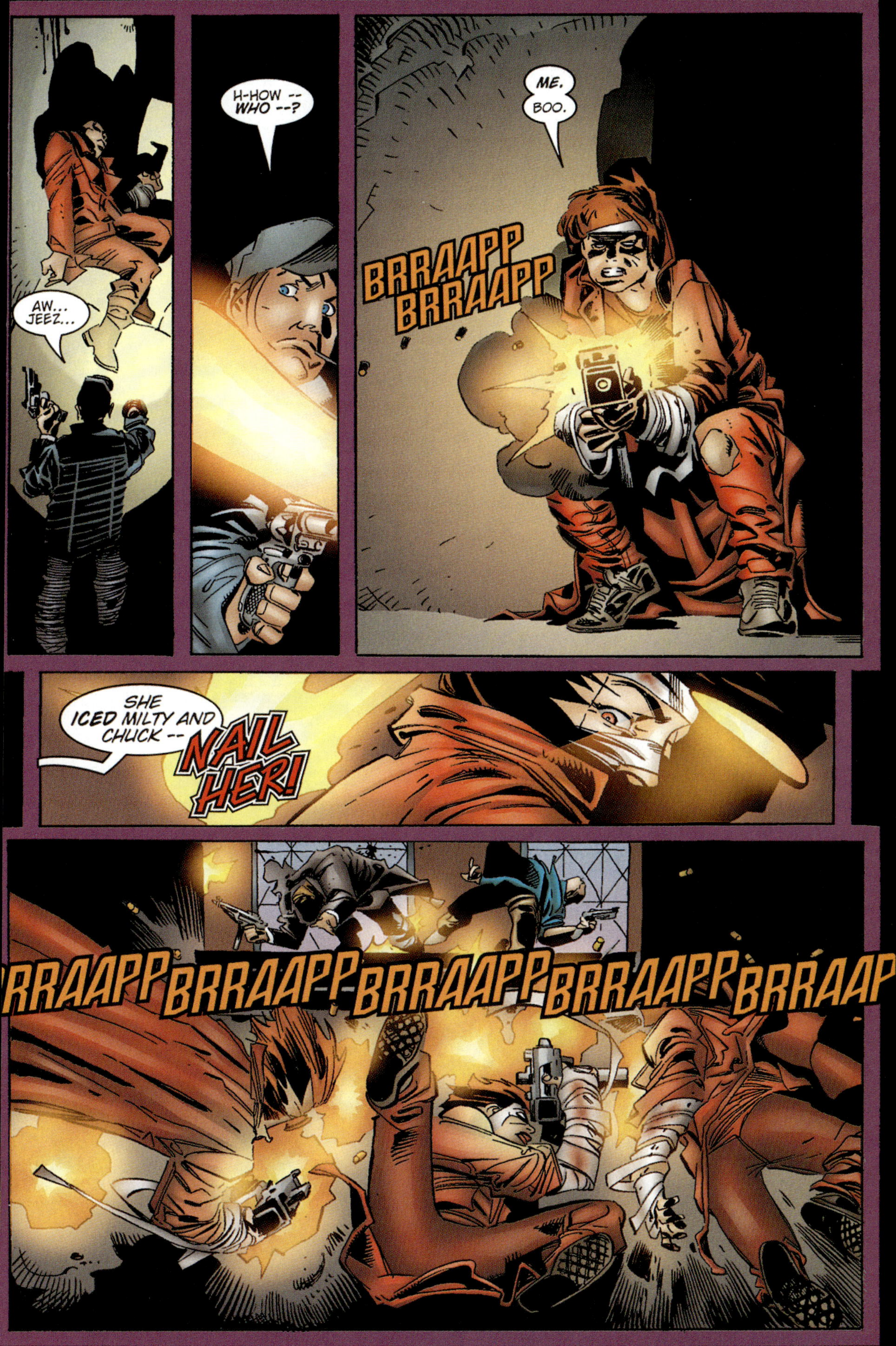

AW... JEEZ...
H-HOW -- WHO --?
ME. BOO.
BRRAAPP BRRAAPP
SHE ICED MILTY AND CHUCK -- NAIL HER!
RRAAPP BRRAAPP BRRAAPP BRRAAPP BRRAAP

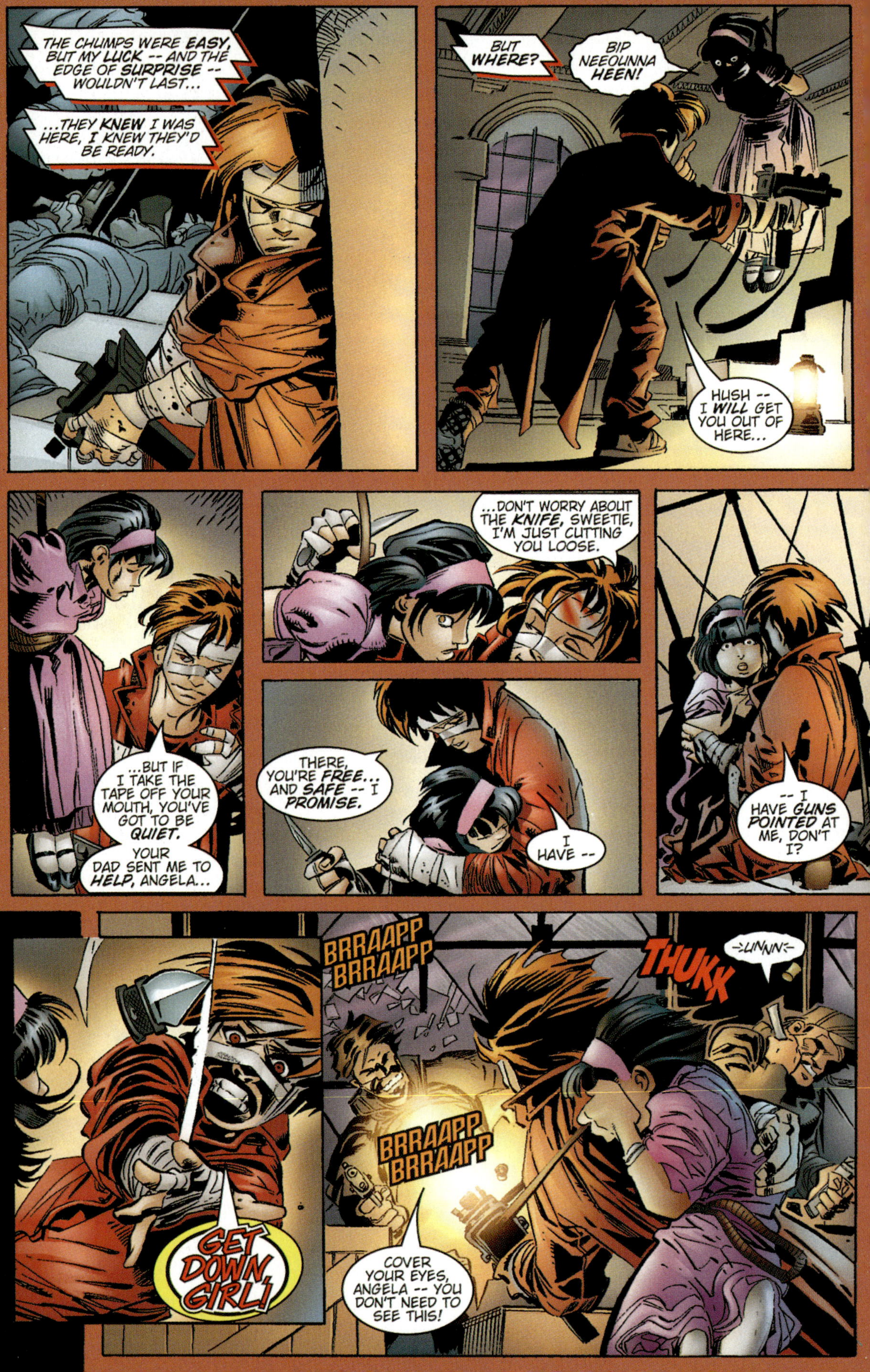
THE CHUMPS WERE EASY, BUT MY LUCK -- AND THE EDGE OF SURPRISE -- WOULDN'T LAST...
...THEY KNEW I WAS HERE, I KNEW THEY'D BE READY.
BUT WHERE?
BIP NEEOUNNA HEEN!
HUSH -- I WILL GET YOU OUT OF HERE...
...BUT IF I TAKE THE TAPE OFF YOUR MOUTH, YOU'VE GOT TO BE QUIET.
YOUR DAD SENT ME TO HELP, ANGELA...
...DON'T WORRY ABOUT THE KNIFE, SWEETIE, I'M JUST CUTTING YOU LOOSE.
THERE, YOU'RE FREE... AND SAFE -- I PROMISE.
I HAVE --
-- I HAVE GUNS POINTED AT ME, DON'T I?
GET DOWN, GIRL!
BRRAAPP BRRAAPP
BRRAAPP BRRAAPP
THUKK
UNNN
COVER YOUR EYES, ANGELA -- YOU DON'T NEED TO SEE THIS!

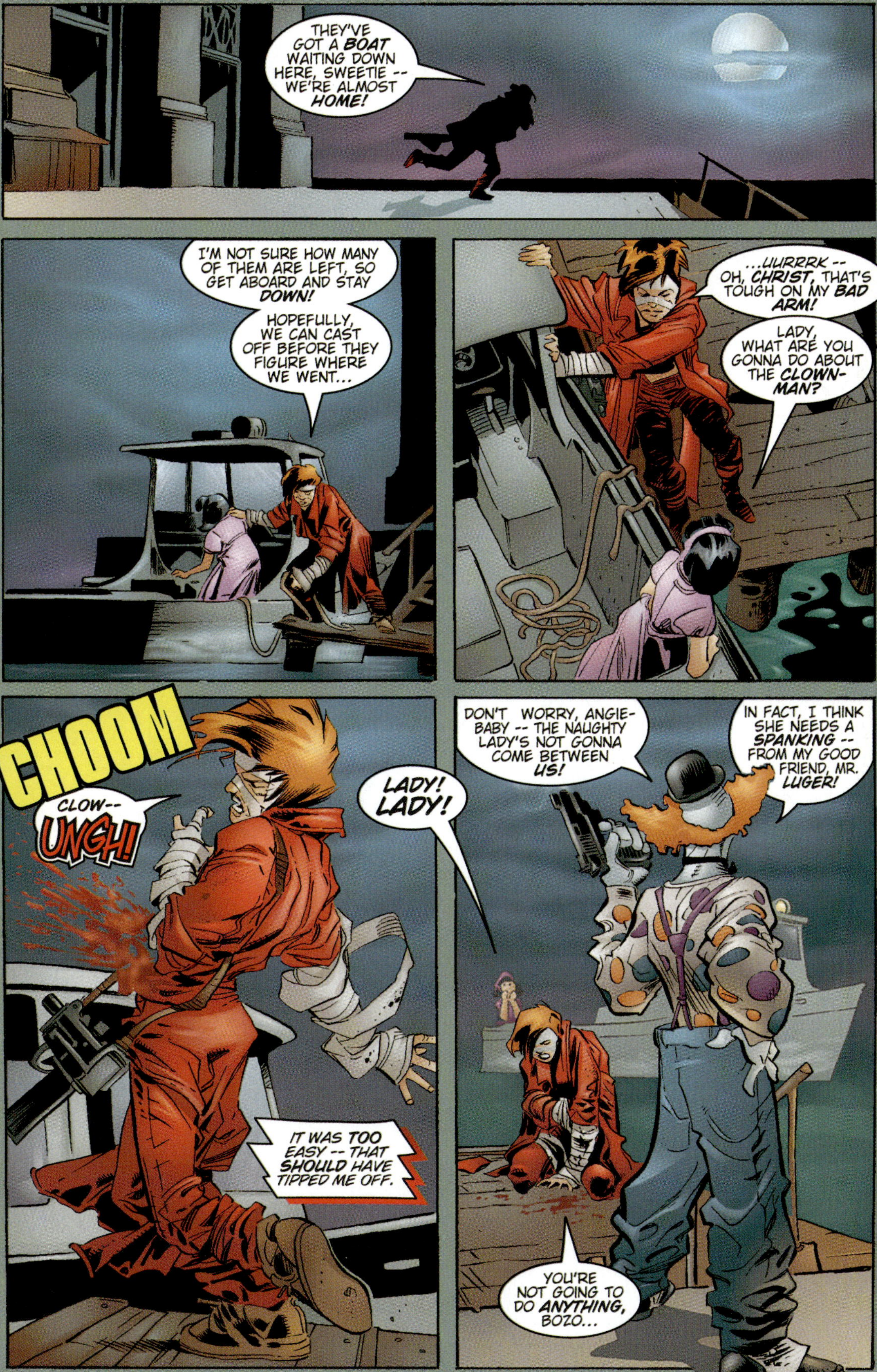
THEY'VE GOT A BOAT WAITING DOWN HERE, SWEETIE -- WE'RE ALMOST HOME!
I'M NOT SURE HOW MANY OF THEM ARE LEFT, SO GET ABOARD AND STAY DOWN!
HOPEFULLY, WE CAN CAST OFF BEFORE THEY FIGURE WHERE WE WENT...
...UURRRK -- OH, CHRIST, THAT'S TOUGH ON MY BAD ARM!
LADY, WHAT ARE YOU GONNA DO ABOUT THE CLOWN-MAN?
CHOOM
CLOW--
UNGH!
LADY! LADY!
IT WAS TOO EASY -- THAT SHOULD HAVE TIPPED ME OFF.
DON'T WORRY, ANGIE-BABY -- THE NAUGHTY LADY'S NOT GONNA COME BETWEEN US!
IN FACT, I THINK SHE NEEDS A SPANKING -- FROM MY GOOD FRIEND, MR. LUGER!
YOU'RE NOT GOING TO DO ANYTHING, BOZO...

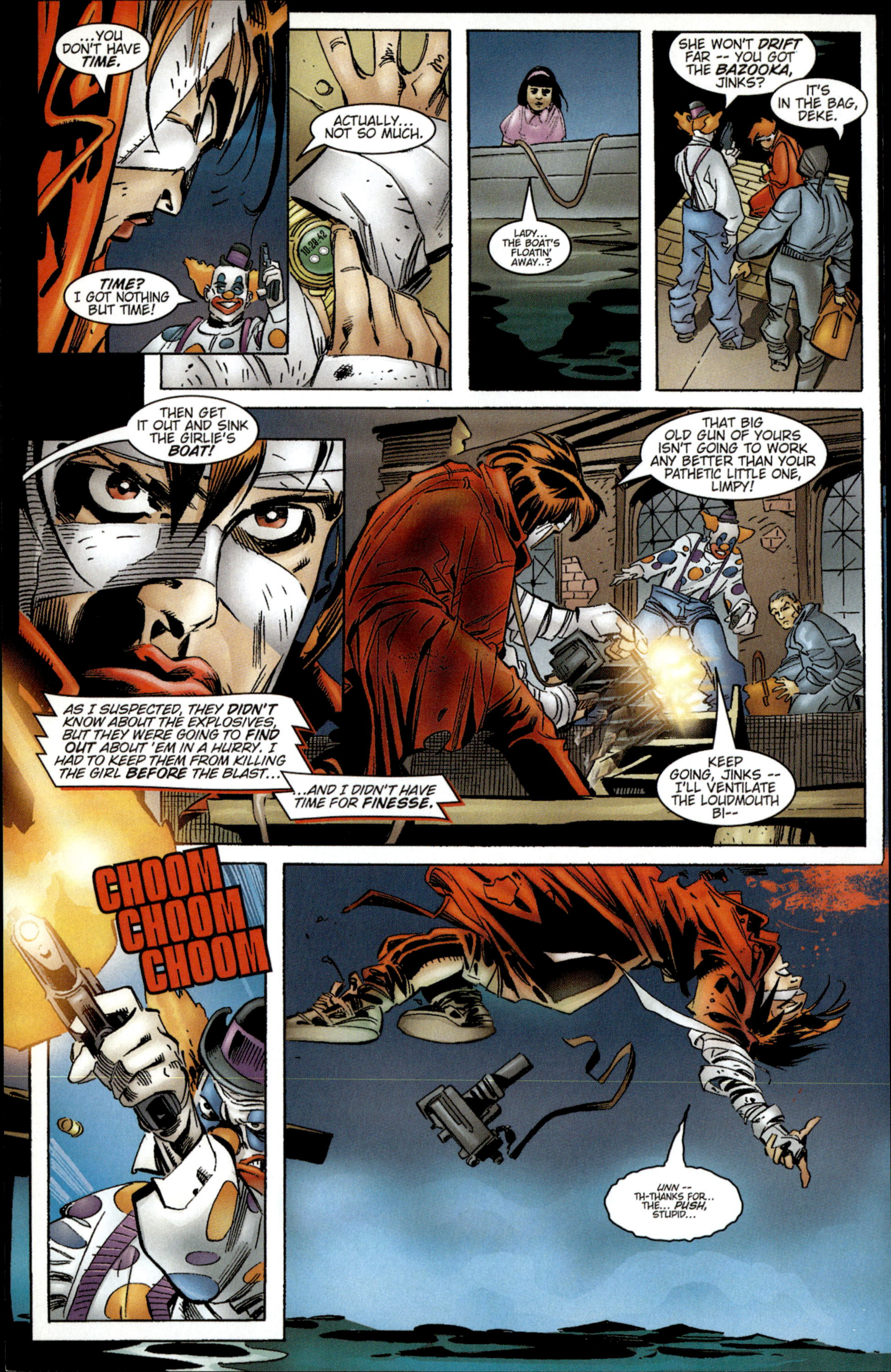

...YOU DON'T HAVE *TIME.*
TIME? I GOT NOTHING BUT TIME!
ACTUALLY... NOT SO MUCH.
LADY... THE BOAT'S FLOATIN' AWAY..?
SHE WON'T *DRIFT* FAR -- YOU GOT THE *BAZOOKA,* JINKS?
IT'S IN THE BAG, DEKE.
THEN GET IT OUT AND SINK THE GIRLIE'S *BOAT!*
THAT BIG OLD GUN OF YOURS ISN'T GOING TO WORK ANY BETTER THAN YOUR PATHETIC LITTLE ONE, LIMPY!
AS I SUSPECTED, THEY *DIDN'T* KNOW ABOUT THE EXPLOSIVES, BUT THEY WERE GOING TO *FIND OUT* ABOUT 'EM IN A HURRY. I HAD TO KEEP THEM FROM KILLING THE GIRL *BEFORE* THE BLAST...
...AND I DIDN'T HAVE TIME FOR *FINESSE.*
KEEP GOING, JINKS -- I'LL VENTILATE THE LOUDMOUTH BI--
CHOOM CHOOM CHOOM
UNN -- TH-THANKS FOR... THE... *PUSH,* STUPID...

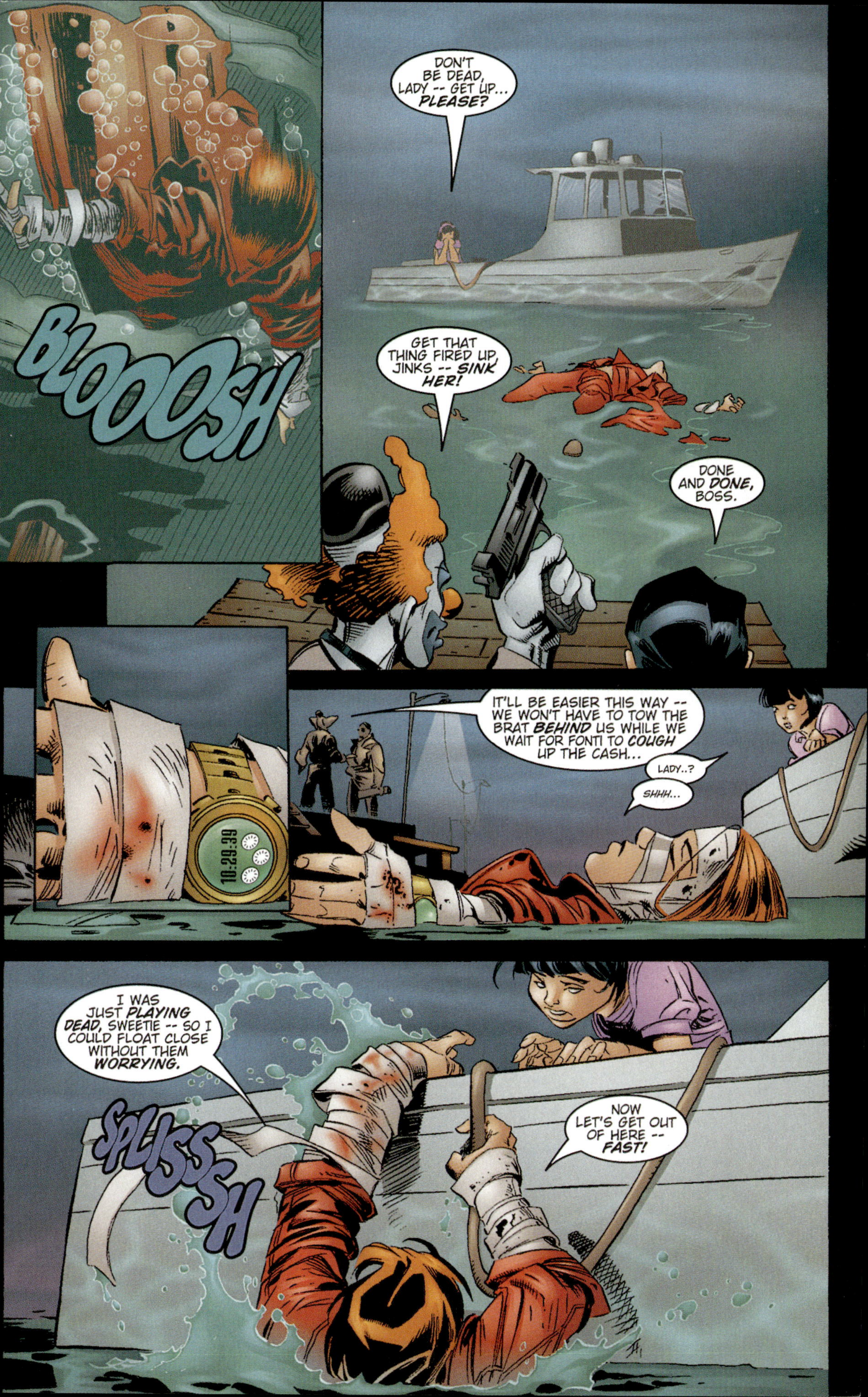
BLOOOSH
DON'T BE DEAD, LADY -- GET UP... PLEASE?
GET THAT THING FIRED UP, JINKS -- SINK HER!
DONE AND DONE, BOSS.
10:29:99
IT'LL BE EASIER THIS WAY -- WE WON'T HAVE TO TOW THE BRAT BEHIND US WHILE WE WAIT FOR FONTI TO COUGH UP THE CASH...
LADY..?
SHHH...
I WAS JUST PLAYING DEAD, SWEETIE -- SO I COULD FLOAT CLOSE WITHOUT THEM WORRYING.
SPLISSSH
NOW LET'S GET OUT OF HERE -- FAST!

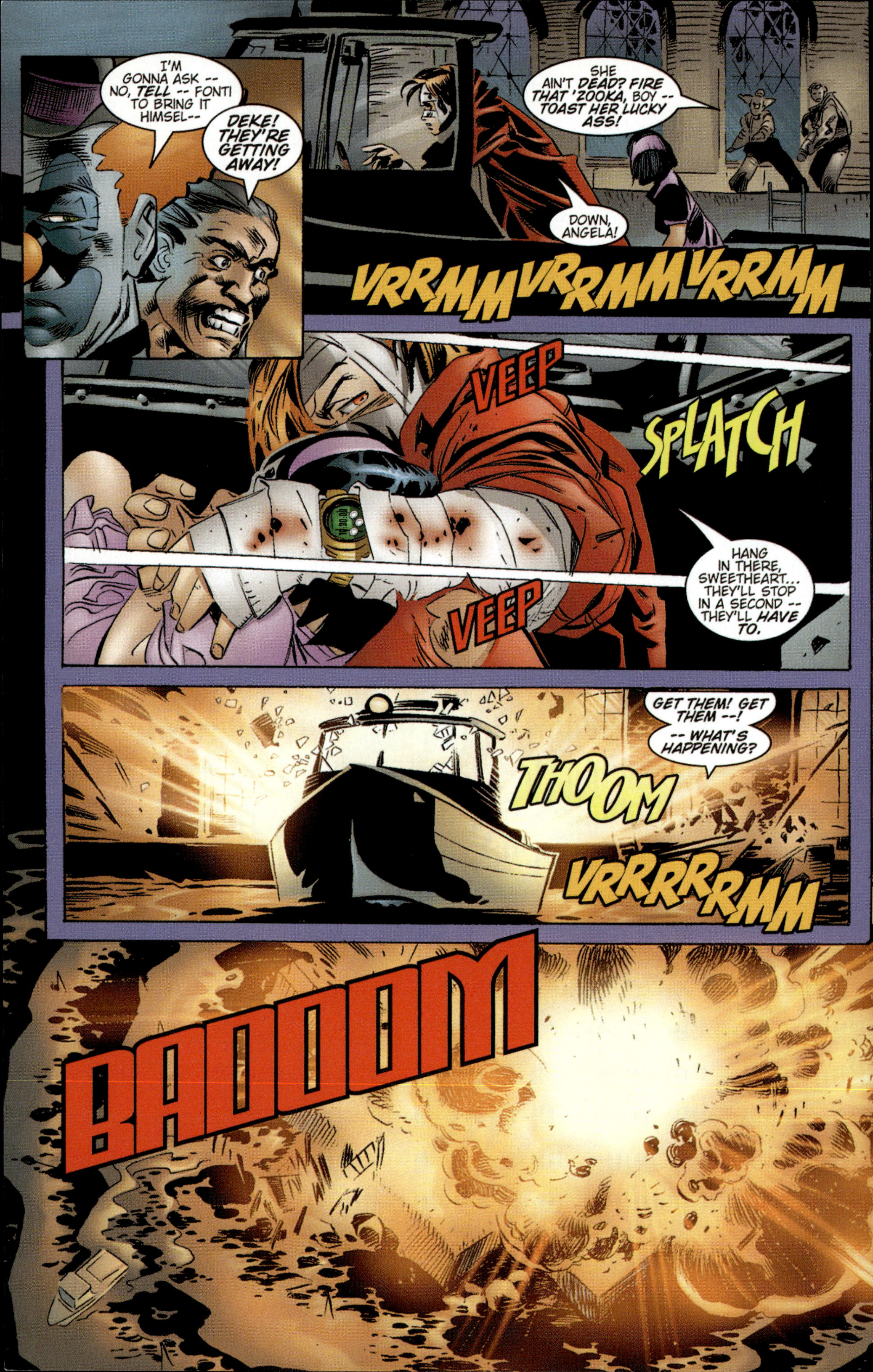
I'M GONNA ASK -- NO, TELL -- FONTI TO BRING IT HIMSEL--
DEKE! THEY'RE GETTING AWAY!
SHE AIN'T DEAD? FIRE THAT 'ZOOKA, BOY -- TOAST HER LUCKY ASS!
DOWN, ANGELA!
VRRMM VRRMM VRRMM
VEEP
SPLATCH
HANG IN THERE, SWEETHEART... THEY'LL STOP IN A SECOND -- THEY'LL HAVE TO.
VEEP
GET THEM! GET THEM --!
-- WHAT'S HAPPENING?
THOOM
VRRRRRMM
BADOOM

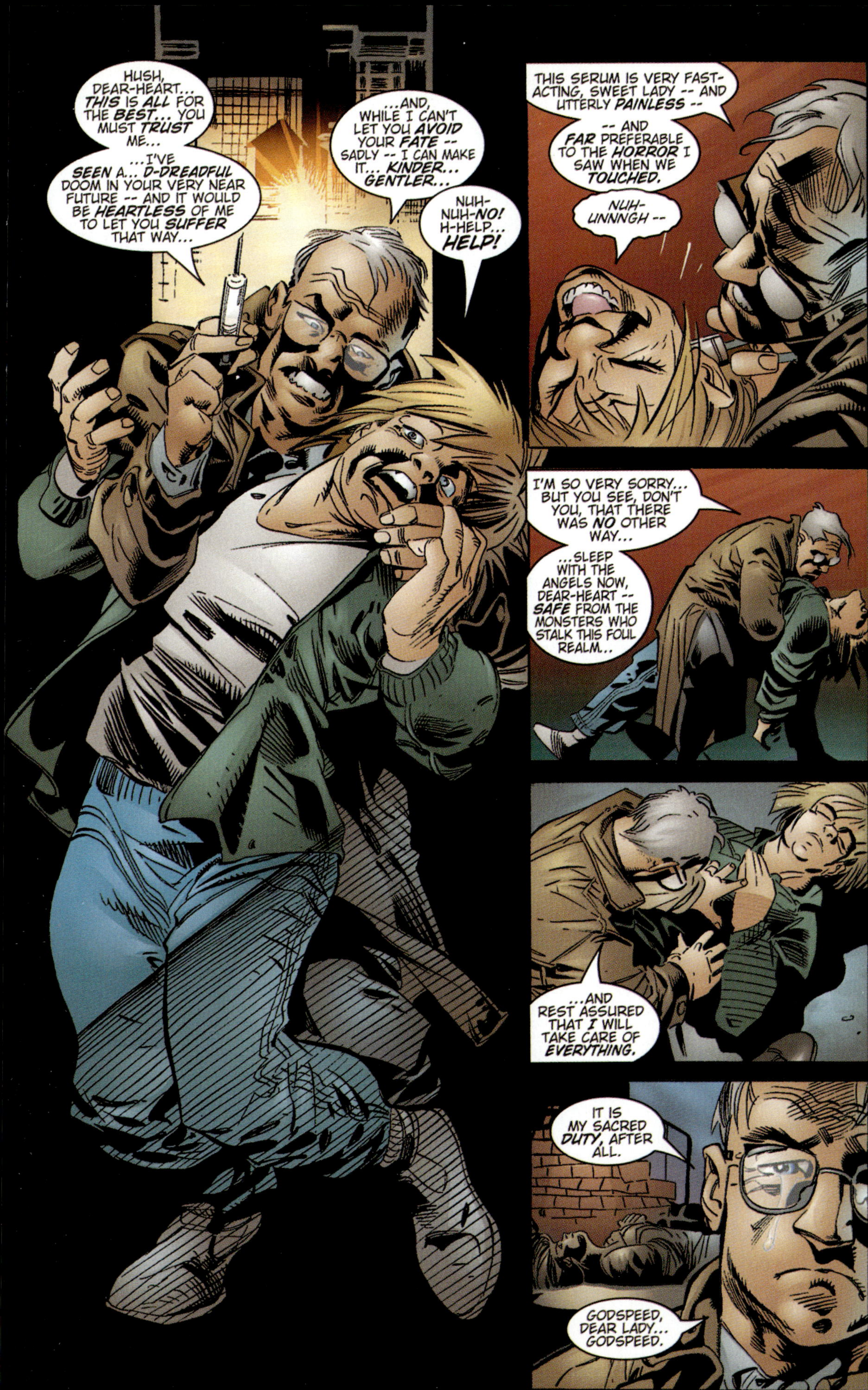
HUSH, DEAR-HEART... THIS IS ALL FOR THE BEST... YOU MUST TRUST ME...
...I'VE SEEN A... D-DREADFUL DOOM IN YOUR VERY NEAR FUTURE -- AND IT WOULD BE HEARTLESS OF ME TO LET YOU SUFFER THAT WAY...
...AND, WHILE I CAN'T LET YOU AVOID YOUR FATE -- SADLY -- I CAN MAKE IT... KINDER... GENTLER...
NUH-NUH-NO! H-HELP... HELP!
THIS SERUM IS VERY FAST-ACTING, SWEET LADY -- AND UTTERLY PAINLESS --
-- AND FAR PREFERABLE TO THE HORROR I SAW WHEN WE TOUCHED.
NUH-UNNNGH --
I'M SO VERY SORRY... BUT YOU SEE, DON'T YOU, THAT THERE WAS NO OTHER WAY...
...SLEEP WITH THE ANGELS NOW, DEAR-HEART -- SAFE FROM THE MONSTERS WHO STALK THIS FOUL REALM...
...AND REST ASSURED THAT I WILL TAKE CARE OF EVERYTHING.
IT IS MY SACRED DUTY, AFTER ALL.
GODSPEED, DEAR LADY... GODSPEED.

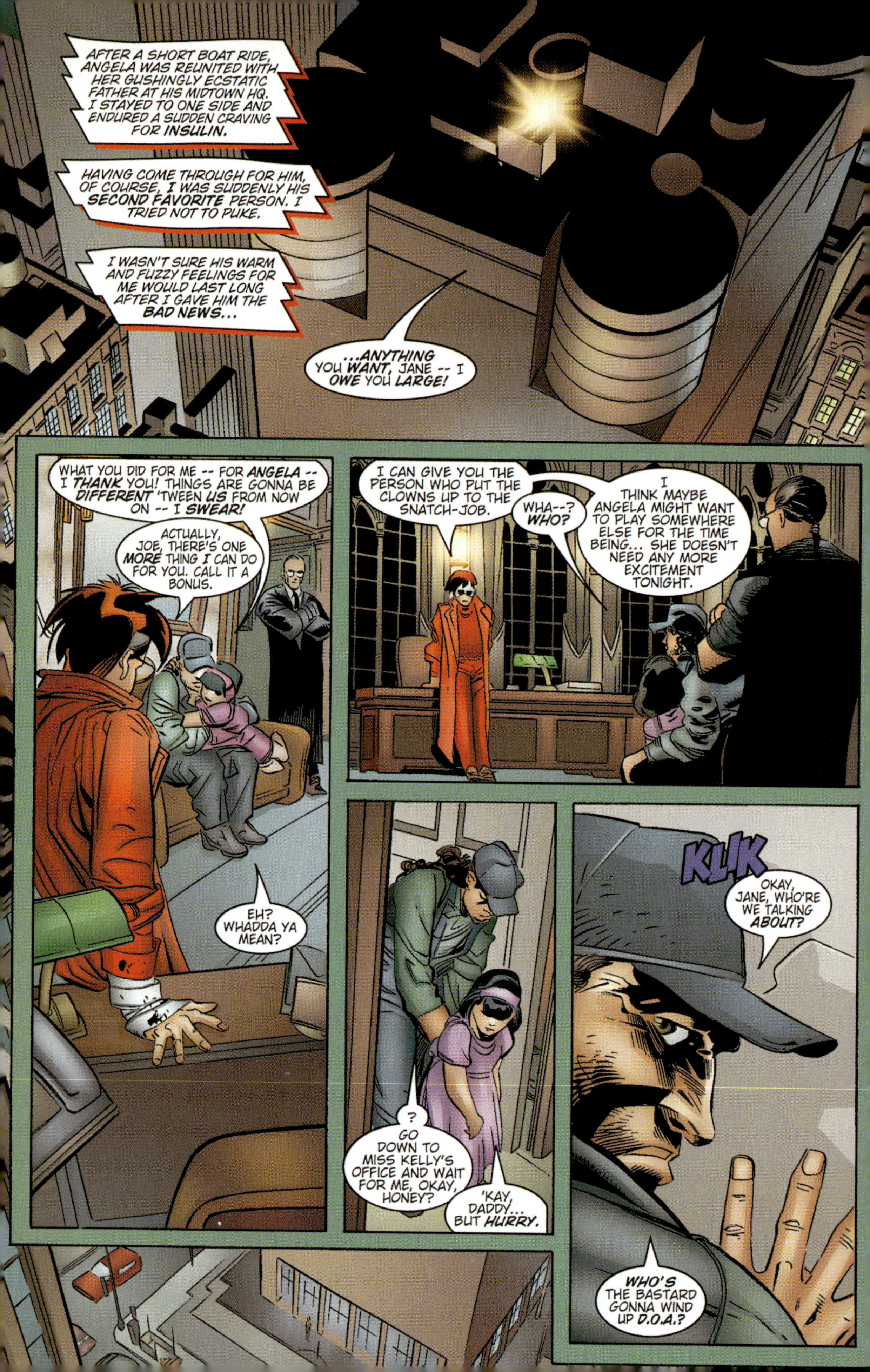
AFTER A SHORT BOAT RIDE, ANGELA WAS REUNITED WITH HER GUSHINGLY ECSTATIC FATHER AT HIS MIDTOWN HQ. I STAYED TO ONE SIDE AND ENDURED A SUDDEN CRAVING FOR INSULIN.
HAVING COME THROUGH FOR HIM, OF COURSE, I WAS SUDDENLY HIS SECOND FAVORITE PERSON. I TRIED NOT TO PUKE.
I WASN'T SURE HIS WARM AND FUZZY FEELINGS FOR ME WOULD LAST LONG AFTER I GAVE HIM THE BAD NEWS...
...ANYTHING YOU WANT, JANE -- I OWE YOU LARGE!
WHAT YOU DID FOR ME -- FOR ANGELA -- I THANK YOU! THINGS ARE GONNA BE DIFFERENT 'TWEEN US FROM NOW ON -- I SWEAR!
ACTUALLY, JOE, THERE'S ONE MORE THING I CAN DO FOR YOU. CALL IT A BONUS.
EH? WHADDA YA MEAN?
I CAN GIVE YOU THE PERSON WHO PUT THE CLOWNS UP TO THE SNATCH-JOB.
WHA--? WHO?
I THINK MAYBE ANGELA MIGHT WANT TO PLAY SOMEWHERE ELSE FOR THE TIME BEING... SHE DOESN'T NEED ANY MORE EXCITEMENT TONIGHT.
?
GO DOWN TO MISS KELLY'S OFFICE AND WAIT FOR ME, OKAY, HONEY?
'KAY, DADDY... BUT HURRY.
KLIK
OKAY, JANE, WHO'RE WE TALKING ABOUT?
WHO'S THE BASTARD GONNA WIND UP D.O.A.?

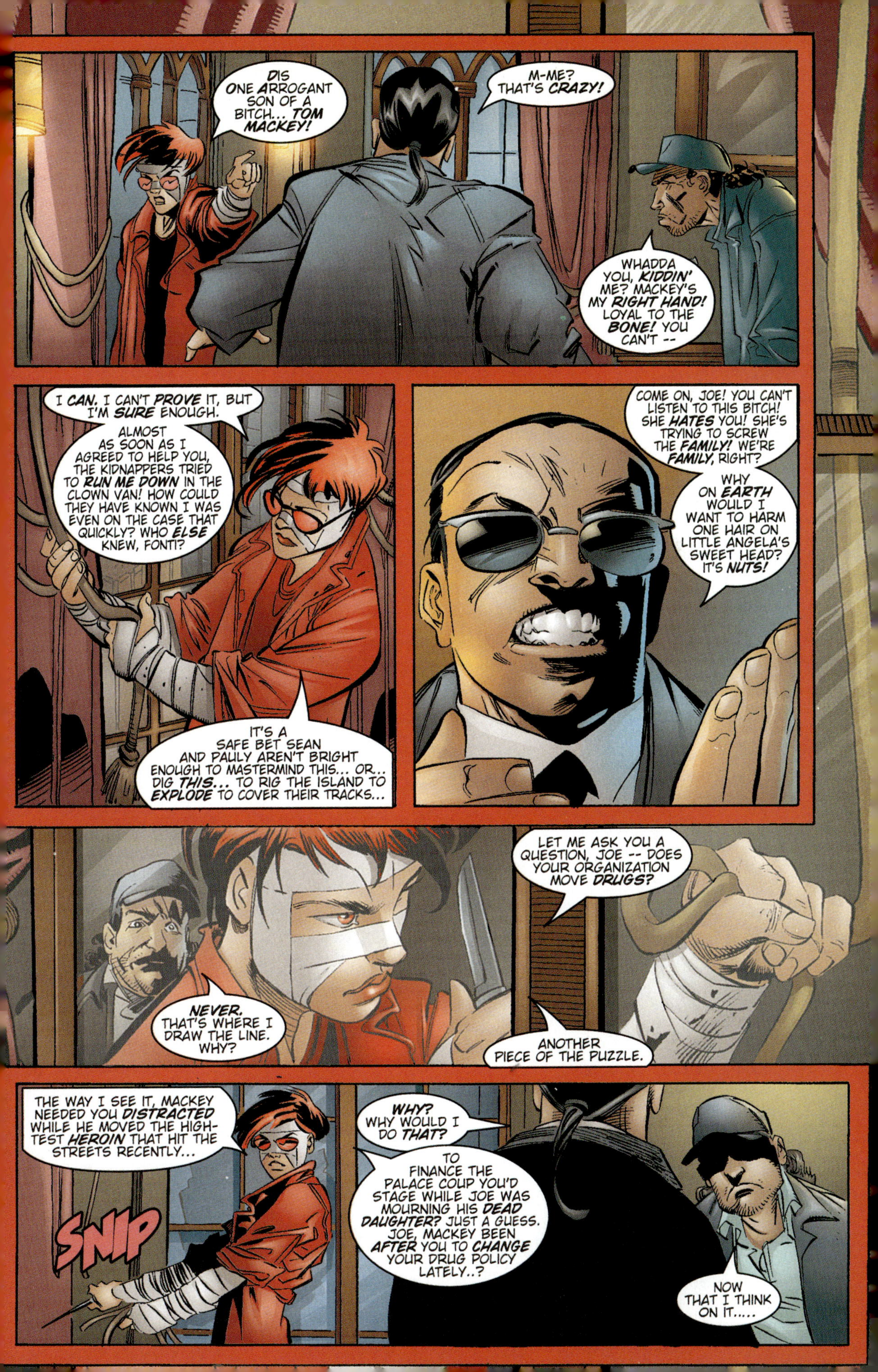
DIS ONE ARROGANT SON OF A BITCH... TOM MACKEY!
M-ME? THAT'S CRAZY!
WHADDA YOU, KIDDIN' ME? MACKEY'S MY RIGHT HAND! LOYAL TO THE BONE! YOU CAN'T --
I CAN. I CAN'T PROVE IT, BUT I'M SURE ENOUGH.
ALMOST AS SOON AS I AGREED TO HELP YOU, THE KIDNAPPERS TRIED TO RUN ME DOWN IN THE CLOWN VAN! HOW COULD THEY HAVE KNOWN I WAS EVEN ON THE CASE THAT QUICKLY? WHO ELSE KNEW, FONTI?
IT'S A SAFE BET SEAN AND PAULY AREN'T BRIGHT ENOUGH TO MASTERMIND THIS... OR... DIG THIS... TO RIG THE ISLAND TO EXPLODE TO COVER THEIR TRACKS...
COME ON, JOE! YOU CAN'T LISTEN TO THIS BITCH! SHE HATES YOU! SHE'S TRYING TO SCREW THE FAMILY! WE'RE FAMILY, RIGHT?
WHY ON EARTH WOULD I WANT TO HARM ONE HAIR ON LITTLE ANGELA'S SWEET HEAD? IT'S NUTS!
LET ME ASK YOU A QUESTION, JOE -- DOES YOUR ORGANIZATION MOVE DRUGS?
NEVER. THAT'S WHERE I DRAW THE LINE. WHY?
ANOTHER PIECE OF THE PUZZLE.
THE WAY I SEE IT, MACKEY NEEDED YOU DISTRACTED WHILE HE MOVED THE HIGH-TEST HEROIN THAT HIT THE STREETS RECENTLY...
SNIP
WHY? WHY WOULD I DO THAT?
TO FINANCE THE PALACE COUP YOU'D STAGE WHILE JOE WAS MOURNING HIS DEAD DAUGHTER? JUST A GUESS. JOE, MACKEY BEEN AFTER YOU TO CHANGE YOUR DRUG POLICY LATELY..?
NOW THAT I THINK ON IT.....

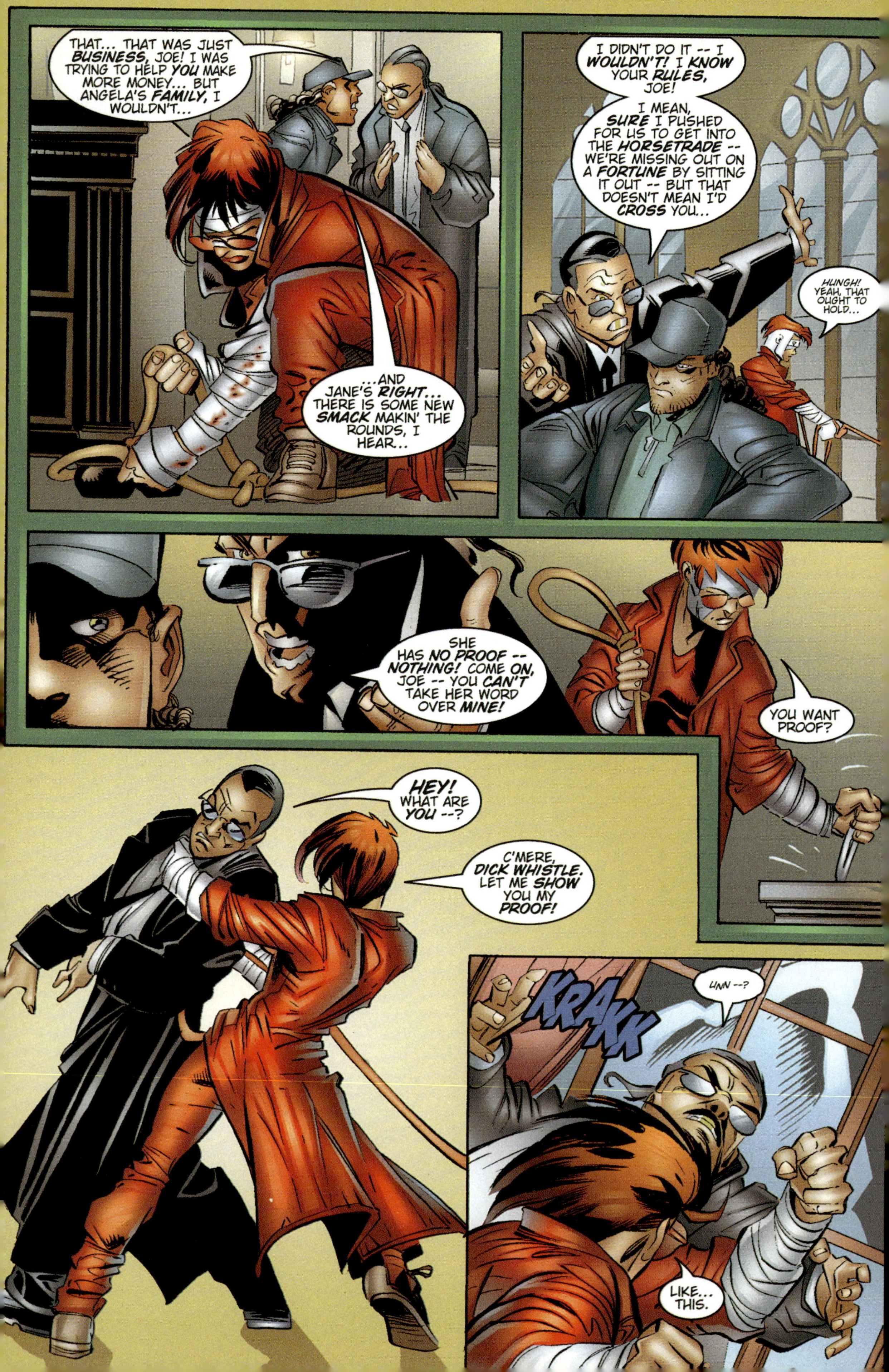

THAT... THAT WAS JUST BUSINESS, JOE! I WAS TRYING TO HELP YOU MAKE MORE MONEY... BUT ANGELA'S FAMILY, I WOULDN'T...
...AND JANE'S RIGHT... THERE IS SOME NEW SMACK MAKIN' THE ROUNDS, I HEAR...
I DIDN'T DO IT -- I WOULDN'T! I KNOW YOUR RULES, JOE!
I MEAN, SURE I PUSHED FOR US TO GET INTO THE HORSETRADE -- WE'RE MISSING OUT ON A FORTUNE BY SITTING IT OUT -- BUT THAT DOESN'T MEAN I'D CROSS YOU...
HUNGH! YEAH, THAT OUGHT TO HOLD...
SHE HAS NO PROOF -- NOTHING! COME ON, JOE -- YOU CAN'T TAKE HER WORD OVER MINE!
YOU WANT PROOF?
HEY! WHAT ARE YOU --?
C'MERE, DICK WHISTLE. LET ME SHOW YOU MY PROOF!
KRAKK
UNN --?
LIKE... THIS.

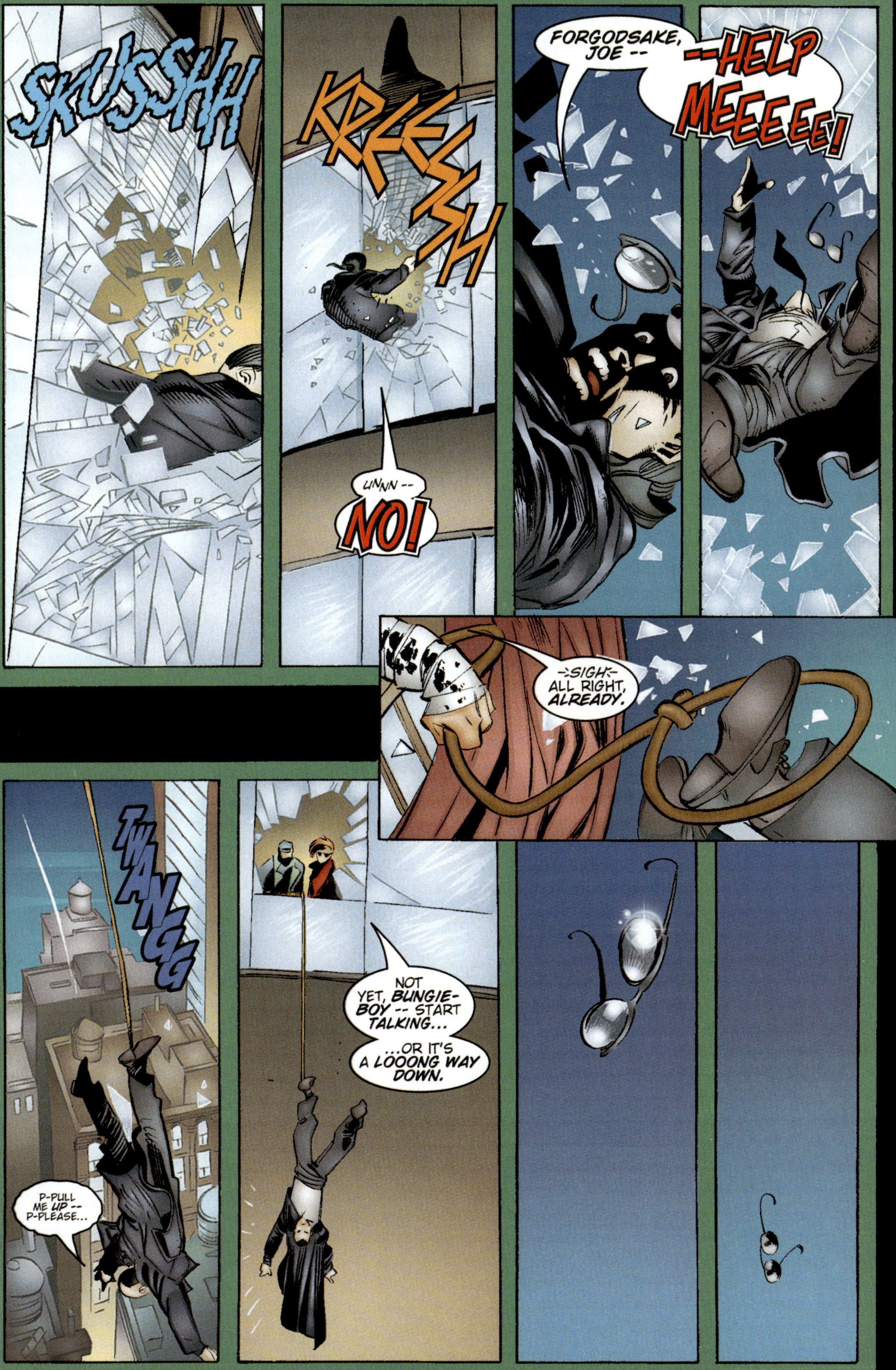

SKUSSHH
KREESSH
UNNN --
NO!
FORGODSAKE, JOE --
--HELP MEEEEEE!
-SIGH- ALL RIGHT, ALREADY.
TWANGG
P-PULL ME UP -- P-PLEASE...
NOT YET, BUNGIE-BOY -- START TALKING...
...OR IT'S A LOOONG WAY DOWN.

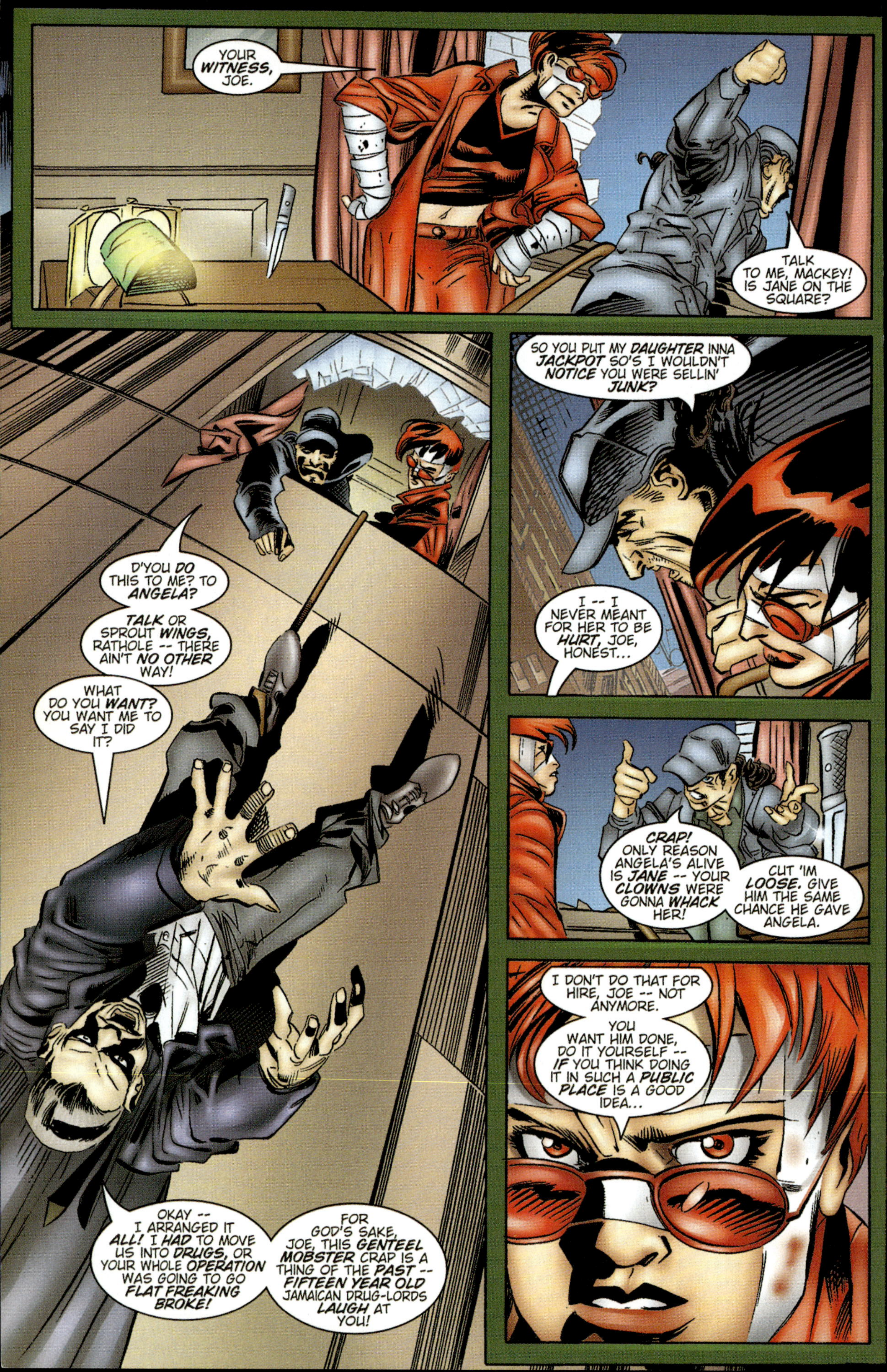
YOUR WITNESS, JOE.
TALK TO ME, MACKEY! IS JANE ON THE SQUARE?
D'YOU DO THIS TO ME? TO ANGELA?
TALK OR SPROUT WINGS, RATHOLE -- THERE AIN'T NO OTHER WAY!
WHAT DO YOU WANT? YOU WANT ME TO SAY I DID IT?
OKAY -- I ARRANGED IT ALL! I HAD TO MOVE US INTO DRUGS, OR YOUR WHOLE OPERATION WAS GOING TO GO FLAT FREAKING BROKE!
FOR GOD'S SAKE, JOE, THIS GENTEEL MOBSTER CRAP IS A THING OF THE PAST -- FIFTEEN YEAR OLD JAMAICAN DRUG-LORDS LAUGH AT YOU!
SO YOU PUT MY DAUGHTER INNA JACKPOT SO'S I WOULDN'T NOTICE YOU WERE SELLIN' JUNK?
I -- I NEVER MEANT FOR HER TO BE HURT, JOE, HONEST...
CRAP! ONLY REASON ANGELA'S ALIVE IS JANE -- YOUR CLOWNS WERE GONNA WHACK HER!
CUT 'IM LOOSE. GIVE HIM THE SAME CHANCE HE GAVE ANGELA.
I DON'T DO THAT FOR HIRE, JOE -- NOT ANYMORE.
YOU WANT HIM DONE, DO IT YOURSELF -- IF YOU THINK DOING IT IN SUCH A PUBLIC PLACE IS A GOOD IDEA...

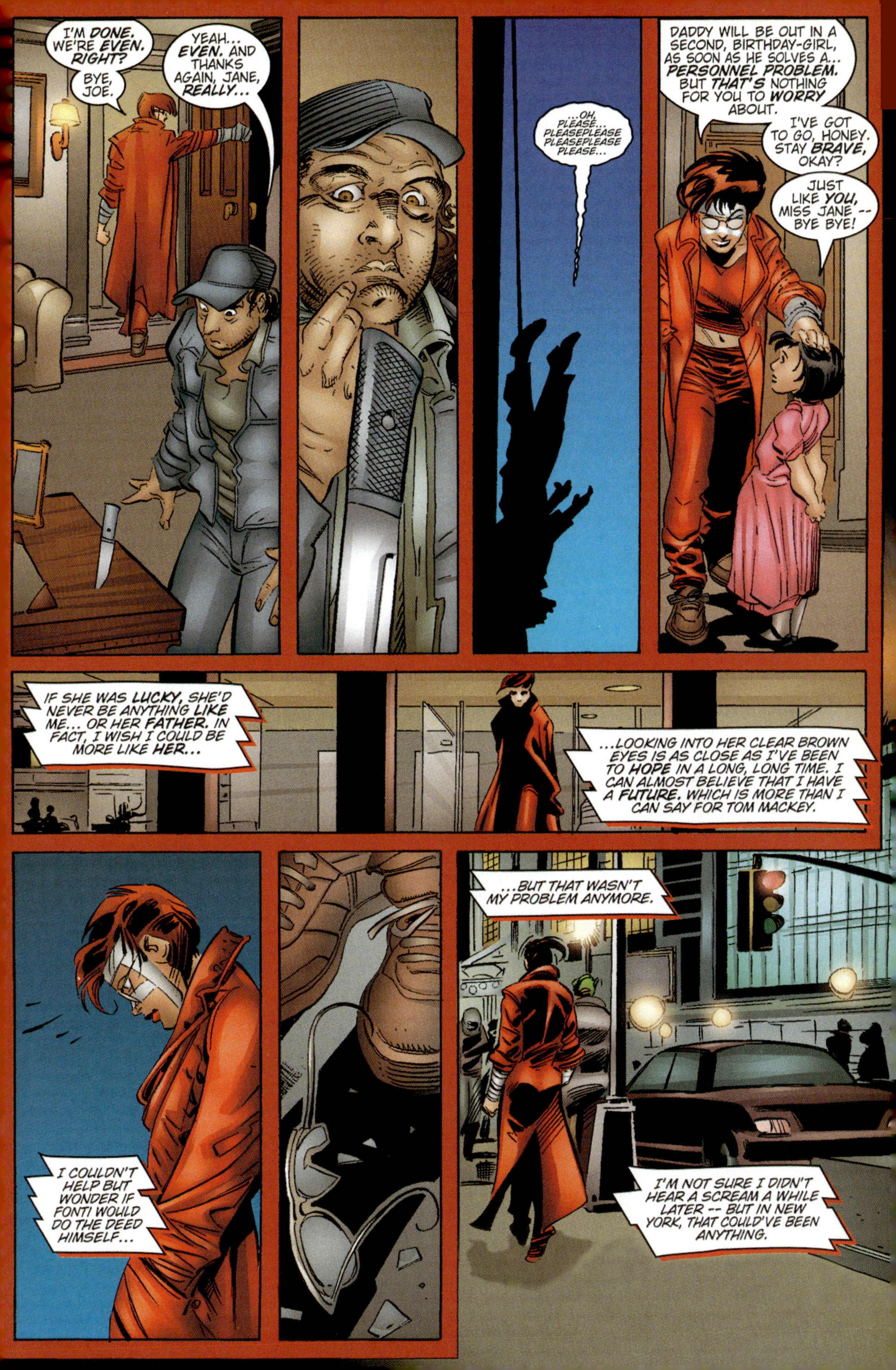

I'M DONE. WE'RE EVEN. RIGHT?
BYE, JOE.
YEAH... EVEN. AND THANKS AGAIN, JANE, REALLY...
...OH, PLEASE... PLEASEPLEASE PLEASEPLEASE PLEASE...
DADDY WILL BE OUT IN A SECOND, BIRTHDAY-GIRL, AS SOON AS HE SOLVES A... PERSONNEL PROBLEM. BUT THAT'S NOTHING FOR YOU TO WORRY ABOUT.
I'VE GOT TO GO, HONEY. STAY BRAVE, OKAY?
JUST LIKE YOU, MISS JANE -- BYE BYE!
IF SHE WAS LUCKY, SHE'D NEVER BE ANYTHING LIKE ME... OR HER FATHER. IN FACT, I WISH I COULD BE MORE LIKE HER...
...LOOKING INTO HER CLEAR BROWN EYES IS AS CLOSE AS I'VE BEEN TO HOPE IN A LONG, LONG TIME. I CAN ALMOST BELIEVE THAT I HAVE A FUTURE. WHICH IS MORE THAN I CAN SAY FOR TOM MACKEY.
I COULDN'T HELP BUT WONDER IF FONTI WOULD DO THE DEED HIMSELF...
...BUT THAT WASN'T MY PROBLEM ANYMORE.
I'M NOT SURE I DIDN'T HEAR A SCREAM A WHILE LATER -- BUT IN NEW YORK, THAT COULD'VE BEEN ANYTHING.

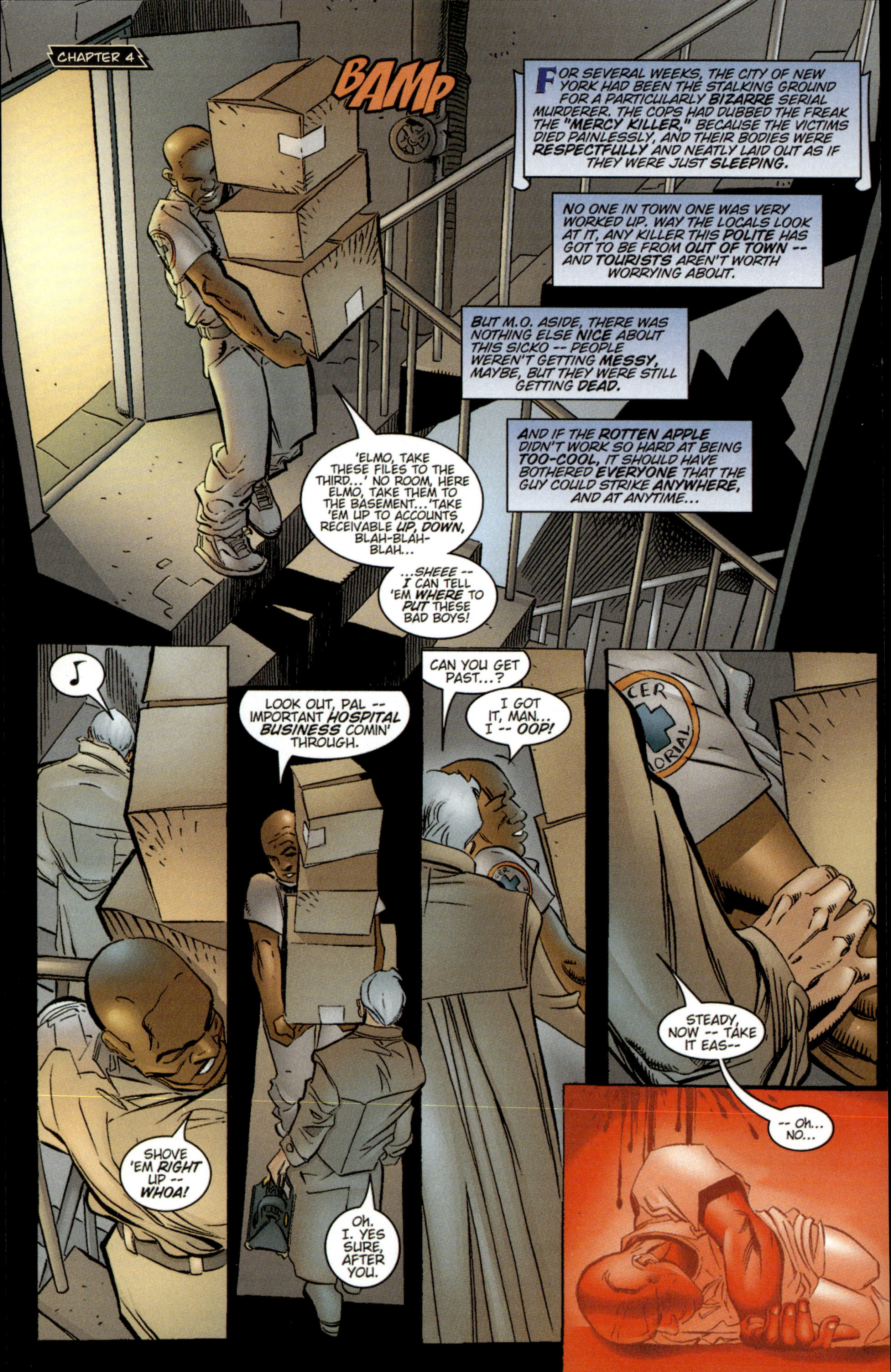
CHAPTER 4
BAMP
FOR SEVERAL WEEKS, THE CITY OF NEW YORK HAD BEEN THE STALKING GROUND FOR A PARTICULARLY BIZARRE SERIAL MURDERER. THE COPS HAD DUBBED THE FREAK THE "MERCY KILLER," BECAUSE THE VICTIMS DIED PAINLESSLY, AND THEIR BODIES WERE RESPECTFULLY AND NEATLY LAID OUT AS IF THEY WERE JUST SLEEPING.
NO ONE IN TOWN ONE WAS VERY WORKED UP. WAY THE LOCALS LOOK AT IT, ANY KILLER THIS POLITE HAS GOT TO BE FROM OUT OF TOWN -- AND TOURISTS AREN'T WORTH WORRYING ABOUT.
BUT M.O. ASIDE, THERE WAS NOTHING ELSE NICE ABOUT THIS SICKO -- PEOPLE WEREN'T GETTING MESSY, MAYBE, BUT THEY WERE STILL GETTING DEAD.
AND IF THE ROTTEN APPLE DIDN'T WORK SO HARD AT BEING TOO-COOL, IT SHOULD HAVE BOTHERED EVERYONE THAT THE GUY COULD STRIKE ANYWHERE, AND AT ANYTIME...
'ELMO, TAKE THESE FILES TO THE THIRD...' NO ROOM, HERE ELMO, TAKE THEM TO THE BASEMENT...'TAKE 'EM UP TO ACCOUNTS RECEIVABLE UP, DOWN, BLAH-BLAH-BLAH...
...SHEEE -- I CAN TELL 'EM WHERE TO PUT THESE BAD BOYS!
♪
SHOVE 'EM RIGHT UP -- WHOA!
LOOK OUT, PAL -- IMPORTANT HOSPITAL BUSINESS COMIN' THROUGH.
Oh. I. YES SURE, AFTER YOU.
CAN YOU GET PAST...?
I GOT IT, MAN... I -- OOP!
STEADY, NOW -- TAKE IT EAS--
-- Oh... NO...

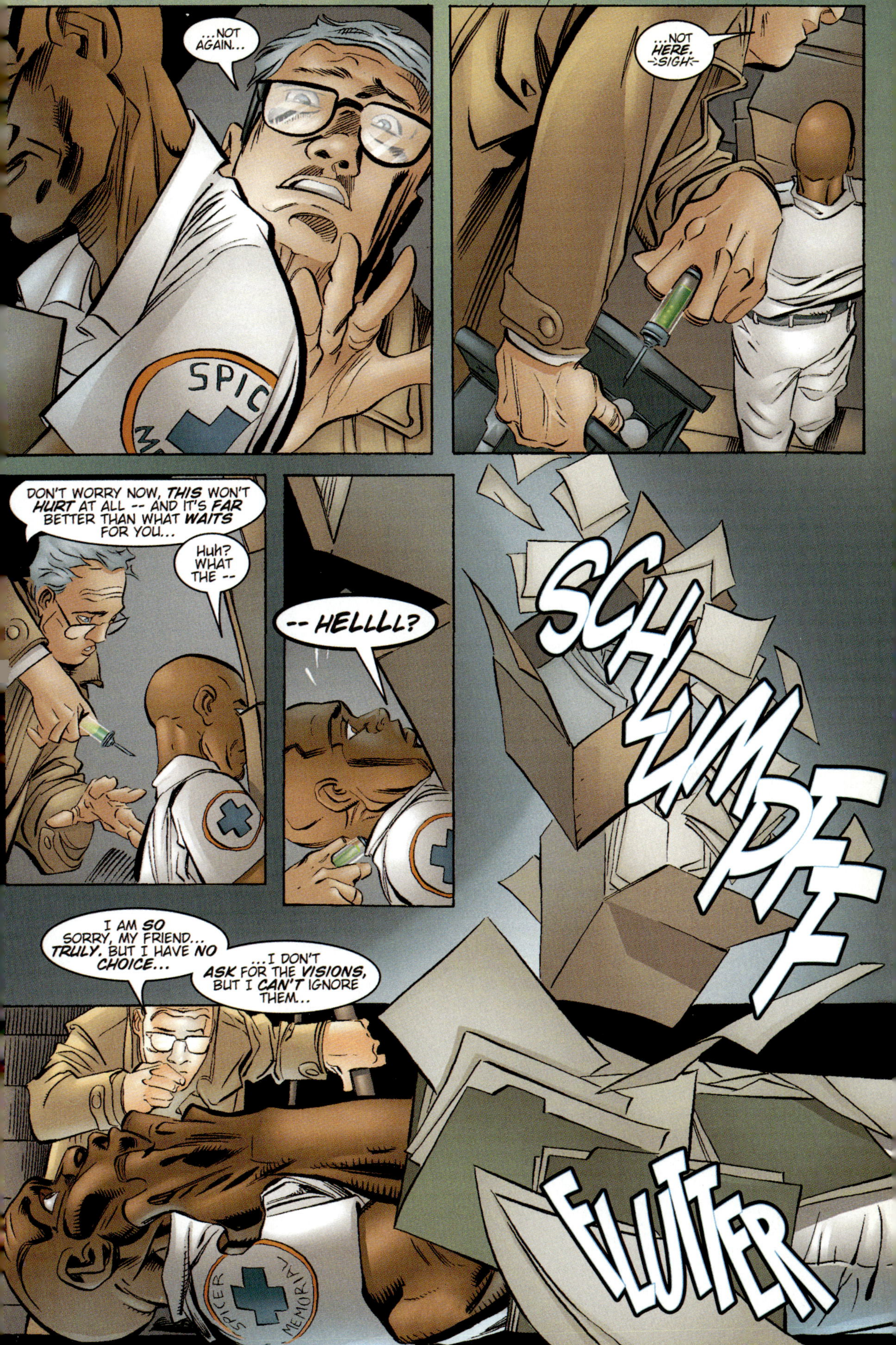
...NOT AGAIN...
SPIC
...NOT HERE. -SIGH-
DON'T WORRY NOW, THIS WON'T HURT AT ALL -- AND IT'S FAR BETTER THAN WHAT WAITS FOR YOU...
Huh? WHAT THE --
-- HELLLL?
SCHLUMPFF
I AM SO SORRY, MY FRIEND... TRULY. BUT I HAVE NO CHOICE...
...I DON'T ASK FOR THE VISIONS, BUT I CAN'T IGNORE THEM...
SPICER MEMORIAL
FLUTTER

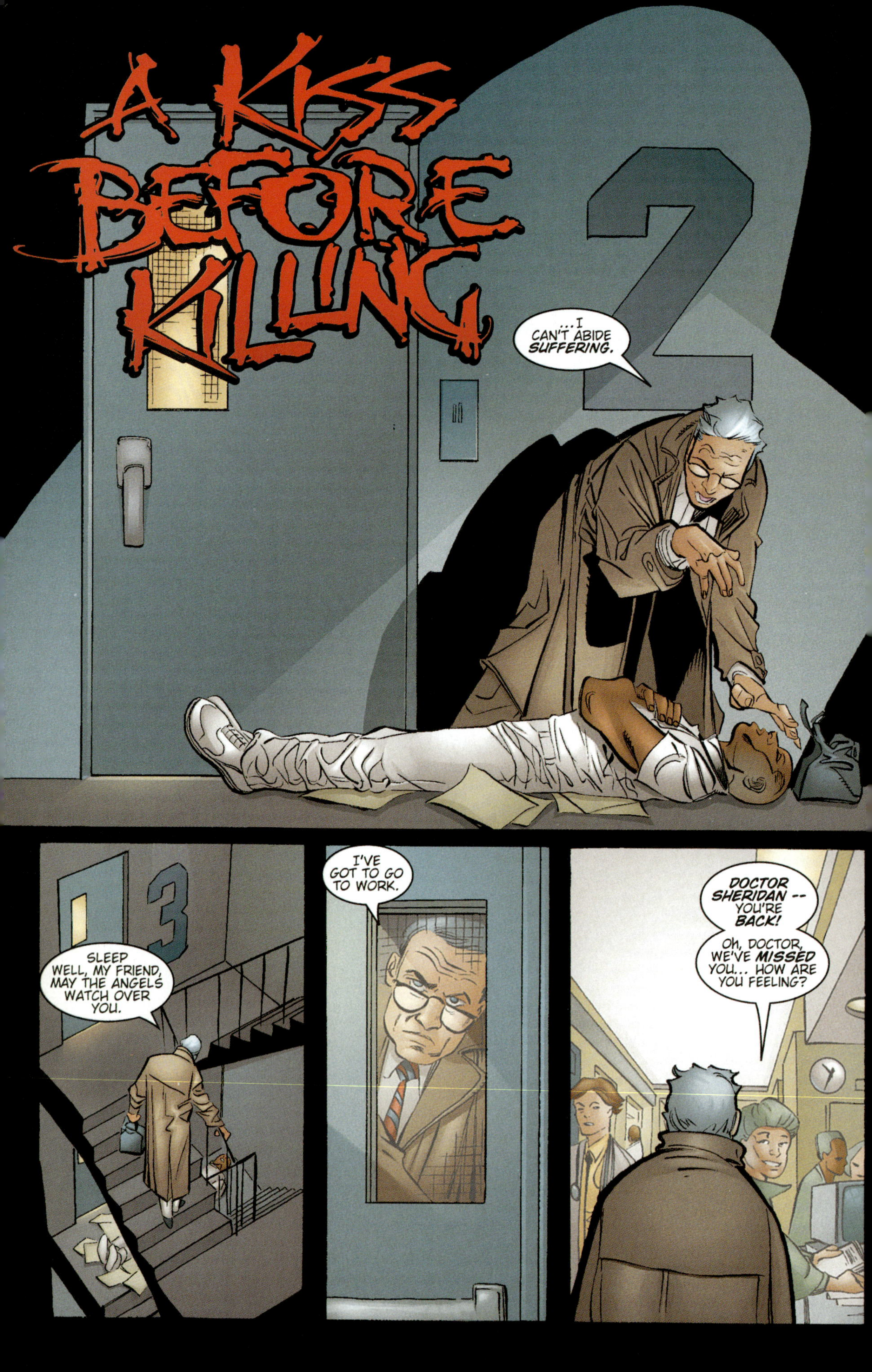
A KISS BEFORE KILLING
2
...I CAN'T ABIDE SUFFERING.
SLEEP WELL, MY FRIEND, MAY THE ANGELS WATCH OVER YOU.
3
I'VE GOT TO GO TO WORK.
DOCTOR SHERIDAN -- YOU'RE BACK!
Oh, DOCTOR, WE'VE MISSED YOU... HOW ARE YOU FEELING?

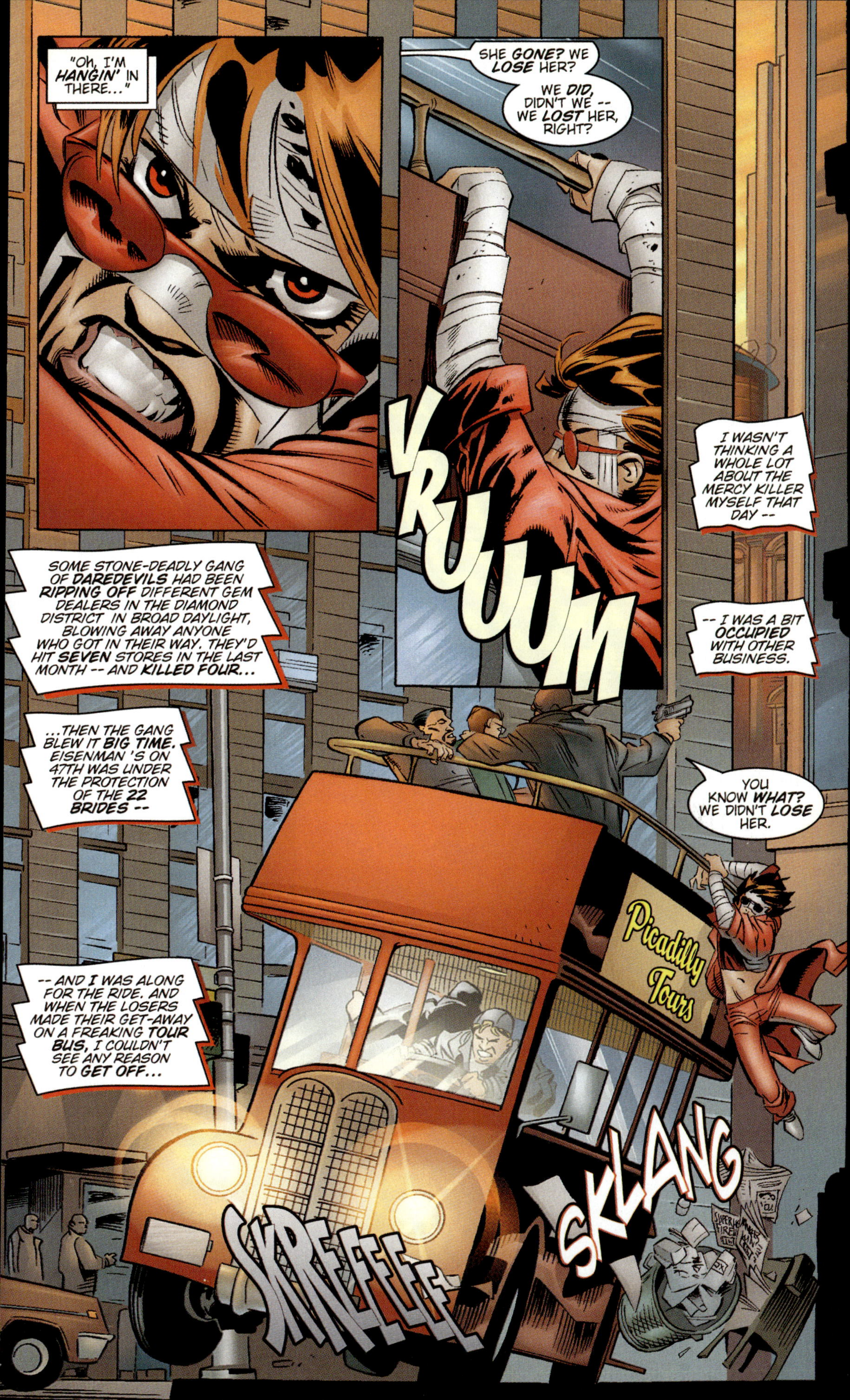

"Oh, I'M HANGIN' IN THERE..."
SHE GONE? WE LOSE HER?
WE DID, DIDN'T WE -- WE LOST HER, RIGHT?
VRUUUUM
I WASN'T THINKING A WHOLE LOT ABOUT THE MERCY KILLER MYSELF THAT DAY --
-- I WAS A BIT OCCUPIED WITH OTHER BUSINESS.
SOME STONE-DEADLY GANG OF DAREDEVILS HAD BEEN RIPPING OFF DIFFERENT GEM DEALERS IN THE DIAMOND DISTRICT IN BROAD DAYLIGHT, BLOWING AWAY ANYONE WHO GOT IN THEIR WAY. THEY'D HIT SEVEN STORES IN THE LAST MONTH -- AND KILLED FOUR...
...THEN THE GANG BLEW IT BIG TIME. EISENMAN'S ON 47TH WAS UNDER THE PROTECTION OF THE 22 BRIDES --
YOU KNOW WHAT? WE DIDN'T LOSE HER.
Picadilly Tours
-- AND I WAS ALONG FOR THE RIDE. AND WHEN THE LOSERS MADE THEIR GET-AWAY ON A FREAKING TOUR BUS, I COULDN'T SEE ANY REASON TO GET OFF...
SKREEEEEE
SKLANG

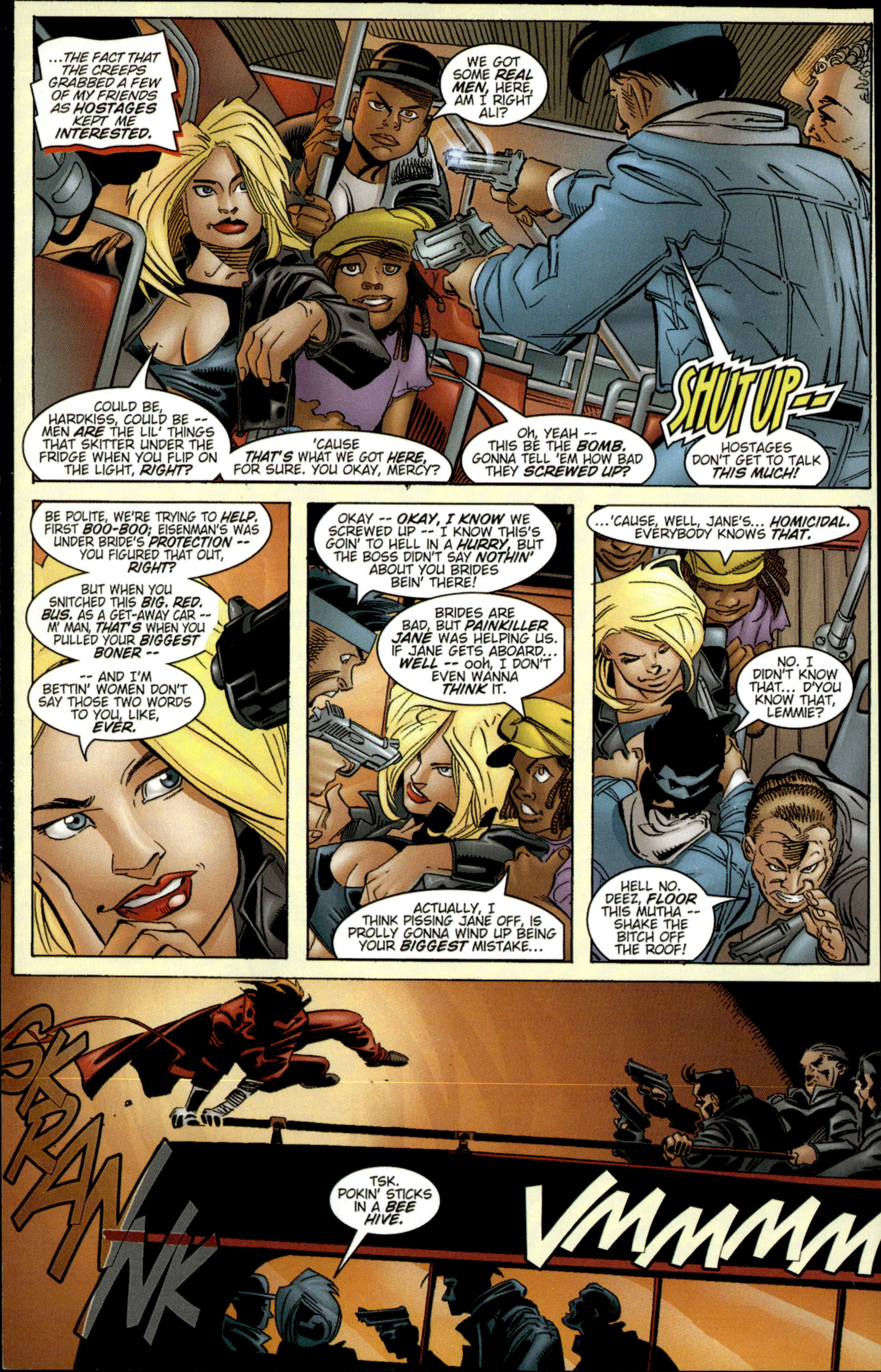

...THE FACT THAT THE CREEPS GRABBED A FEW OF MY FRIENDS AS HOSTAGES KEPT ME INTERESTED.
WE GOT SOME REAL MEN, HERE, AM I RIGHT ALI?
COULD BE, HARDKISS, COULD BE -- MEN ARE THE LIL' THINGS THAT SKITTER UNDER THE FRIDGE WHEN YOU FLIP ON THE LIGHT, RIGHT?
'CAUSE THAT'S WHAT WE GOT HERE, FOR SURE. YOU OKAY, MERCY?
Oh, YEAH -- THIS BE THE BOMB. GONNA TELL 'EM HOW BAD THEY SCREWED UP?
SHUT UP --
HOSTAGES DON'T GET TO TALK THIS MUCH!
BE POLITE, WE'RE TRYING TO HELP. FIRST BOO-BOO; EISENMAN'S WAS UNDER BRIDE'S PROTECTION -- YOU FIGURED THAT OUT, RIGHT?
BUT WHEN YOU SNITCHED THIS BIG. RED. BUS. AS A GET-AWAY CAR -- M' MAN, THAT'S WHEN YOU PULLED YOUR BIGGEST BONER --
-- AND I'M BETTIN' WOMEN DON'T SAY THOSE TWO WORDS TO YOU, LIKE, EVER.
OKAY -- OKAY, I KNOW WE SCREWED UP -- I KNOW THIS'S GOIN' TO HELL IN A HURRY, BUT THE BOSS DIDN'T SAY NOTHIN' ABOUT YOU BRIDES BEIN' THERE!
BRIDES ARE BAD, BUT PAINKILLER JANE WAS HELPING US. IF JANE GETS ABOARD... WELL -- ooh, I DON'T EVEN WANNA THINK IT.
ACTUALLY, I THINK PISSING JANE OFF, IS PROLLY GONNA WIND UP BEING YOUR BIGGEST MISTAKE...
...'CAUSE, WELL, JANE'S... HOMICIDAL. EVERYBODY KNOWS THAT.
NO. I DIDN'T KNOW THAT... D'YOU KNOW THAT, LEMMIE?
HELL NO. DEEZ, FLOOR THIS MUTHA -- SHAKE THE BITCH OFF THE ROOF!
SKRANNK
TSK. POKIN' STICKS IN A BEE HIVE.
VMMMM

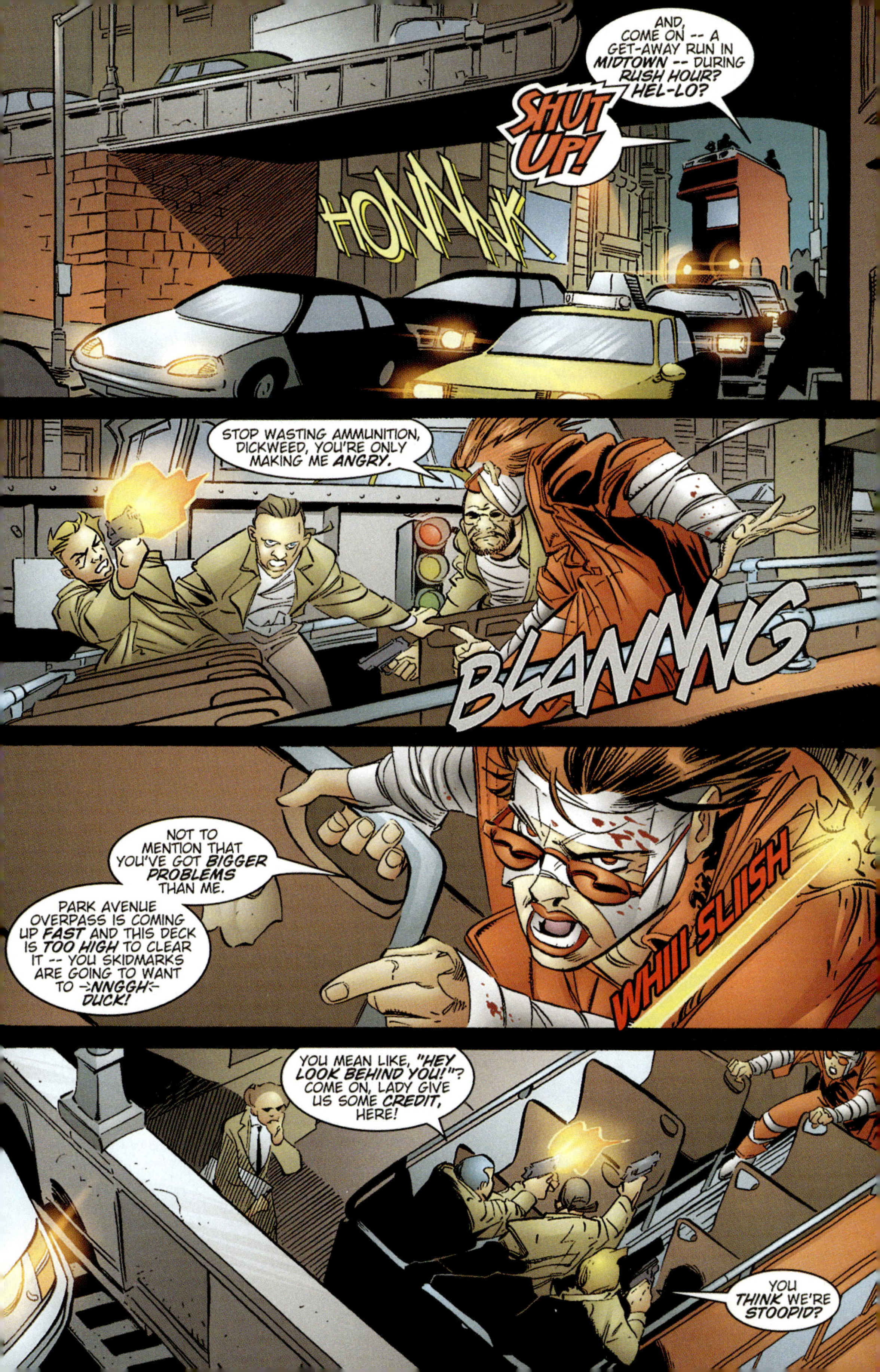
AND, COME ON -- A GET-AWAY RUN IN MIDTOWN -- DURING RUSH HOUR? HEL-LO?
SHUT UP!
HONNNK
STOP WASTING AMMUNITION, DICKWEED, YOU'RE ONLY MAKING ME ANGRY.
BLANNNG
NOT TO MENTION THAT YOU'VE GOT BIGGER PROBLEMS THAN ME.
PARK AVENUE OVERPASS IS COMING UP FAST AND THIS DECK IS TOO HIGH TO CLEAR IT -- YOU SKIDMARKS ARE GOING TO WANT TO -NNGGH- DUCK!
WHIII SLIISH
YOU MEAN LIKE, "HEY LOOK BEHIND YOU!"? COME ON, LADY GIVE US SOME CREDIT, HERE!
YOU THINK WE'RE STOOPID?

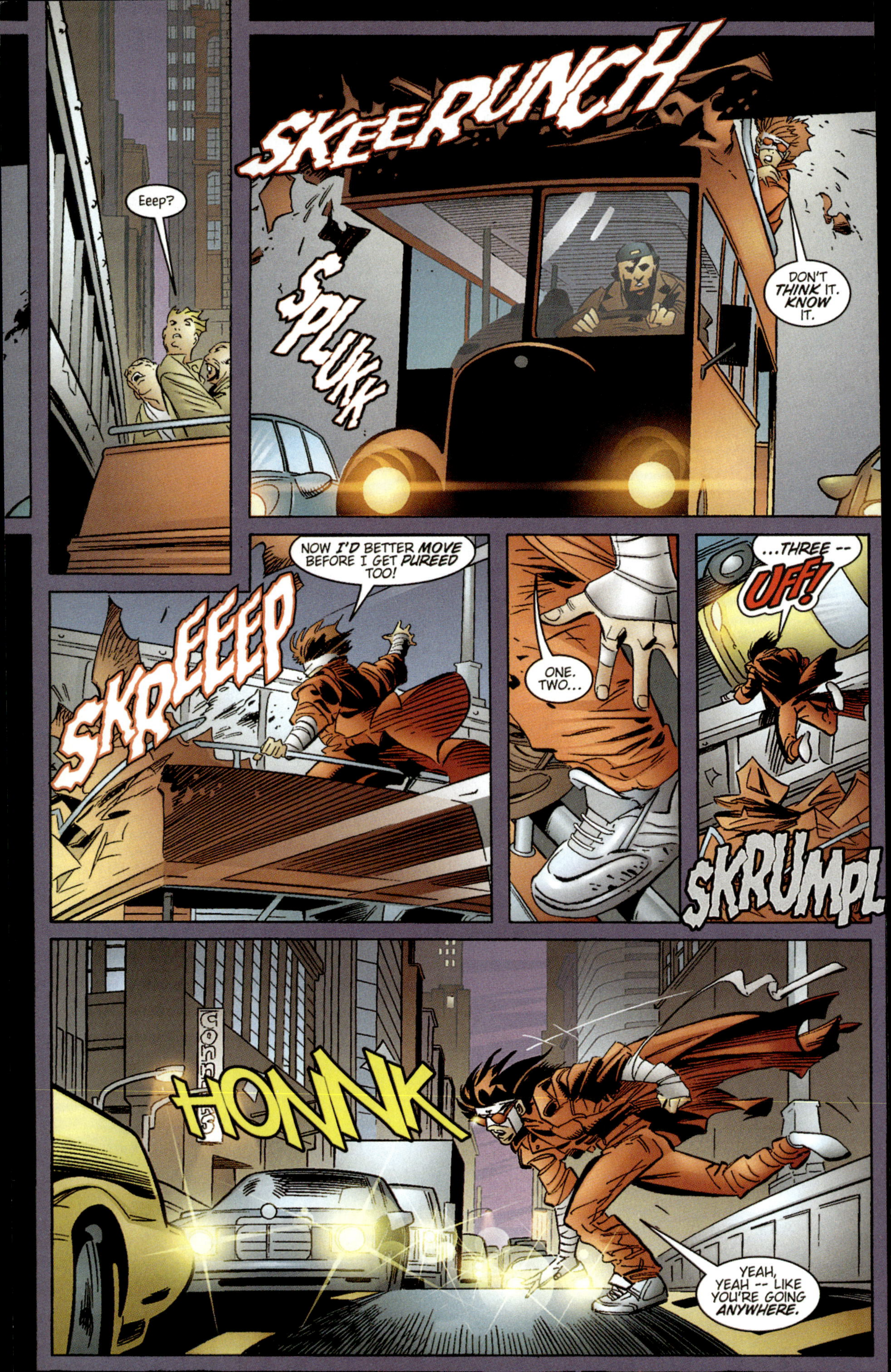
Eeep?
SKEERUNCH
SPLUKK
DON'T THINK IT. KNOW IT.
NOW I'D BETTER MOVE BEFORE I GET PUREED TOO!
SKREEEP
ONE. TWO...
...THREE --
UFF!
SKRUMPL
HONNK
YEAH, YEAH -- LIKE YOU'RE GOING ANYWHERE.

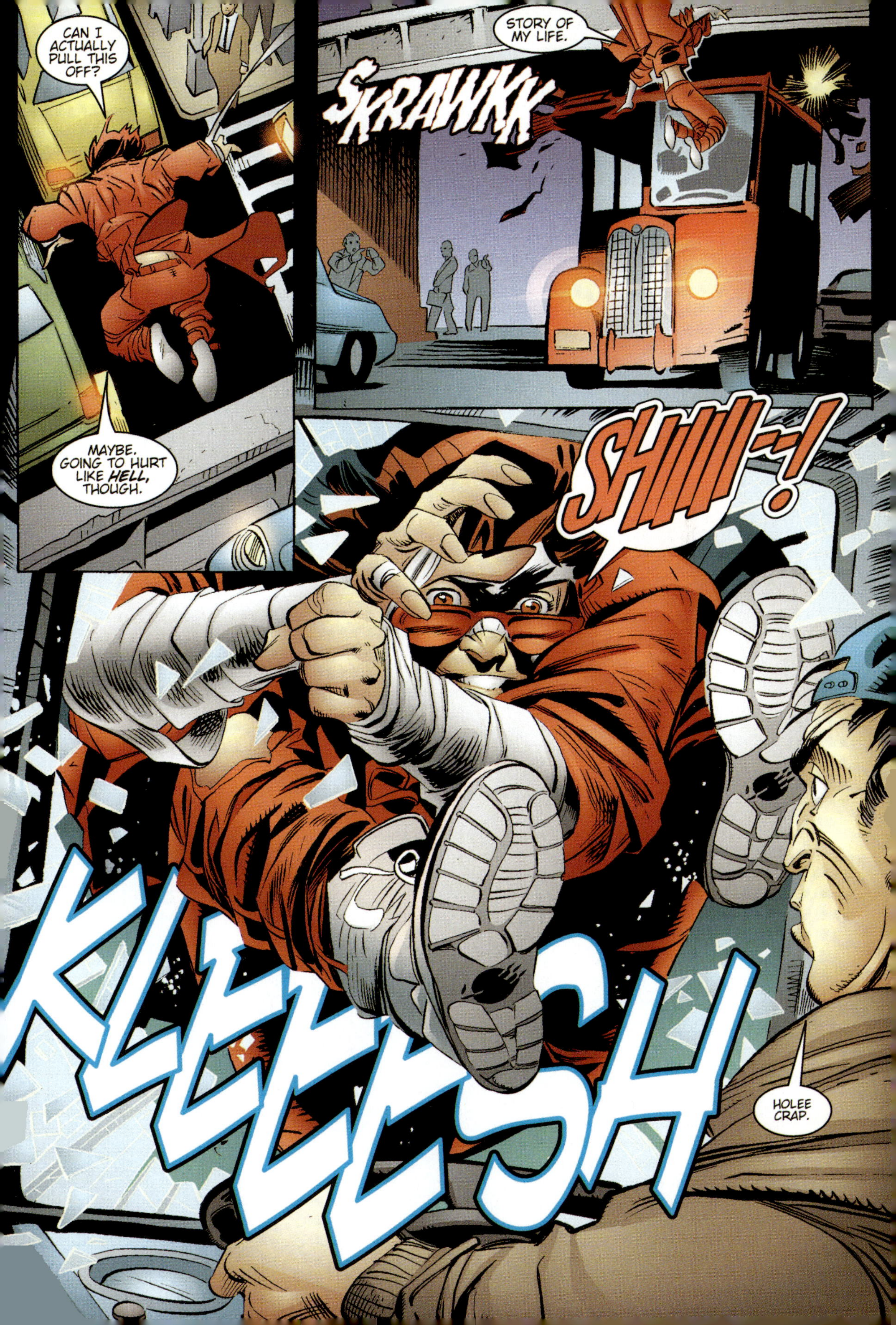
CAN I ACTUALLY PULL THIS OFF?
MAYBE. GOING TO HURT LIKE *HELL,* THOUGH.
STORY OF MY LIFE.
SKRAWKK
SHIIII--!
KLEEEESH
HOLEE CRAP.

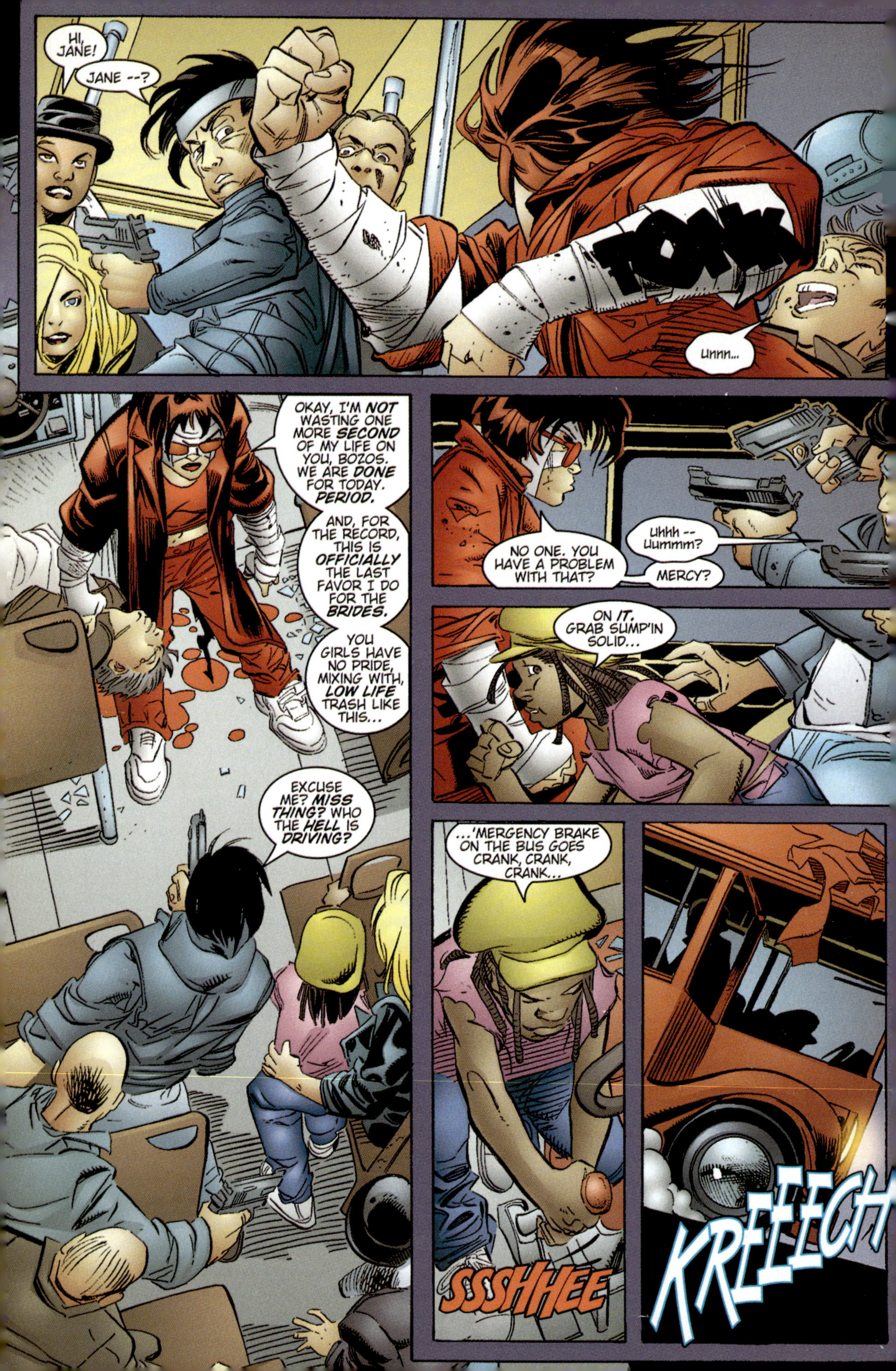
HI, JANE!
JANE --?
TONK
Unnn...
OKAY, I'M NOT WASTING ONE MORE SECOND OF MY LIFE ON YOU, BOZOS. WE ARE DONE FOR TODAY. PERIOD.
AND, FOR THE RECORD, THIS IS OFFICIALLY THE LAST FAVOR I DO FOR THE BRIDES.
YOU GIRLS HAVE NO PRIDE, MIXING WITH, LOW LIFE TRASH LIKE THIS...
EXCUSE ME? MISS THING? WHO THE HELL IS DRIVING?
NO ONE. YOU HAVE A PROBLEM WITH THAT?
Uhhh -- Uummm?
MERCY?
ON IT. GRAB SUMP'IN SOLID...
...'MERGENCY BRAKE ON THE BUS GOES CRANK, CRANK, CRANK...
SSSHHEE
KREEECH

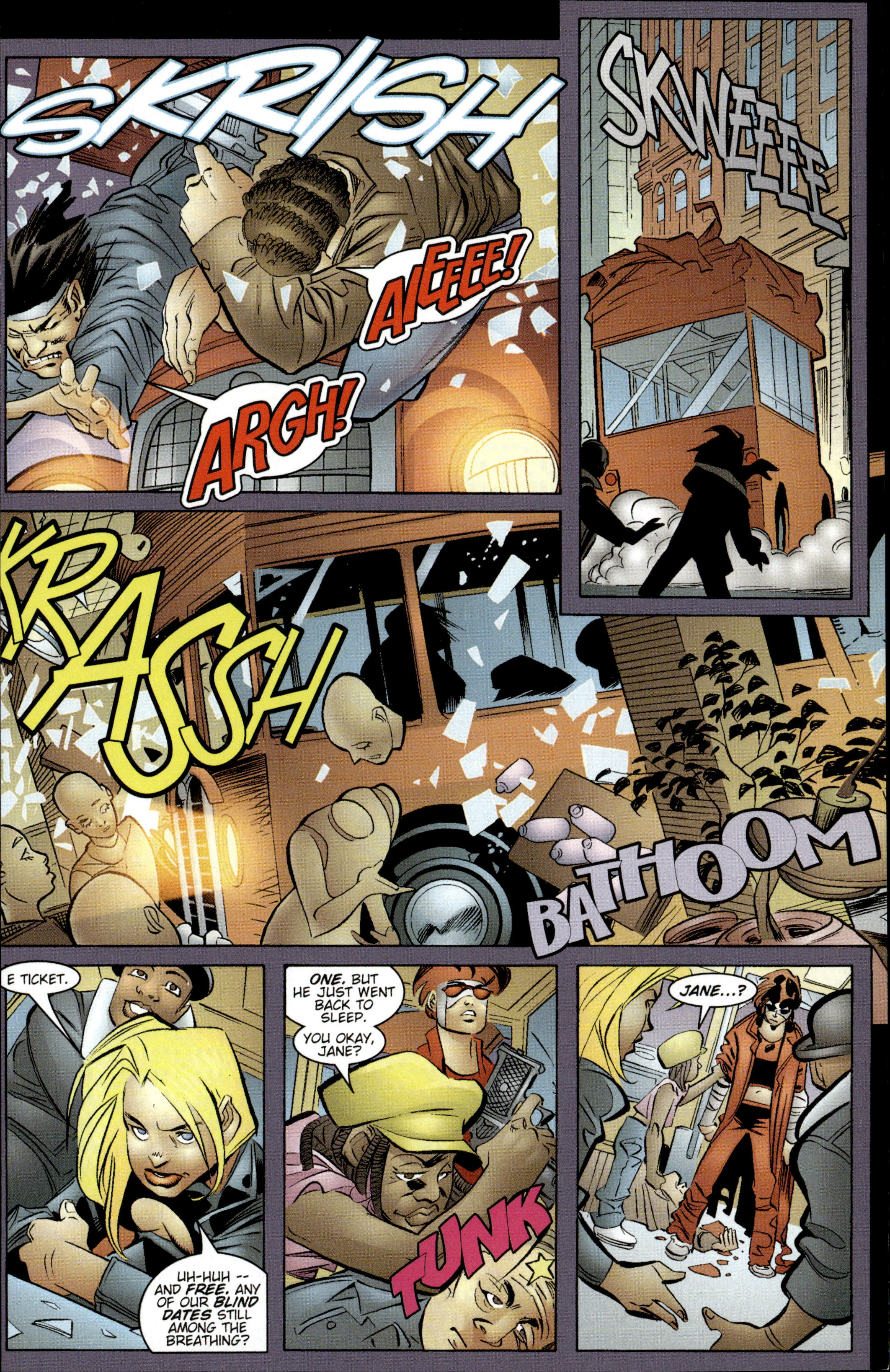
SKRIISH
AIEEEE!
ARGH!
SKWEEEE
KRASSH
BATHOOM
E TICKET.
UH-HUH -- AND FREE. ANY OF OUR BLIND DATES STILL AMONG THE BREATHING?
ONE. BUT HE JUST WENT BACK TO SLEEP.
YOU OKAY, JANE?
TUNK
JANE...?

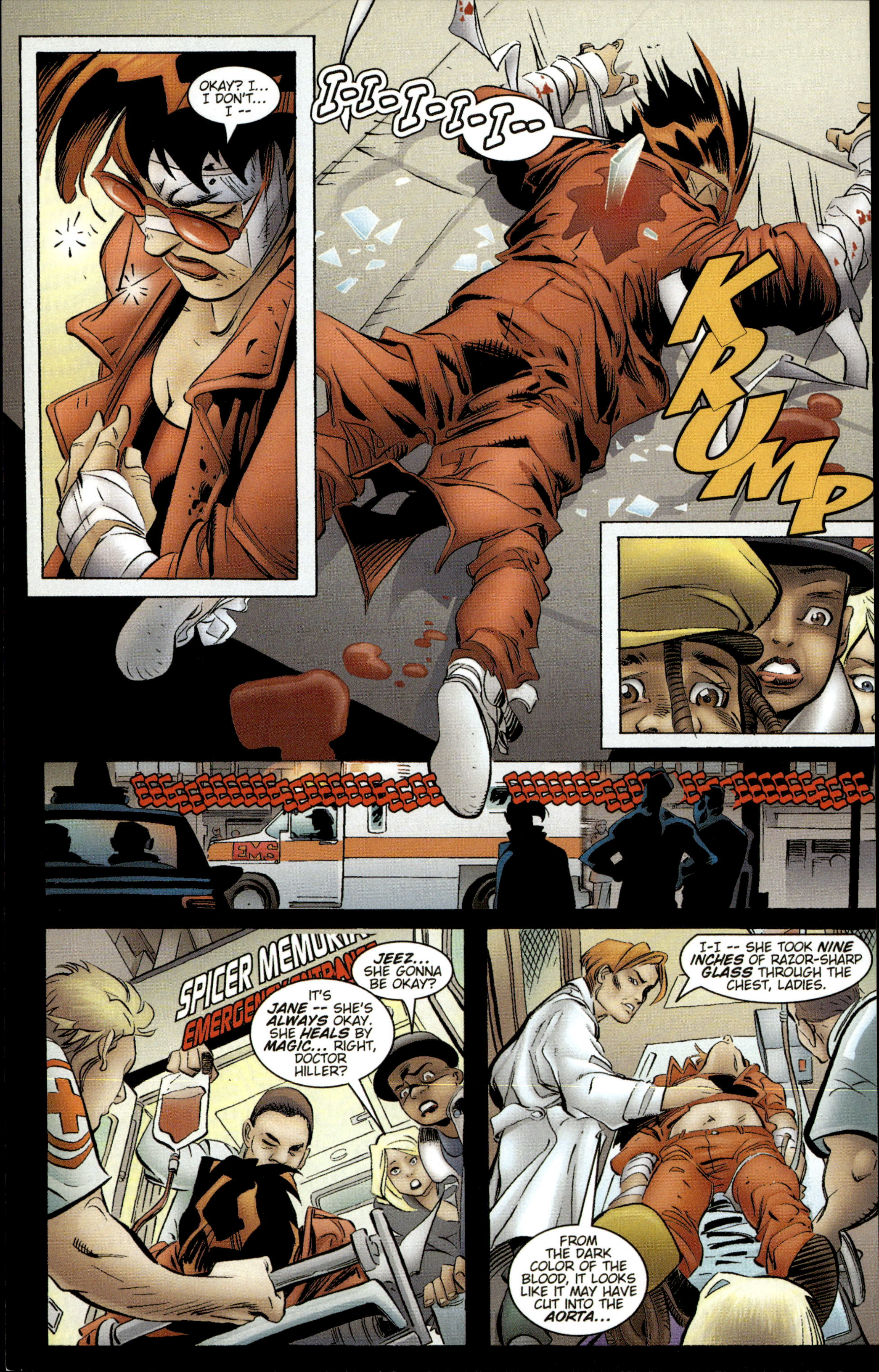
OKAY? I... I DON'T... I --
I-I-I-I-I..
KRUMP
EEEEEEEEEEEEEEEEEEEEEEEEEEEEE
EEEEEEEEEEEE
EEEEEEEEEEEEE
SPICER MEMORIAL
JEEZ... SHE GONNA BE OKAY?
IT'S JANE -- SHE'S ALWAYS OKAY. SHE HEALS BY MAGIC... RIGHT, DOCTOR HILLER?
I-I -- SHE TOOK NINE INCHES OF RAZOR-SHARP GLASS THROUGH THE CHEST, LADIES.
FROM THE DARK COLOR OF THE BLOOD, IT LOOKS LIKE IT MAY HAVE CUT INTO THE AORTA...

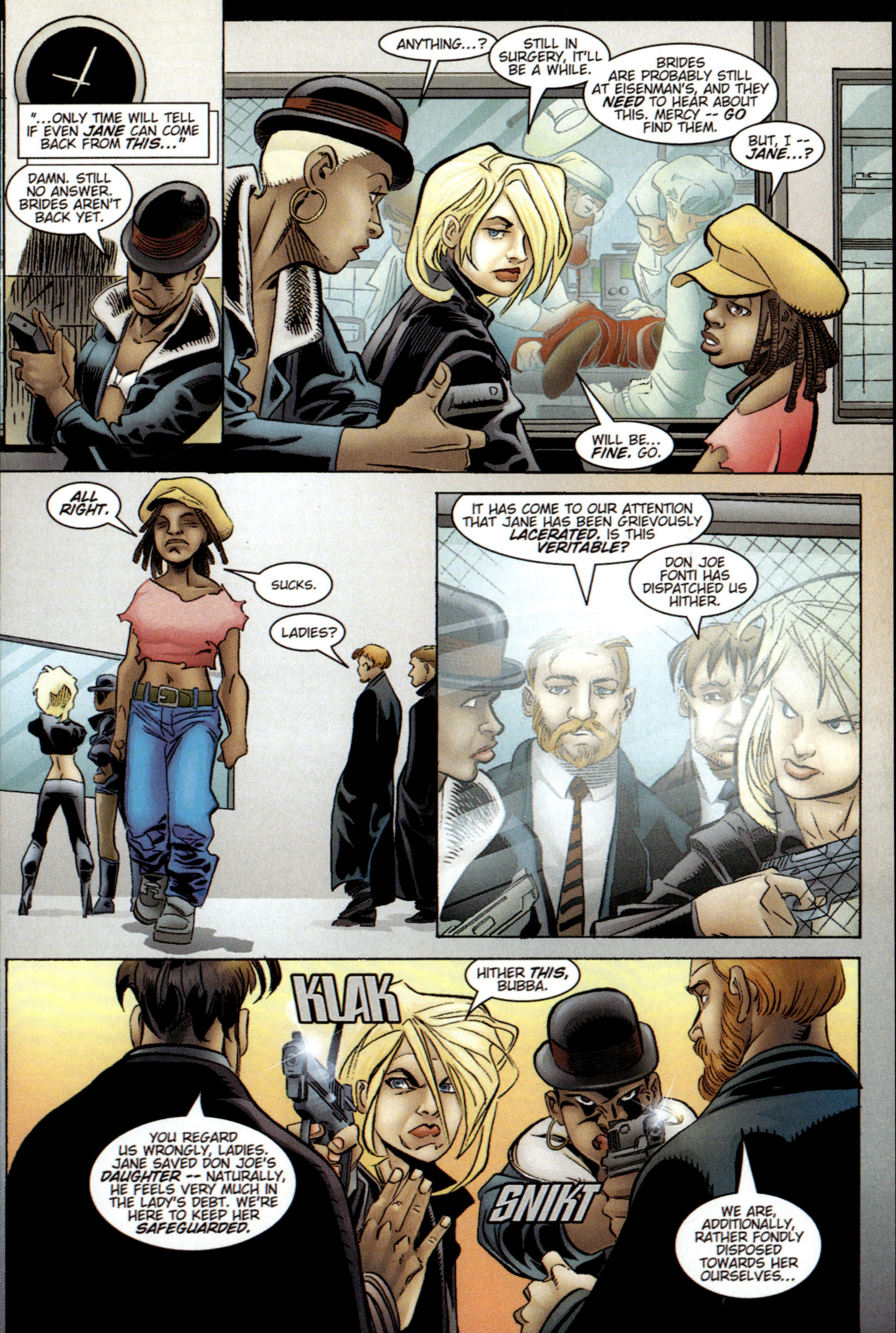
"...ONLY TIME WILL TELL IF EVEN JANE CAN COME BACK FROM THIS..."
DAMN. STILL NO ANSWER. BRIDES AREN'T BACK YET.
ANYTHING...?
STILL IN SURGERY, IT'LL BE A WHILE.
BRIDES ARE PROBABLY STILL AT EISENMAN'S, AND THEY NEED TO HEAR ABOUT THIS. MERCY -- GO FIND THEM.
BUT, I -- JANE...?
WILL BE... FINE. GO.
ALL RIGHT.
SUCKS.
LADIES?
IT HAS COME TO OUR ATTENTION THAT JANE HAS BEEN GRIEVOUSLY LACERATED. IS THIS VERITABLE?
DON JOE FONTI HAS DISPATCHED US HITHER.
KLAK
HITHER THIS, BUBBA.
YOU REGARD US WRONGLY, LADIES. JANE SAVED DON JOE'S DAUGHTER -- NATURALLY, HE FEELS VERY MUCH IN THE LADY'S DEBT. WE'RE HERE TO KEEP HER SAFEGUARDED.
SNIKT
WE ARE, ADDITIONALLY, RATHER FONDLY DISPOSED TOWARDS HER OURSELVES...

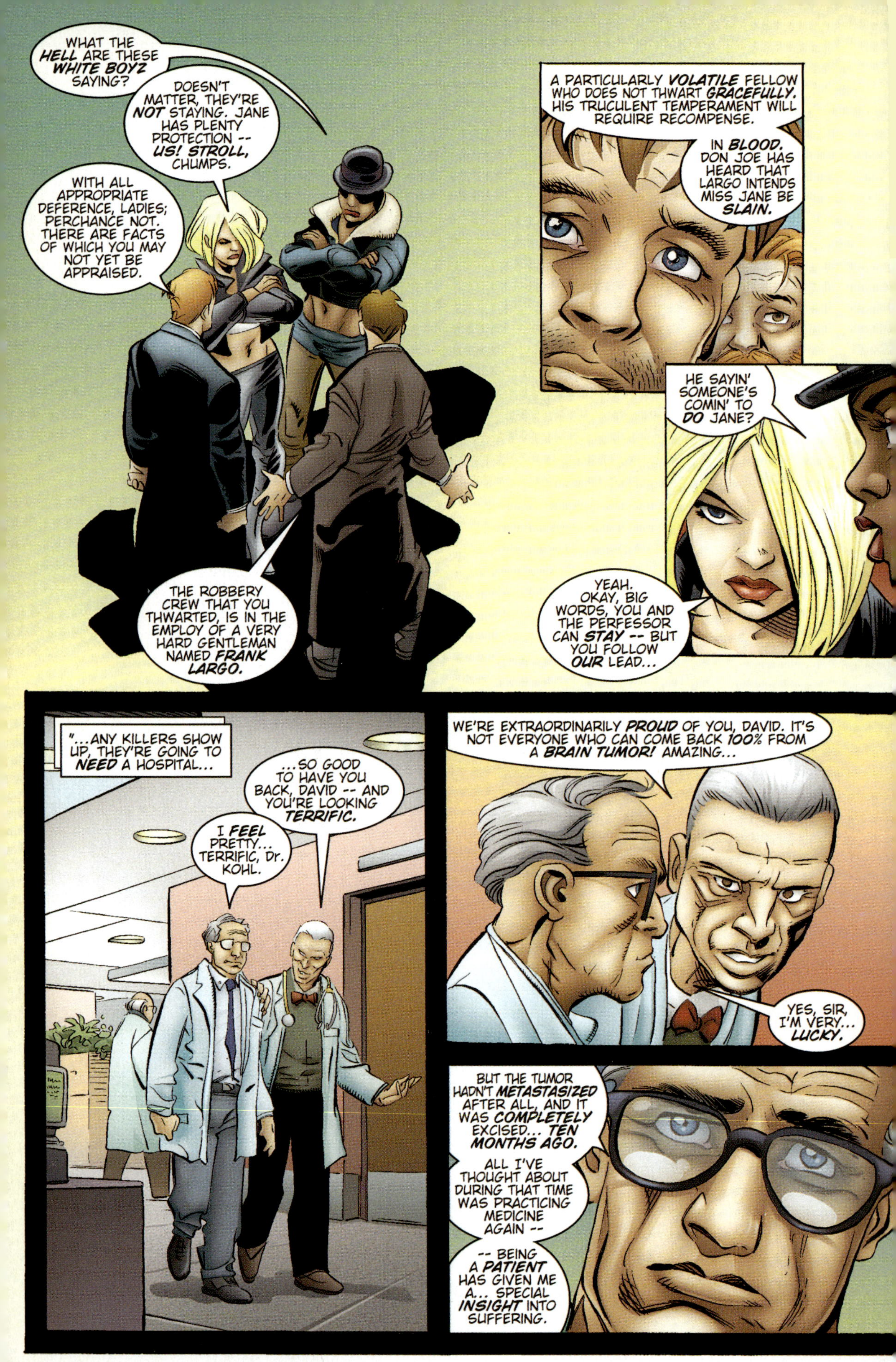

WHAT THE HELL ARE THESE WHITE BOYZ SAYING?
DOESN'T MATTER, THEY'RE NOT STAYING. JANE HAS PLENTY PROTECTION -- US! STROLL, CHUMPS.
WITH ALL APPROPRIATE DEFERENCE, LADIES; PERCHANCE NOT. THERE ARE FACTS OF WHICH YOU MAY NOT YET BE APPRAISED.
THE ROBBERY CREW THAT YOU THWARTED, IS IN THE EMPLOY OF A VERY HARD GENTLEMAN NAMED FRANK LARGO.
A PARTICULARLY VOLATILE FELLOW WHO DOES NOT THWART GRACEFULLY. HIS TRUCULENT TEMPERAMENT WILL REQUIRE RECOMPENSE.
IN BLOOD. DON JOE HAS HEARD THAT LARGO INTENDS MISS JANE BE SLAIN.
HE SAYIN' SOMEONE'S COMIN' TO DO JANE?
YEAH. OKAY, BIG WORDS, YOU AND THE PERFESSOR CAN STAY -- BUT YOU FOLLOW OUR LEAD...
"...ANY KILLERS SHOW UP, THEY'RE GOING TO NEED A HOSPITAL...
...SO GOOD TO HAVE YOU BACK, DAVID -- AND YOU'RE LOOKING TERRIFIC.
I FEEL PRETTY... TERRIFIC, Dr. KOHL.
WE'RE EXTRAORDINARILY PROUD OF YOU, DAVID. IT'S NOT EVERYONE WHO CAN COME BACK 100% FROM A BRAIN TUMOR! AMAZING...
YES, SIR, I'M VERY... LUCKY.
BUT THE TUMOR HADN'T METASTASIZED AFTER ALL, AND IT WAS COMPLETELY EXCISED... TEN MONTHS AGO.
ALL I'VE THOUGHT ABOUT DURING THAT TIME WAS PRACTICING MEDICINE AGAIN --
-- BEING A PATIENT HAS GIVEN ME A... SPECIAL INSIGHT INTO SUFFERING.

Panel 1:
"WONDERFUL, WONDERFUL -- HAVING BEATEN *CANCER* ALSO GIVES YOU THE RIGHT *TOUCH* AROUND HERE...

...JUST TELLING YOUR STORY WILL BOLSTER SPIRITS TREMENDOUSLY."

ONCOLOGY

Panel 2:
"YOU CAN START *HERE*. PERHAPS YOU REMEMBER MR. GANNON?"

"YES...?"

"HE'S... MUCH WORSE."

Panel 3:
"...

...AH, MR. GANNON.

WELL THEN, DAVID, I'LL... LEAVE YOU TO IT, THEN..."

Panel 4:
"YES, I-I... OH..."

Panel 5:
"...MY. GOD.

WHAT WAS I *THINKING* COMING BACK? HOW CAN I EVEN *BE* HERE?

SO. MUCH. DEATH."

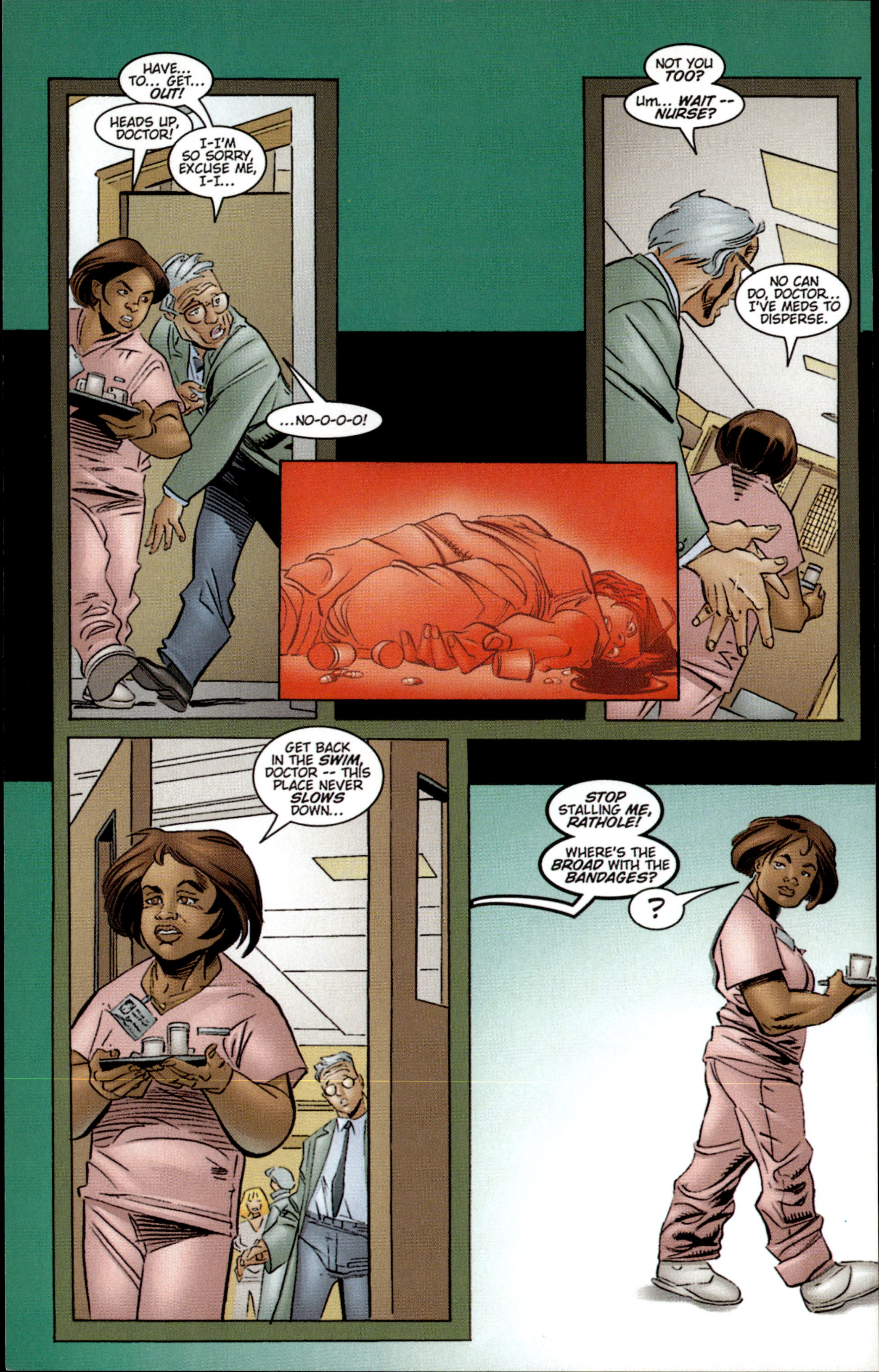
HAVE... TO... GET... OUT!
HEADS UP, DOCTOR!
I-I'M SO SORRY, EXCUSE ME, I-I...
...NO-O-O-O!
NOT YOU TOO?
Um... WAIT -- NURSE?
NO CAN DO, DOCTOR... I'VE MEDS TO DISPERSE.
GET BACK IN THE SWIM, DOCTOR -- THIS PLACE NEVER SLOWS DOWN...
STOP STALLING ME, RATHOLE!
WHERE'S THE BROAD WITH THE BANDAGES?
?

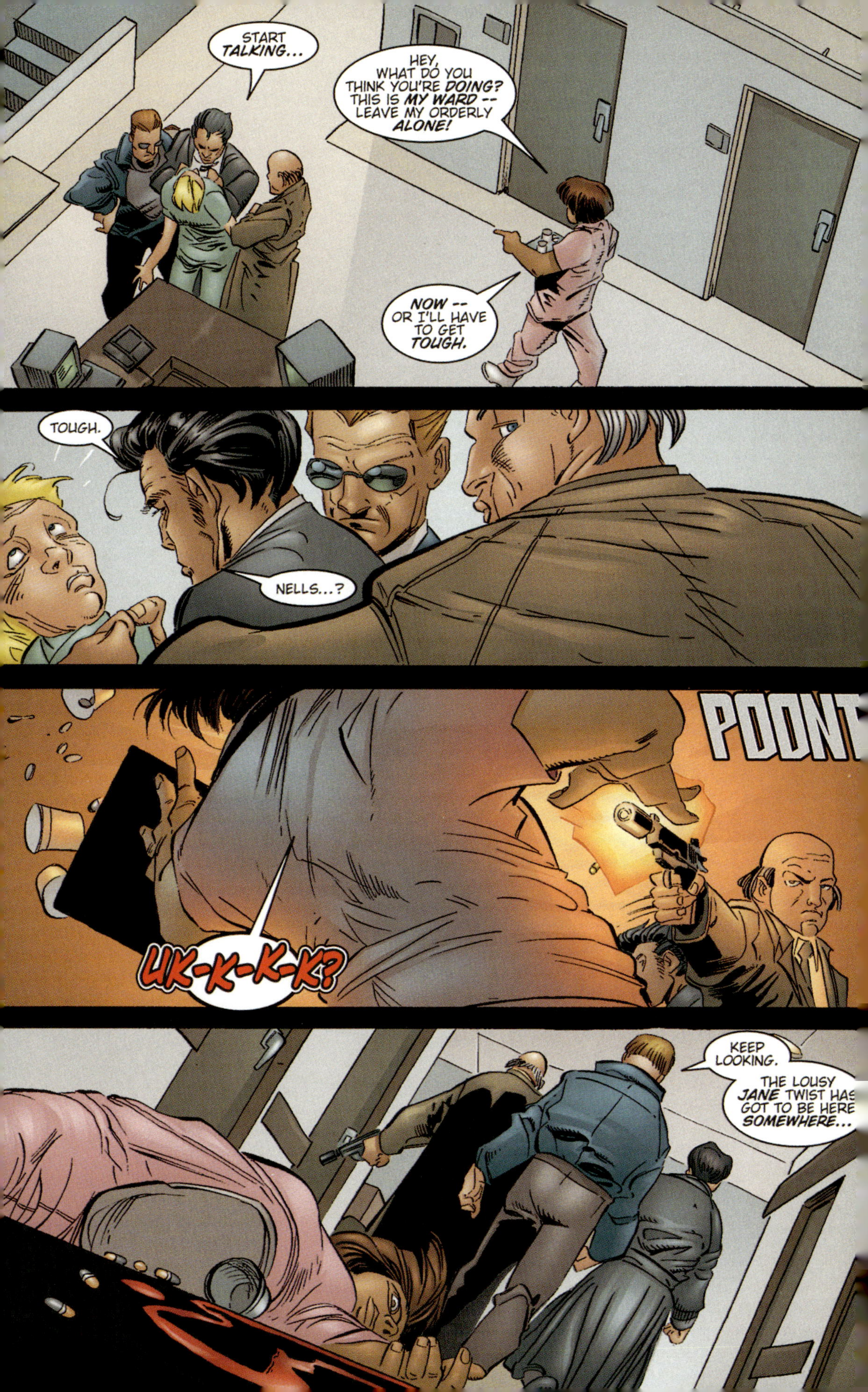
START TALKING...
HEY, WHAT DO YOU THINK YOU'RE DOING? THIS IS MY WARD -- LEAVE MY ORDERLY ALONE!
NOW -- OR I'LL HAVE TO GET TOUGH.
TOUGH.
NELLS...?
POONT
UK-K-K-K?
KEEP LOOKING.
THE LOUSY JANE TWIST HAS GOT TO BE HERE SOMEWHERE...

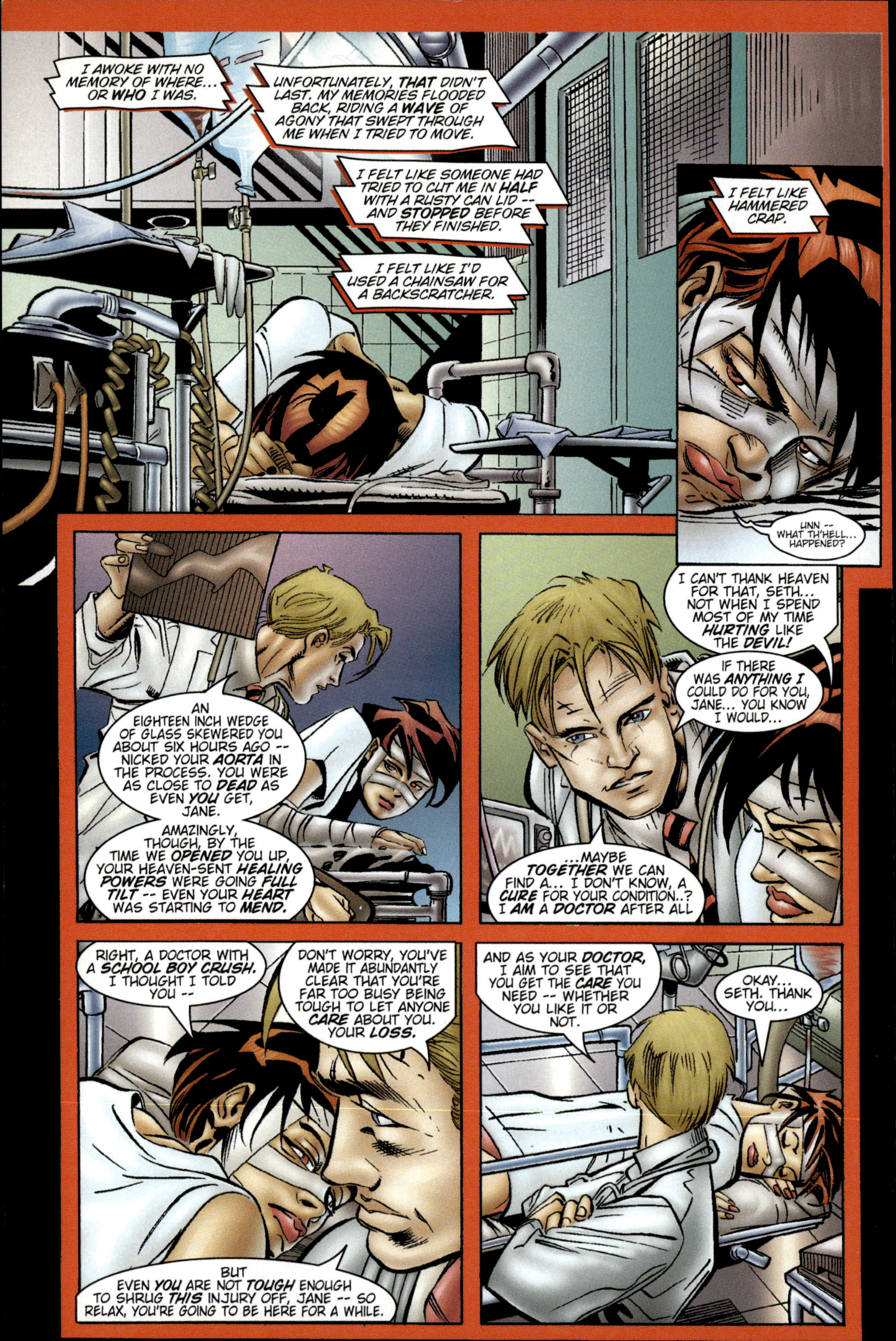
I AWOKE WITH NO MEMORY OF WHERE... OR WHO I WAS.
UNFORTUNATELY, THAT DIDN'T LAST. MY MEMORIES FLOODED BACK, RIDING A WAVE OF AGONY THAT SWEPT THROUGH ME WHEN I TRIED TO MOVE.
I FELT LIKE SOMEONE HAD TRIED TO CUT ME IN HALF WITH A RUSTY CAN LID -- AND STOPPED BEFORE THEY FINISHED.
I FELT LIKE I'D USED A CHAINSAW FOR A BACKSCRATCHER.
I FELT LIKE HAMMERED CRAP.
UNN -- WHAT TH'HELL... HAPPENED?
AN EIGHTEEN INCH WEDGE OF GLASS SKEWERED YOU ABOUT SIX HOURS AGO -- NICKED YOUR AORTA IN THE PROCESS. YOU WERE AS CLOSE TO DEAD AS EVEN YOU GET, JANE.
AMAZINGLY, THOUGH, BY THE TIME WE OPENED YOU UP, YOUR HEAVEN-SENT HEALING POWERS WERE GOING FULL TILT -- EVEN YOUR HEART WAS STARTING TO MEND.
I CAN'T THANK HEAVEN FOR THAT, SETH... NOT WHEN I SPEND MOST OF MY TIME HURTING LIKE THE DEVIL!
IF THERE WAS ANYTHING I COULD DO FOR YOU, JANE... YOU KNOW I WOULD...
...MAYBE TOGETHER WE CAN FIND A... I DON'T KNOW, A CURE FOR YOUR CONDITION..? I AM A DOCTOR AFTER ALL
RIGHT, A DOCTOR WITH A SCHOOL BOY CRUSH. I THOUGHT I TOLD YOU --
DON'T WORRY, YOU'VE MADE IT ABUNDANTLY CLEAR THAT YOU'RE FAR TOO BUSY BEING TOUGH TO LET ANYONE CARE ABOUT YOU. YOUR LOSS.
BUT EVEN YOU ARE NOT TOUGH ENOUGH TO SHRUG THIS INJURY OFF, JANE -- SO RELAX, YOU'RE GOING TO BE HERE FOR A WHILE.
AND AS YOUR DOCTOR, I AIM TO SEE THAT YOU GET THE CARE YOU NEED -- WHETHER YOU LIKE IT OR NOT.
OKAY... SETH. THANK YOU...

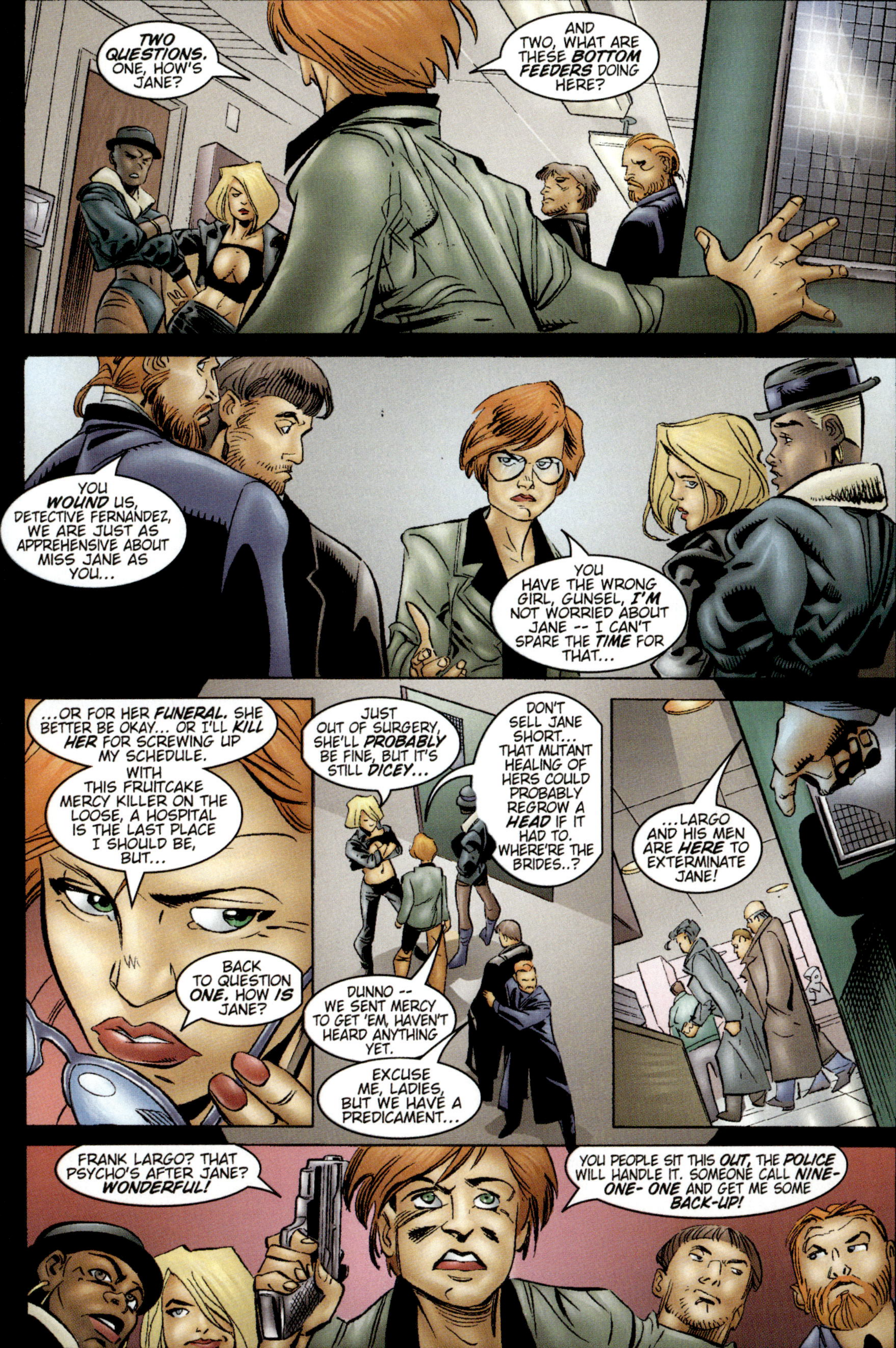
TWO QUESTIONS. ONE, HOW'S JANE?
AND TWO, WHAT ARE THESE BOTTOM FEEDERS DOING HERE?
YOU WOUND US, DETECTIVE FERNANDEZ, WE ARE JUST AS APPREHENSIVE ABOUT MISS JANE AS YOU...
YOU HAVE THE WRONG GIRL, GUNSEL, I'M NOT WORRIED ABOUT JANE -- I CAN'T SPARE THE TIME FOR THAT...
...OR FOR HER FUNERAL. SHE BETTER BE OKAY... OR I'LL KILL HER FOR SCREWING UP MY SCHEDULE.
WITH THIS FRUITCAKE MERCY KILLER ON THE LOOSE, A HOSPITAL IS THE LAST PLACE I SHOULD BE, BUT...
BACK TO QUESTION ONE. HOW IS JANE?
JUST OUT OF SURGERY, SHE'LL PROBABLY BE FINE, BUT IT'S STILL DICEY...
DON'T SELL JANE SHORT... THAT MUTANT HEALING OF HERS COULD PROBABLY REGROW A HEAD IF IT HAD TO. WHERE'RE THE BRIDES..?
DUNNO -- WE SENT MERCY TO GET 'EM, HAVEN'T HEARD ANYTHING YET.
EXCUSE ME, LADIES, BUT WE HAVE A PREDICAMENT...
...LARGO AND HIS MEN ARE HERE TO EXTERMINATE JANE!
FRANK LARGO? THAT PSYCHO'S AFTER JANE? WONDERFUL!
YOU PEOPLE SIT THIS OUT, THE POLICE WILL HANDLE IT. SOMEONE CALL NINE-ONE- ONE AND GET ME SOME BACK-UP!

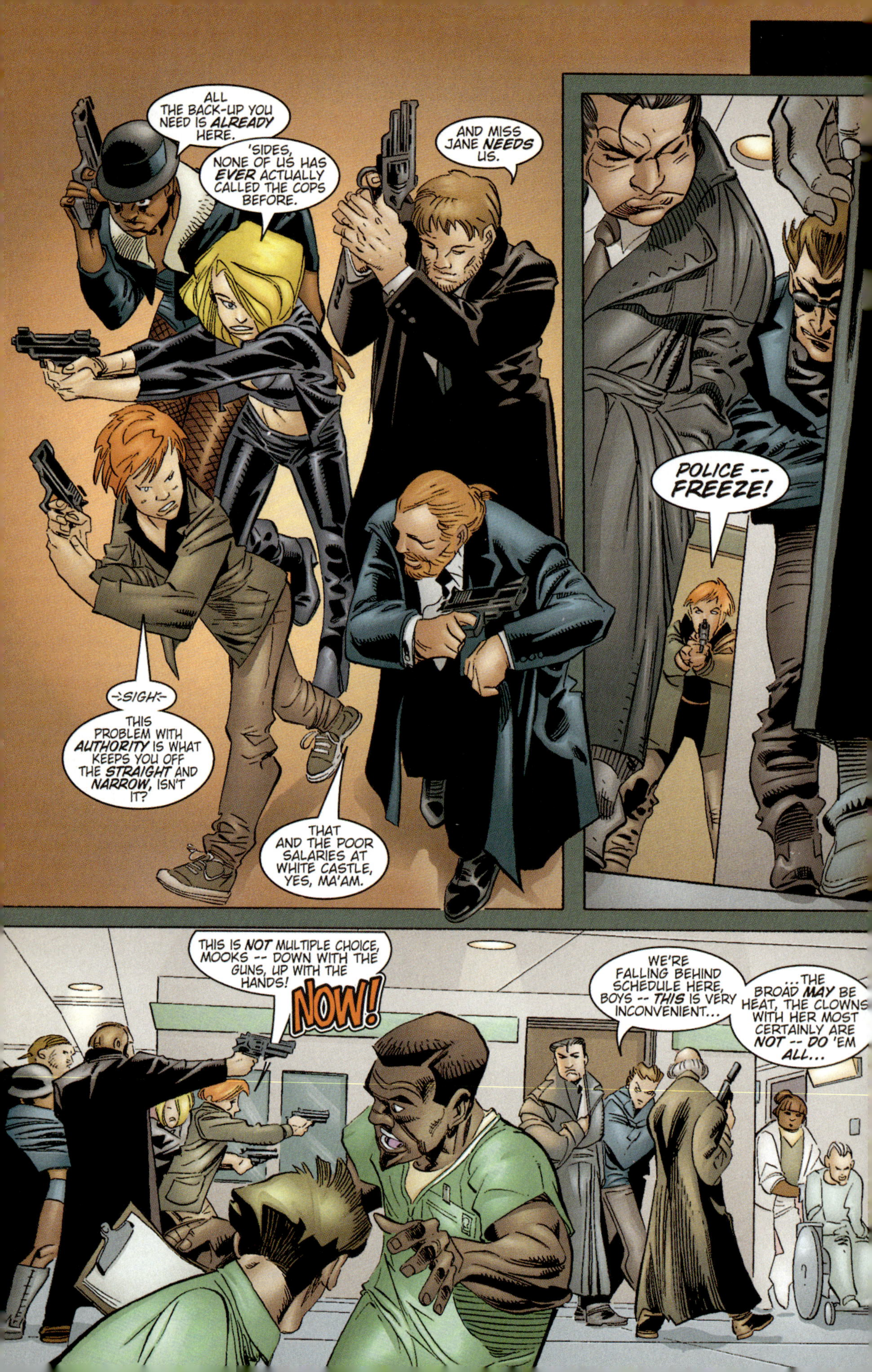

ALL THE BACK-UP YOU NEED IS *ALREADY* HERE.
'SIDES, NONE OF US HAS *EVER* ACTUALLY CALLED THE COPS BEFORE.
AND MISS JANE *NEEDS* US.
POLICE -- FREEZE!
-SIGH-
THIS PROBLEM WITH *AUTHORITY* IS WHAT KEEPS YOU OFF THE *STRAIGHT* AND *NARROW,* ISN'T IT?
THAT AND THE POOR SALARIES AT WHITE CASTLE, YES, MA'AM.
THIS IS *NOT* MULTIPLE CHOICE, MOOKS -- DOWN WITH THE GUNS, UP WITH THE HANDS!
NOW!
WE'RE FALLING BEHIND SCHEDULE HERE, BOYS -- *THIS* IS VERY INCONVENIENT...
...THE BROAD *MAY* BE HEAT, THE CLOWNS WITH HER MOST CERTAINLY ARE *NOT* -- *DO* 'EM *ALL*...

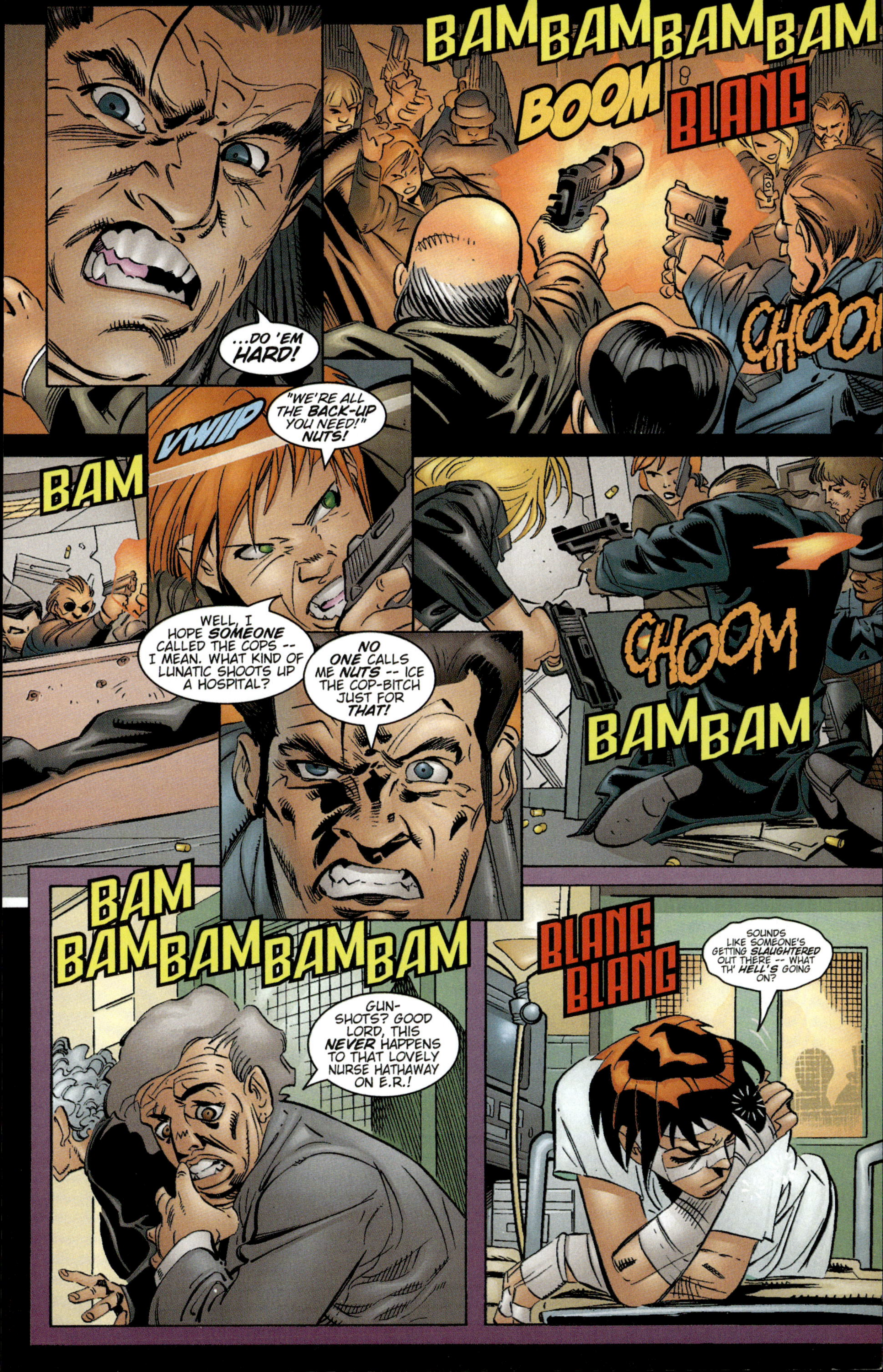
...DO 'EM HARD!
BAMBAMBAMBAM
BOOM
BLANG
CHOOM
VWIP
"WE'RE ALL THE BACK-UP YOU NEED!" NUTS!
BAM
WELL, I HOPE SOMEONE CALLED THE COPS -- I MEAN. WHAT KIND OF LUNATIC SHOOTS UP A HOSPITAL?
NO ONE CALLS ME NUTS -- ICE THE COP-BITCH JUST FOR THAT!
CHOOM
BAMBAM
BAM
BAMBAMBAMBAM
GUN-SHOTS? GOOD LORD, THIS NEVER HAPPENS TO THAT LOVELY NURSE HATHAWAY ON E.R.!
BLANG BLANG
SOUNDS LIKE SOMEONE'S GETTING SLAUGHTERED OUT THERE -- WHAT TH' HELL'S GOING ON?

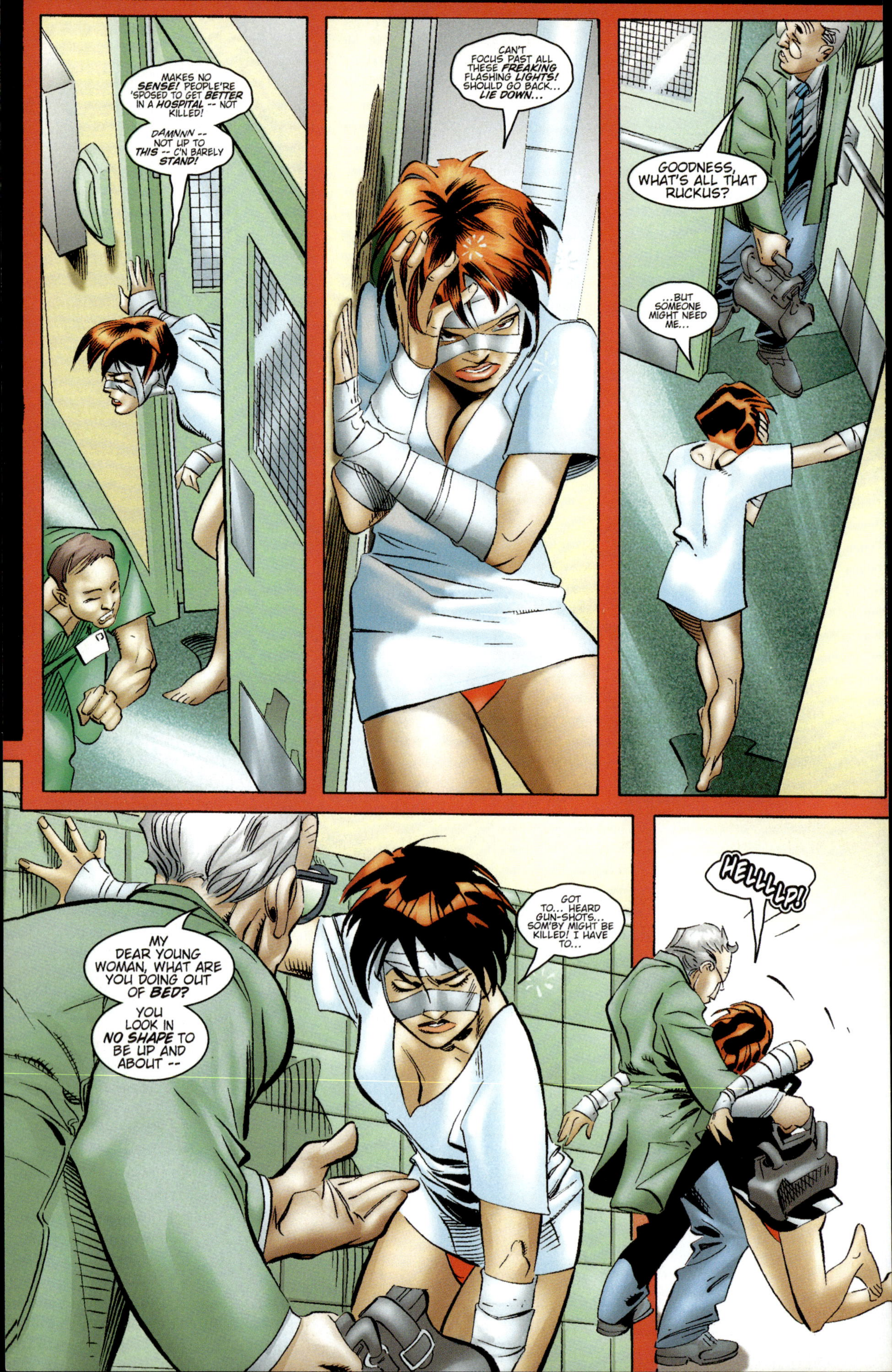

MAKES NO SENSE! PEOPLE'RE 'SPOSED TO GET BETTER IN A HOSPITAL -- NOT KILLED!
DAMNNN -- NOT UP TO THIS -- C'N BARELY STAND!
CAN'T FOCUS PAST ALL THESE FREAKING FLASHING LIGHTS! SHOULD GO BACK... LIE DOWN...
GOODNESS, WHAT'S ALL THAT RUCKUS?
...BUT SOMEONE MIGHT NEED ME...
MY DEAR YOUNG WOMAN, WHAT ARE YOU DOING OUT OF BED?
YOU LOOK IN NO SHAPE TO BE UP AND ABOUT --
GOT TO... HEARD GUN-SHOTS... SOM'BY MIGHT BE KILLED! I HAVE TO...
HELLLLP!

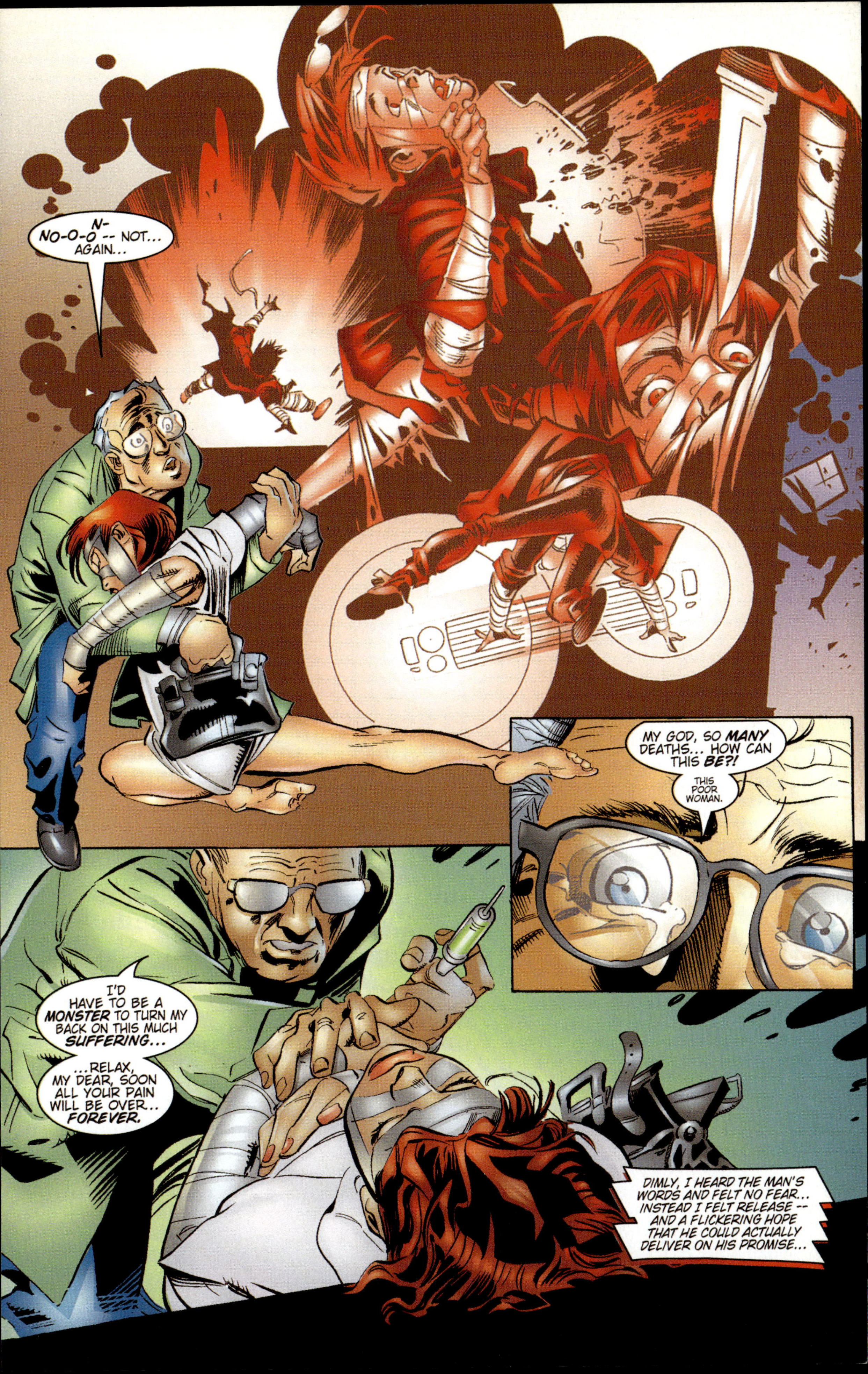
N-
NO-O-O -- NOT... AGAIN...
MY GOD, SO MANY DEATHS... HOW CAN THIS BE?!
THIS POOR WOMAN.
I'D HAVE TO BE A MONSTER TO TURN MY BACK ON THIS MUCH SUFFERING...
...RELAX, MY DEAR, SOON ALL YOUR PAIN WILL BE OVER... FOREVER.
DIMLY, I HEARD THE MAN'S WORDS AND FELT NO FEAR... INSTEAD I FELT RELEASE -- AND A FLICKERING HOPE THAT HE COULD ACTUALLY DELIVER ON HIS PROMISE...

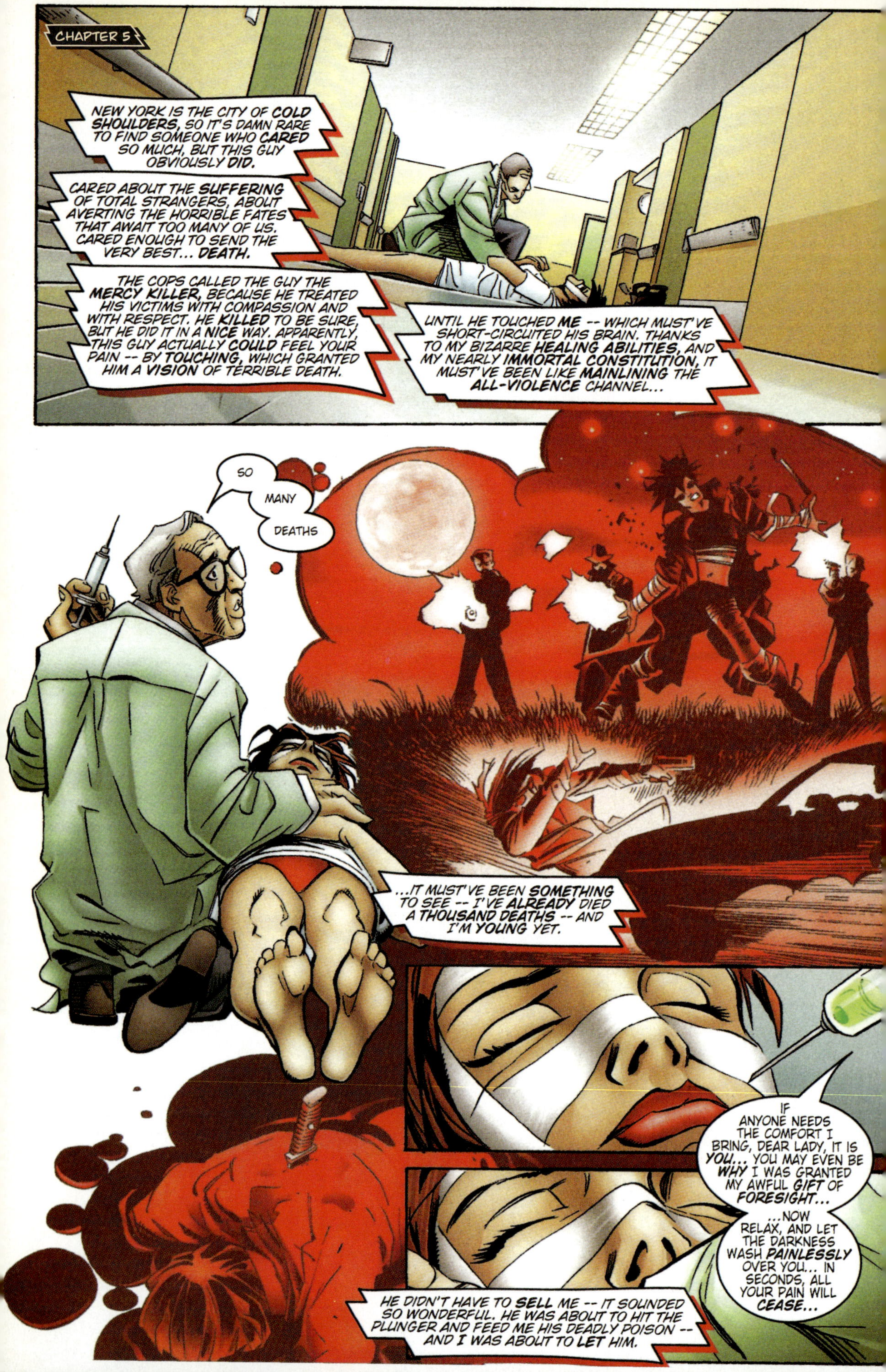
CHAPTER 5
NEW YORK IS THE CITY OF COLD SHOULDERS, SO IT'S DAMN RARE TO FIND SOMEONE WHO CARED SO MUCH, BUT THIS GUY OBVIOUSLY DID.
CARED ABOUT THE SUFFERING OF TOTAL STRANGERS, ABOUT AVERTING THE HORRIBLE FATES THAT AWAIT TOO MANY OF US. CARED ENOUGH TO SEND THE VERY BEST... DEATH.
THE COPS CALLED THE GUY THE MERCY KILLER, BECAUSE HE TREATED HIS VICTIMS WITH COMPASSION AND WITH RESPECT. HE KILLED TO BE SURE, BUT HE DID IT IN A NICE WAY. APPARENTLY, THIS GUY ACTUALLY COULD FEEL YOUR PAIN -- BY TOUCHING, WHICH GRANTED HIM A VISION OF TERRIBLE DEATH.
UNTIL HE TOUCHED ME -- WHICH MUST'VE SHORT-CIRCUITED HIS BRAIN. THANKS TO MY BIZARRE HEALING ABILITIES, AND MY NEARLY IMMORTAL CONSTITUTION, IT MUST'VE BEEN LIKE MAINLINING THE ALL-VIOLENCE CHANNEL...
SO
MANY
DEATHS
...IT MUST'VE BEEN SOMETHING TO SEE -- I'VE ALREADY DIED A THOUSAND DEATHS -- AND I'M YOUNG YET.
IF ANYONE NEEDS THE COMFORT I BRING, DEAR LADY, IT IS YOU... YOU MAY EVEN BE WHY I WAS GRANTED MY AWFUL GIFT OF FORESIGHT...
...NOW RELAX, AND LET THE DARKNESS WASH PAINLESSLY OVER YOU... IN SECONDS, ALL YOUR PAIN WILL CEASE...
HE DIDN'T HAVE TO SELL ME -- IT SOUNDED SO WONDERFUL. HE WAS ABOUT TO HIT THE PLUNGER AND FEED ME HIS DEADLY POISON -- AND I WAS ABOUT TO LET HIM.

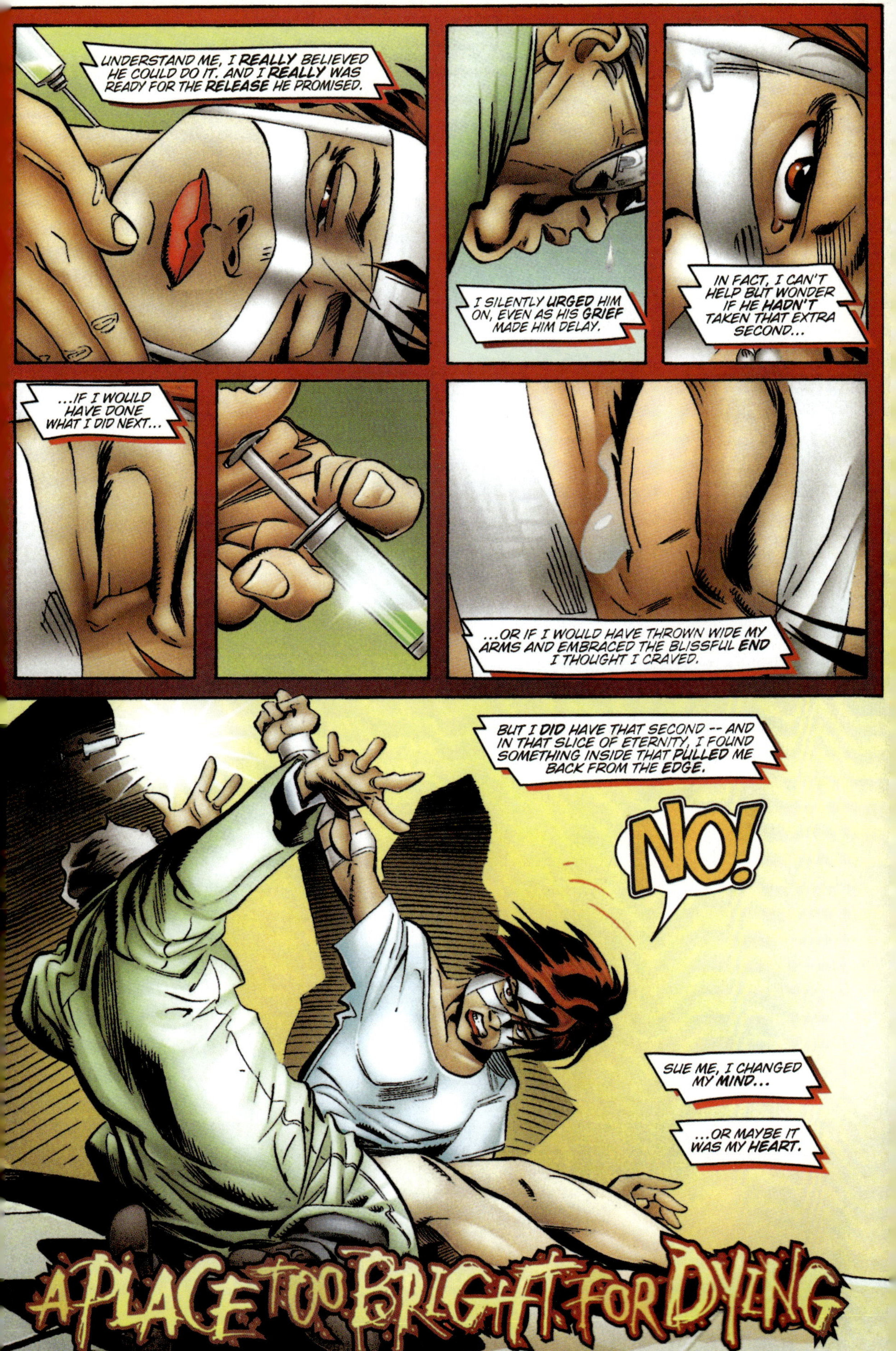
UNDERSTAND ME, I REALLY BELIEVED HE COULD DO IT. AND I REALLY WAS READY FOR THE RELEASE HE PROMISED.
I SILENTLY URGED HIM ON, EVEN AS HIS GRIEF MADE HIM DELAY.
IN FACT, I CAN'T HELP BUT WONDER IF HE HADN'T TAKEN THAT EXTRA SECOND...
...IF I WOULD HAVE DONE WHAT I DID NEXT...
...OR IF I WOULD HAVE THROWN WIDE MY ARMS AND EMBRACED THE BLISSFUL END I THOUGHT I CRAVED.
BUT I DID HAVE THAT SECOND -- AND IN THAT SLICE OF ETERNITY, I FOUND SOMETHING INSIDE THAT PULLED ME BACK FROM THE EDGE.
NO!
SUE ME, I CHANGED MY MIND...
...OR MAYBE IT WAS MY HEART.
A PLACE TOO BRIGHT FOR DYING

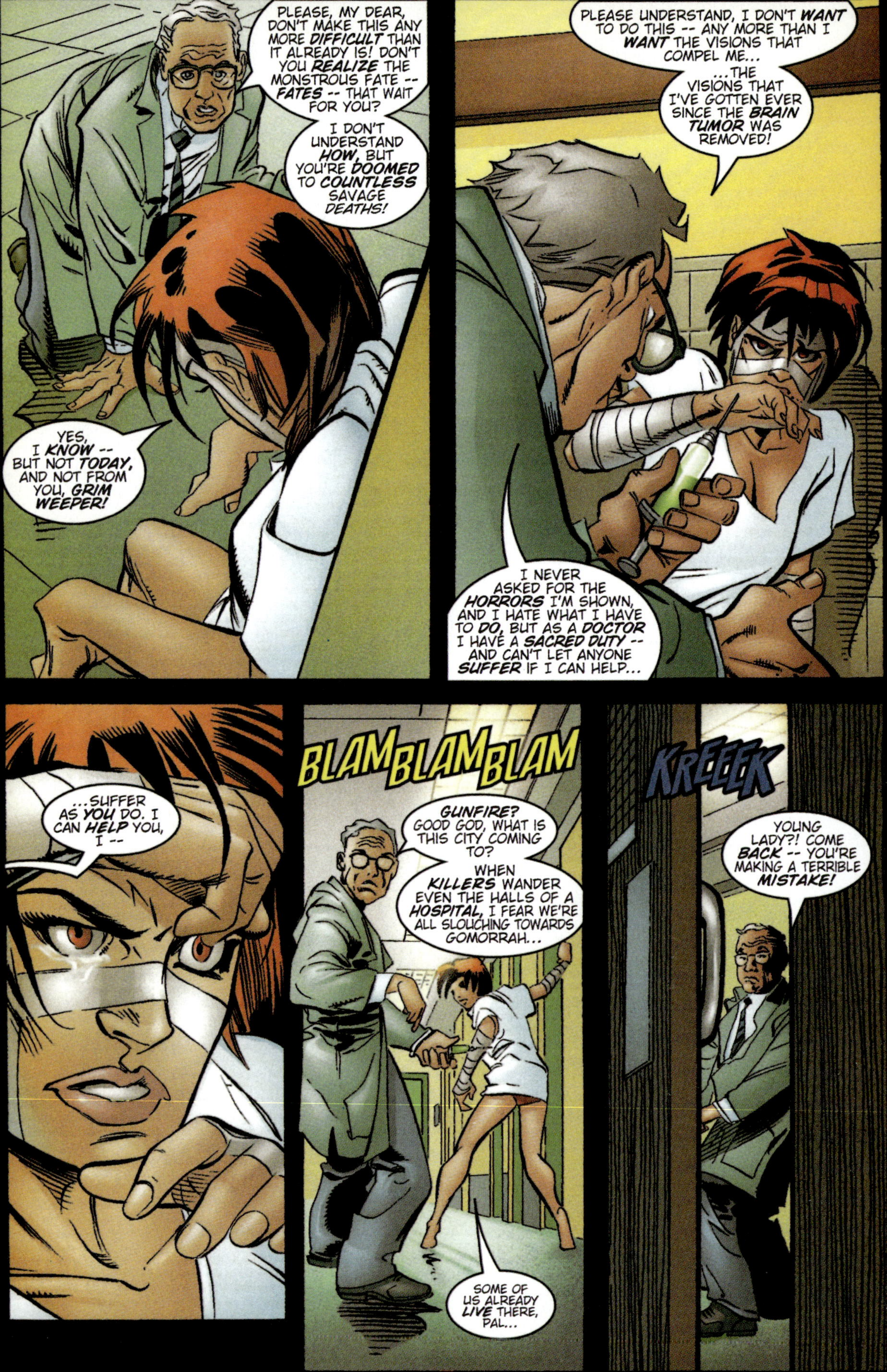
PLEASE, MY DEAR, DON'T MAKE THIS ANY MORE DIFFICULT THAN IT ALREADY IS! DON'T YOU REALIZE THE MONSTROUS FATE -- FATES -- THAT WAIT FOR YOU?
I DON'T UNDERSTAND HOW, BUT YOU'RE DOOMED TO COUNTLESS SAVAGE DEATHS!
YES, I KNOW -- BUT NOT TODAY, AND NOT FROM YOU, GRIM WEEPER!
PLEASE UNDERSTAND, I DON'T WANT TO DO THIS -- ANY MORE THAN I WANT THE VISIONS THAT COMPEL ME...
...THE VISIONS THAT I'VE GOTTEN EVER SINCE THE BRAIN TUMOR WAS REMOVED!
I NEVER ASKED FOR THE HORRORS I'M SHOWN, AND I HATE WHAT I HAVE TO DO, BUT AS A DOCTOR I HAVE A SACRED DUTY -- AND CAN'T LET ANYONE SUFFER IF I CAN HELP...
...SUFFER AS YOU DO. I CAN HELP YOU, I --
BLAMBLAMBLAM
GUNFIRE? GOOD GOD, WHAT IS THIS CITY COMING TO?
WHEN KILLERS WANDER EVEN THE HALLS OF A HOSPITAL, I FEAR WE'RE ALL SLOUCHING TOWARDS GOMORRAH...
SOME OF US ALREADY LIVE THERE, PAL...
KREEEK
YOUNG LADY?! COME BACK -- YOU'RE MAKING A TERRIBLE MISTAKE!

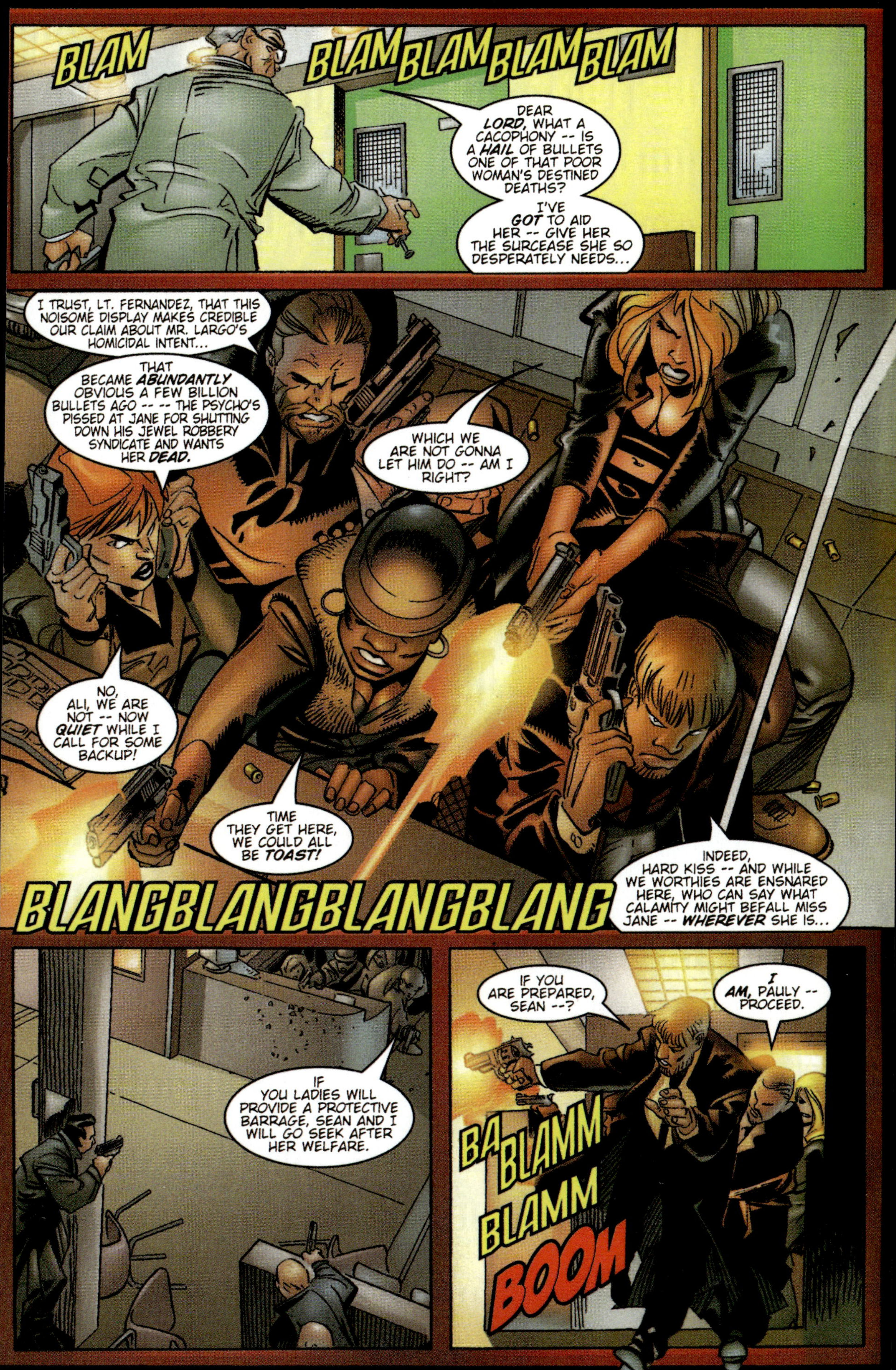
BLAM
BLAM BLAM BLAM BLAM
DEAR LORD, WHAT A CACOPHONY -- IS A HAIL OF BULLETS ONE OF THAT POOR WOMAN'S DESTINED DEATHS?
I'VE GOT TO AID HER -- GIVE HER THE SURCEASE SHE SO DESPERATELY NEEDS...
I TRUST, LT. FERNANDEZ, THAT THIS NOISOME DISPLAY MAKES CREDIBLE OUR CLAIM ABOUT MR. LARGO'S HOMICIDAL INTENT...
THAT BECAME ABUNDANTLY OBVIOUS A FEW BILLION BULLETS AGO -- -- THE PSYCHO'S PISSED AT JANE FOR SHUTTING DOWN HIS JEWEL ROBBERY SYNDICATE AND WANTS HER DEAD.
WHICH WE ARE NOT GONNA LET HIM DO -- AM I RIGHT?
NO, ALI, WE ARE NOT -- NOW QUIET WHILE I CALL FOR SOME BACKUP!
TIME THEY GET HERE, WE COULD ALL BE TOAST!
BLANGBLANGBLANGBLANG
INDEED, HARD KISS -- AND WHILE WE WORTHIES ARE ENSNARED HERE, WHO CAN SAY WHAT CALAMITY MIGHT BEFALL MISS JANE -- WHEREVER SHE IS...
IF YOU LADIES WILL PROVIDE A PROTECTIVE BARRAGE, SEAN AND I WILL GO SEEK AFTER HER WELFARE.
IF YOU ARE PREPARED, SEAN --?
I AM, PAULY -- PROCEED.
BA BLAMM
BLAMM
BOOM

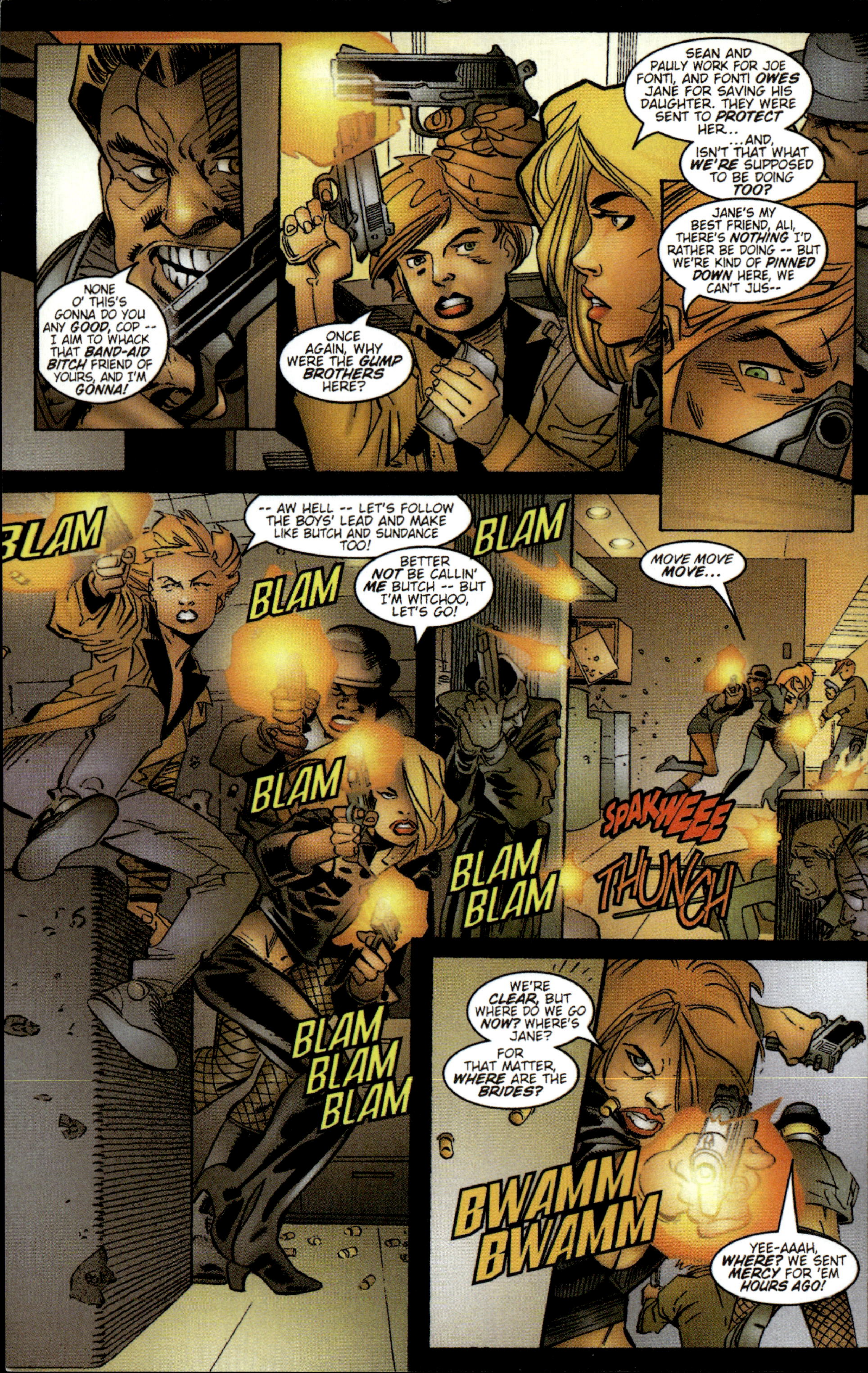
NONE O' THIS'S GONNA DO YOU ANY GOOD, COP -- I AIM TO WHACK THAT BAND-AID BITCH FRIEND OF YOURS, AND I'M GONNA!
ONCE AGAIN, WHY WERE THE GUMP BROTHERS HERE?
SEAN AND PAULY WORK FOR JOE FONTI, AND FONTI OWES JANE FOR SAVING HIS DAUGHTER. THEY WERE SENT TO PROTECT HER...
...AND, ISN'T THAT WHAT WE'RE SUPPOSED TO BE DOING TOO?
JANE'S MY BEST FRIEND, ALI, THERE'S NOTHING I'D RATHER BE DOING -- BUT WE'RE KIND OF PINNED DOWN HERE, WE CAN'T JUS--
BLAM
-- AW HELL -- LET'S FOLLOW THE BOYS' LEAD AND MAKE LIKE BUTCH AND SUNDANCE TOO!
BLAM
BETTER NOT BE CALLIN' ME BUTCH -- BUT I'M WITCHOO, LET'S GO!
BLAM
MOVE MOVE MOVE...
BLAM
SPAKWEEE
BLAM BLAM
THUNCH
BLAM BLAM BLAM
WE'RE CLEAR, BUT WHERE DO WE GO NOW? WHERE'S JANE?
FOR THAT MATTER, WHERE ARE THE BRIDES?
BWAMM BWAMM
YEE-AAAH, WHERE? WE SENT MERCY FOR 'EM HOURS AGO!

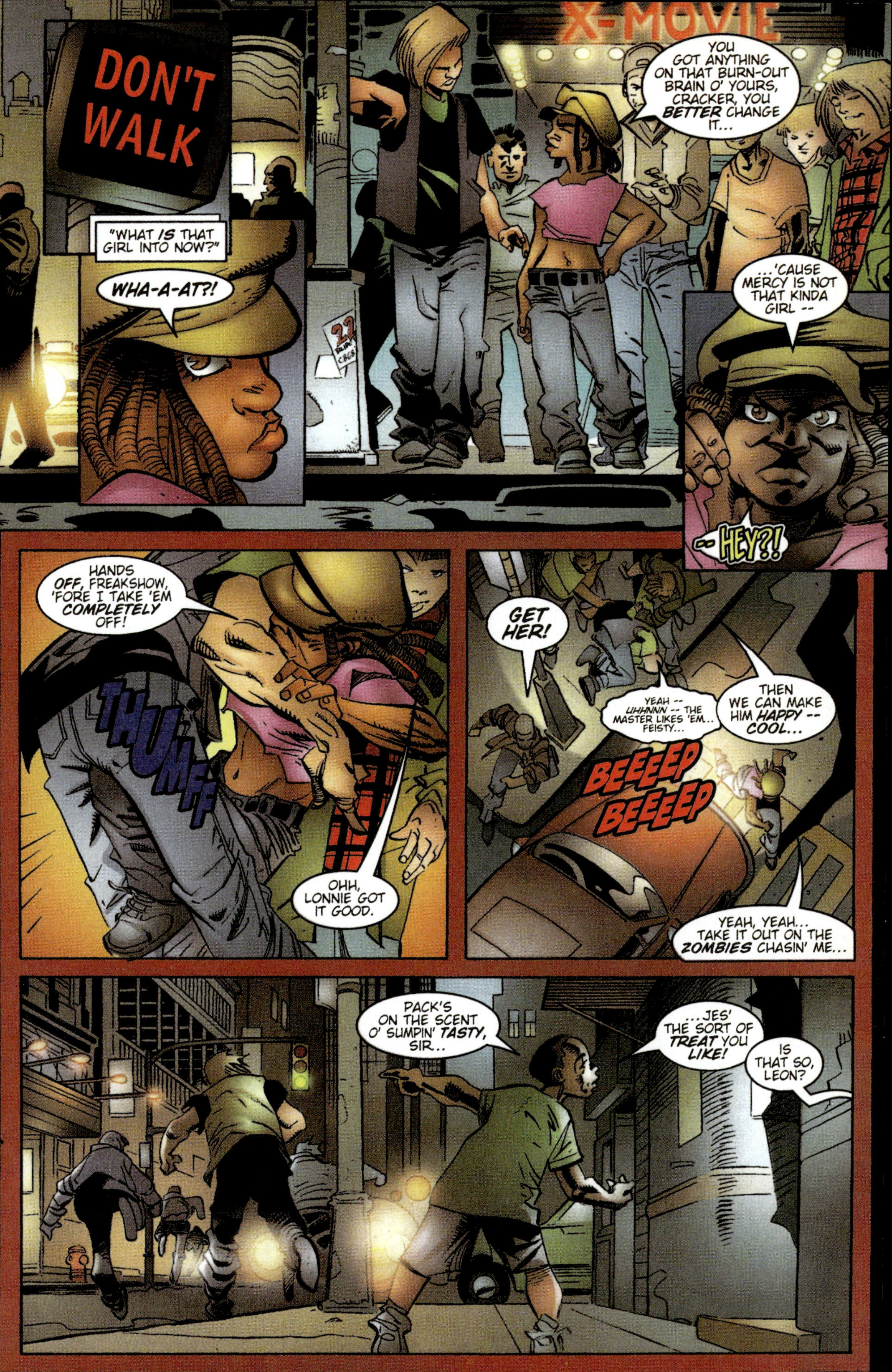

X-MOVIE
DON'T WALK
"WHAT IS THAT GIRL INTO NOW?"
WHA-A-AT?!
YOU GOT ANYTHING ON THAT BURN-OUT BRAIN O' YOURS, CRACKER, YOU BETTER CHANGE IT...
...'CAUSE MERCY IS NOT THAT KINDA GIRL --
-- HEY?!
HANDS OFF, FREAKSHOW, 'FORE I TAKE 'EM COMPLETELY OFF!
THUMFF
OHH, LONNIE GOT IT GOOD.
GET HER!
YEAH -- UHHNNN -- THE MASTER LIKES 'EM... FEISTY...
THEN WE CAN MAKE HIM HAPPY -- COOL...
BEEEEP BEEEEP
YEAH, YEAH... TAKE IT OUT ON THE ZOMBIES CHASIN' ME...
PACK'S ON THE SCENT O' SUMPIN' TASTY, SIR...
...JES' THE SORT OF TREAT YOU LIKE!
IS THAT SO, LEON?

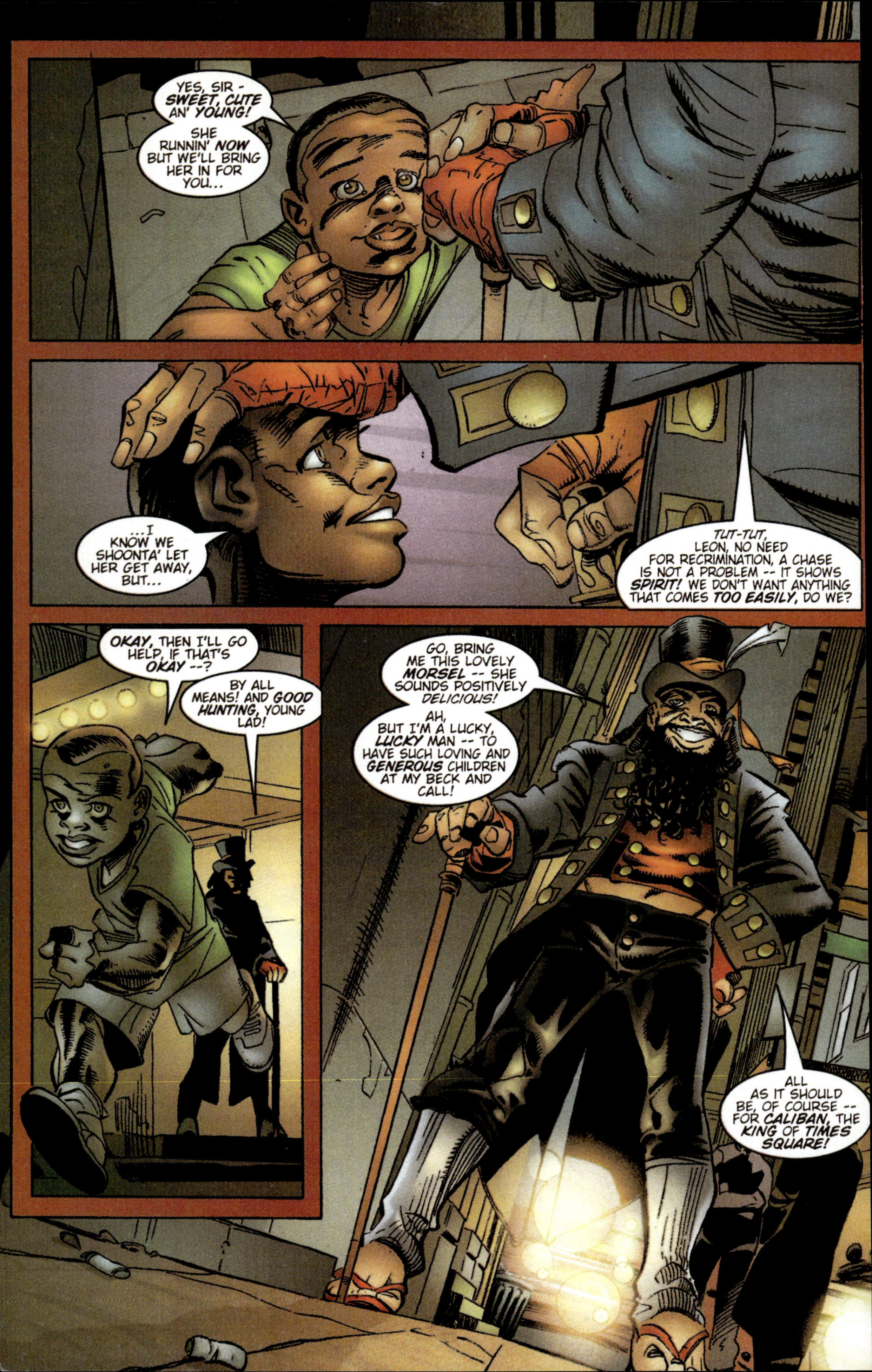
YES, SIR - SWEET, CUTE AN' YOUNG! SHE RUNNIN' NOW BUT WE'LL BRING HER IN FOR YOU...
...I KNOW WE SHOONTA' LET HER GET AWAY, BUT...
TUT-TUT, LEON, NO NEED FOR RECRIMINATION, A CHASE IS NOT A PROBLEM -- IT SHOWS SPIRIT! WE DON'T WANT ANYTHING THAT COMES TOO EASILY, DO WE?
OKAY, THEN I'LL GO HELP, IF THAT'S OKAY --?
BY ALL MEANS! AND GOOD HUNTING, YOUNG LAD!
GO, BRING ME THIS LOVELY MORSEL -- SHE SOUNDS POSITIVELY DELICIOUS!
AH, BUT I'M A LUCKY, LUCKY MAN -- TO HAVE SUCH LOVING AND GENEROUS CHILDREN AT MY BECK AND CALL!
ALL AS IT SHOULD BE, OF COURSE -- FOR CALIBAN, THE KING OF TIMES SQUARE!

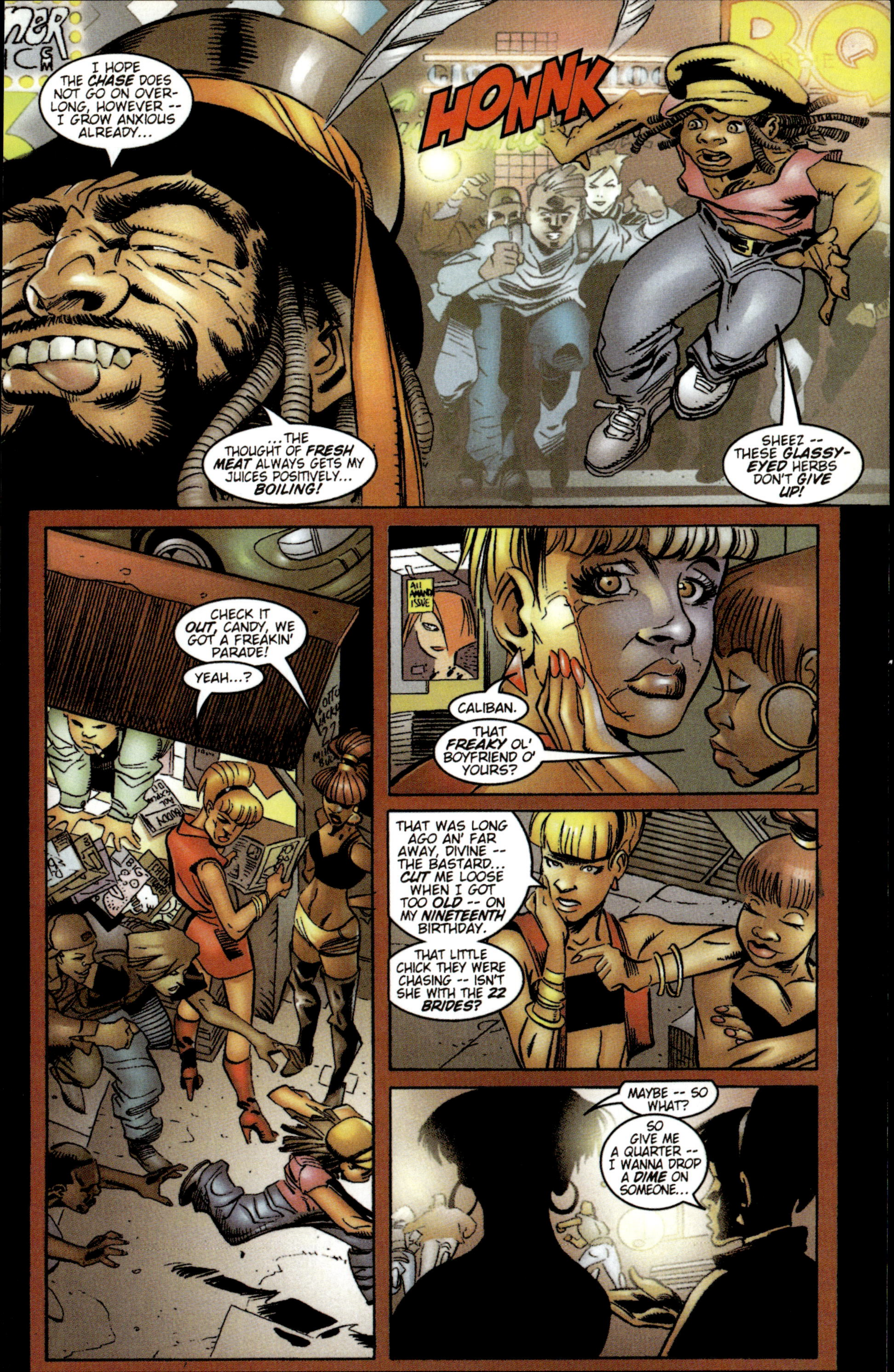
I HOPE THE CHASE DOES NOT GO ON OVER-LONG, HOWEVER -- I GROW ANXIOUS ALREADY...
...THE THOUGHT OF FRESH MEAT ALWAYS GETS MY JUICES POSITIVELY... BOILING!
HONNK
SHEEZ -- THESE GLASSY-EYED HERBS DON'T GIVE UP!
CHECK IT OUT, CANDY, WE GOT A FREAKIN' PARADE!
YEAH...?
CALIBAN.
THAT FREAKY OL' BOYFRIEND O' YOURS?
THAT WAS LONG AGO AN' FAR AWAY, DIVINE -- THE BASTARD... CUT ME LOOSE WHEN I GOT TOO OLD -- ON MY NINETEENTH BIRTHDAY.
THAT LITTLE CHICK THEY WERE CHASING -- ISN'T SHE WITH THE 22 BRIDES?
MAYBE -- SO WHAT?
SO GIVE ME A QUARTER -- I WANNA DROP A DIME ON SOMEONE...

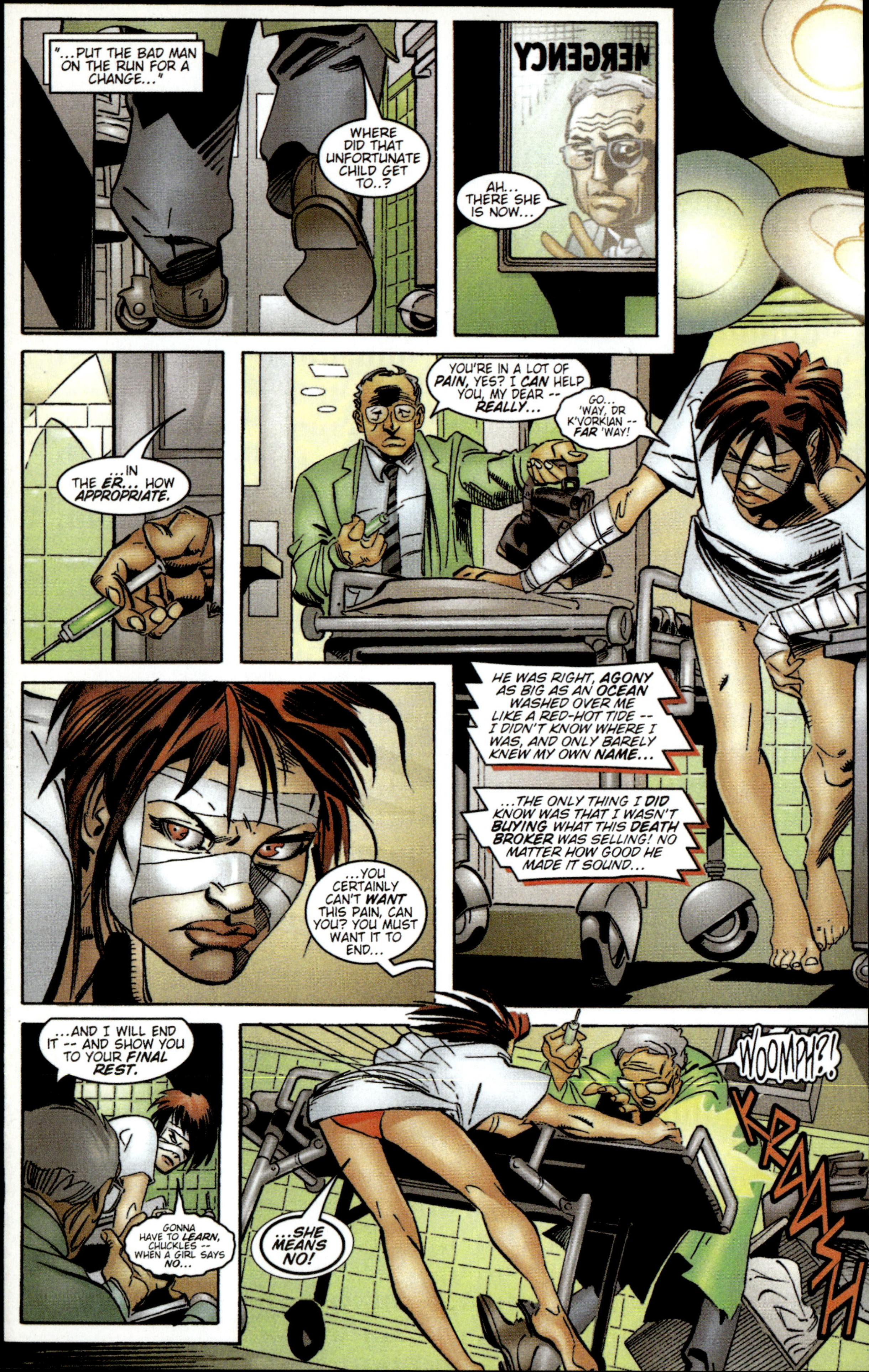
"...PUT THE BAD MAN ON THE RUN FOR A CHANGE..."
WHERE DID THAT UNFORTUNATE CHILD GET TO..?
AH... THERE SHE IS NOW...
...IN THE ER... HOW APPROPRIATE.
YOU'RE IN A LOT OF PAIN, YES? I CAN HELP YOU, MY DEAR -- REALLY...
GO... 'WAY, DR K'VORKIAN -- FAR 'WAY!
HE WAS RIGHT, AGONY AS BIG AS AN OCEAN WASHED OVER ME LIKE A RED-HOT TIDE -- I DIDN'T KNOW WHERE I WAS, AND ONLY BARELY KNEW MY OWN NAME...
...THE ONLY THING I DID KNOW WAS THAT I WASN'T BUYING WHAT THIS DEATH BROKER WAS SELLING! NO MATTER HOW GOOD HE MADE IT SOUND...
...YOU CERTAINLY CAN'T WANT THIS PAIN, CAN YOU? YOU MUST WANT IT TO END...
...AND I WILL END IT -- AND SHOW YOU TO YOUR FINAL REST.
GONNA HAVE TO LEARN, CHUCKLES -- WHEN A GIRL SAYS NO...
...SHE MEANS NO!
WOOMPH?!
KRAASH

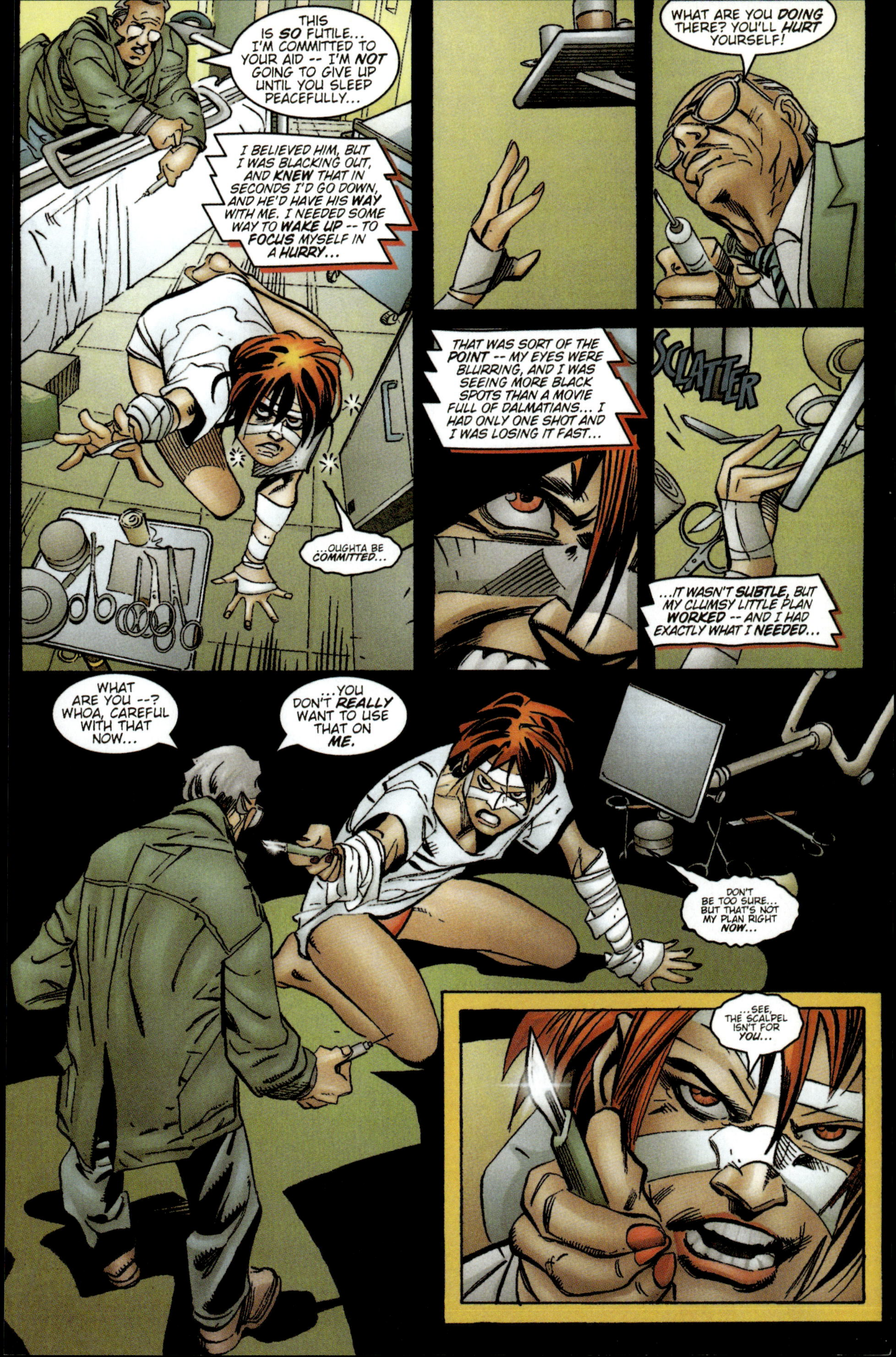
THIS IS SO FUTILE... I'M COMMITTED TO YOUR AID -- I'M NOT GOING TO GIVE UP UNTIL YOU SLEEP PEACEFULLY...
I BELIEVED HIM, BUT I WAS BLACKING OUT, AND KNEW THAT IN SECONDS I'D GO DOWN, AND HE'D HAVE HIS WAY WITH ME. I NEEDED SOME WAY TO WAKE UP -- TO FOCUS MYSELF IN A HURRY...
...OUGHTA BE COMMITTED...
WHAT ARE YOU DOING THERE? YOU'LL HURT YOURSELF!
THAT WAS SORT OF THE POINT -- MY EYES WERE BLURRING, AND I WAS SEEING MORE BLACK SPOTS THAN A MOVIE FULL OF DALMATIANS... I HAD ONLY ONE SHOT AND I WAS LOSING IT FAST...
SCLATTER
...IT WASN'T SUBTLE, BUT MY CLUMSY LITTLE PLAN WORKED -- AND I HAD EXACTLY WHAT I NEEDED...
WHAT ARE YOU --? WHOA, CAREFUL WITH THAT NOW...
...YOU DON'T REALLY WANT TO USE THAT ON ME.
DON'T BE TOO SURE... BUT THAT'S NOT MY PLAN RIGHT NOW...
...SEE, THE SCALPEL ISN'T FOR YOU...

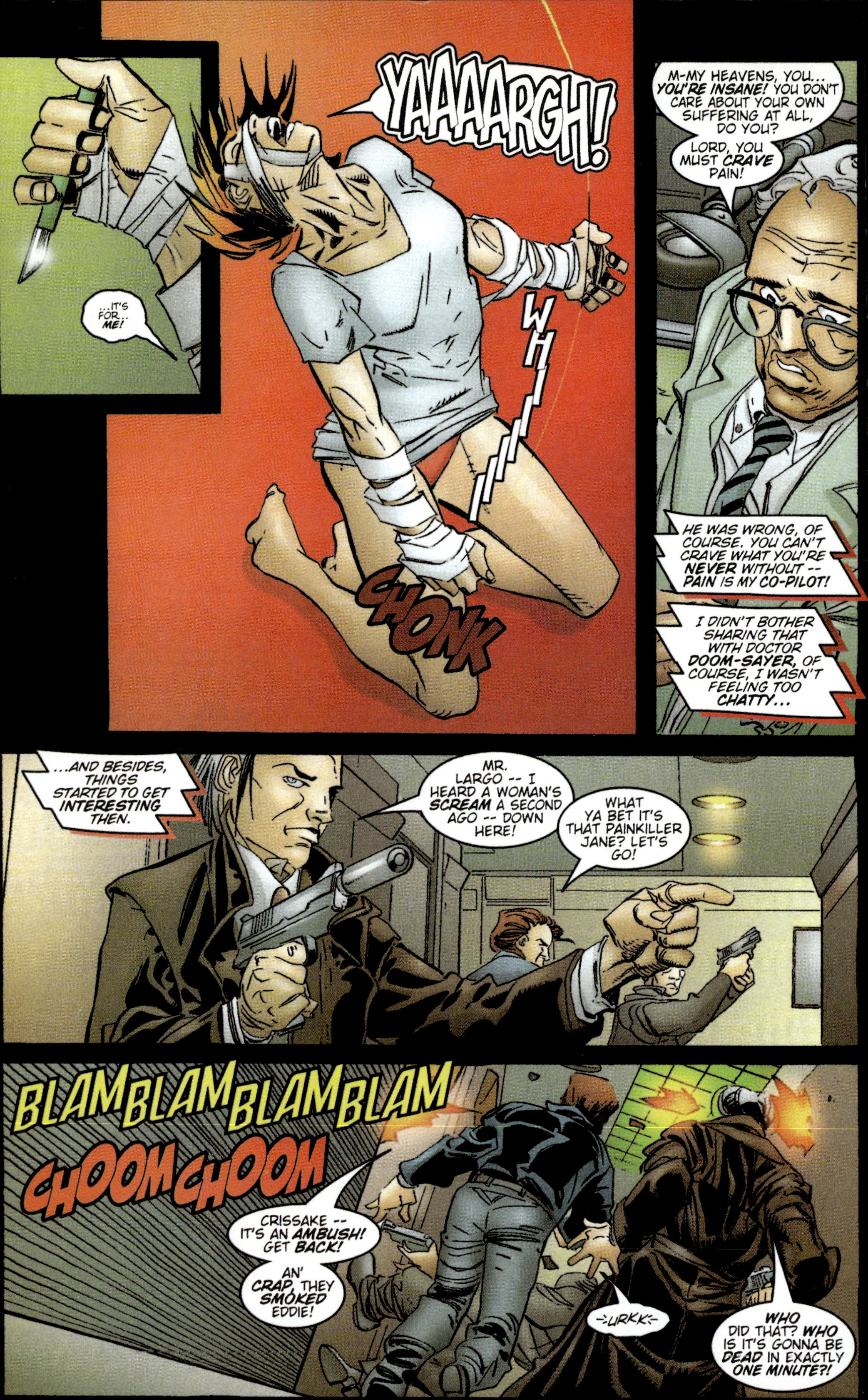
YAAAARGH!
...IT'S FOR... ME!
WHHHH
CHONK
M-MY HEAVENS, YOU... YOU'RE INSANE! YOU DON'T CARE ABOUT YOUR OWN SUFFERING AT ALL, DO YOU?
LORD, YOU MUST CRAVE PAIN!
HE WAS WRONG, OF COURSE. YOU CAN'T CRAVE WHAT YOU'RE NEVER WITHOUT -- PAIN IS MY CO-PILOT!
I DIDN'T BOTHER SHARING THAT WITH DOCTOR DOOM-SAYER, OF COURSE, I WASN'T FEELING TOO CHATTY...
...AND BESIDES, THINGS STARTED TO GET INTERESTING THEN.
MR. LARGO -- I HEARD A WOMAN'S SCREAM A SECOND AGO -- DOWN HERE!
WHAT YA BET IT'S THAT PAINKILLER JANE? LET'S GO!
BLAMBLAMBLAMBLAM
CHOOMCHOOM
CRISSAKE -- IT'S AN AMBUSH! GET BACK!
AN' CRAP, THEY SMOKED EDDIE!
URKK
WHO DID THAT? WHO IS IT'S GONNA BE DEAD IN EXACTLY ONE MINUTE?!

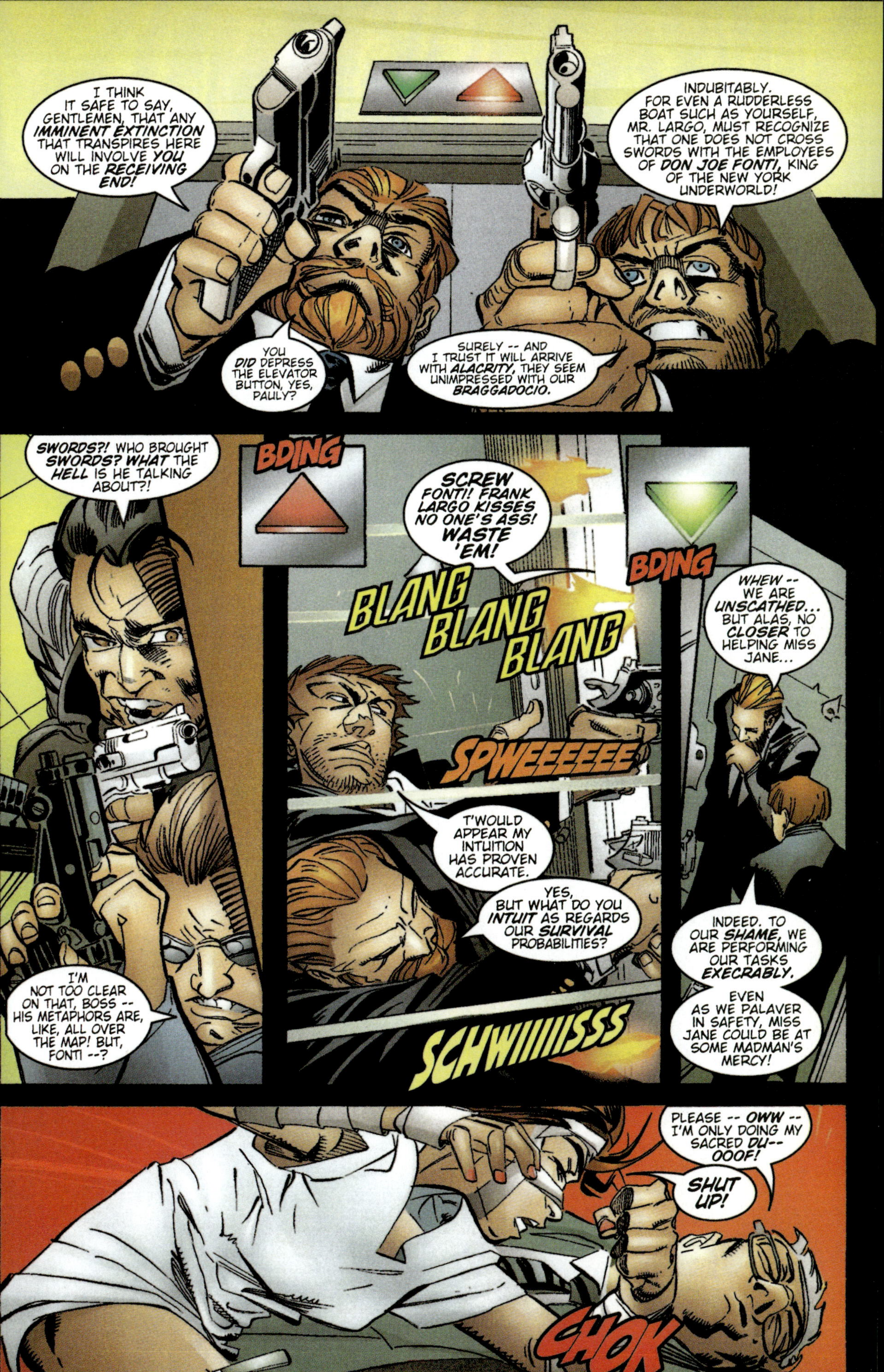

I THINK IT SAFE TO SAY, GENTLEMEN, THAT ANY IMMINENT EXTINCTION THAT TRANSPIRES HERE WILL INVOLVE YOU ON THE RECEIVING END!
INDUBITABLY. FOR EVEN A RUDDERLESS BOAT SUCH AS YOURSELF, MR. LARGO, MUST RECOGNIZE THAT ONE DOES NOT CROSS SWORDS WITH THE EMPLOYEES OF DON JOE FONTI, KING OF THE NEW YORK UNDERWORLD!
YOU DID DEPRESS THE ELEVATOR BUTTON, YES, PAULY?
SURELY -- AND I TRUST IT WILL ARRIVE WITH ALACRITY, THEY SEEM UNIMPRESSED WITH OUR BRAGGADOCIO.
SWORDS?! WHO BROUGHT SWORDS? WHAT THE HELL IS HE TALKING ABOUT?!
I'M NOT TOO CLEAR ON THAT, BOSS -- HIS METAPHORS ARE, LIKE, ALL OVER THE MAP! BUT, FONTI --?
BDING
SCREW FONTI!! FRANK LARGO KISSES NO ONE'S ASS! WASTE 'EM!
BLANG BLANG BLANG
SPWEEEEEE
T'WOULD APPEAR MY INTUITION HAS PROVEN ACCURATE.
YES, BUT WHAT DO YOU INTUIT AS REGARDS OUR SURVIVAL PROBABILITIES?
SCHWIIIIISSS
BDING
WHEW -- WE ARE UNSCATHED... BUT ALAS, NO CLOSER TO HELPING MISS JANE...
INDEED. TO OUR SHAME, WE ARE PERFORMING OUR TASKS EXECRABLY.
EVEN AS WE PALAVER IN SAFETY, MISS JANE COULD BE AT SOME MADMAN'S MERCY!
PLEASE -- OWW -- I'M ONLY DOING MY SACRED DU-- OOOF!
SHUT UP!
CHOK

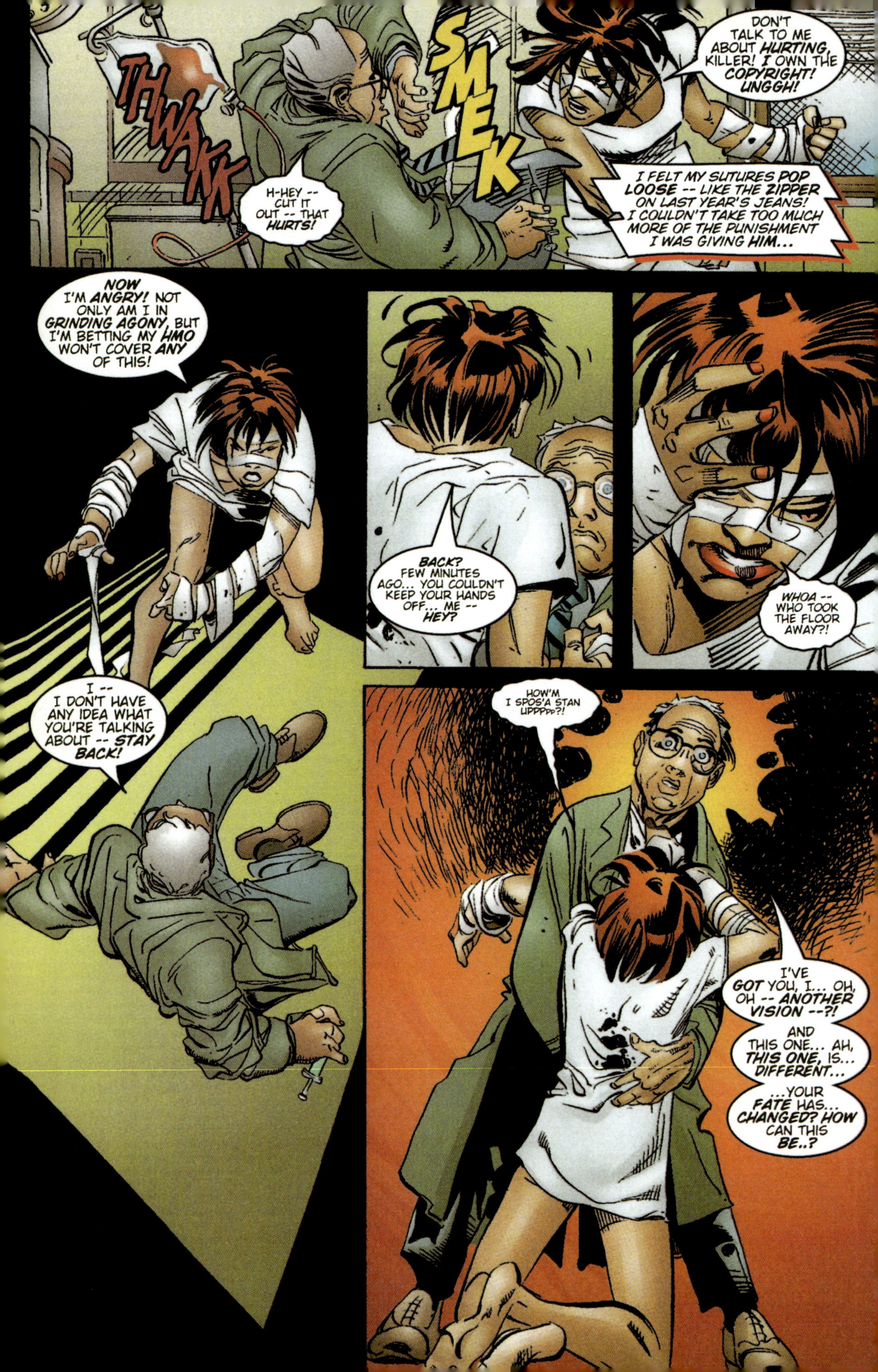
THWAKK
SMEK
DON'T TALK TO ME ABOUT HURTING, KILLER! I OWN THE COPYRIGHT! UNGGH!
H-HEY -- CUT IT OUT -- THAT HURTS!
I FELT MY SUTURES POP LOOSE -- LIKE THE ZIPPER ON LAST YEAR'S JEANS! I COULDN'T TAKE TOO MUCH MORE OF THE PUNISHMENT I WAS GIVING HIM...
NOW I'M ANGRY! NOT ONLY AM I IN GRINDING AGONY, BUT I'M BETTING MY HMO WON'T COVER ANY OF THIS!
I -- I DON'T HAVE ANY IDEA WHAT YOU'RE TALKING ABOUT -- STAY BACK!
BACK? FEW MINUTES AGO... YOU COULDN'T KEEP YOUR HANDS OFF... ME -- HEY?
WHOA -- WHO TOOK THE FLOOR AWAY?!
HOW'M I SPOS'A STAN UPPPPP?!
I'VE GOT YOU, I... OH, OH -- ANOTHER VISION --?!
AND THIS ONE... AH, THIS ONE, IS... DIFFERENT...
...YOUR FATE HAS... CHANGED? HOW CAN THIS BE..?

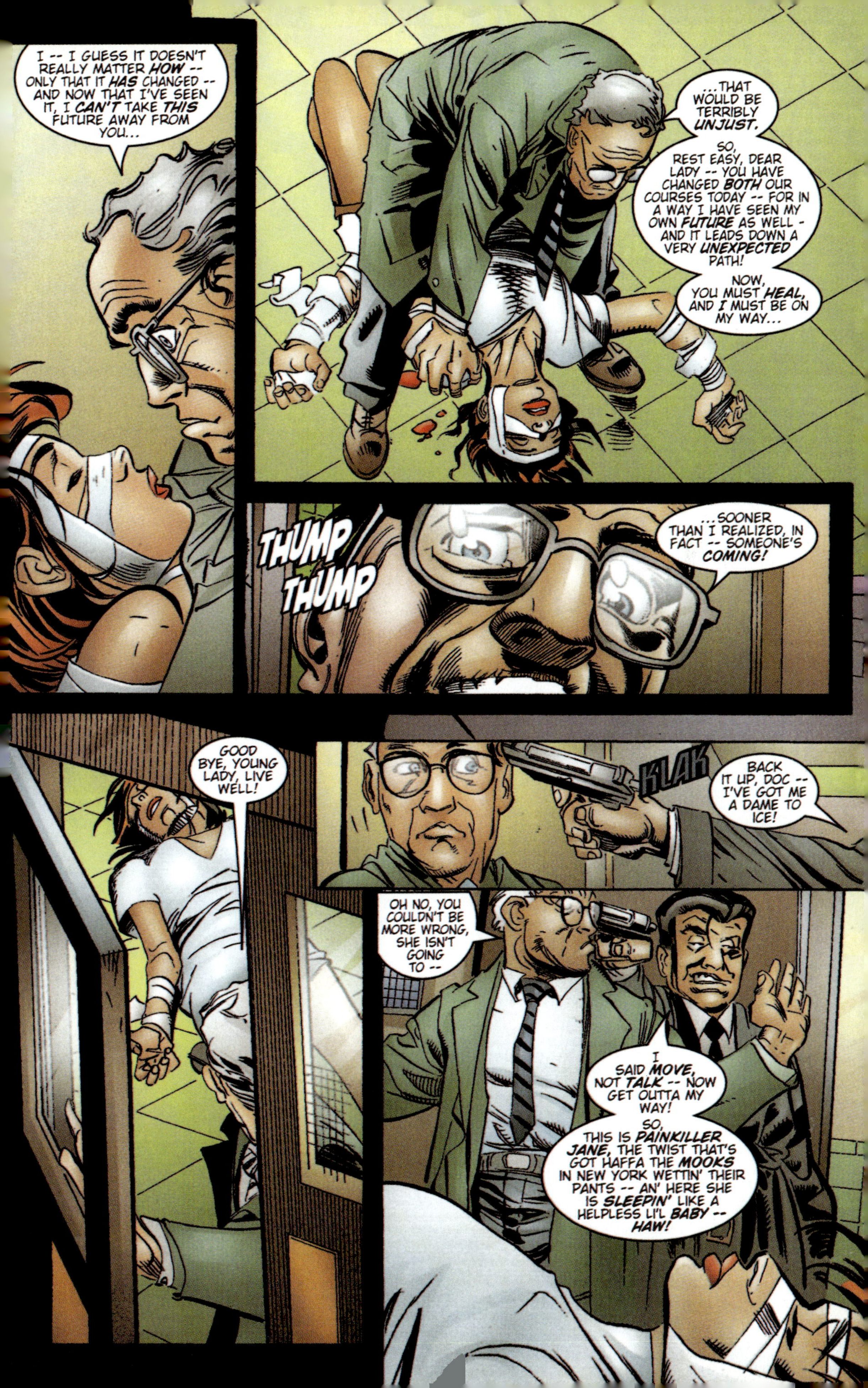
I -- I GUESS IT DOESN'T REALLY MATTER HOW -- ONLY THAT IT HAS CHANGED -- AND NOW THAT I'VE SEEN IT, I CAN'T TAKE THIS FUTURE AWAY FROM YOU...
...THAT WOULD BE TERRIBLY UNJUST.
SO, REST EASY, DEAR LADY -- YOU HAVE CHANGED BOTH OUR COURSES TODAY -- FOR IN A WAY I HAVE SEEN MY OWN FUTURE AS WELL - AND IT LEADS DOWN A VERY UNEXPECTED PATH!
NOW, YOU MUST HEAL, AND I MUST BE ON MY WAY...
THUMP THUMP
...SOONER THAN I REALIZED, IN FACT -- SOMEONE'S COMING!
GOOD BYE, YOUNG LADY, LIVE WELL!
KLAK
BACK IT UP, DOC -- I'VE GOT ME A DAME TO ICE!
OH NO, YOU COULDN'T BE MORE WRONG, SHE ISN'T GOING TO --
I SAID MOVE, NOT TALK -- NOW GET OUTTA MY WAY!
SO, THIS IS PAINKILLER JANE, THE TWIST THAT'S GOT HAFFA THE MOOKS IN NEW YORK WETTIN' THEIR PANTS -- AN' HERE SHE IS SLEEPIN' LIKE A HELPLESS LI'L BABY -- HAW!

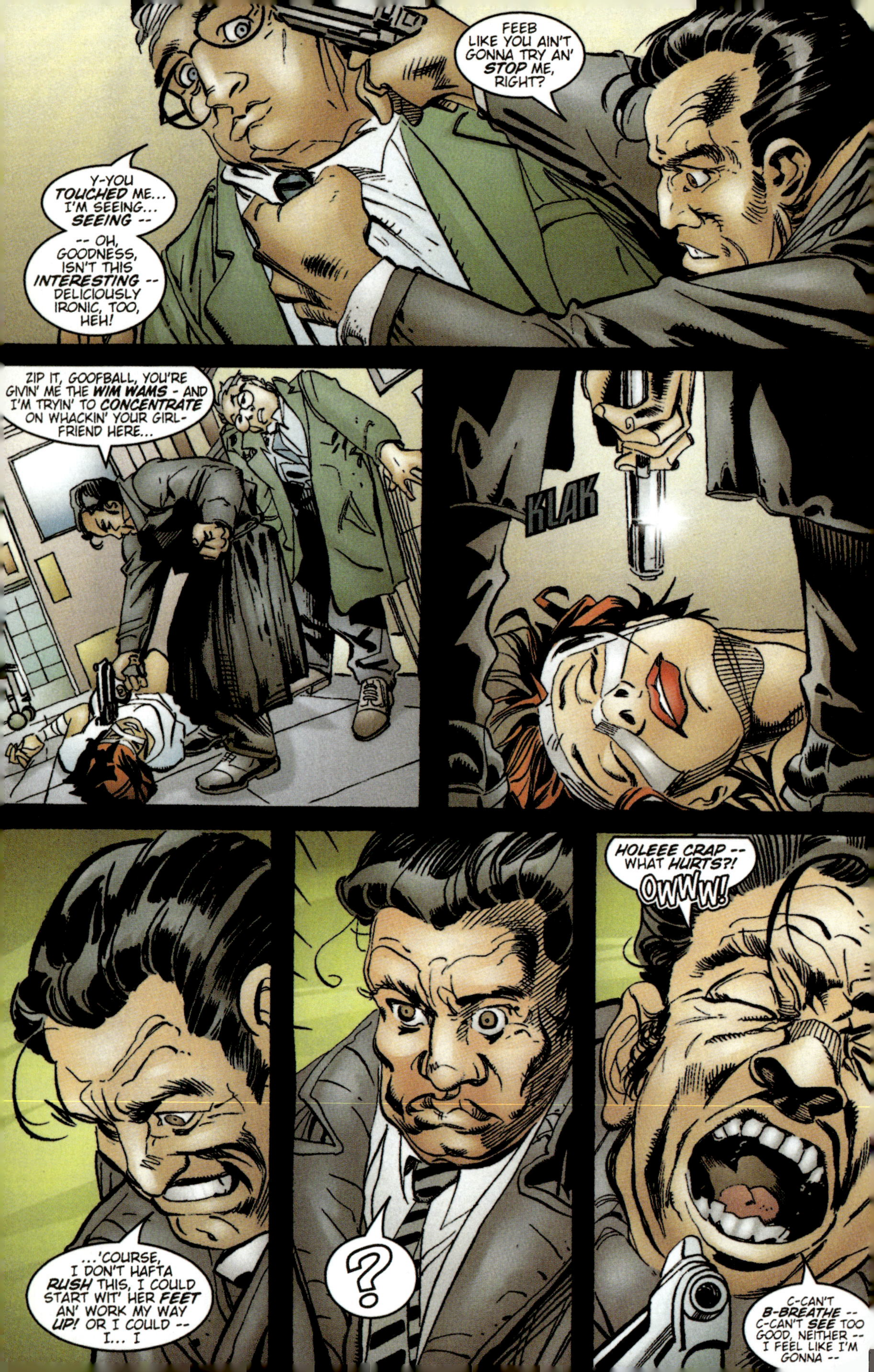
FEEB LIKE YOU AIN'T GONNA TRY AN' STOP ME, RIGHT?
Y-YOU TOUCHED ME... I'M SEEING... SEEING --
-- OH, GOODNESS, ISN'T THIS INTERESTING -- DELICIOUSLY IRONIC, TOO, HEH!
ZIP IT, GOOFBALL, YOU'RE GIVIN' ME THE WIM WAMS - AND I'M TRYIN' TO CONCENTRATE ON WHACKIN' YOUR GIRL-FRIEND HERE...
KLAK
...'COURSE, I DON'T HAFTA RUSH THIS, I COULD START WIT' HER FEET AN' WORK MY WAY UP! OR I COULD -- I... I
?
HOLEEE CRAP -- WHAT HURTS?!
OWWW!
C-CAN'T B-BREATHE -- C-CAN'T SEE TOO GOOD, NEITHER -- I FEEL LIKE I'M GONNA --

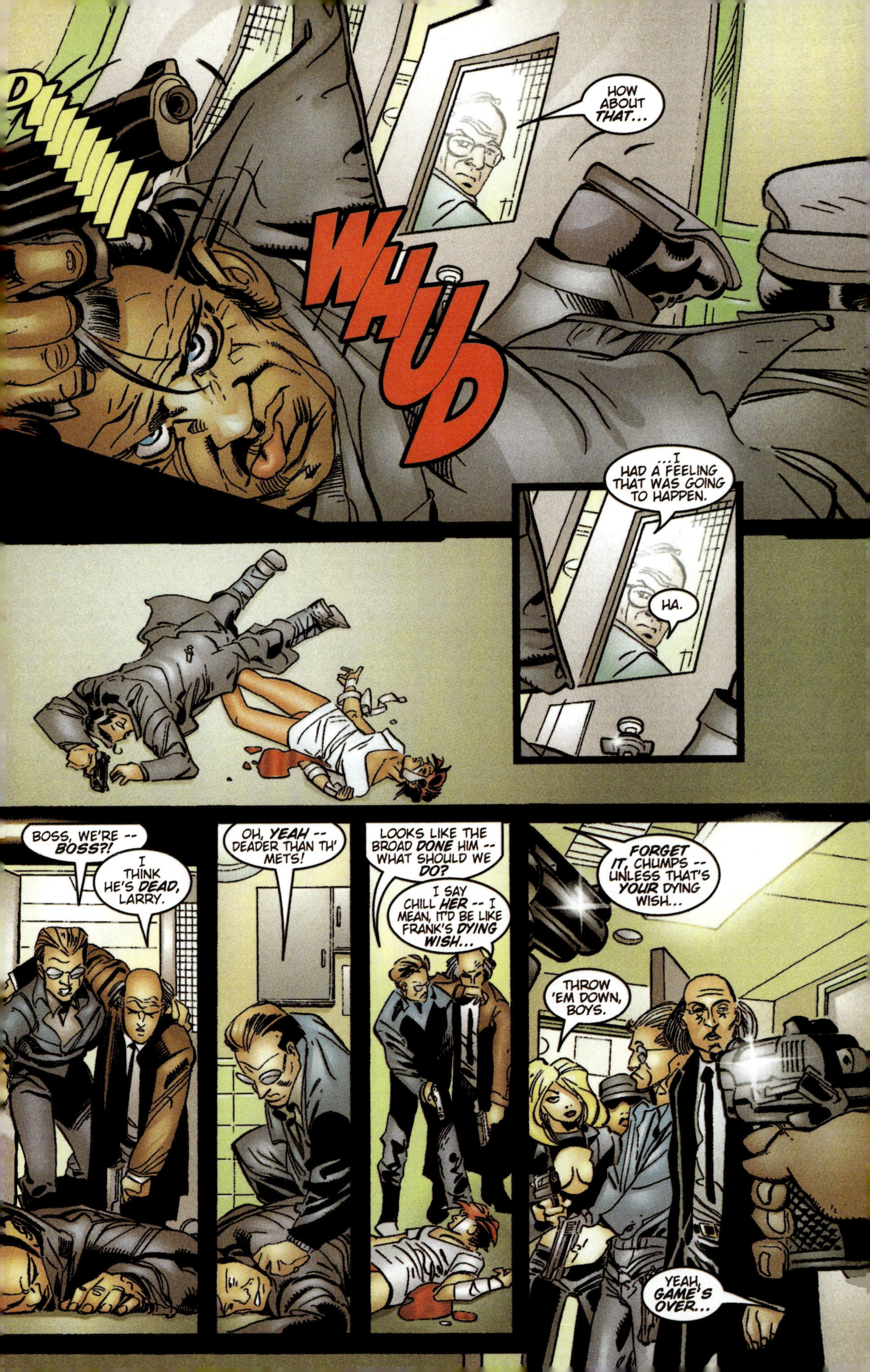
DHHHHHH!!
HOW ABOUT THAT...
WHUD
...I HAD A FEELING THAT WAS GOING TO HAPPEN.
HA.
BOSS, WE'RE -- BOSS?!
I THINK HE'S DEAD, LARRY.
OH, YEAH -- DEADER THAN TH' METS!
LOOKS LIKE THE BROAD DONE HIM -- WHAT SHOULD WE DO?
I SAY CHILL HER -- I MEAN, IT'D BE LIKE FRANK'S DYING WISH...
FORGET IT, CHUMPS -- UNLESS THAT'S YOUR DYING WISH...
THROW 'EM DOWN, BOYS.
YEAH, GAME'S OVER...

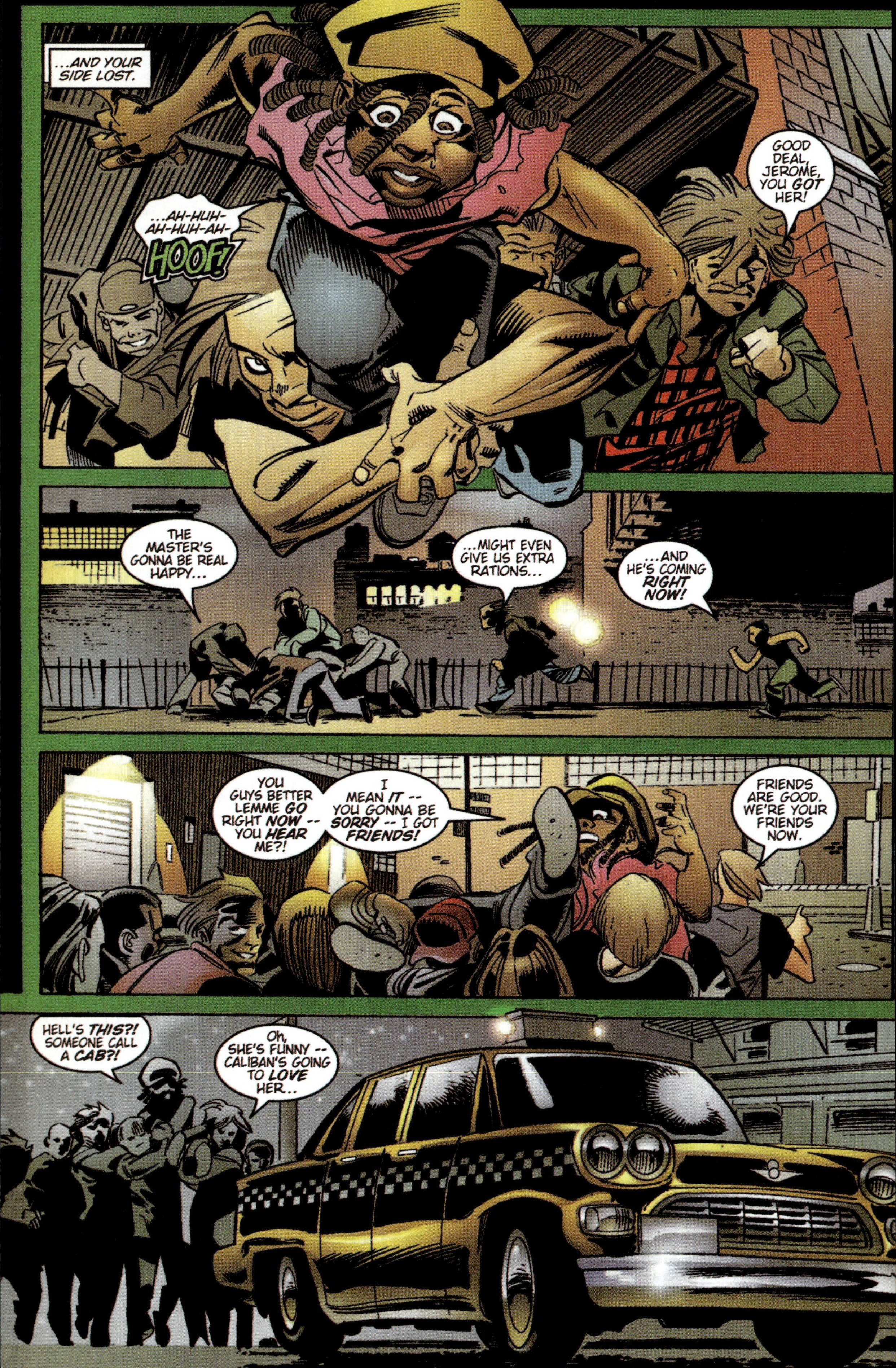
...AND YOUR SIDE LOST.
...AH-HUH-AH-HUH-AH-
HOOF!
GOOD DEAL, JEROME, YOU GOT HER!
THE MASTER'S GONNA BE REAL HAPPY...
...MIGHT EVEN GIVE US EXTRA RATIONS...
...AND HE'S COMING RIGHT NOW!
YOU GUYS BETTER LEMME GO RIGHT NOW -- YOU HEAR ME?!
I MEAN IT -- YOU GONNA BE SORRY -- I GOT FRIENDS!
FRIENDS ARE GOOD. WE'RE YOUR FRIENDS NOW.
HELL'S THIS?! SOMEONE CALL A CAB?!
Oh, SHE'S FUNNY -- CALIBAN'S GOING TO LOVE HER..

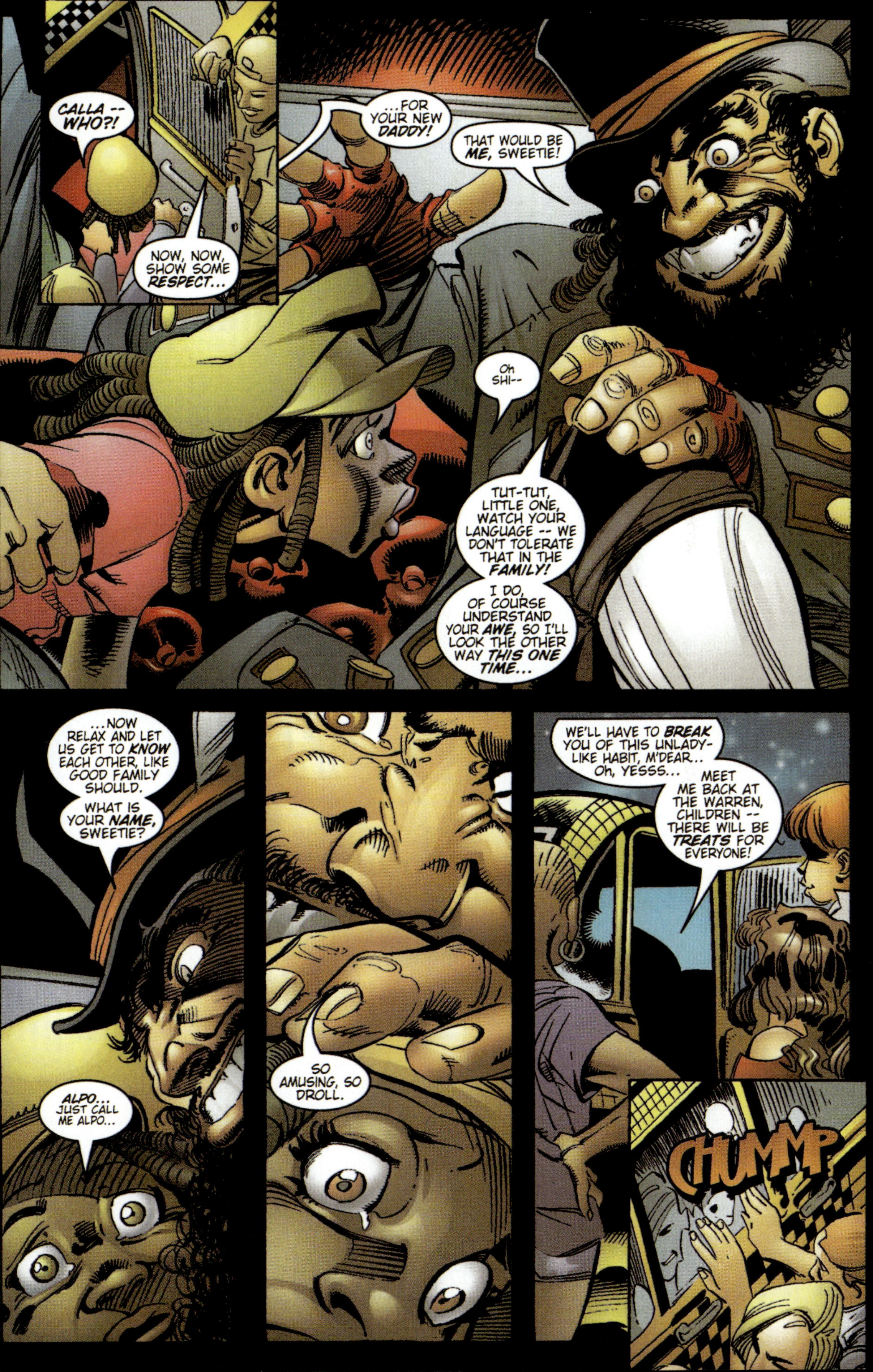
CALLA -- WHO?!
NOW, NOW, SHOW SOME RESPECT...
...FOR YOUR NEW DADDY!
THAT WOULD BE ME, SWEETIE!
Oh SHI--
TUT-TUT, LITTLE ONE, WATCH YOUR LANGUAGE -- WE DON'T TOLERATE THAT IN THE FAMILY!
I DO, OF COURSE UNDERSTAND YOUR AWE, SO I'LL LOOK THE OTHER WAY THIS ONE TIME...
...NOW RELAX AND LET US GET TO KNOW EACH OTHER, LIKE GOOD FAMILY SHOULD.
WHAT IS YOUR NAME, SWEETIE?
ALPO... JUST CALL ME ALPO...
SO AMUSING, SO DROLL.
WE'LL HAVE TO BREAK YOU OF THIS UNLADY-LIKE HABIT, M'DEAR... Oh, YESSS...
MEET ME BACK AT THE WARREN, CHILDREN -- THERE WILL BE TREATS FOR EVERYONE!
CHUMMP

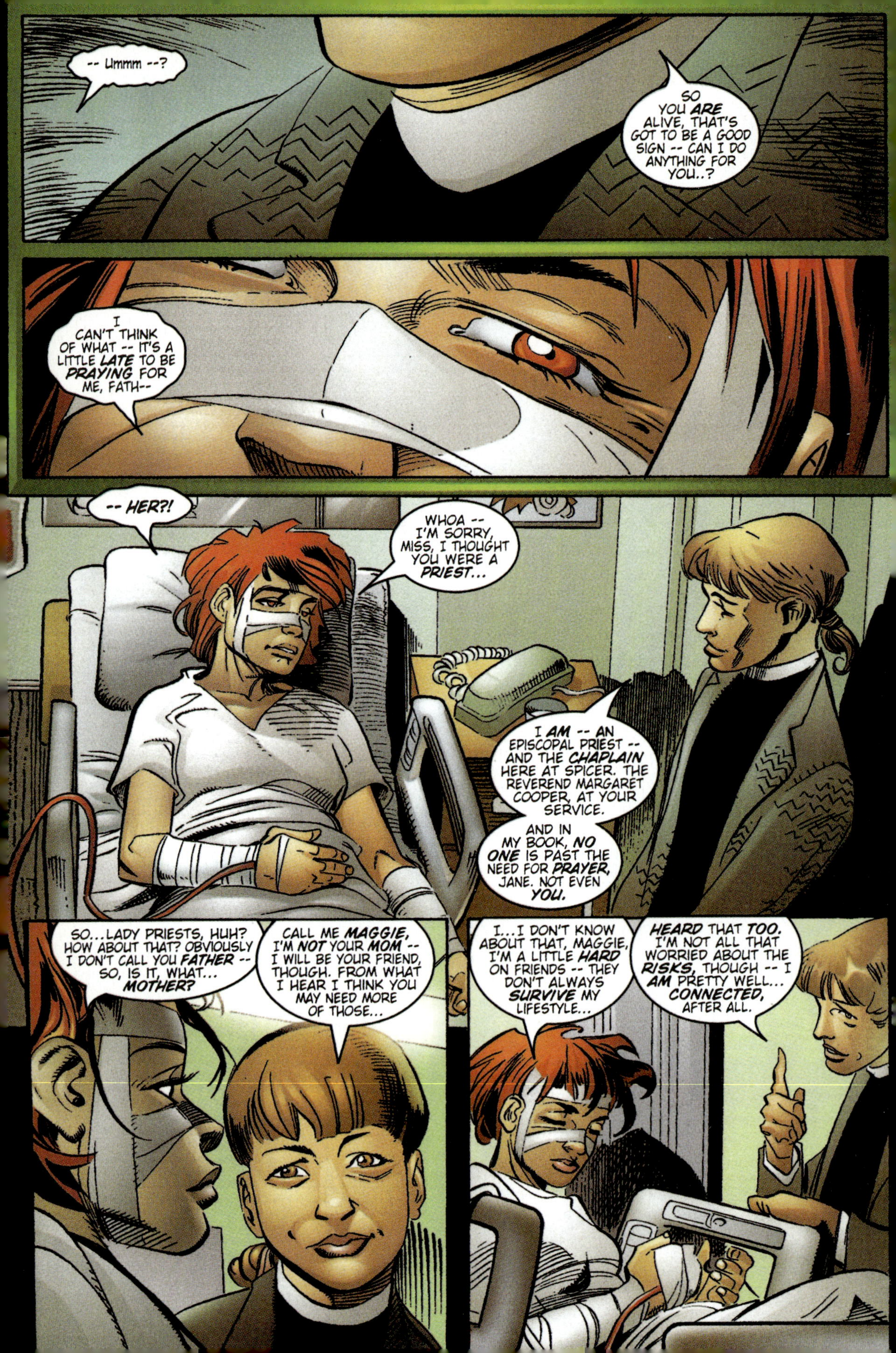
-- Ummm --?
SO YOU ARE ALIVE, THAT'S GOT TO BE A GOOD SIGN -- CAN I DO ANYTHING FOR YOU..?
I CAN'T THINK OF WHAT -- IT'S A LITTLE LATE TO BE PRAYING FOR ME, FATH--
-- HER?!
WHOA -- I'M SORRY, MISS, I THOUGHT YOU WERE A PRIEST...
I AM -- AN EPISCOPAL PRIEST -- AND THE CHAPLAIN HERE AT SPICER. THE REVEREND MARGARET COOPER, AT YOUR SERVICE.
AND IN MY BOOK, NO ONE IS PAST THE NEED FOR PRAYER, JANE. NOT EVEN YOU.
SO...LADY PRIESTS, HUH? HOW ABOUT THAT? OBVIOUSLY I DON'T CALL YOU FATHER -- SO, IS IT, WHAT... MOTHER?
CALL ME MAGGIE, I'M NOT YOUR MOM -- I WILL BE YOUR FRIEND, THOUGH. FROM WHAT I HEAR I THINK YOU MAY NEED MORE OF THOSE...
I...I DON'T KNOW ABOUT THAT, MAGGIE, I'M A LITTLE HARD ON FRIENDS -- THEY DON'T ALWAYS SURVIVE MY LIFESTYLE...
HEARD THAT TOO. I'M NOT ALL THAT WORRIED ABOUT THE RISKS, THOUGH -- I AM PRETTY WELL... CONNECTED, AFTER ALL.

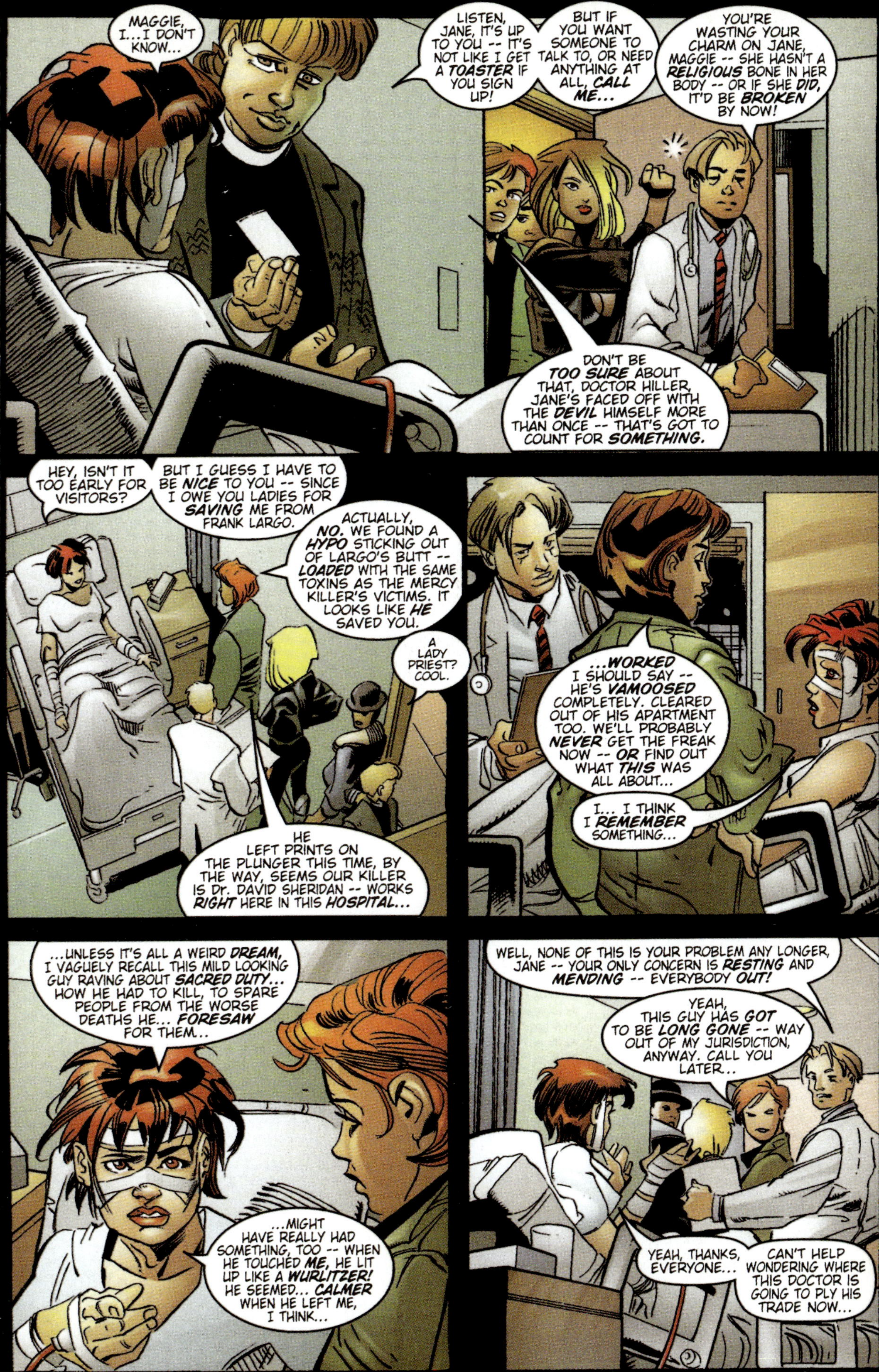
MAGGIE, I... I DON'T KNOW...
LISTEN, JANE, IT'S UP TO YOU -- IT'S NOT LIKE I GET A TOASTER IF YOU SIGN UP!
BUT IF YOU WANT SOMEONE TO TALK TO, OR NEED ANYTHING AT ALL, CALL ME...
YOU'RE WASTING YOUR CHARM ON JANE, MAGGIE -- SHE HASN'T A RELIGIOUS BONE IN HER BODY -- OR IF SHE DID, IT'D BE BROKEN BY NOW!
DON'T BE TOO SURE ABOUT THAT, DOCTOR HILLER. JANE'S FACED OFF WITH THE DEVIL HIMSELF MORE THAN ONCE -- THAT'S GOT TO COUNT FOR SOMETHING.
HEY, ISN'T IT TOO EARLY FOR VISITORS?
BUT I GUESS I HAVE TO BE NICE TO YOU -- SINCE I OWE YOU LADIES FOR SAVING ME FROM FRANK LARGO.
ACTUALLY, NO. WE FOUND A HYPO STICKING OUT OF LARGO'S BUTT -- LOADED WITH THE SAME TOXINS AS THE MERCY KILLER'S VICTIMS. IT LOOKS LIKE HE SAVED YOU.
A LADY PRIEST? COOL.
HE LEFT PRINTS ON THE PLUNGER THIS TIME, BY THE WAY, SEEMS OUR KILLER IS Dr. DAVID SHERIDAN -- WORKS RIGHT HERE IN THIS HOSPITAL...
...WORKED I SHOULD SAY -- HE'S VAMOOSED COMPLETELY. CLEARED OUT OF HIS APARTMENT TOO. WE'LL PROBABLY NEVER GET THE FREAK NOW -- OR FIND OUT WHAT THIS WAS ALL ABOUT...
I... I THINK I REMEMBER SOMETHING...
...UNLESS IT'S ALL A WEIRD DREAM, I VAGUELY RECALL THIS MILD LOOKING GUY RAVING ABOUT SACRED DUTY... HOW HE HAD TO KILL, TO SPARE PEOPLE FROM THE WORSE DEATHS HE... FORESAW FOR THEM...
...MIGHT HAVE REALLY HAD SOMETHING, TOO -- WHEN HE TOUCHED ME, HE LIT UP LIKE A WURLITZER! HE SEEMED... CALMER WHEN HE LEFT ME, I THINK...
WELL, NONE OF THIS IS YOUR PROBLEM ANY LONGER, JANE -- YOUR ONLY CONCERN IS RESTING AND MENDING -- EVERYBODY OUT!
YEAH, THIS GUY HAS GOT TO BE LONG GONE -- WAY OUT OF MY JURISDICTION, ANYWAY. CALL YOU LATER...
YEAH, THANKS, EVERYONE...
CAN'T HELP WONDERING WHERE THIS DOCTOR IS GOING TO PLY HIS TRADE NOW...

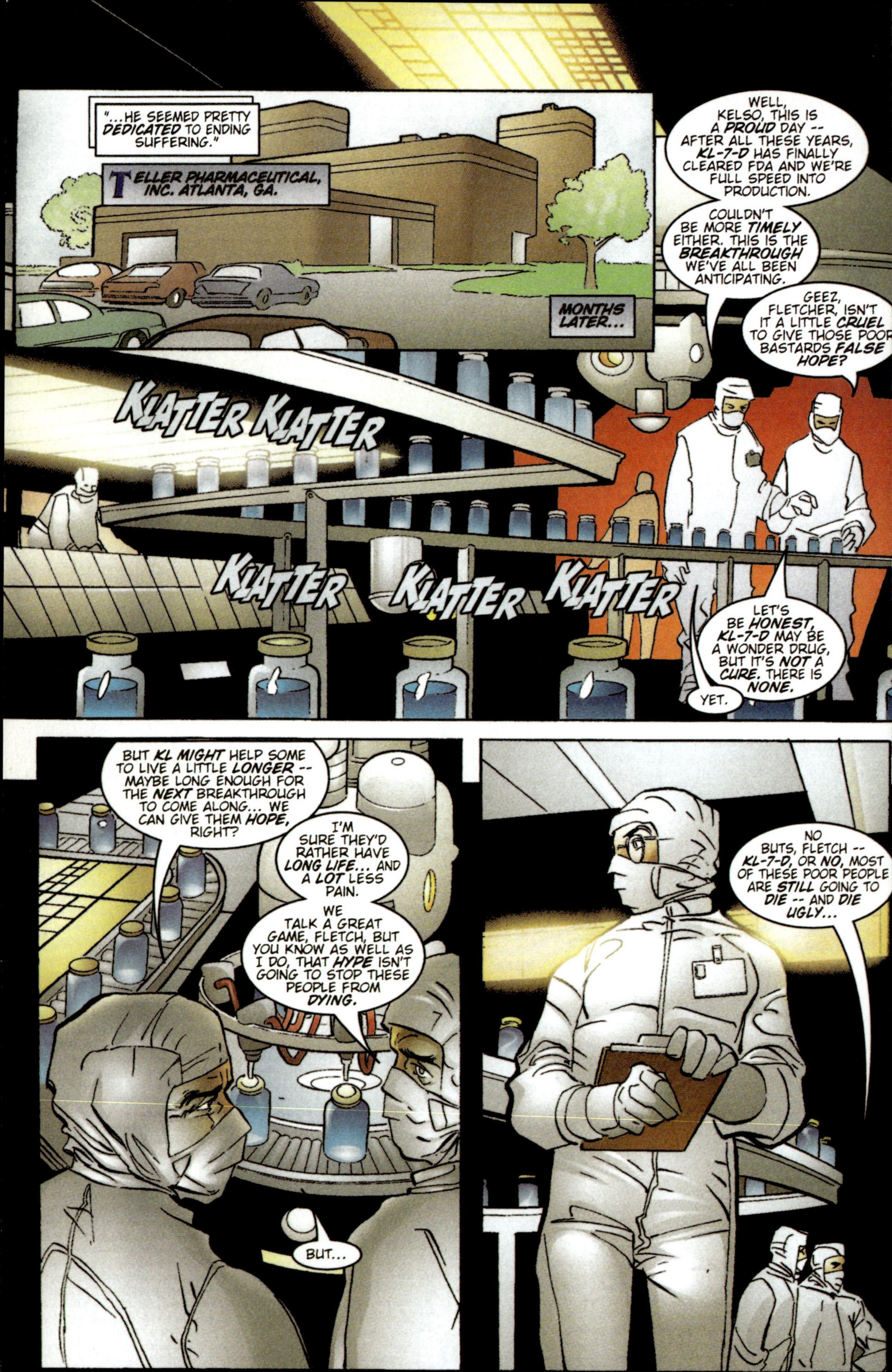
"...HE SEEMED PRETTY DEDICATED TO ENDING SUFFERING."
TELLER PHARMACEUTICAL, INC. ATLANTA, GA.
MONTHS LATER...
WELL, KELSO, THIS IS A PROUD DAY -- AFTER ALL THESE YEARS, KL-7-D HAS FINALLY CLEARED FDA AND WE'RE FULL SPEED INTO PRODUCTION.
COULDN'T BE MORE TIMELY EITHER. THIS IS THE BREAKTHROUGH WE'VE ALL BEEN ANTICIPATING.
GEEZ, FLETCHER, ISN'T IT A LITTLE CRUEL TO GIVE THOSE POOR BASTARDS FALSE HOPE?
KLATTER KLATTER
KLATTER KLATTER KLATTER
LET'S BE HONEST, KL-7-D MAY BE A WONDER DRUG, BUT IT'S NOT A CURE. THERE IS NONE.
YET.
BUT KL MIGHT HELP SOME TO LIVE A LITTLE LONGER -- MAYBE LONG ENOUGH FOR THE NEXT BREAKTHROUGH TO COME ALONG... WE CAN GIVE THEM HOPE, RIGHT?
I'M SURE THEY'D RATHER HAVE LONG LIFE... AND A LOT LESS PAIN.
WE TALK A GREAT GAME, FLETCH, BUT YOU KNOW AS WELL AS I DO, THAT HYPE ISN'T GOING TO STOP THESE PEOPLE FROM DYING.
BUT...
NO BUTS, FLETCH -- KL-7-D, OR NO, MOST OF THESE POOR PEOPLE ARE STILL GOING TO DIE -- AND DIE UGLY...

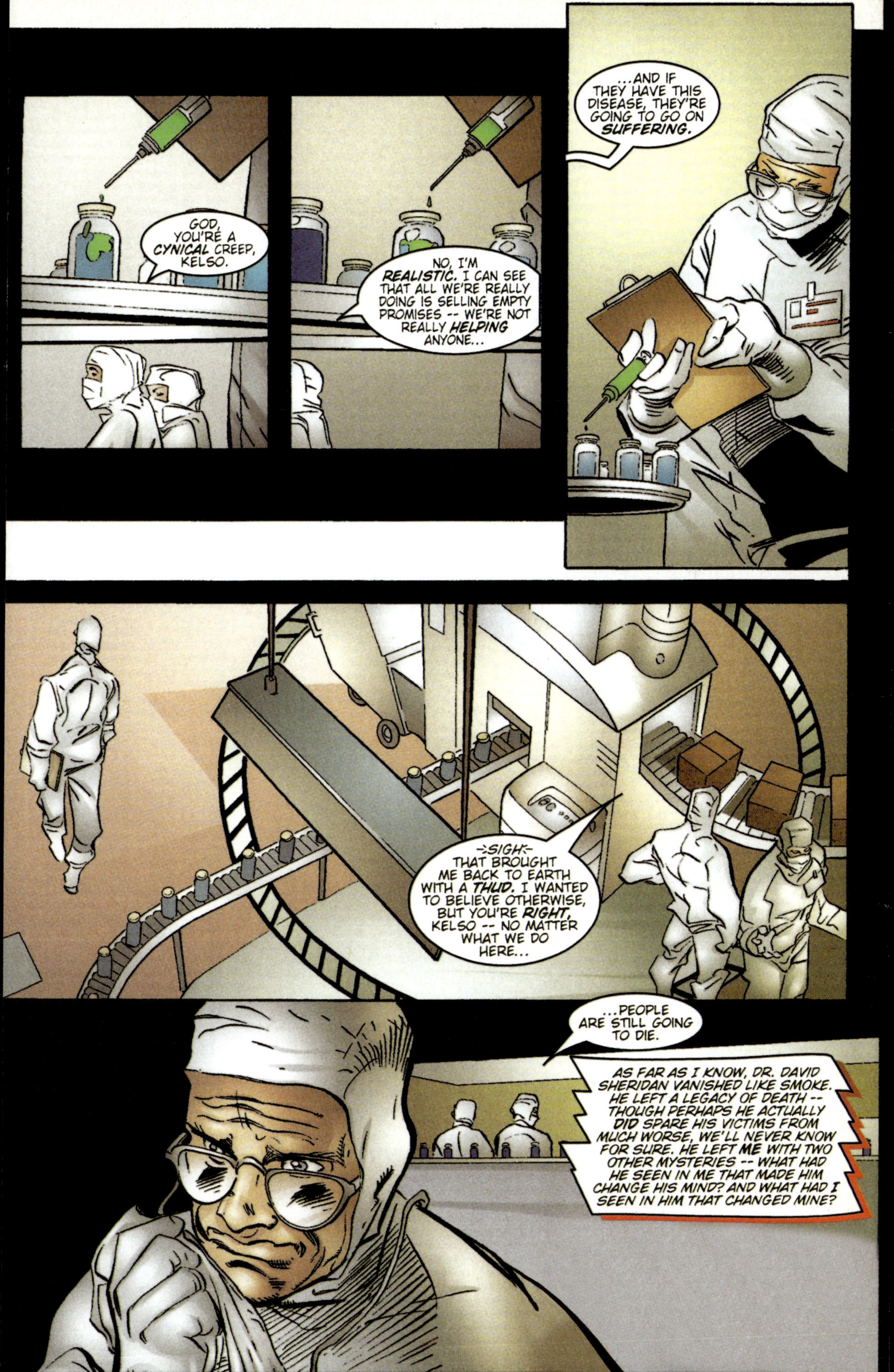
GOD, YOU'RE A CYNICAL CREEP, KELSO.
NO, I'M REALISTIC. I CAN SEE THAT ALL WE'RE REALLY DOING IS SELLING EMPTY PROMISES -- WE'RE NOT REALLY HELPING ANYONE...
...AND IF THEY HAVE THIS DISEASE, THEY'RE GOING TO GO ON SUFFERING.
-SIGH- THAT BROUGHT ME BACK TO EARTH WITH A THUD. I WANTED TO BELIEVE OTHERWISE, BUT YOU'RE RIGHT, KELSO -- NO MATTER WHAT WE DO HERE...
...PEOPLE ARE STILL GOING TO DIE.
AS FAR AS I KNOW, DR. DAVID SHERIDAN VANISHED LIKE SMOKE. HE LEFT A LEGACY OF DEATH -- THOUGH PERHAPS HE ACTUALLY DID SPARE HIS VICTIMS FROM MUCH WORSE, WE'LL NEVER KNOW FOR SURE. HE LEFT ME WITH TWO OTHER MYSTERIES -- WHAT HAD HE SEEN IN ME THAT MADE HIM CHANGE HIS MIND? AND WHAT HAD I SEEN IN HIM THAT CHANGED MINE?

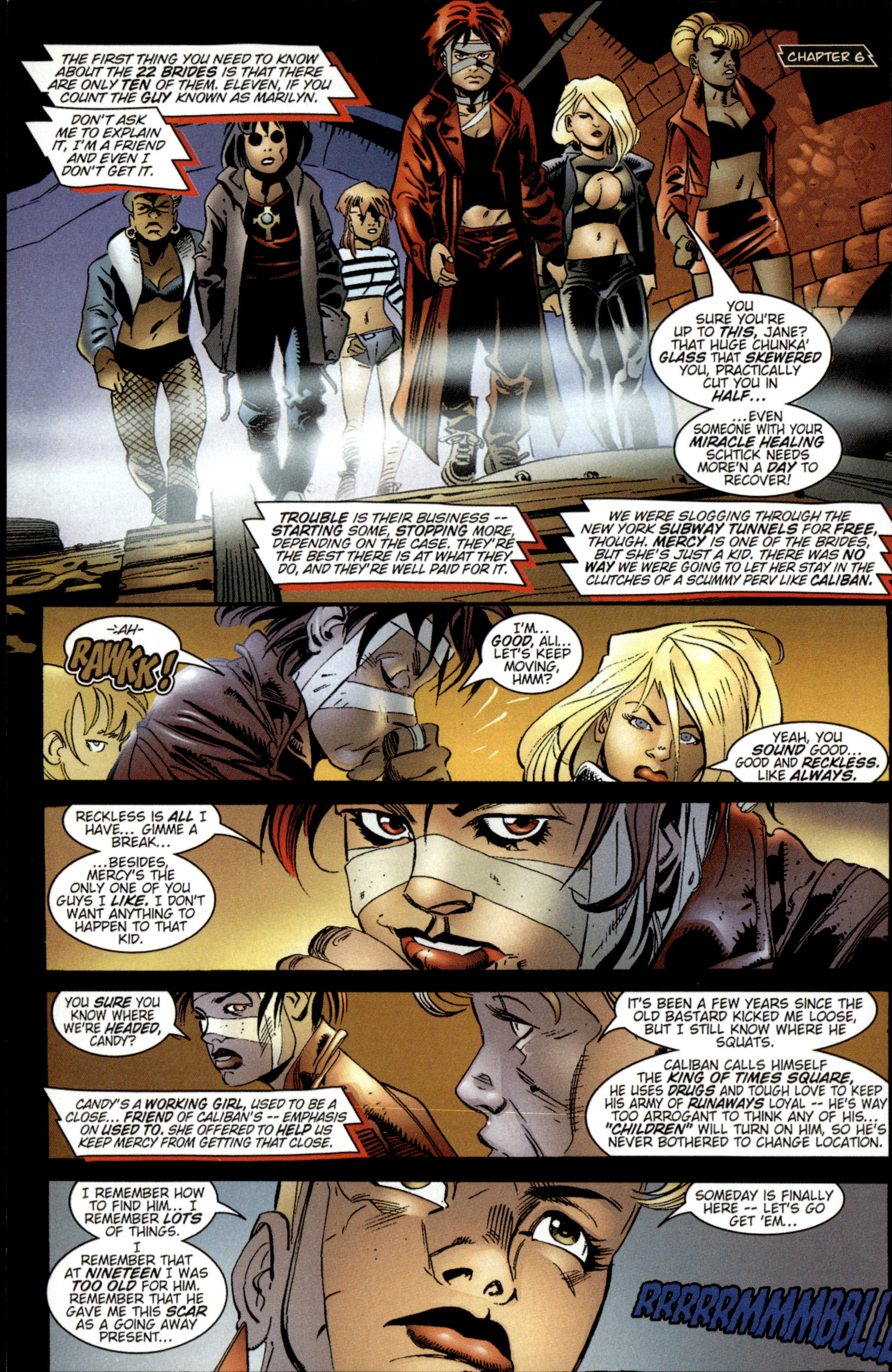
CHAPTER 6
THE FIRST THING YOU NEED TO KNOW ABOUT THE 22 BRIDES IS THAT THERE ARE ONLY TEN OF THEM. ELEVEN, IF YOU COUNT THE GUY KNOWN AS MARILYN.
DON'T ASK ME TO EXPLAIN IT, I'M A FRIEND AND EVEN I DON'T GET IT.
YOU SURE YOU'RE UP TO THIS, JANE? THAT HUGE CHUNKA' GLASS THAT SKEWERED YOU, PRACTICALLY CUT YOU IN HALF...
...EVEN SOMEONE WITH YOUR MIRACLE HEALING SCHTICK NEEDS MORE'N A DAY TO RECOVER!
TROUBLE IS THEIR BUSINESS -- STARTING SOME, STOPPING MORE, DEPENDING ON THE CASE. THEY'RE THE BEST THERE IS AT WHAT THEY DO, AND THEY'RE WELL PAID FOR IT.
WE WERE SLOGGING THROUGH THE NEW YORK SUBWAY TUNNELS FOR FREE, THOUGH. MERCY IS ONE OF THE BRIDES, BUT SHE'S JUST A KID. THERE WAS NO WAY WE WERE GOING TO LET HER STAY IN THE CLUTCHES OF A SCUMMY PERV LIKE CALIBAN.
-AH-
RAWKK!
I'M... GOOD, ALL... LET'S KEEP MOVING, HMM?
YEAH, YOU SOUND GOOD... GOOD AND RECKLESS. LIKE ALWAYS.
RECKLESS IS ALL I HAVE... GIMME A BREAK...
...BESIDES, MERCY'S THE ONLY ONE OF YOU GUYS I LIKE. I DON'T WANT ANYTHING TO HAPPEN TO THAT KID.
YOU SURE YOU KNOW WHERE WE'RE HEADED, CANDY?
IT'S BEEN A FEW YEARS SINCE THE OLD BASTARD KICKED ME LOOSE, BUT I STILL KNOW WHERE HE SQUATS.
CALIBAN CALLS HIMSELF THE KING OF TIMES SQUARE. HE USES DRUGS AND TOUGH LOVE TO KEEP HIS ARMY OF RUNAWAYS LOYAL -- HE'S WAY TOO ARROGANT TO THINK ANY OF HIS... "CHILDREN" WILL TURN ON HIM, SO HE'S NEVER BOTHERED TO CHANGE LOCATION.
CANDY'S A WORKING GIRL, USED TO BE A CLOSE... FRIEND OF CALIBAN'S -- EMPHASIS ON USED TO. SHE OFFERED TO HELP US KEEP MERCY FROM GETTING THAT CLOSE.
I REMEMBER HOW TO FIND HIM... I REMEMBER LOTS OF THINGS.
I REMEMBER THAT AT NINETEEN I WAS TOO OLD FOR HIM. REMEMBER THAT HE GAVE ME THIS SCAR AS A GOING AWAY PRESENT...
SOMEDAY IS FINALLY HERE -- LET'S GO GET 'EM...
RRRRRRMMMMBBLL

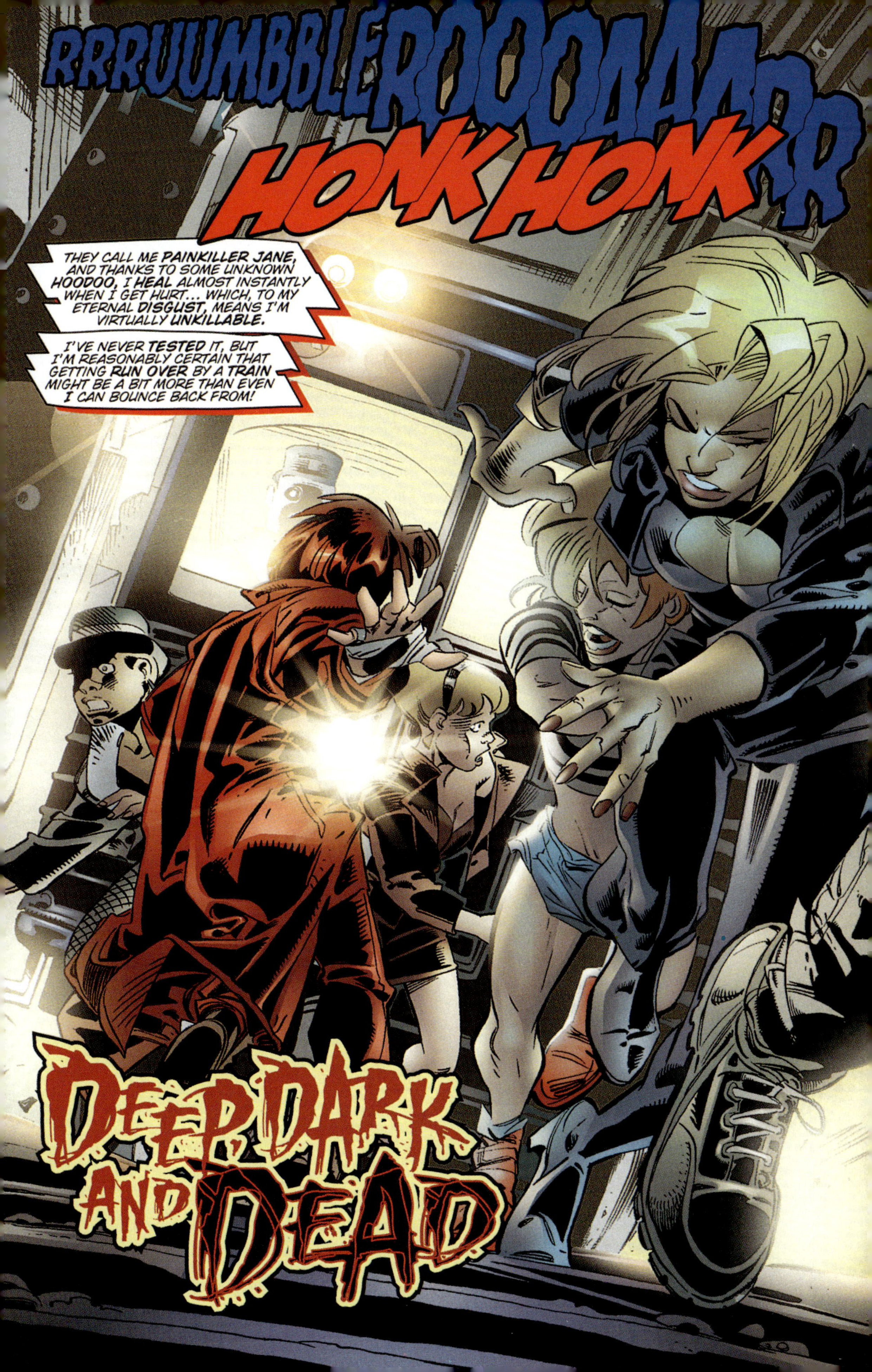
RRRUUMBBLE ROOOAAARR
HONK HONK
THEY CALL ME PAINKILLER JANE, AND THANKS TO SOME UNKNOWN HOODOO, I HEAL ALMOST INSTANTLY WHEN I GET HURT... WHICH, TO MY ETERNAL DISGUST, MEANS I'M VIRTUALLY UNKILLABLE.
I'VE NEVER TESTED IT, BUT I'M REASONABLY CERTAIN THAT GETTING RUN OVER BY A TRAIN MIGHT BE A BIT MORE THAN EVEN I CAN BOUNCE BACK FROM!
DEEP DARK AND DEAD

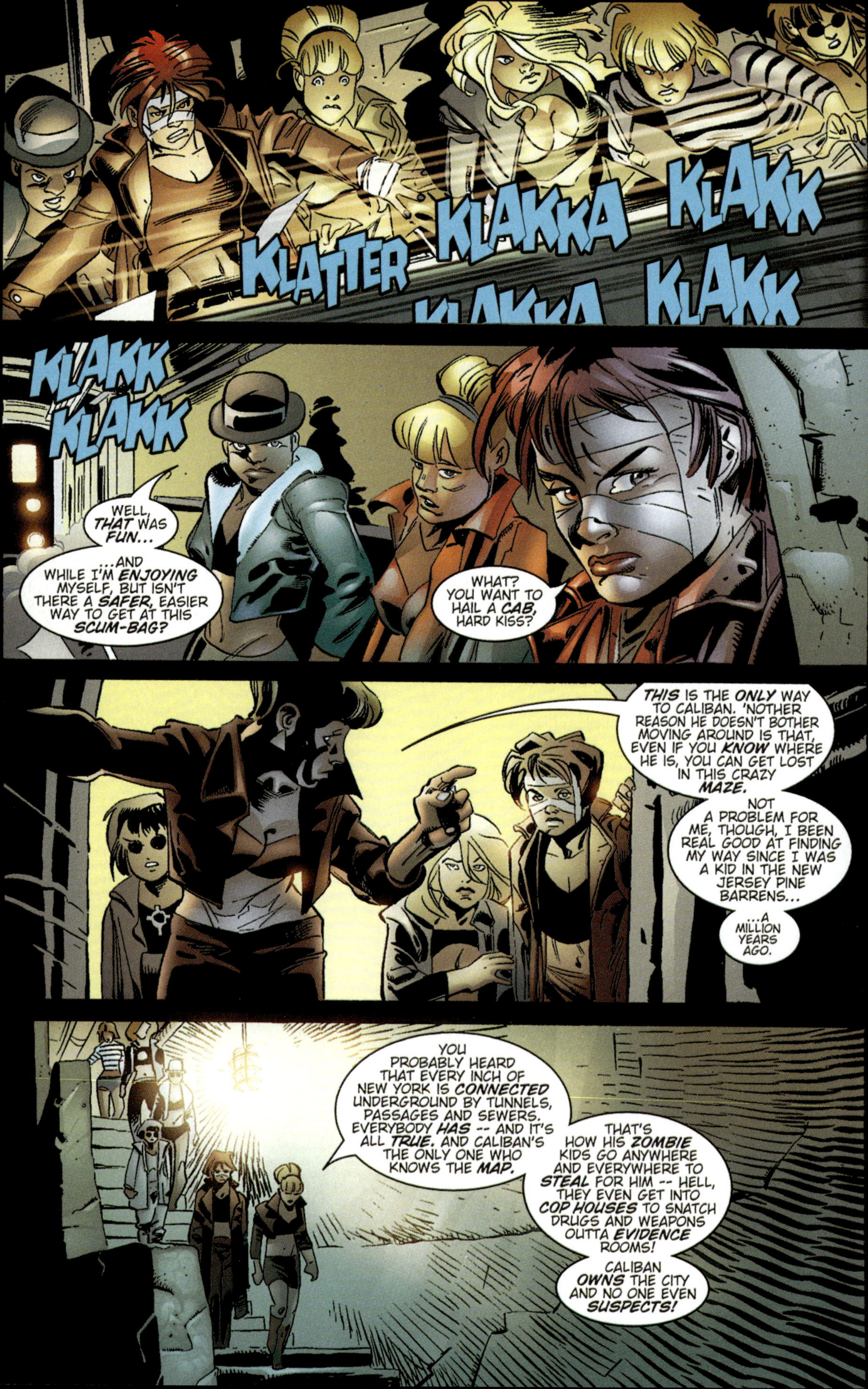
KLATTER KLAKKA KLAKK
KLAKKA KLAKK
KLAKK KLAKK
WELL, THAT WAS FUN...
...AND WHILE I'M ENJOYING MYSELF, BUT ISN'T THERE A SAFER, EASIER WAY TO GET AT THIS SCUM-BAG?
WHAT? YOU WANT TO HAIL A CAB, HARD KISS?
THIS IS THE ONLY WAY TO CALIBAN. 'NOTHER REASON HE DOESN'T BOTHER MOVING AROUND IS THAT, EVEN IF YOU KNOW WHERE HE IS, YOU CAN GET LOST IN THIS CRAZY MAZE.
NOT A PROBLEM FOR ME, THOUGH, I BEEN REAL GOOD AT FINDING MY WAY SINCE I WAS A KID IN THE NEW JERSEY PINE BARRENS...
...A MILLION YEARS AGO.
YOU PROBABLY HEARD THAT EVERY INCH OF NEW YORK IS CONNECTED UNDERGROUND BY TUNNELS, PASSAGES AND SEWERS. EVERYBODY HAS -- AND IT'S ALL TRUE. AND CALIBAN'S THE ONLY ONE WHO KNOWS THE MAP.
THAT'S HOW HIS ZOMBIE KIDS GO ANYWHERE AND EVERYWHERE TO STEAL FOR HIM -- HELL, THEY EVEN GET INTO COP HOUSES TO SNATCH DRUGS AND WEAPONS OUTTA EVIDENCE ROOMS!
CALIBAN OWNS THE CITY AND NO ONE EVEN SUSPECTS!

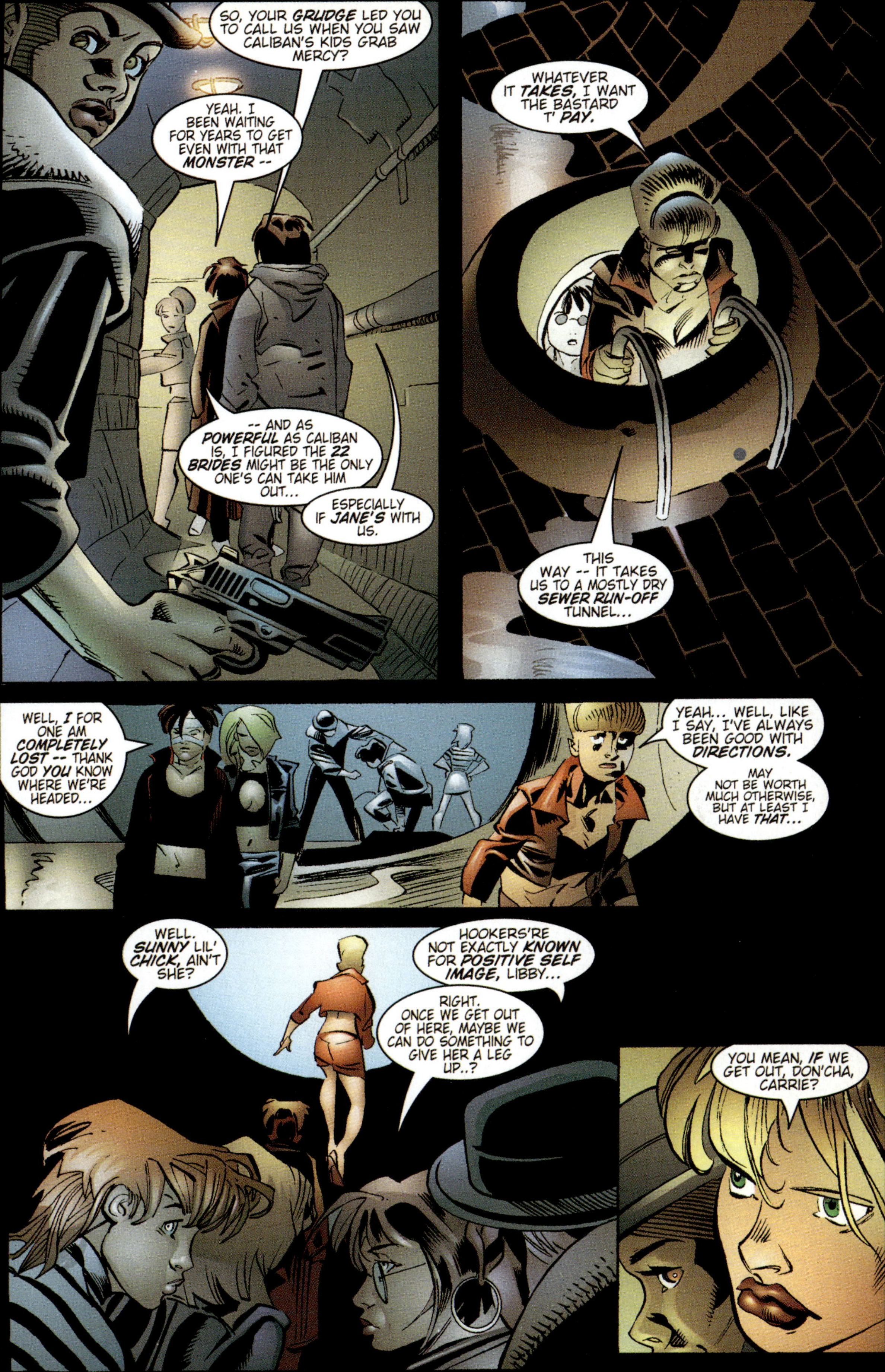
SO, YOUR GRUDGE LED YOU TO CALL US WHEN YOU SAW CALIBAN'S KIDS GRAB MERCY?
YEAH. I BEEN WAITING FOR YEARS TO GET EVEN WITH THAT MONSTER --
-- AND AS POWERFUL AS CALIBAN IS, I FIGURED THE 22 BRIDES MIGHT BE THE ONLY ONE'S CAN TAKE HIM OUT...
ESPECIALLY IF JANE'S WITH US.
WHATEVER IT TAKES, I WANT THE BASTARD T' PAY.
THIS WAY -- IT TAKES US TO A MOSTLY DRY SEWER RUN-OFF TUNNEL...
WELL, I FOR ONE AM COMPLETELY LOST -- THANK GOD YOU KNOW WHERE WE'RE HEADED...
YEAH... WELL, LIKE I SAY, I'VE ALWAYS BEEN GOOD WITH DIRECTIONS.
MAY NOT BE WORTH MUCH OTHERWISE, BUT AT LEAST I HAVE THAT...
WELL. SUNNY LIL' CHICK, AIN'T SHE?
HOOKERS'RE NOT EXACTLY KNOWN FOR POSITIVE SELF IMAGE, LIBBY...
RIGHT. ONCE WE GET OUT OF HERE, MAYBE WE CAN DO SOMETHING TO GIVE HER A LEG UP..?
YOU MEAN, IF WE GET OUT, DON'CHA, CARRIE?

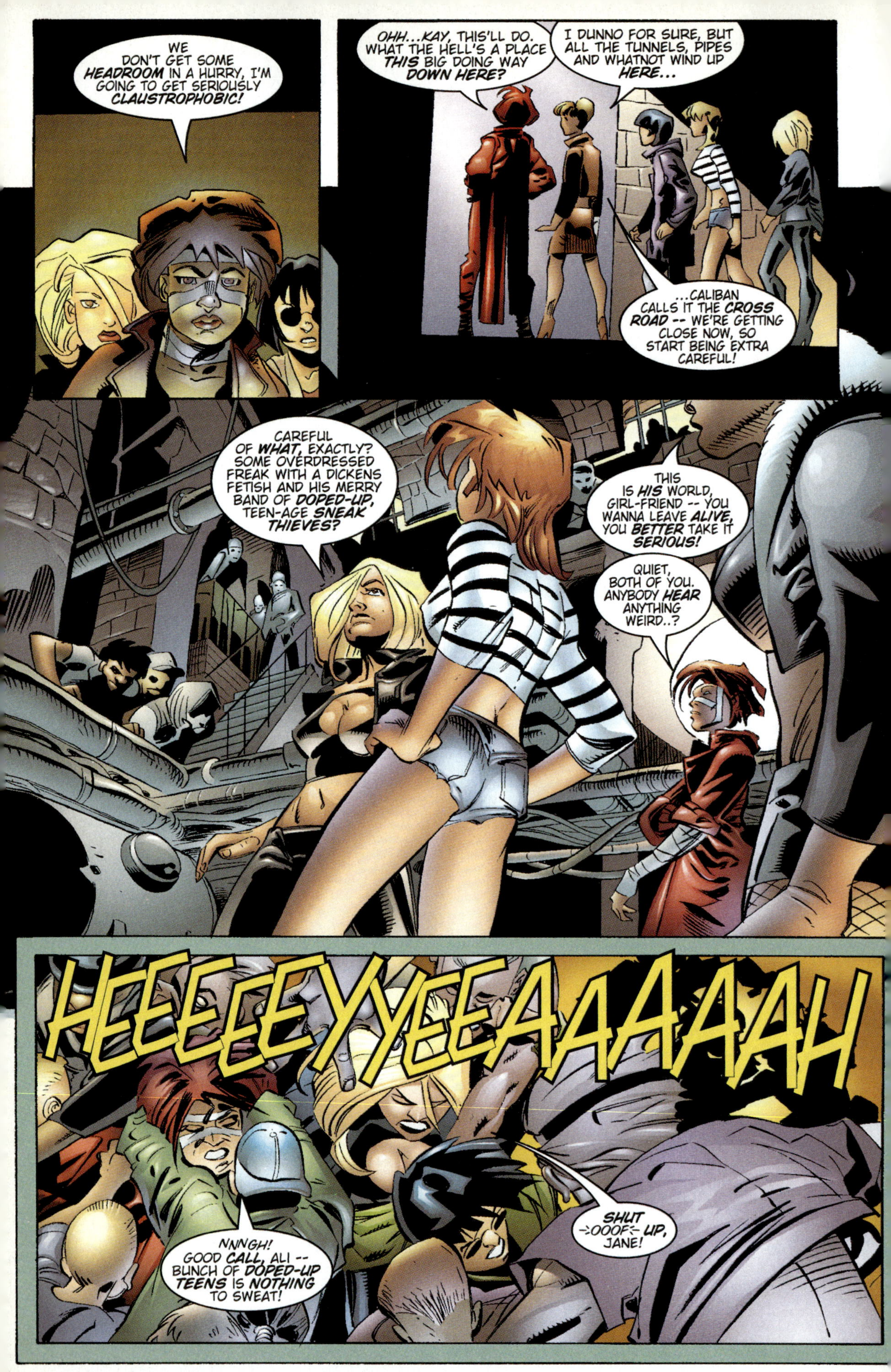
WE DON'T GET SOME HEADROOM IN A HURRY, I'M GOING TO GET SERIOUSLY CLAUSTROPHOBIC!
OHH...KAY, THIS'LL DO. WHAT THE HELL'S A PLACE THIS BIG DOING WAY DOWN HERE?
I DUNNO FOR SURE, BUT ALL THE TUNNELS, PIPES AND WHATNOT WIND UP HERE...
...CALIBAN CALLS IT THE CROSS ROAD -- WE'RE GETTING CLOSE NOW, SO START BEING EXTRA CAREFUL!
CAREFUL OF WHAT, EXACTLY? SOME OVERDRESSED FREAK WITH A DICKENS FETISH AND HIS MERRY BAND OF DOPED-UP, TEEN-AGE SNEAK THIEVES?
THIS IS HIS WORLD, GIRL-FRIEND -- YOU WANNA LEAVE ALIVE, YOU BETTER TAKE IT SERIOUS!
QUIET, BOTH OF YOU. ANYBODY HEAR ANYTHING WEIRD..?
HEEEEEYYEEAAAAAH
NNNGH! GOOD CALL, ALI -- BUNCH OF DOPED-UP TEENS IS NOTHING TO SWEAT!
SHUT -OOOF- UP, JANE!

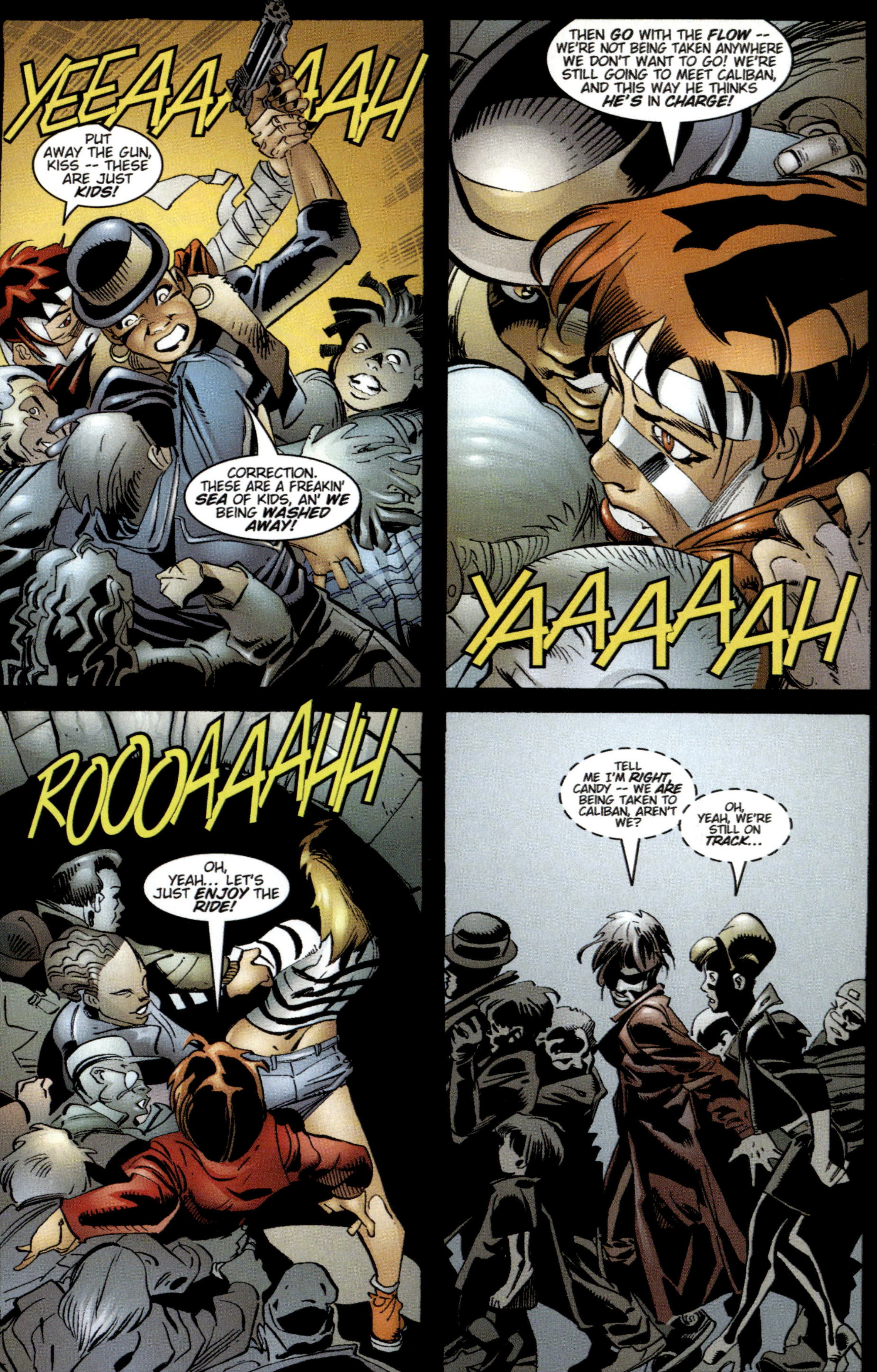
YEEAAAAAH
PUT AWAY THE GUN, KISS -- THESE ARE JUST KIDS!
CORRECTION. THESE ARE A FREAKIN' SEA OF KIDS, AN' WE BEING WASHED AWAY!
THEN GO WITH THE FLOW -- WE'RE NOT BEING TAKEN ANYWHERE WE DON'T WANT TO GO! WE'RE STILL GOING TO MEET CALIBAN, AND THIS WAY HE THINKS HE'S IN CHARGE!
YAAAAAH
ROOOAAAAHH
OH, YEAH... LET'S JUST ENJOY THE RIDE!
TELL ME I'M RIGHT, CANDY -- WE ARE BEING TAKEN TO CALIBAN, AREN'T WE?
OH, YEAH, WE'RE STILL ON TRACK...

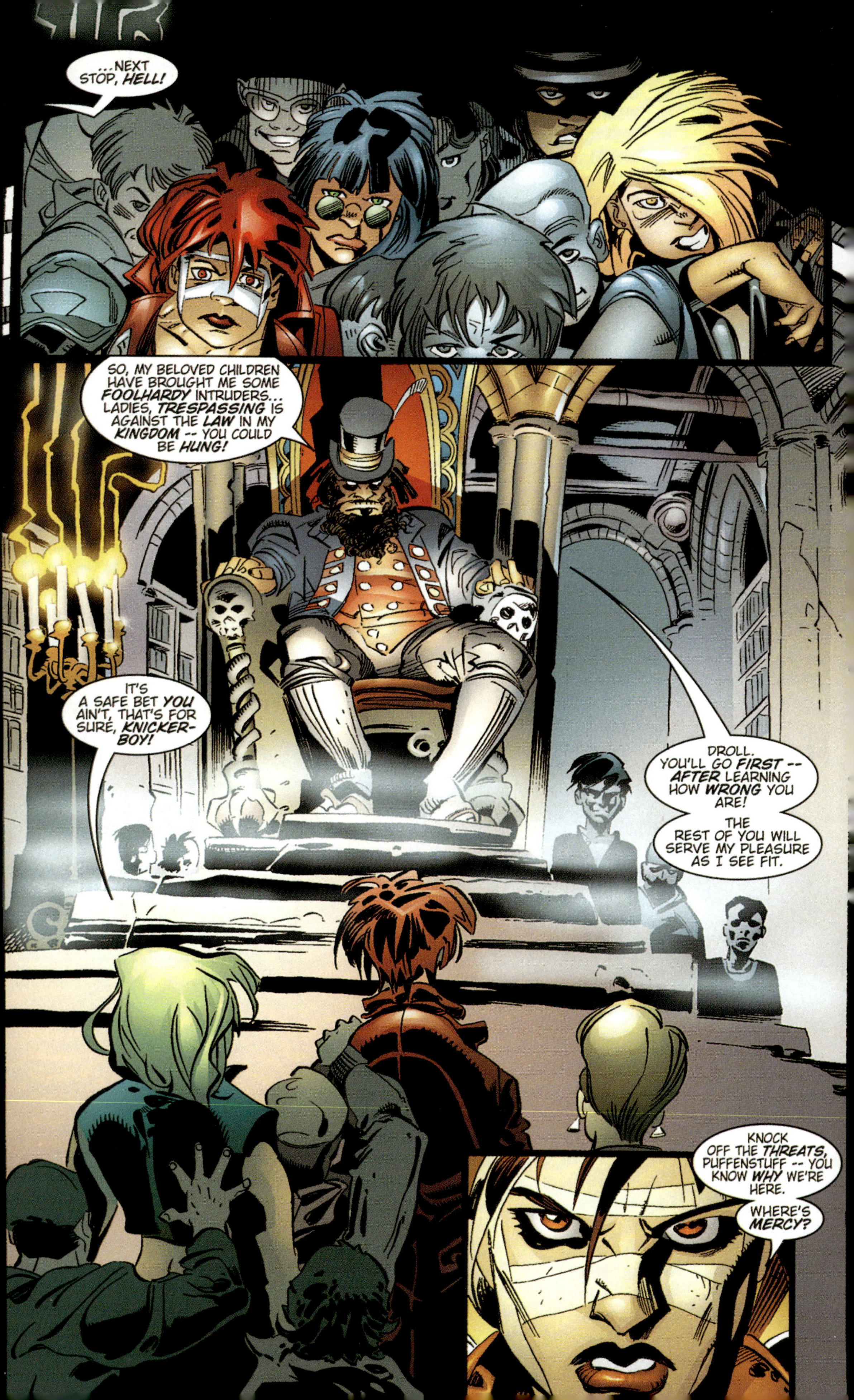
...NEXT STOP, HELL!
SO, MY BELOVED CHILDREN HAVE BROUGHT ME SOME FOOLHARDY INTRUDERS... LADIES, TRESPASSING IS AGAINST THE LAW IN MY KINGDOM -- YOU COULD BE HUNG!
IT'S A SAFE BET YOU AIN'T, THAT'S FOR SURE, KNICKER-BOY!
DROLL. YOU'LL GO FIRST -- AFTER LEARNING HOW WRONG YOU ARE!
THE REST OF YOU WILL SERVE MY PLEASURE AS I SEE FIT.
KNOCK OFF THE THREATS, PUFFENSTUFF -- YOU KNOW WHY WE'RE HERE.
WHERE'S MERCY?

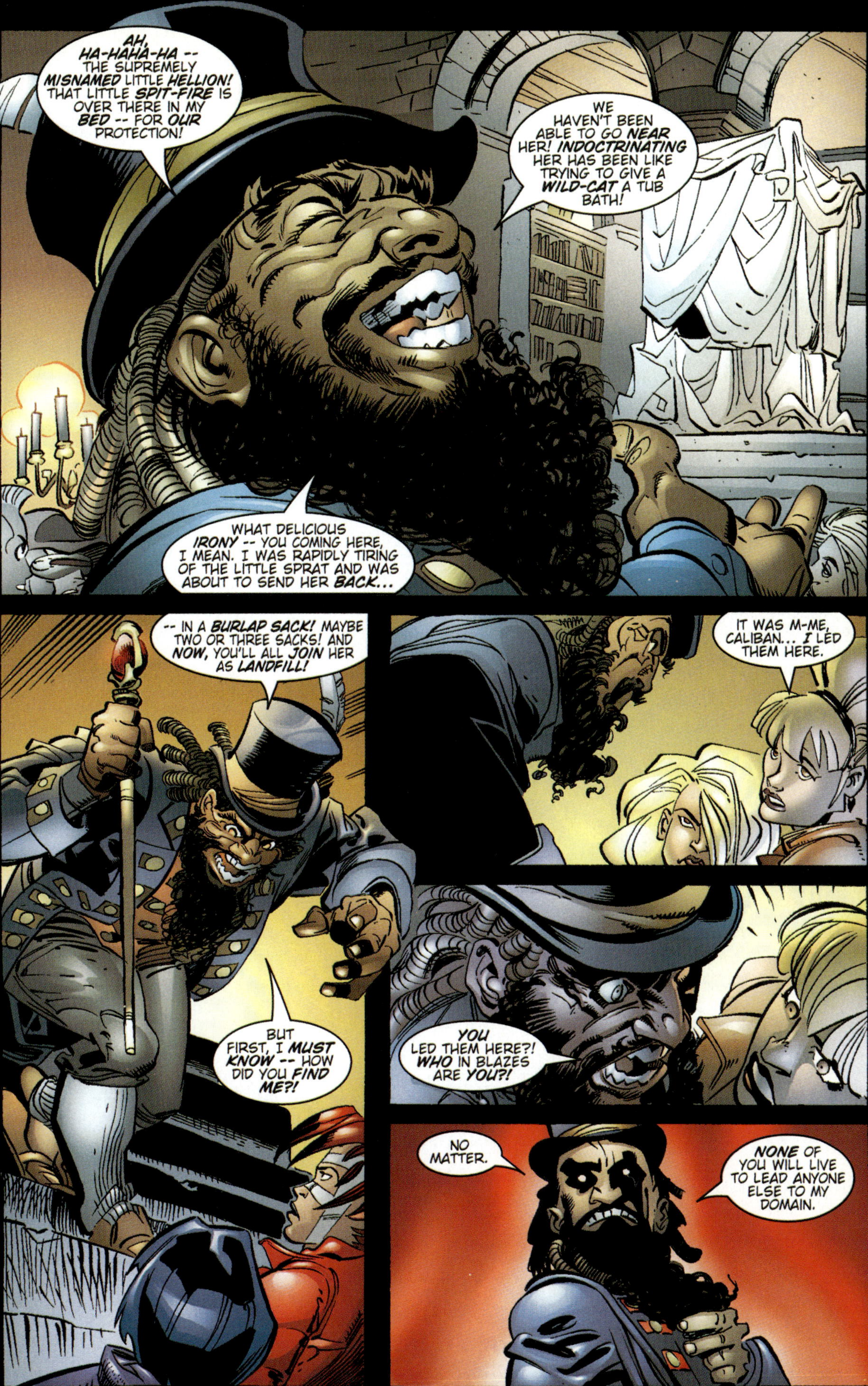
AH, HA-HAHA-HA -- THE SUPREMELY MISNAMED LITTLE HELLION! THAT LITTLE SPIT-FIRE IS OVER THERE IN MY BED -- FOR OUR PROTECTION!
WE HAVEN'T BEEN ABLE TO GO NEAR HER! INDOCTRINATING HER HAS BEEN LIKE TRYING TO GIVE A WILD-CAT A TUB BATH!
WHAT DELICIOUS IRONY -- YOU COMING HERE, I MEAN. I WAS RAPIDLY TIRING OF THE LITTLE SPRAT AND WAS ABOUT TO SEND HER BACK...
-- IN A BURLAP SACK! MAYBE TWO OR THREE SACKS! AND NOW, YOU'LL ALL JOIN HER AS LANDFILL!
BUT FIRST, I MUST KNOW -- HOW DID YOU FIND ME?!
IT WAS M-ME, CALIBAN... I LED THEM HERE.
YOU LED THEM HERE?! WHO IN BLAZES ARE YOU?!
NO MATTER.
NONE OF YOU WILL LIVE TO LEAD ANYONE ELSE TO MY DOMAIN.

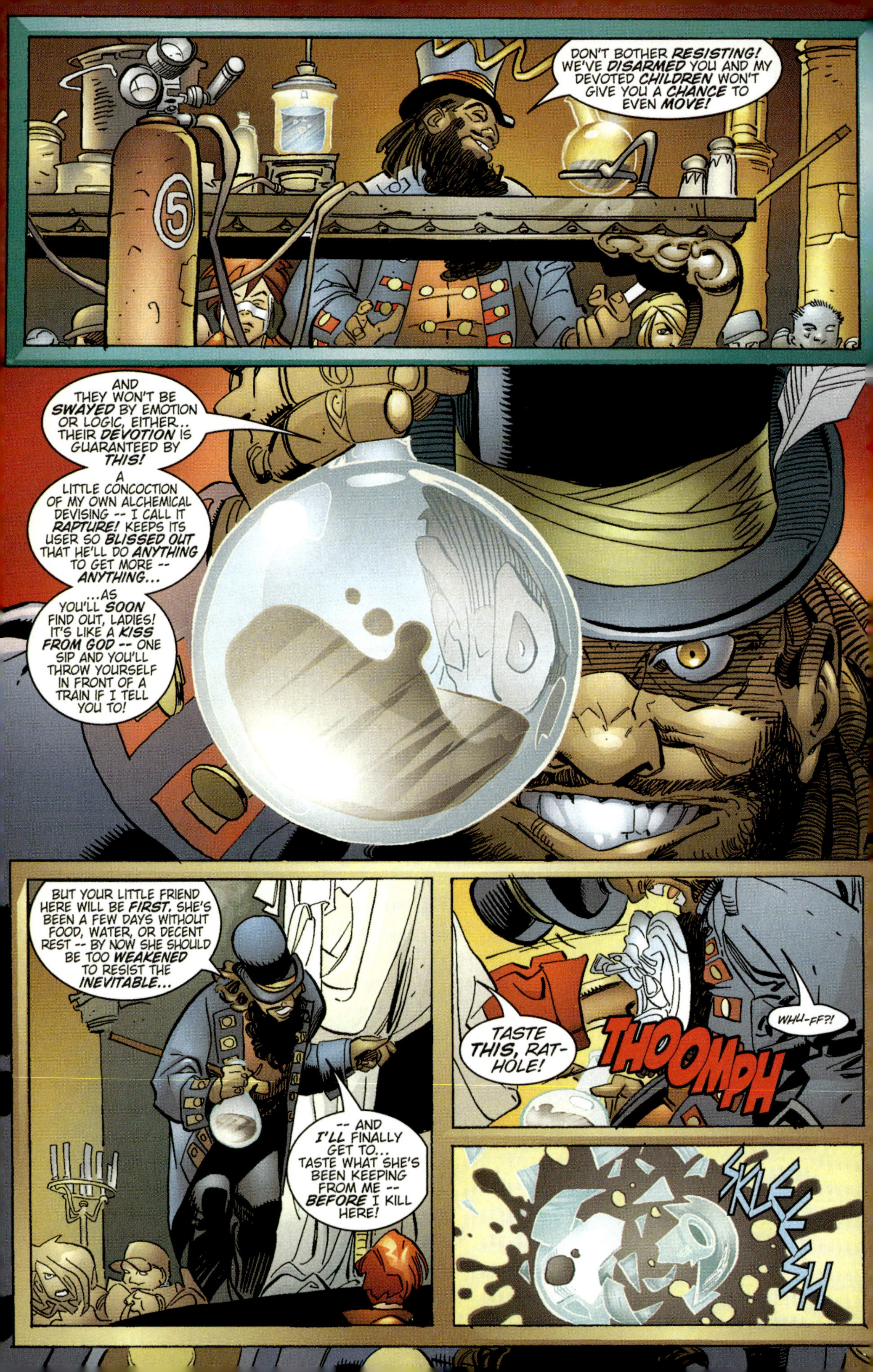
DON'T BOTHER RESISTING! WE'VE DISARMED YOU AND MY DEVOTED CHILDREN WON'T GIVE YOU A CHANCE TO EVEN MOVE!
AND THEY WON'T BE SWAYED BY EMOTION OR LOGIC, EITHER.. THEIR DEVOTION IS GUARANTEED BY THIS!
A LITTLE CONCOCTION OF MY OWN ALCHEMICAL DEVISING -- I CALL IT RAPTURE! KEEPS ITS USER SO BLISSED OUT THAT HE'LL DO ANYTHING TO GET MORE -- ANYTHING...
...AS YOU'LL SOON FIND OUT, LADIES! IT'S LIKE A KISS FROM GOD -- ONE SIP AND YOU'LL THROW YOURSELF IN FRONT OF A TRAIN IF I TELL YOU TO!
BUT YOUR LITTLE FRIEND HERE WILL BE FIRST. SHE'S BEEN A FEW DAYS WITHOUT FOOD, WATER, OR DECENT REST -- BY NOW SHE SHOULD BE TOO WEAKENED TO RESIST THE INEVITABLE...
-- AND I'LL FINALLY GET TO... TASTE WHAT SHE'S BEEN KEEPING FROM ME -- BEFORE I KILL HERE!
TASTE THIS, RAT-HOLE!
THOOMPH
WHU--FF?!
SKLEESH

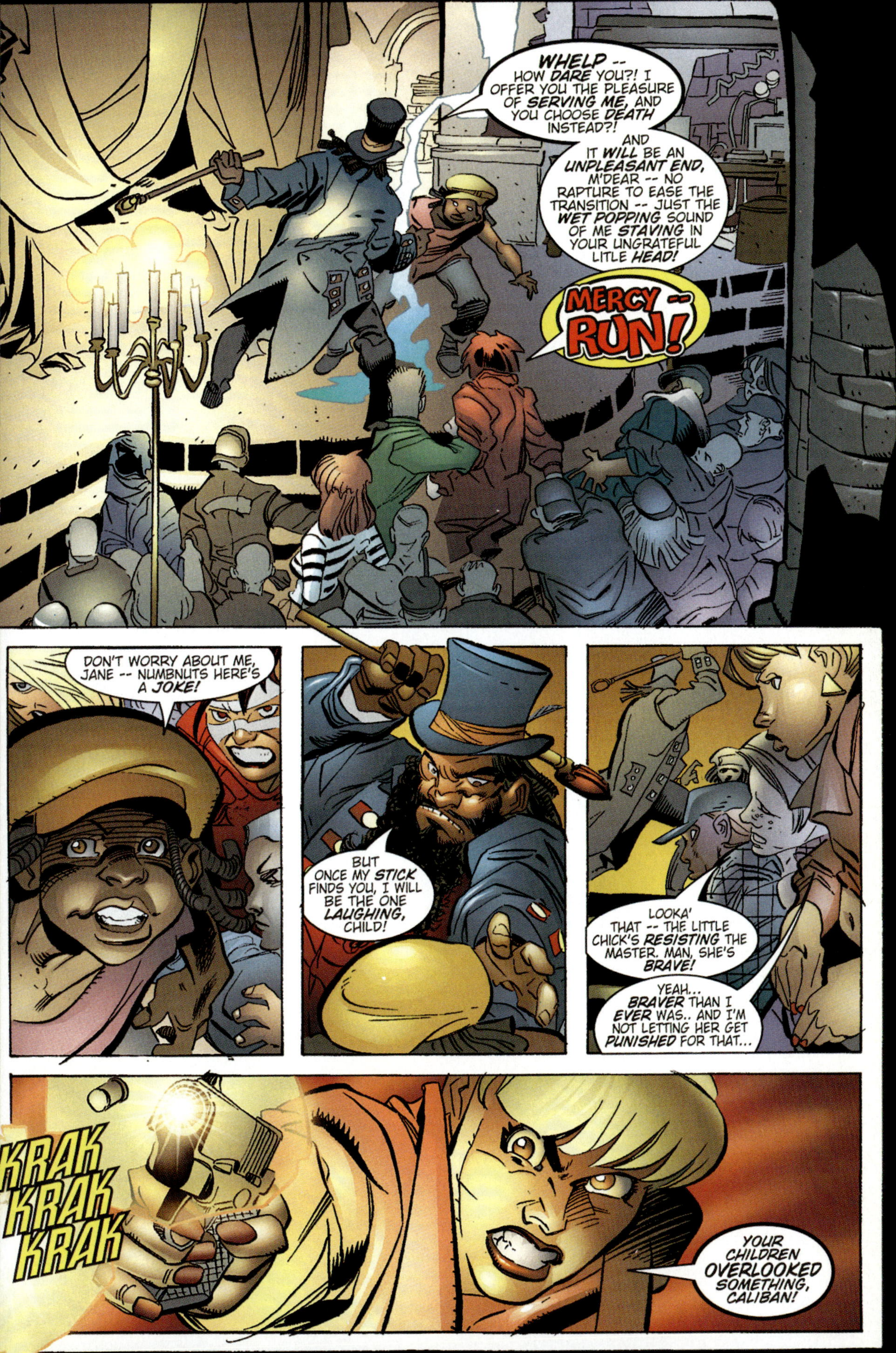
WHELP -- HOW DARE YOU?! I OFFER YOU THE PLEASURE OF SERVING ME, AND YOU CHOOSE DEATH INSTEAD?!
AND IT WILL BE AN UNPLEASANT END, M'DEAR -- NO RAPTURE TO EASE THE TRANSITION -- JUST THE WET POPPING SOUND OF ME STAVING IN YOUR UNGRATEFUL LITTLE HEAD!
MERCY -- RUN!
DON'T WORRY ABOUT ME, JANE -- NUMBNUTS HERE'S A JOKE!
BUT ONCE MY STICK FINDS YOU, I WILL BE THE ONE LAUGHING, CHILD!
LOOKA' THAT -- THE LITTLE CHICK'S RESISTING THE MASTER. MAN, SHE'S BRAVE!
YEAH... BRAVER THAN I EVER WAS.. AND I'M NOT LETTING HER GET PUNISHED FOR THAT...
KRAK KRAK KRAK
YOUR CHILDREN OVERLOOKED SOMETHING, CALIBAN!

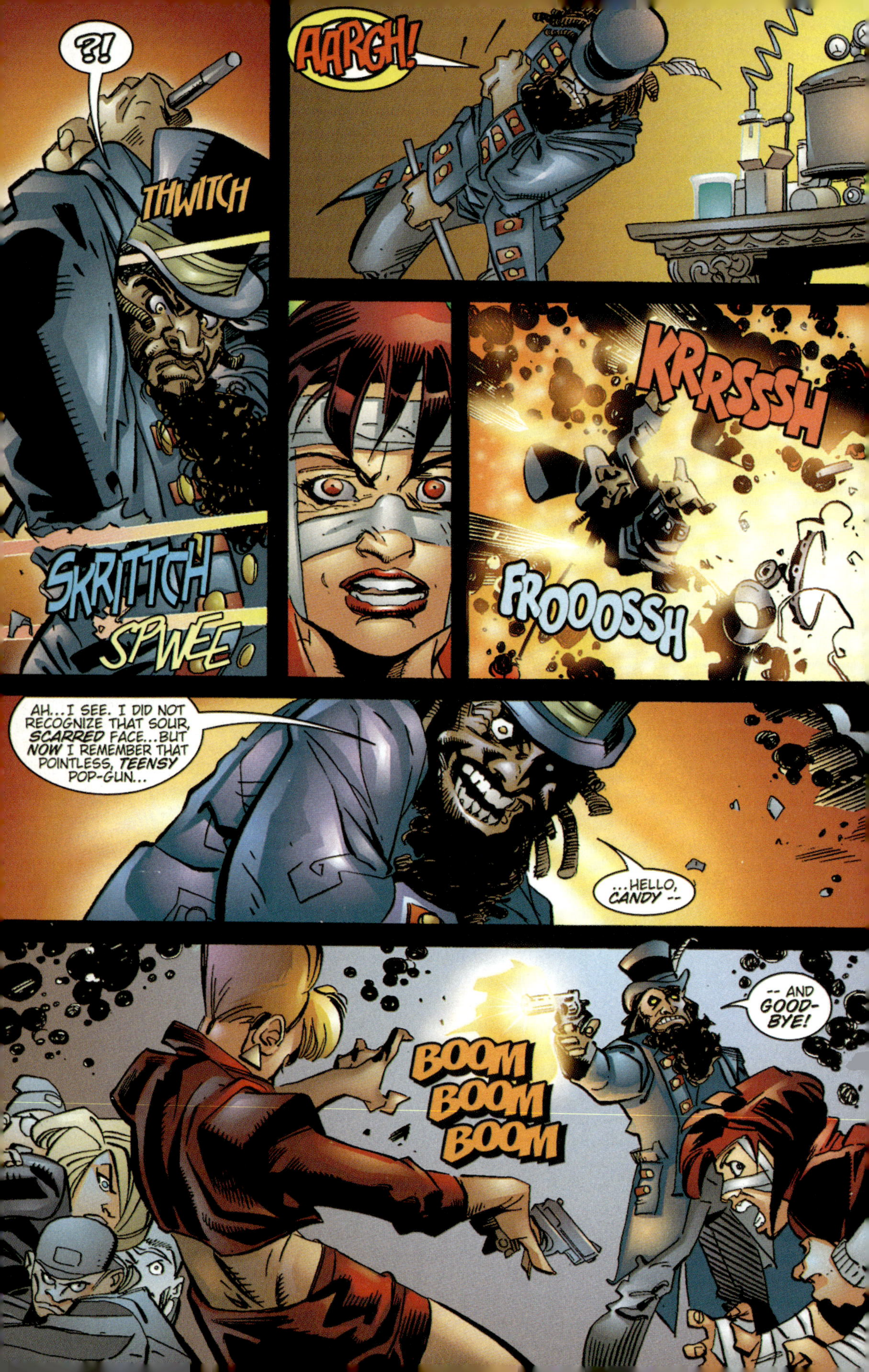
?!
THWITCH
SKRITTCH
SPWEE
AARGH!
KRRSSSH
FROOOSSH
AH...I SEE. I DID NOT RECOGNIZE THAT SOUR, SCARRED FACE...BUT NOW I REMEMBER THAT POINTLESS, TEENSY POP-GUN...
...HELLO, CANDY --
-- AND GOOD-BYE!
BOOM BOOM BOOM

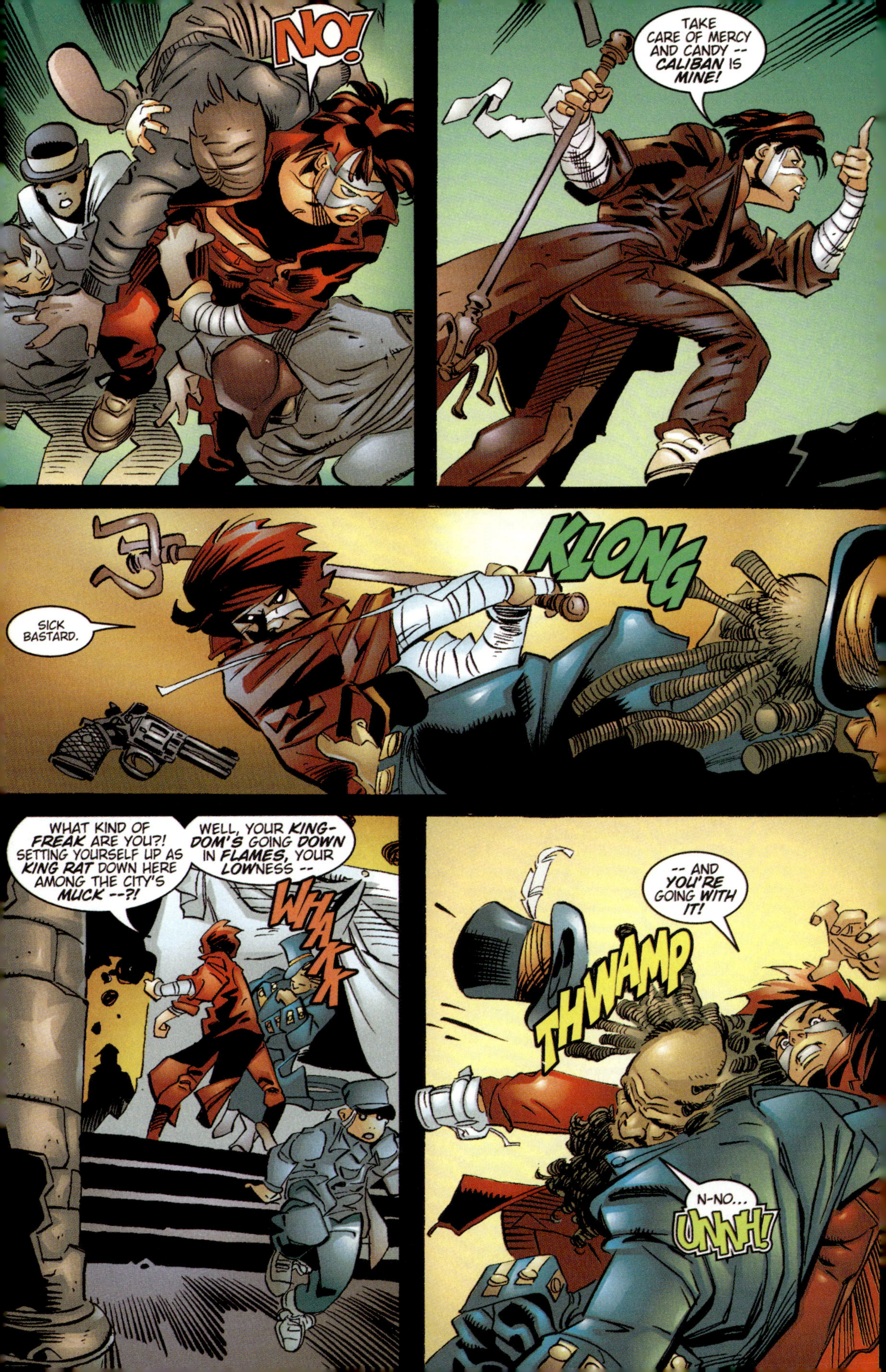
NO!
TAKE CARE OF MERCY AND CANDY -- CALIBAN IS MINE!
KLONG
SICK BASTARD.
WHAT KIND OF FREAK ARE YOU?! SETTING YOURSELF UP AS KING RAT DOWN HERE AMONG THE CITY'S MUCK --?!
WELL, YOUR KING-DOM'S GOING DOWN IN FLAMES, YOUR LOWNESS --
WHAAK
-- AND YOU'RE GOING WITH IT!
THWAMP
N-NO...
UNNH!

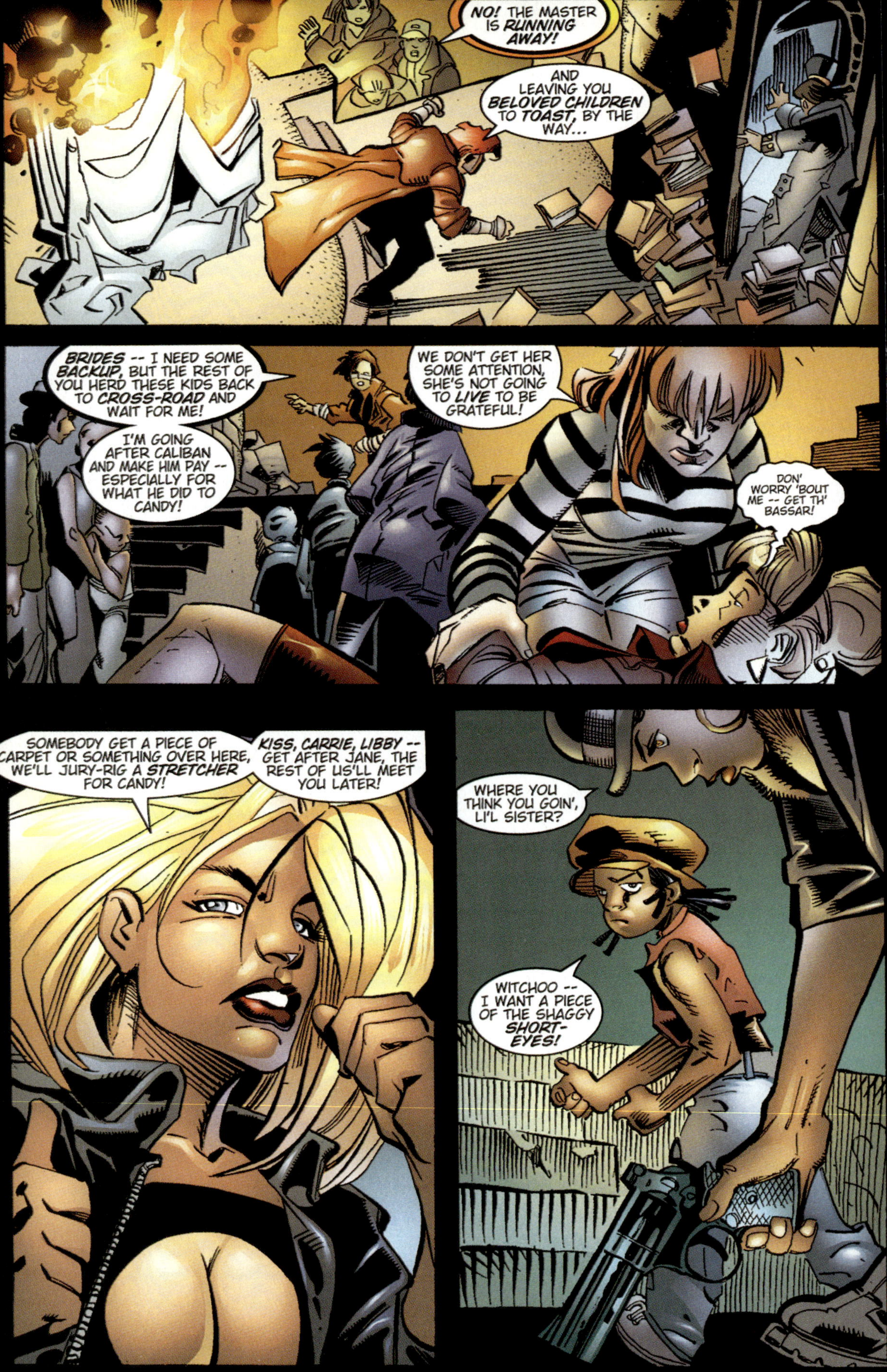
NO! THE MASTER IS RUNNING AWAY!
AND LEAVING YOU BELOVED CHILDREN TO TOAST, BY THE WAY...
BRIDES -- I NEED SOME BACKUP, BUT THE REST OF YOU HERD THESE KIDS BACK TO CROSS-ROAD AND WAIT FOR ME!
I'M GOING AFTER CALIBAN AND MAKE HIM PAY -- ESPECIALLY FOR WHAT HE DID TO CANDY!
WE DON'T GET HER SOME ATTENTION, SHE'S NOT GOING TO LIVE TO BE GRATEFUL!
DON' WORRY 'BOUT ME -- GET TH' BASSAR!
SOMEBODY GET A PIECE OF CARPET OR SOMETHING OVER HERE, WE'LL JURY-RIG A STRETCHER FOR CANDY!
KISS, CARRIE, LIBBY -- GET AFTER JANE, THE REST OF US'LL MEET YOU LATER!
WHERE YOU THINK YOU GOIN', LI'L SISTER?
WITCHOO -- I WANT A PIECE OF THE SHAGGY SHORT-EYES!

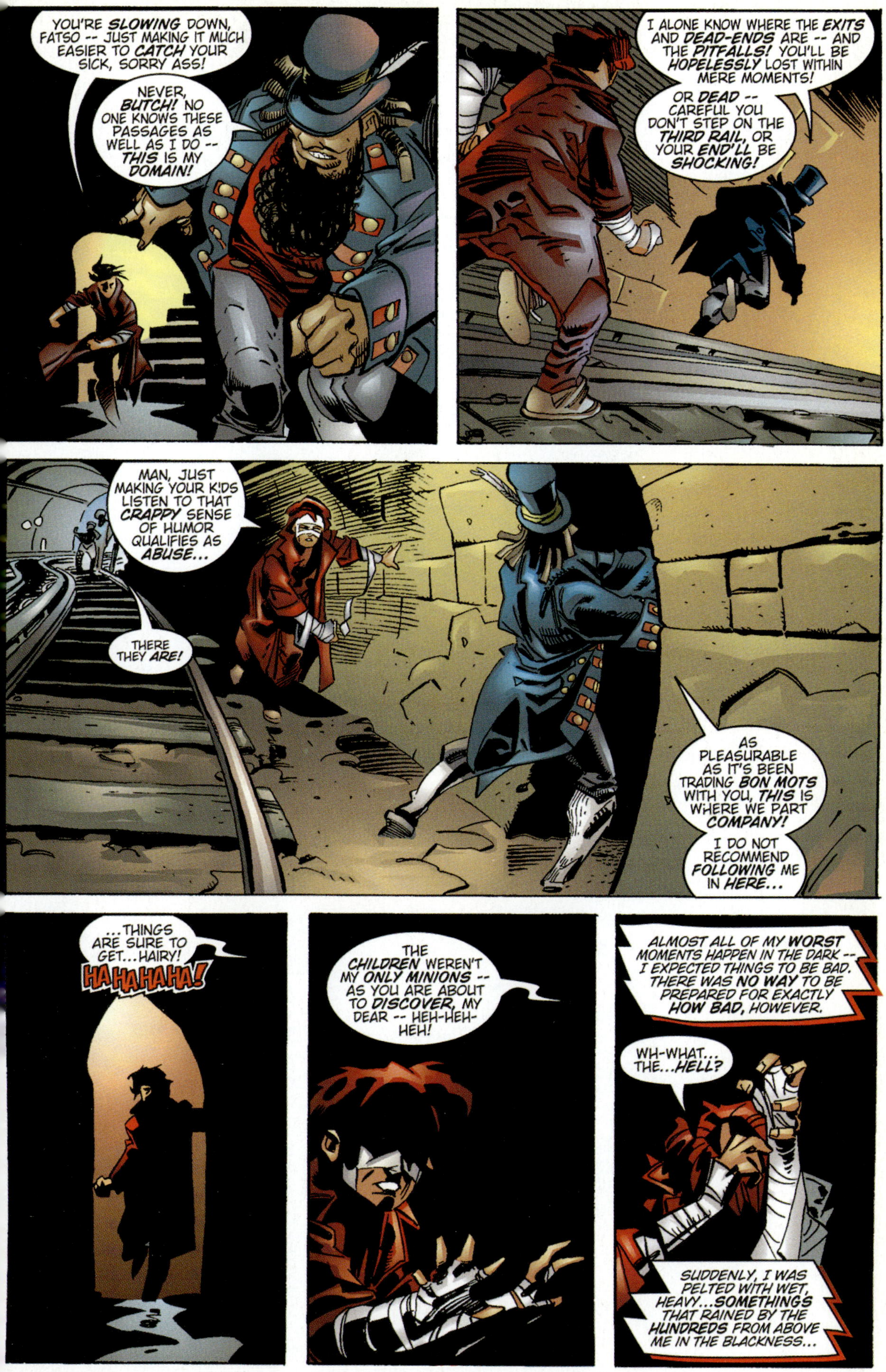
YOU'RE SLOWING DOWN, FATSO -- JUST MAKING IT MUCH EASIER TO CATCH YOUR SICK, SORRY ASS!
NEVER, BUTCH! NO ONE KNOWS THESE PASSAGES AS WELL AS I DO -- THIS IS MY DOMAIN!
I ALONE KNOW WHERE THE EXITS AND DEAD-ENDS ARE -- AND THE PITFALLS! YOU'LL BE HOPELESSLY LOST WITHIN MERE MOMENTS!
OR DEAD -- CAREFUL YOU DON'T STEP ON THE THIRD RAIL, OR YOUR END'LL BE SHOCKING!
MAN, JUST MAKING YOUR KIDS LISTEN TO THAT CRAPPY SENSE OF HUMOR QUALIFIES AS ABUSE...
THERE THEY ARE!
AS PLEASURABLE AS IT'S BEEN TRADING BON MOTS WITH YOU, THIS IS WHERE WE PART COMPANY!
I DO NOT RECOMMEND FOLLOWING ME IN HERE...
...THINGS ARE SURE TO GET...HAIRY!
HAHAHAHA!
THE CHILDREN WEREN'T MY ONLY MINIONS -- AS YOU ARE ABOUT TO DISCOVER, MY DEAR -- HEH-HEH-HEH!
ALMOST ALL OF MY WORST MOMENTS HAPPEN IN THE DARK -- I EXPECTED THINGS TO BE BAD. THERE WAS NO WAY TO BE PREPARED FOR EXACTLY HOW BAD, HOWEVER.
WH-WHAT... THE...HELL?
SUDDENLY, I WAS PELTED WITH WET, HEAVY...SOMETHINGS THAT RAINED BY THE HUNDREDS FROM ABOVE ME IN THE BLACKNESS...

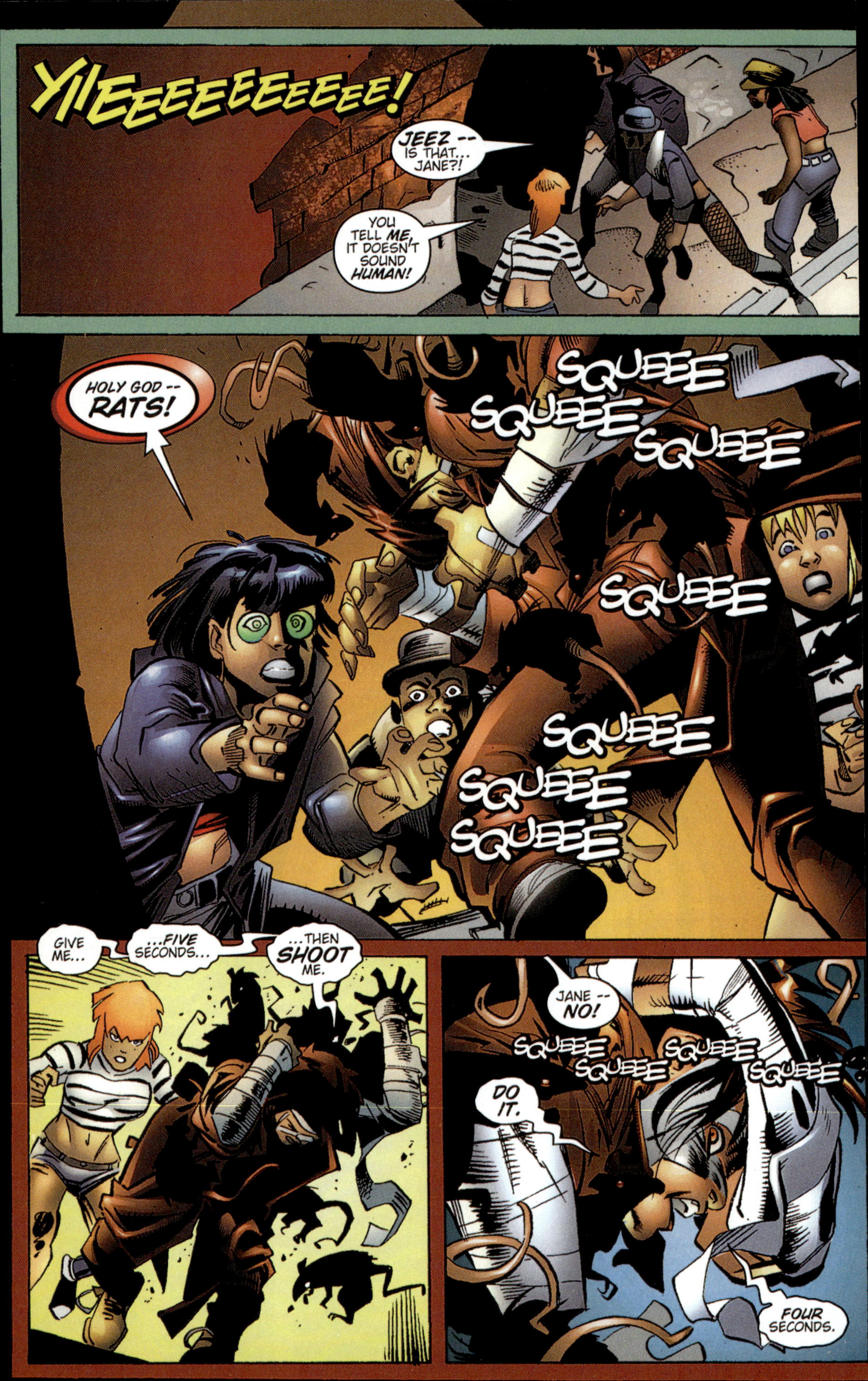

YIIEEEEEEEEEEE!
JEEZ -- IS THAT... JANE?!
YOU TELL ME, IT DOESN'T SOUND HUMAN!
HOLY GOD -- RATS!
SQUEEEE
SQUEEEE
SQUEEEE
SQUEEEE
SQUEEEE
SQUEEEE
SQUEEEE
GIVE ME...
...FIVE SECONDS...
...THEN SHOOT ME.
JANE -- NO!
SQUEEEE SQUEEEE SQUEEEE SQUEEEE
DO IT.
FOUR SECONDS.

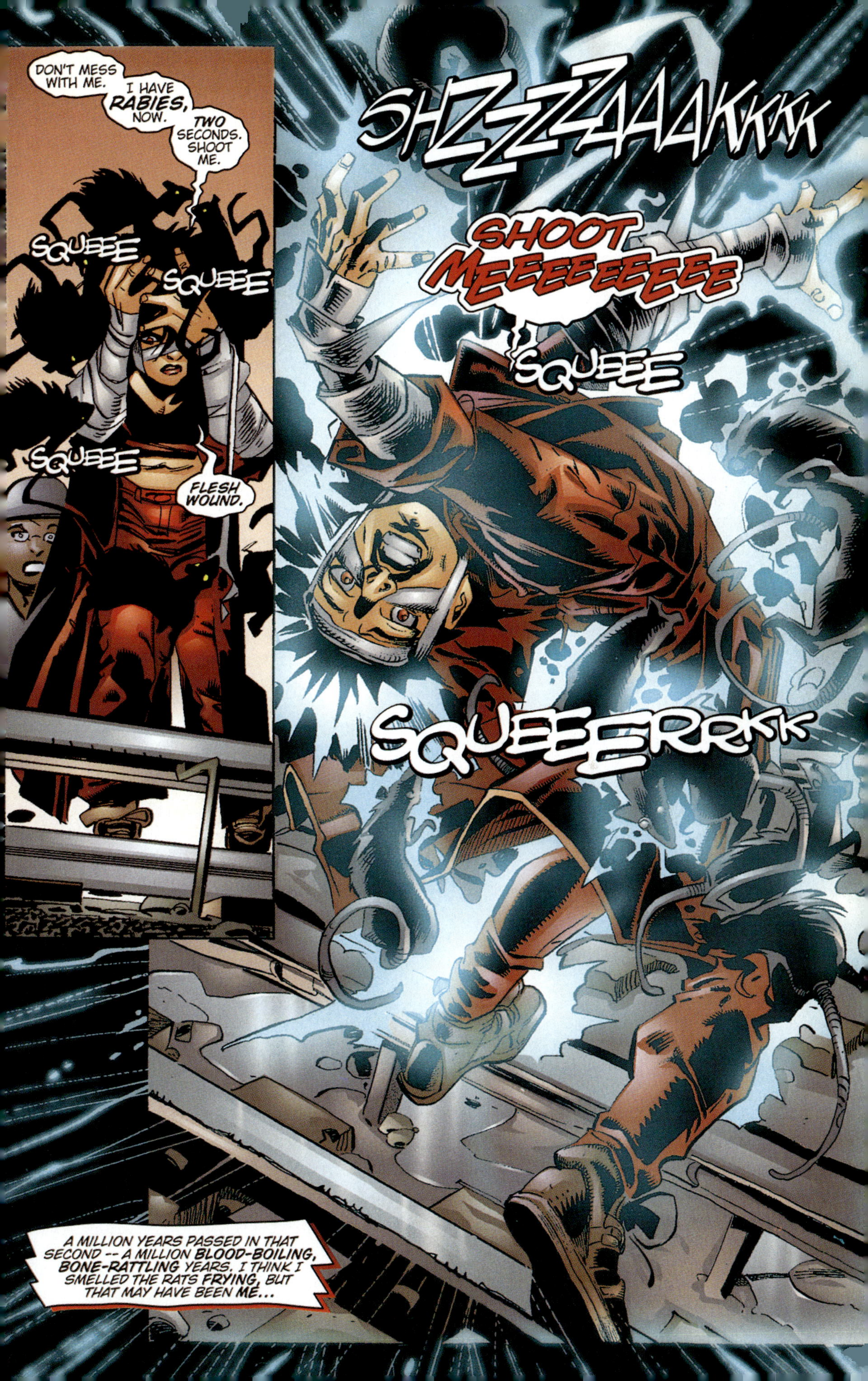

DON'T MESS WITH ME.
I HAVE RABIES, NOW.
TWO SECONDS. SHOOT ME.
SQUEEE
SQUEEE
SQUEEE
FLESH WOUND.
SHZZZZAAAKKKK
SHOOT MEEEEEEEEE
SQUEEE
SQUEEERRKK
A MILLION YEARS PASSED IN THAT SECOND -- A MILLION BLOOD-BOILING, BONE-RATTLING YEARS. I THINK I SMELLED THE RATS FRYING, BUT THAT MAY HAVE BEEN ME...

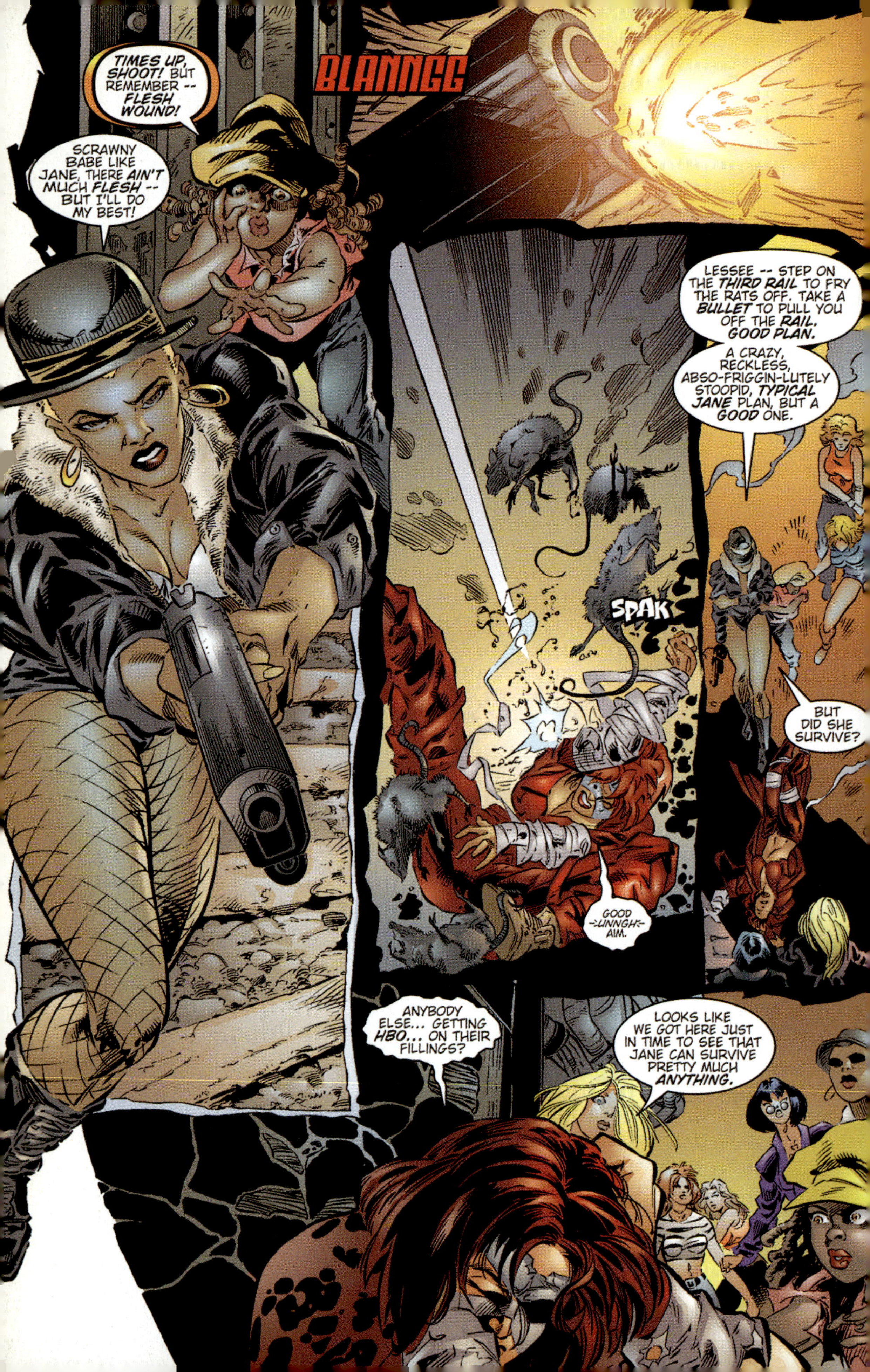
TIMES UP, SHOOT! BUT REMEMBER -- FLESH WOUND!
BLANNGG
SCRAWNY BABE LIKE JANE, THERE AIN'T MUCH FLESH -- BUT I'LL DO MY BEST!
SPAK
GOOD -UNNGH- AIM.
LESSEE -- STEP ON THE THIRD RAIL TO FRY THE RATS OFF. TAKE A BULLET TO PULL YOU OFF THE RAIL. GOOD PLAN.
A CRAZY, RECKLESS, ABSO-FRIGGIN-LUTELY STOOPID, TYPICAL JANE PLAN, BUT A GOOD ONE.
BUT DID SHE SURVIVE?
ANYBODY ELSE... GETTING HBO... ON THEIR FILLINGS?
LOOKS LIKE WE GOT HERE JUST IN TIME TO SEE THAT JANE CAN SURVIVE PRETTY MUCH ANYTHING.

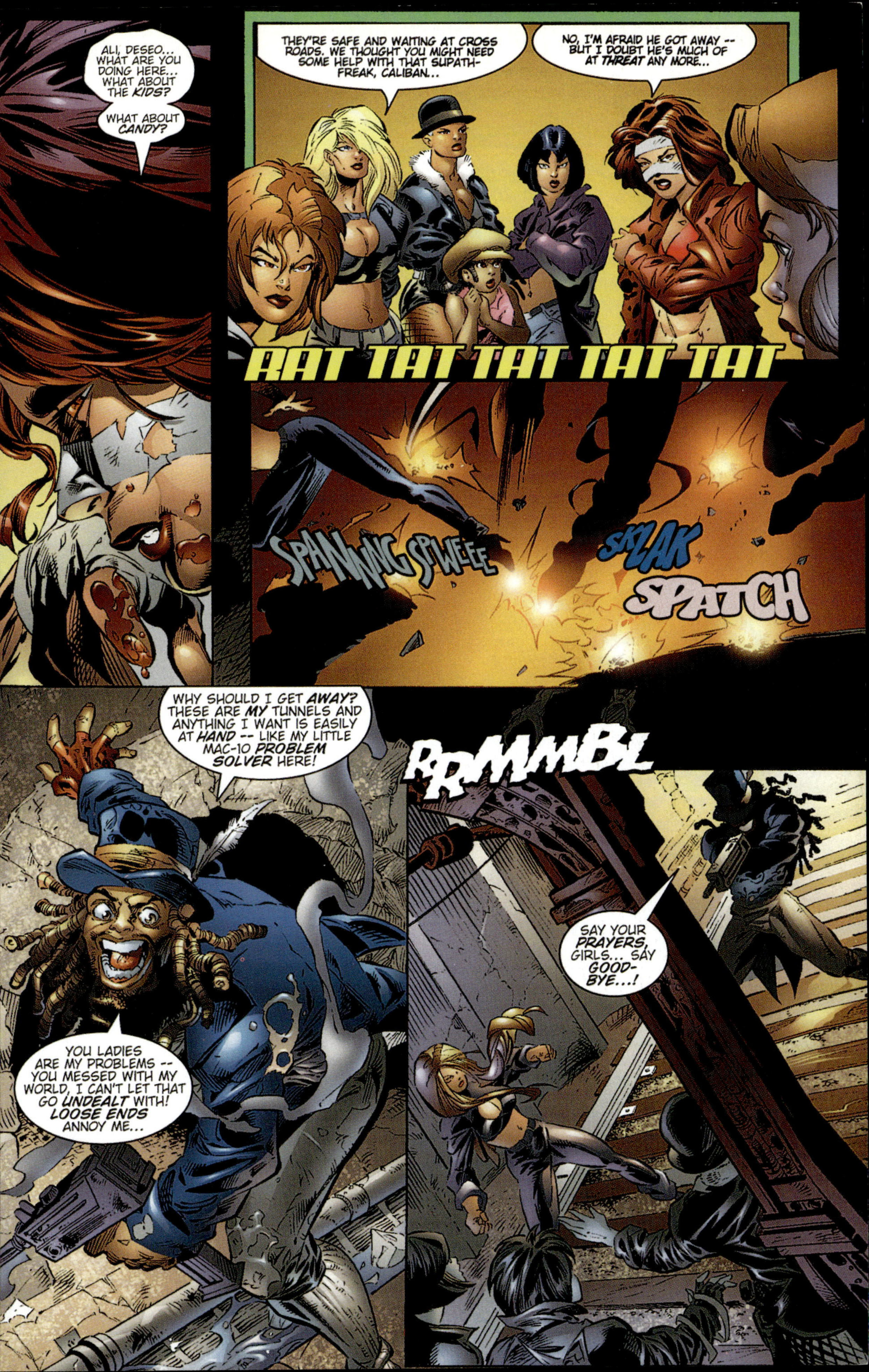

ALI, DESEO... WHAT ARE YOU DOING HERE... WHAT ABOUT THE KIDS?
WHAT ABOUT CANDY?
THEY'RE SAFE AND WAITING AT CROSS ROADS. WE THOUGHT YOU MIGHT NEED SOME HELP WITH THAT SUPATH-FREAK, CALIBAN...
NO, I'M AFRAID HE GOT AWAY -- BUT I DOUBT HE'S MUCH OF AT THREAT ANY MORE...
RAT TAT TAT TAT TAT
SPANNNG SPWEEE
SKLAK
SPATCH
WHY SHOULD I GET AWAY? THESE ARE MY TUNNELS AND ANYTHING I WANT IS EASILY AT HAND -- LIKE MY LITTLE MAC-10 PROBLEM SOLVER HERE!
YOU LADIES ARE MY PROBLEMS -- YOU MESSED WITH MY WORLD, I CAN'T LET THAT GO UNDEALT WITH! LOOSE ENDS ANNOY ME...
RRMMMBL
SAY YOUR PRAYERS, GIRLS... SAY GOOD-BYE...!

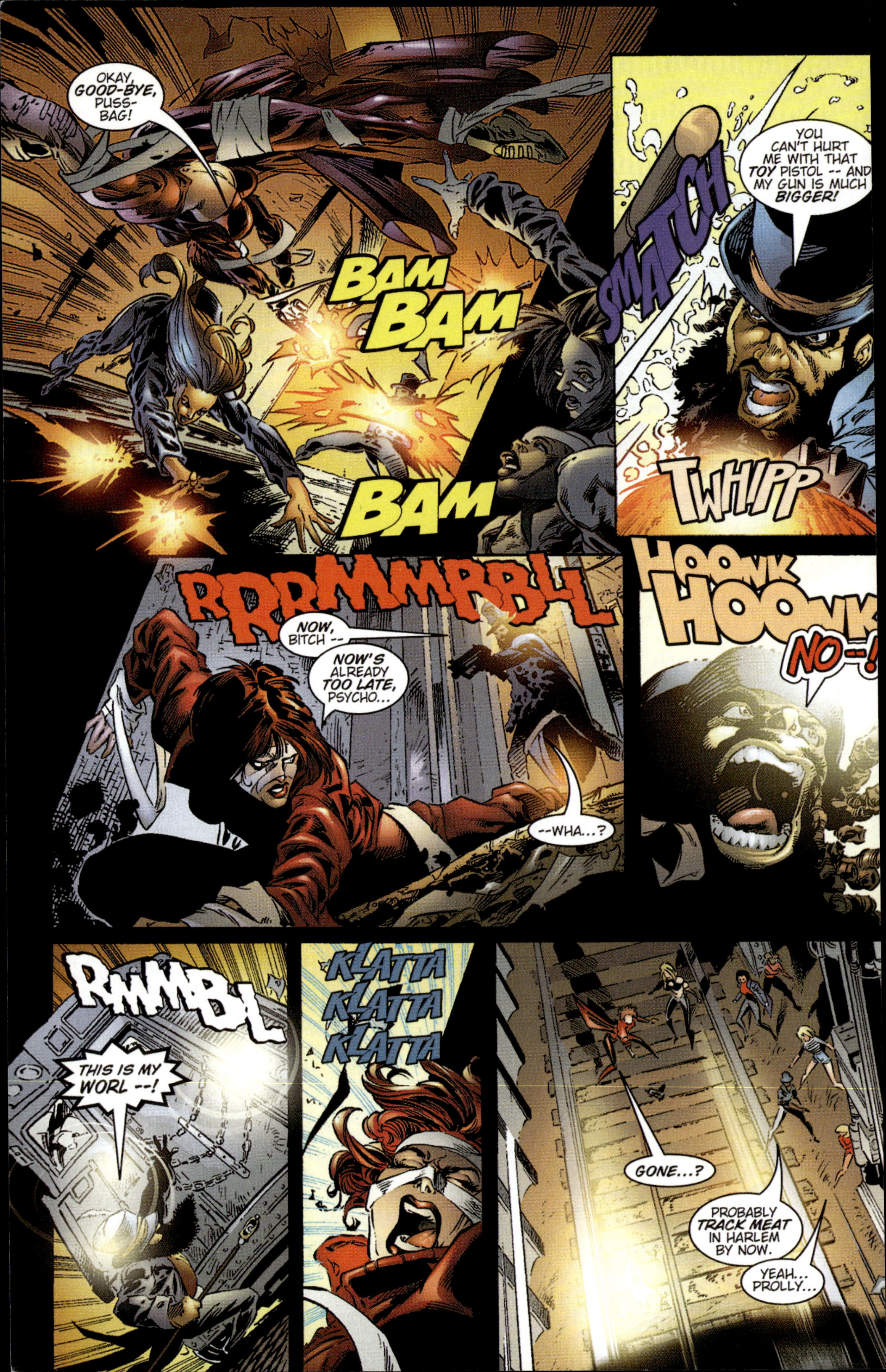
OKAY, GOOD-BYE, PUSS-BAG!
BAM BAM
BAM
SNATCH
YOU CAN'T HURT ME WITH THAT TOY PISTOL -- AND MY GUN IS MUCH BIGGER!
TWHIPP
RRRMMMRBLL
NOW, BITCH --
NOW'S ALREADY TOO LATE, PSYCHO...
--WHA...?
HOONK HOONK
NO--!
RMMBL
THIS IS MY WORL --!
KLATTA KLATTA KLATTA
GONE...?
PROBABLY TRACK MEAT IN HARLEM BY NOW.
YEAH... PROLLY...

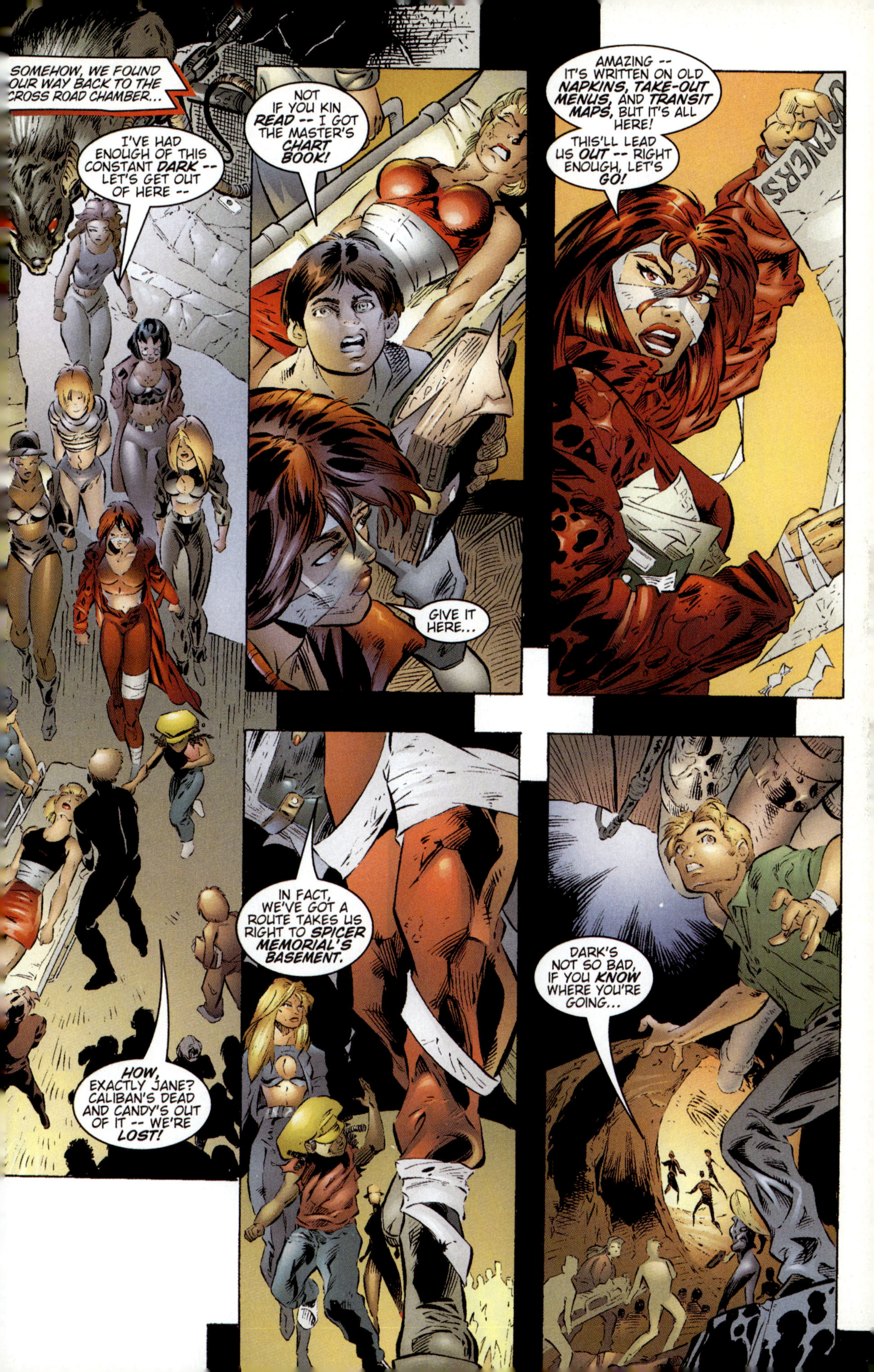
SOMEHOW, WE FOUND OUR WAY BACK TO THE CROSS ROAD CHAMBER...
I'VE HAD ENOUGH OF THIS CONSTANT DARK -- LET'S GET OUT OF HERE --
HOW, EXACTLY JANE? CALIBAN'S DEAD AND CANDY'S OUT OF IT -- WE'RE LOST!
NOT IF YOU KIN READ -- I GOT THE MASTER'S CHART BOOK!
GIVE IT HERE...
AMAZING -- IT'S WRITTEN ON OLD NAPKINS, TAKE-OUT MENUS, AND TRANSIT MAPS, BUT IT'S ALL HERE!
THIS'LL LEAD US OUT -- RIGHT ENOUGH, LET'S GO!
IN FACT, WE'VE GOT A ROUTE TAKES US RIGHT TO SPICER MEMORIAL'S BASEMENT.
DARK'S NOT SO BAD, IF YOU KNOW WHERE YOU'RE GOING...

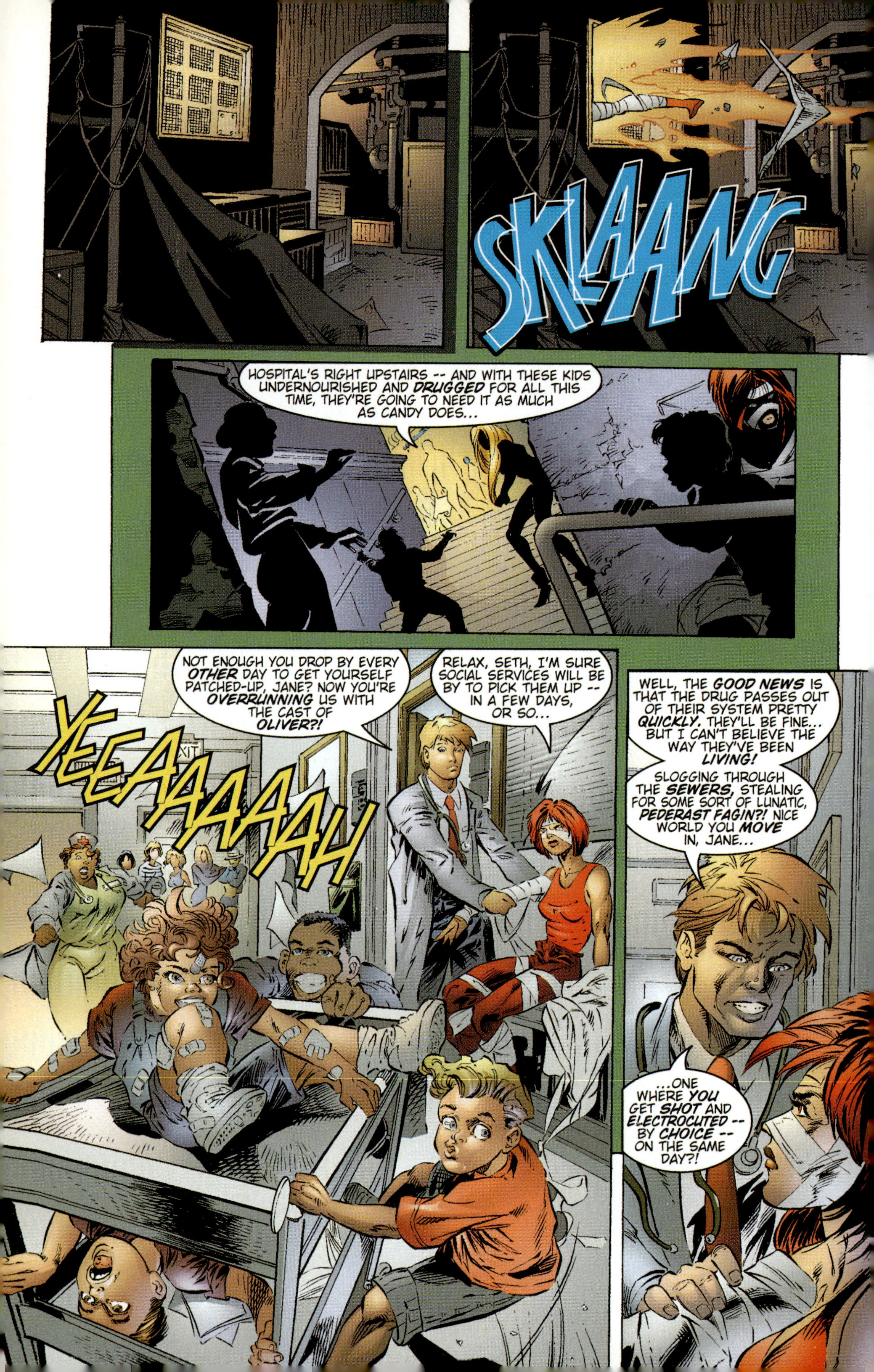
SKLAANG
HOSPITAL'S RIGHT UPSTAIRS -- AND WITH THESE KIDS UNDERNOURISHED AND DRUGGED FOR ALL THIS TIME, THEY'RE GOING TO NEED IT AS MUCH AS CANDY DOES...
YEEAAAAAAH
NOT ENOUGH YOU DROP BY EVERY OTHER DAY TO GET YOURSELF PATCHED-UP, JANE? NOW YOU'RE OVERRUNNING US WITH THE CAST OF OLIVER?!
RELAX, SETH, I'M SURE SOCIAL SERVICES WILL BE BY TO PICK THEM UP -- IN A FEW DAYS, OR SO...
WELL, THE GOOD NEWS IS THAT THE DRUG PASSES OUT OF THEIR SYSTEM PRETTY QUICKLY. THEY'LL BE FINE... BUT I CAN'T BELIEVE THE WAY THEY'VE BEEN LIVING!
SLOGGING THROUGH THE SEWERS, STEALING FOR SOME SORT OF LUNATIC, PEDERAST FAGIN?! NICE WORLD YOU MOVE IN, JANE...
...ONE WHERE YOU GET SHOT AND ELECTROCUTED -- BY CHOICE -- ON THE SAME DAY?!

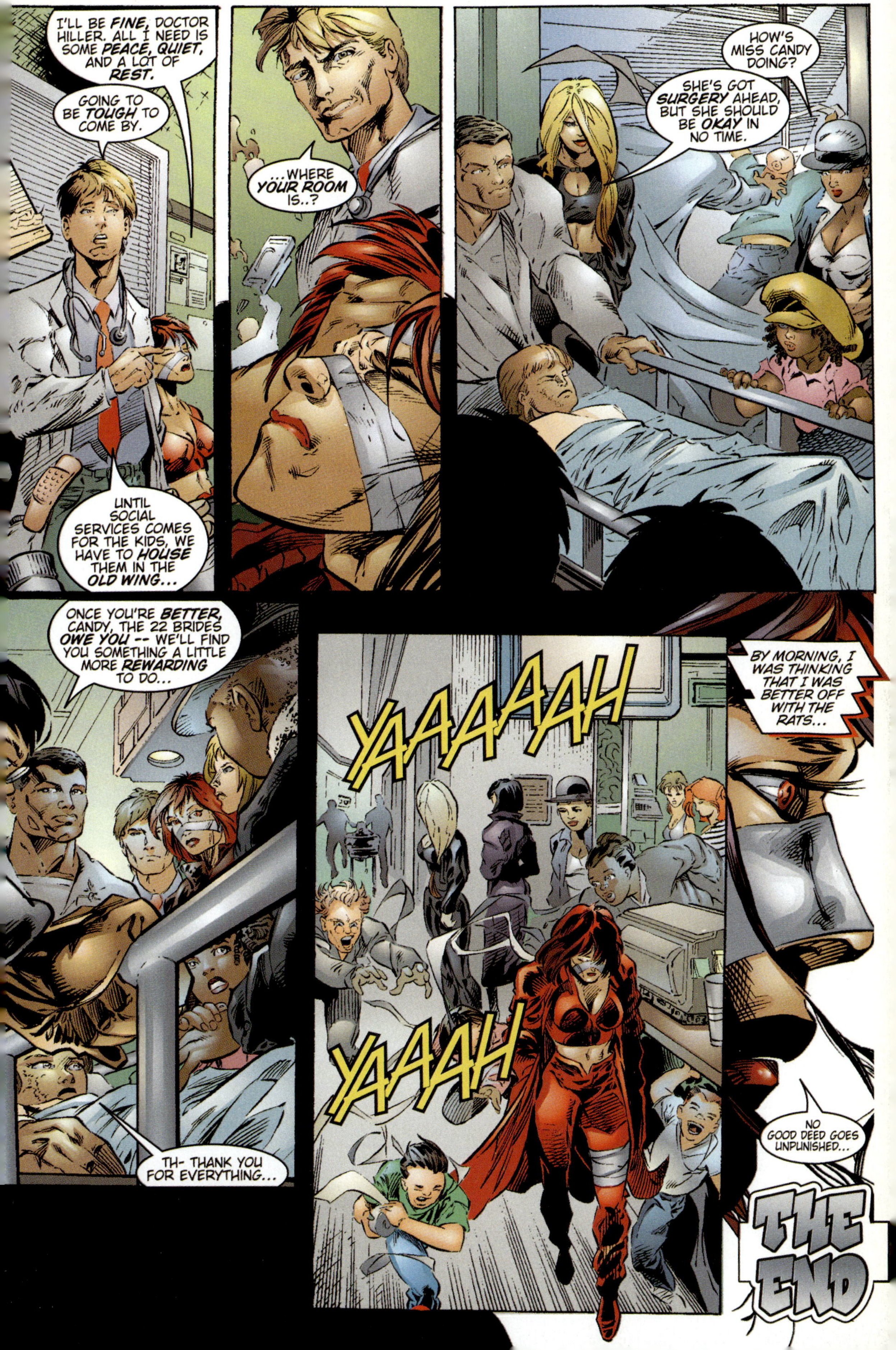
I'LL BE FINE, DOCTOR HILLER. ALL I NEED IS SOME PEACE, QUIET, AND A LOT OF REST.
GOING TO BE TOUGH TO COME BY.
UNTIL SOCIAL SERVICES COMES FOR THE KIDS, WE HAVE TO HOUSE THEM IN THE OLD WING...
...WHERE YOUR ROOM IS..?
HOW'S MISS CANDY DOING?
SHE'S GOT SURGERY AHEAD, BUT SHE SHOULD BE OKAY IN NO TIME.
ONCE YOU'RE BETTER, CANDY, THE 22 BRIDES OWE YOU -- WE'LL FIND YOU SOMETHING A LITTLE MORE REWARDING TO DO...
TH- THANK YOU FOR EVERYTHING...
YAAAAAH
YAAAH
BY MORNING, I WAS THINKING THAT I WAS BETTER OFF WITH THE RATS...
NO GOOD DEED GOES UNPUNISHED...
THE END

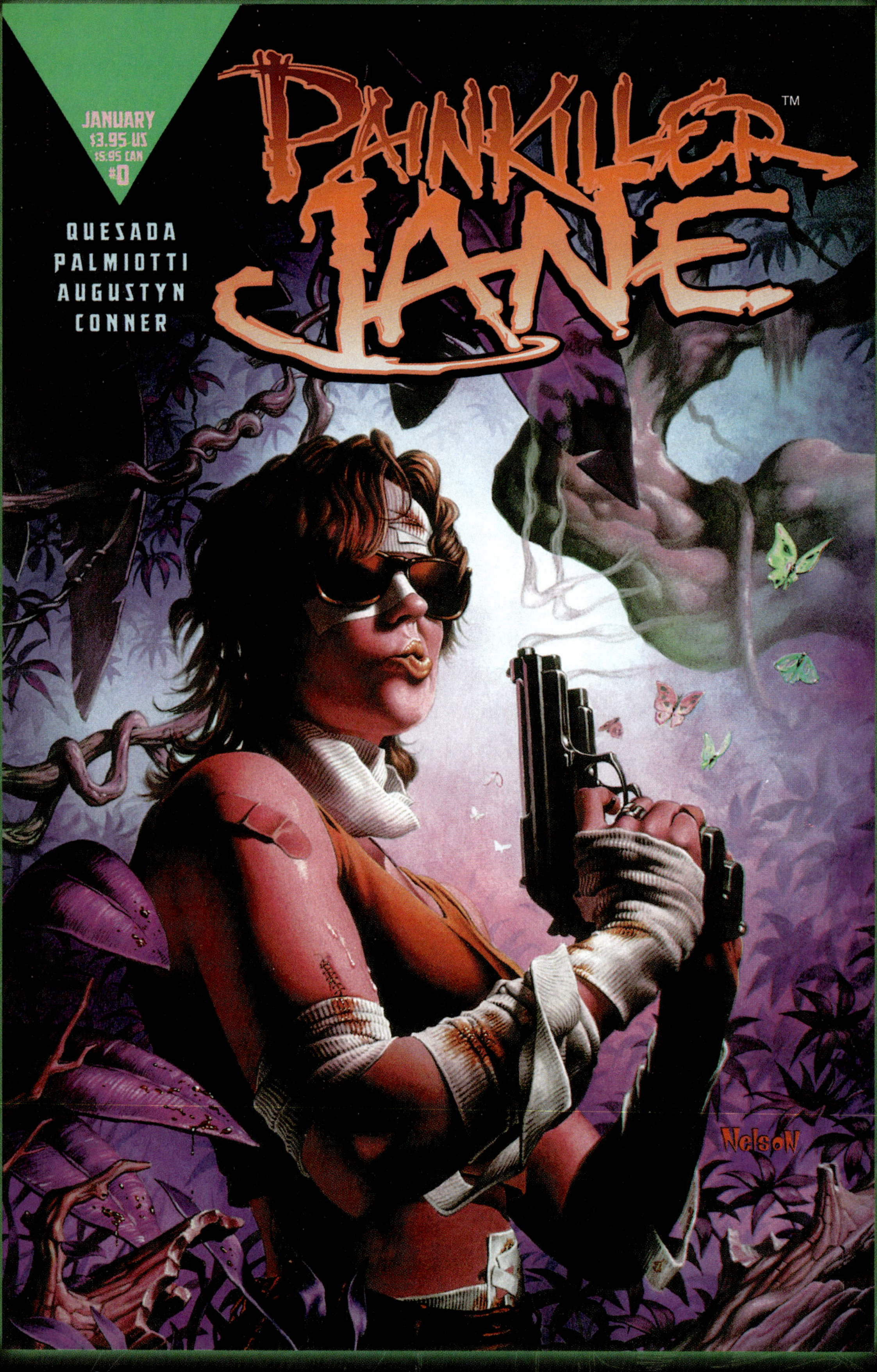
PAINKILLER JANE™
JANUARY
$3.95 US
$5.95 CAN
#0
QUESADA
PALMIOTTI
AUGUSTYN
CONNER
NELSON

Cover for #0 by Nelson

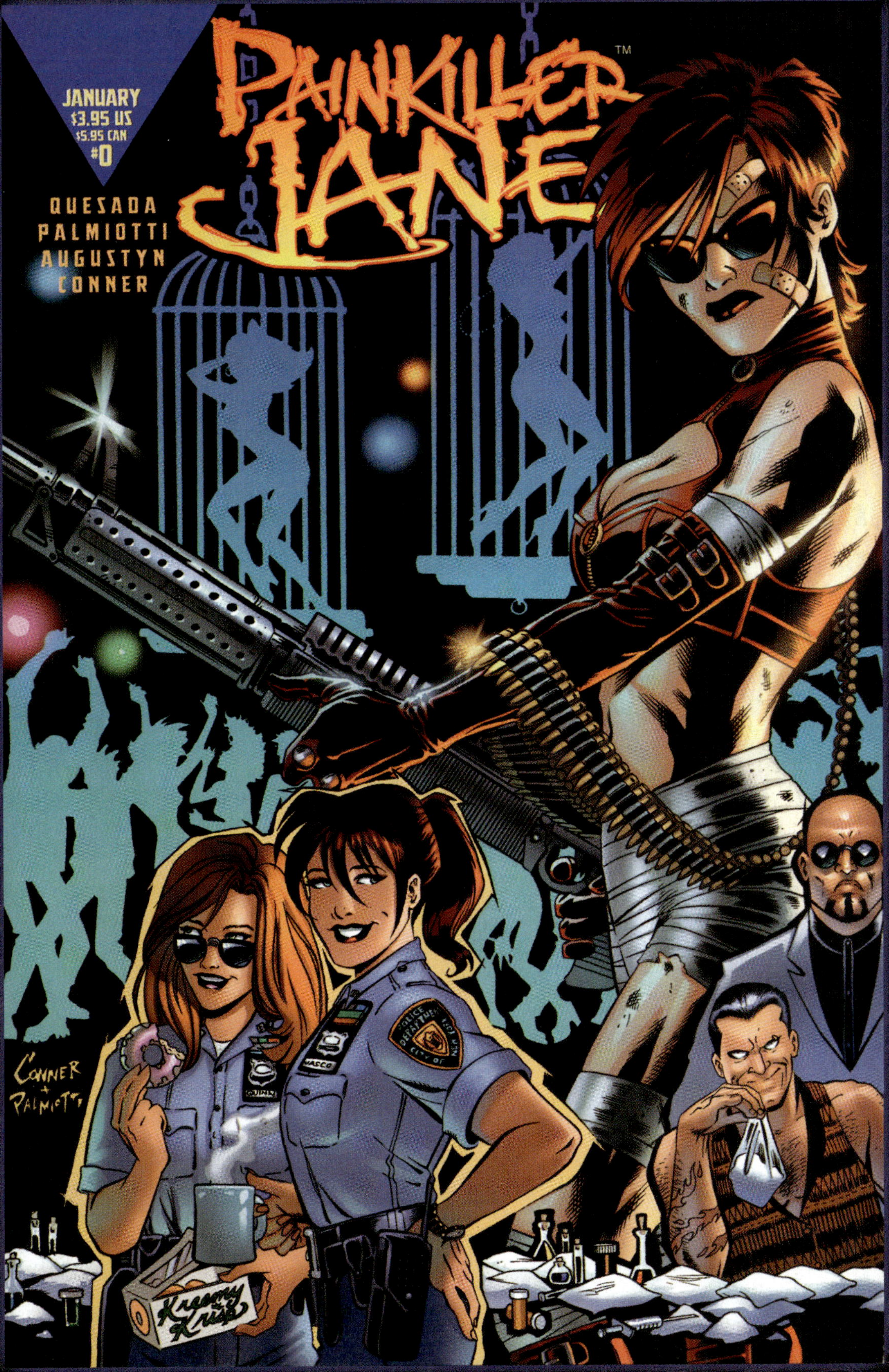
PAINKILLER JANE
JANUARY
$3.95 US
$5.95 CAN
#0
QUESADA
PALMIOTTI
AUGUSTYN
CONNER

Cover for #0 by Amanda Conner & Jimmy Palmiotti

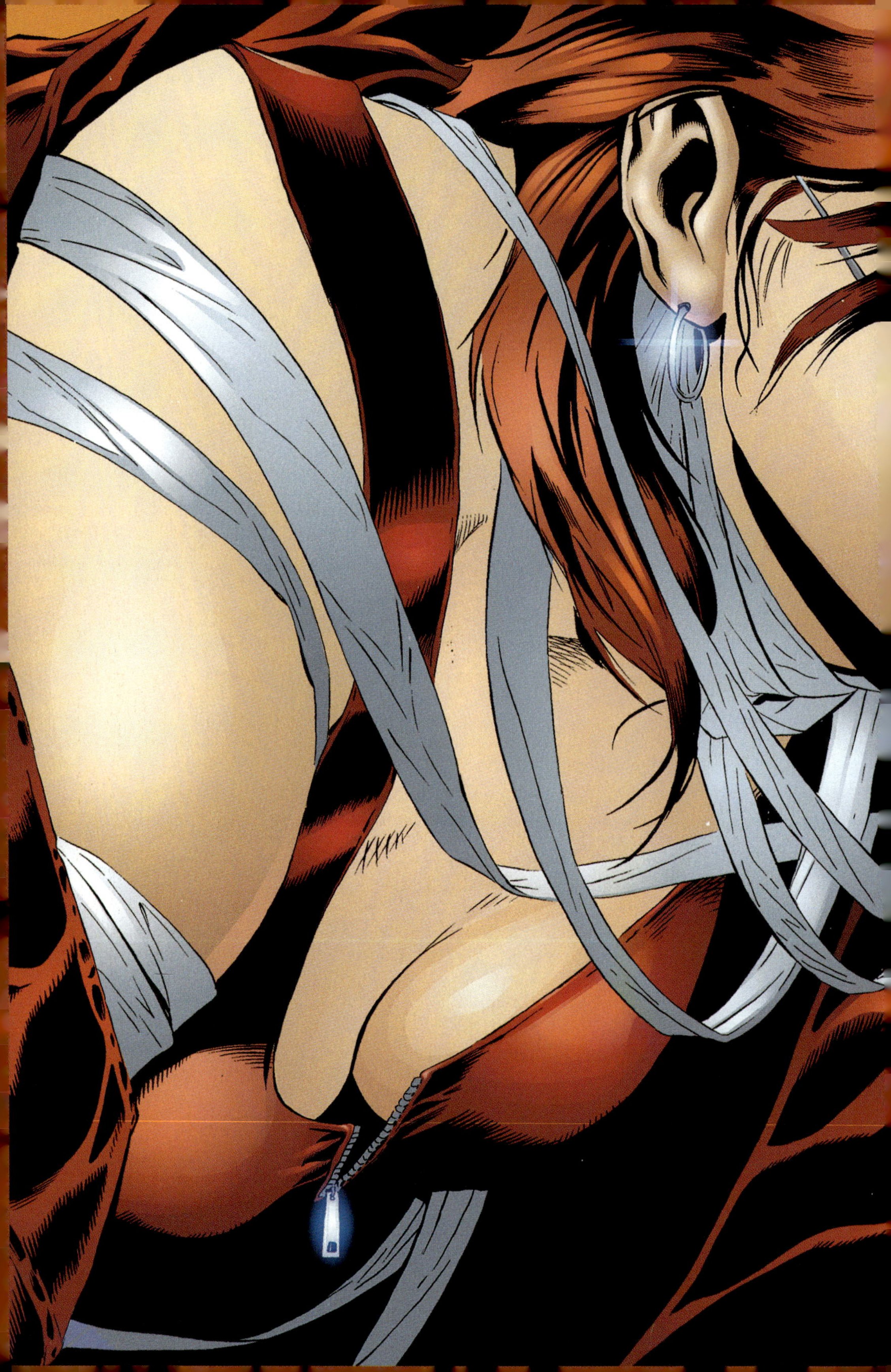

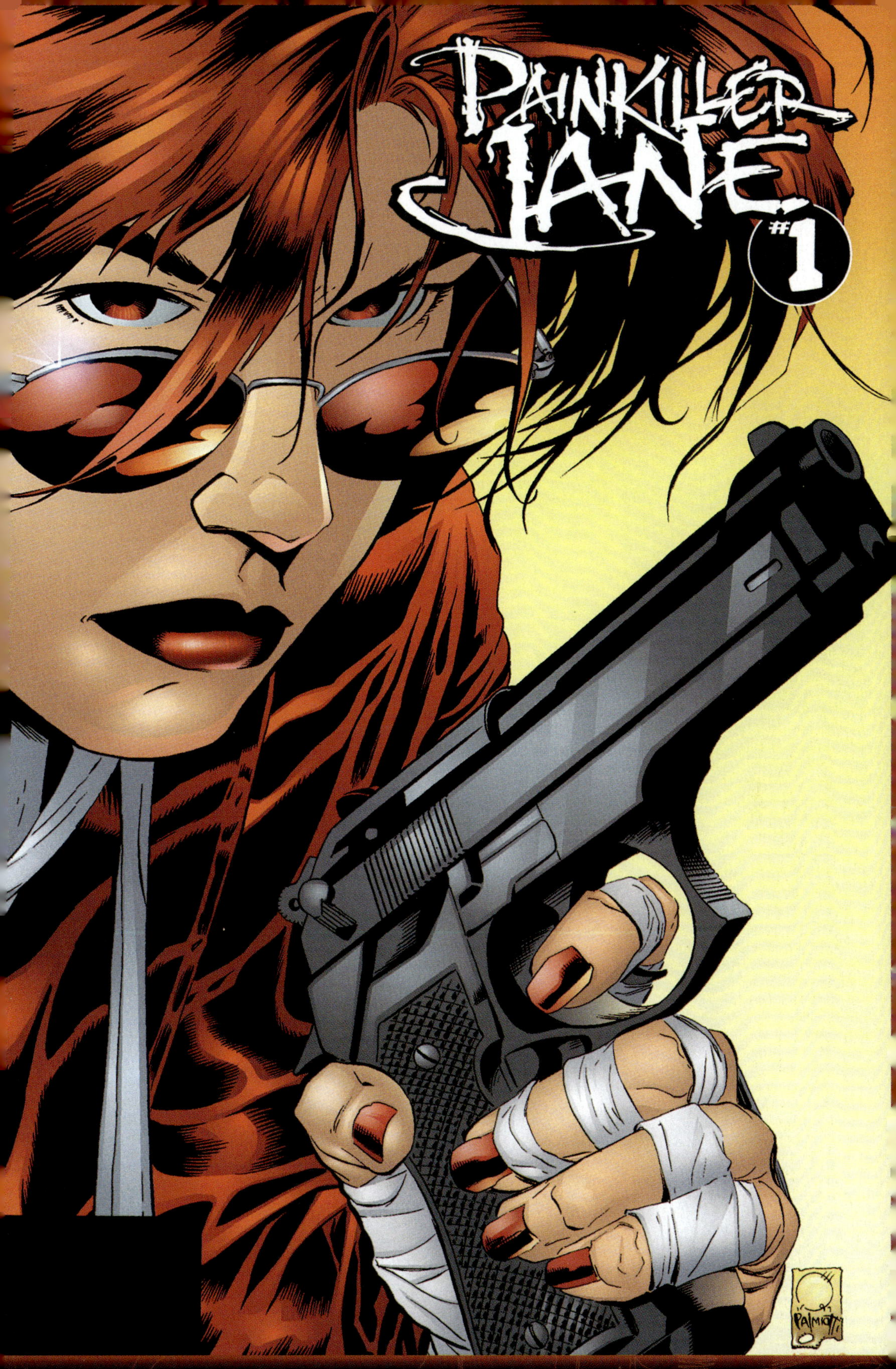
PAINKILLER JANE
#1
PALMIOTTI

Cover #1 by Joe Quesada & Jimmy Palmiotti

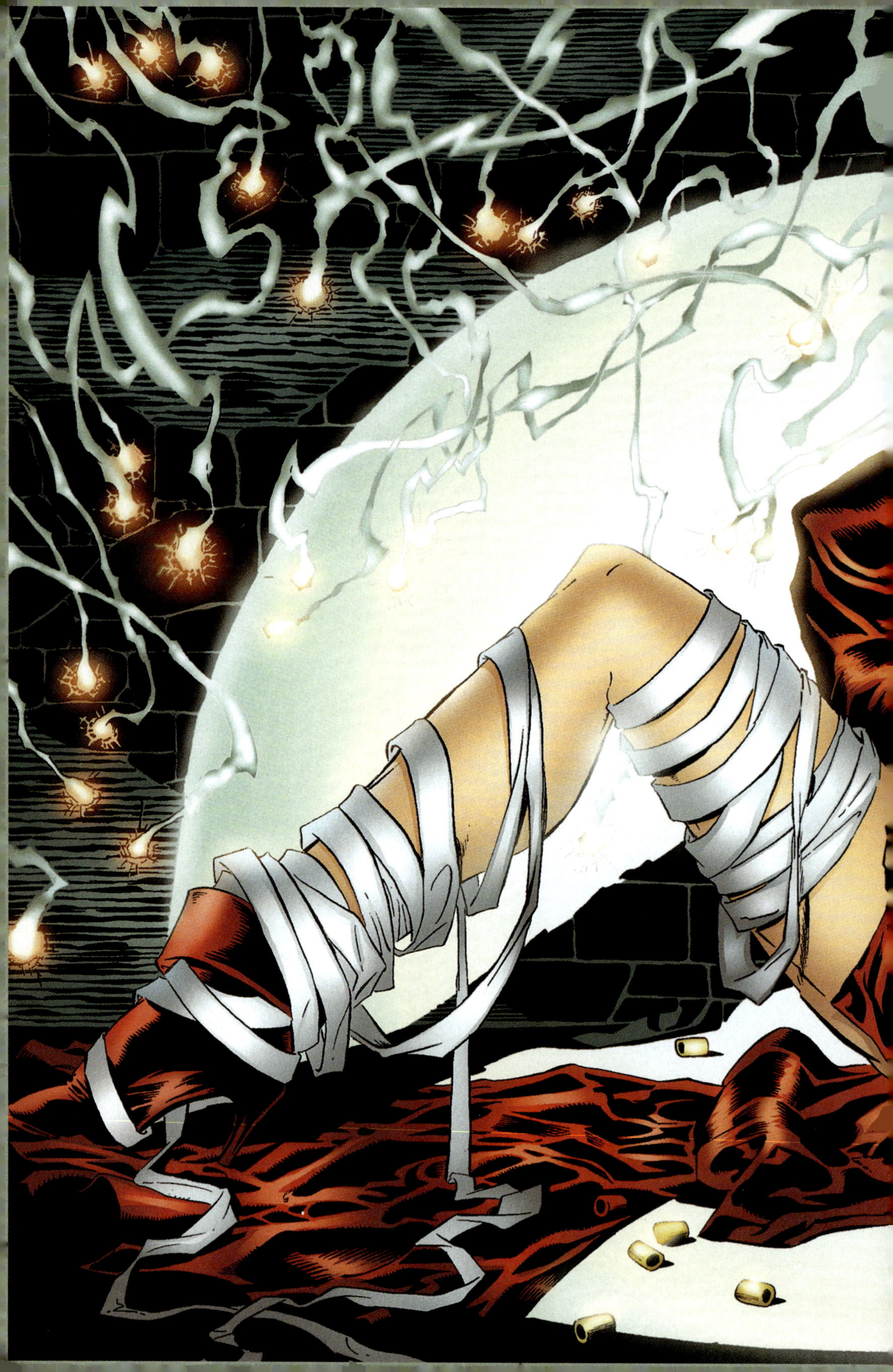

Cover #1 by Joe Quesada & Jimmy Palmiotti

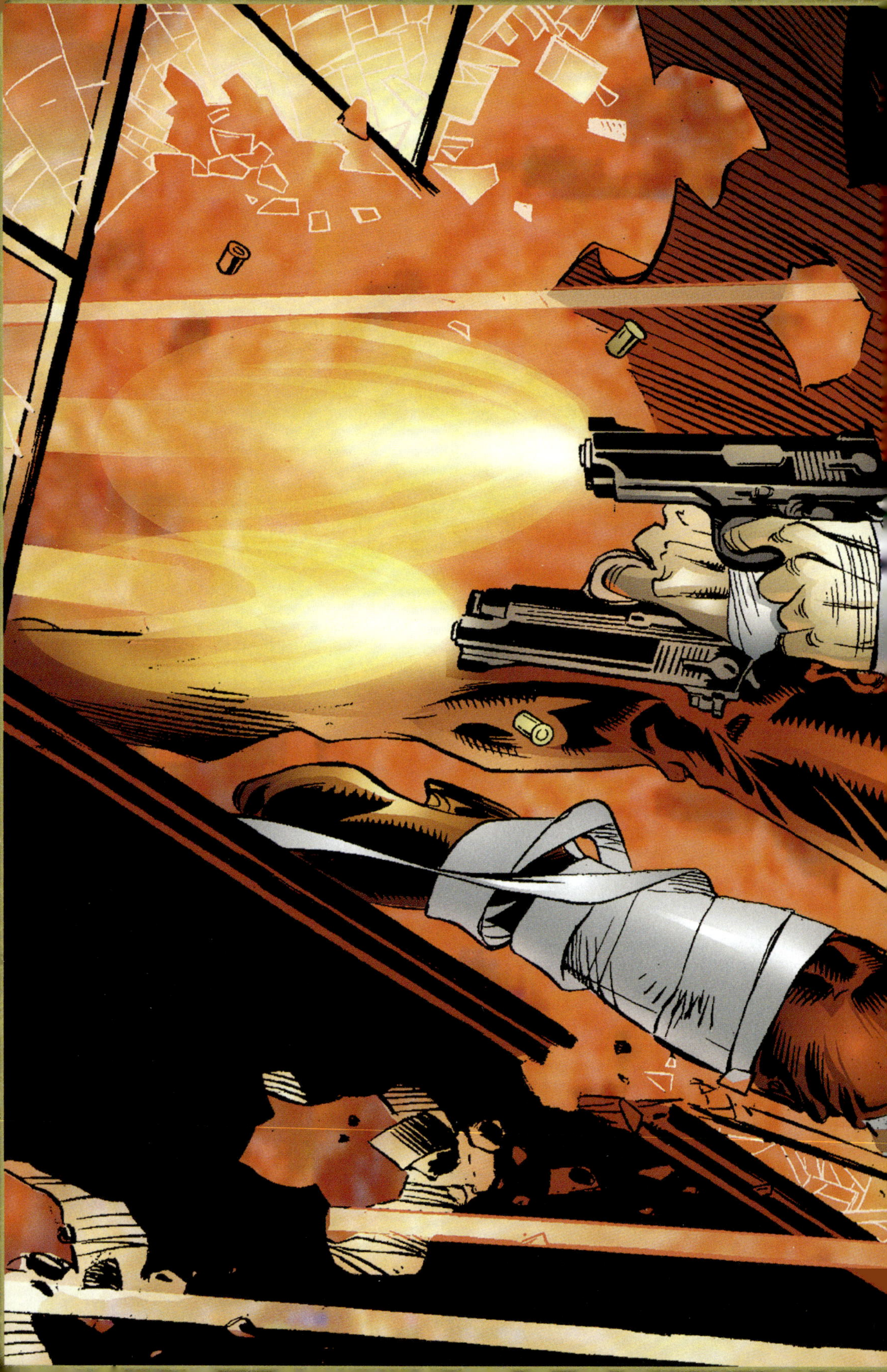

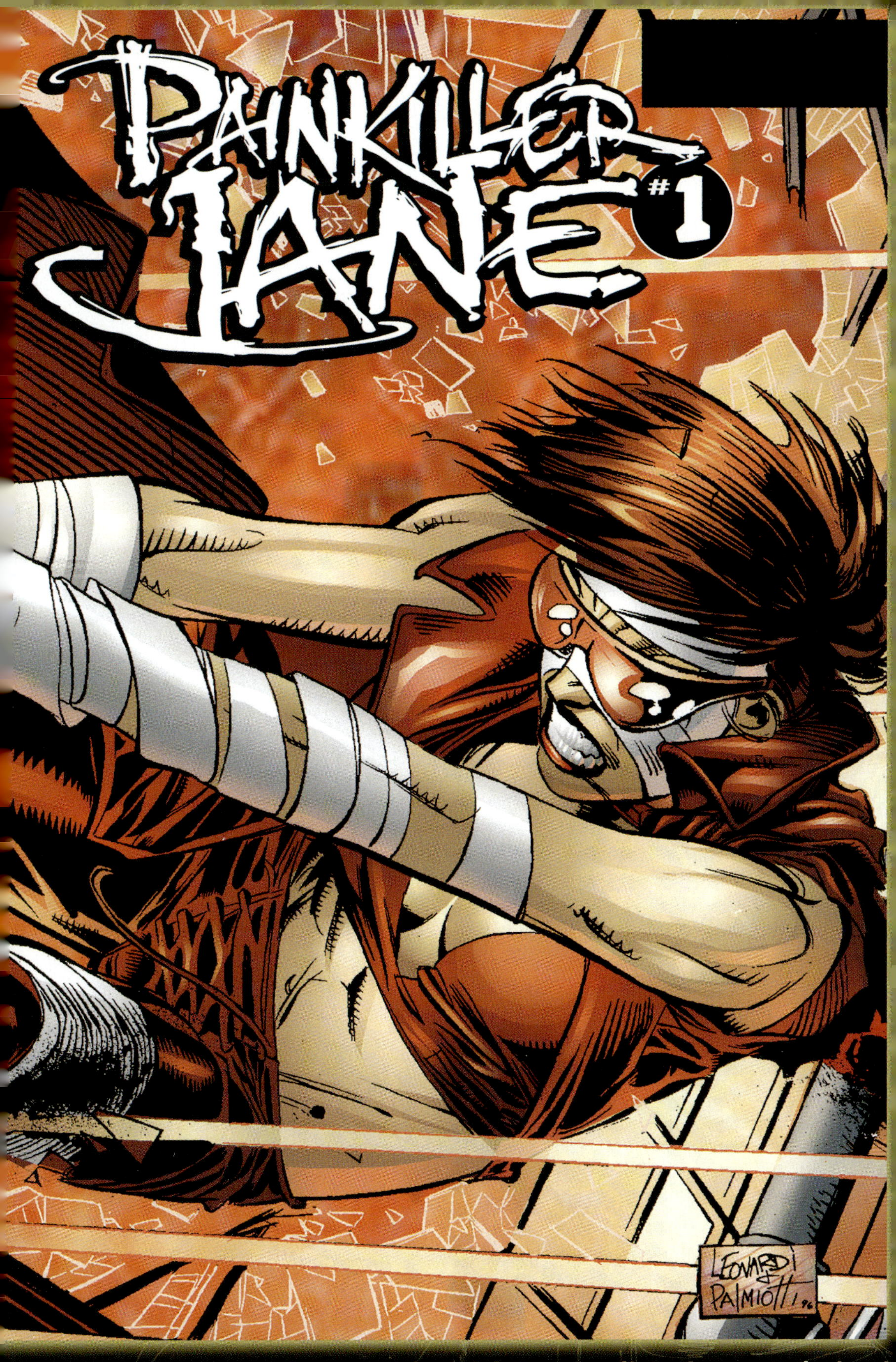
PAINKILLER JANE
#1
LEONARDI
PALMIOTTI

Cover #1 by Rick Leonardi & Jimmy Palmiotti

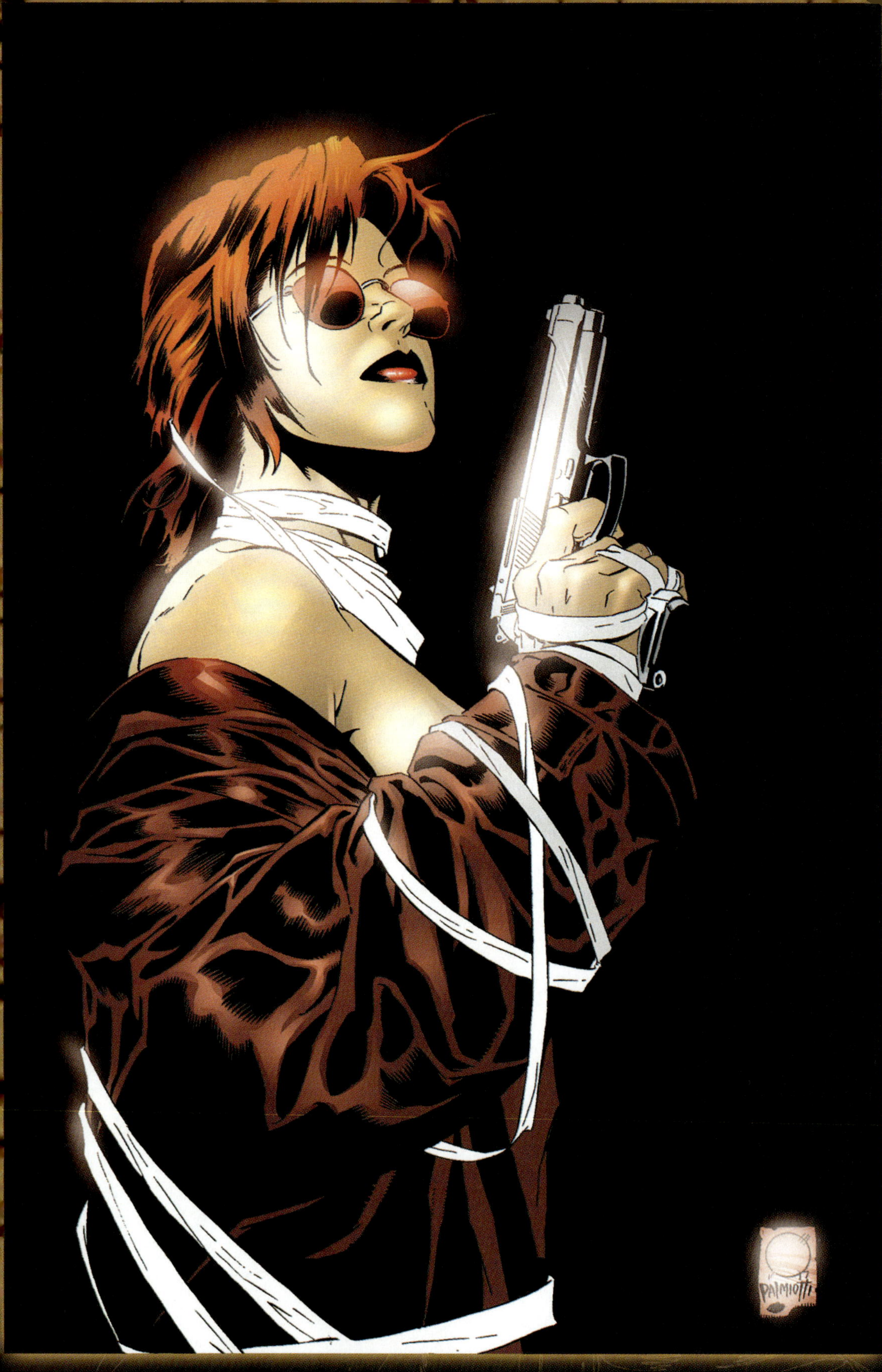
PALMIOTTI

Cover for #1 by Joe Quesada & Jimmy Palmiotti

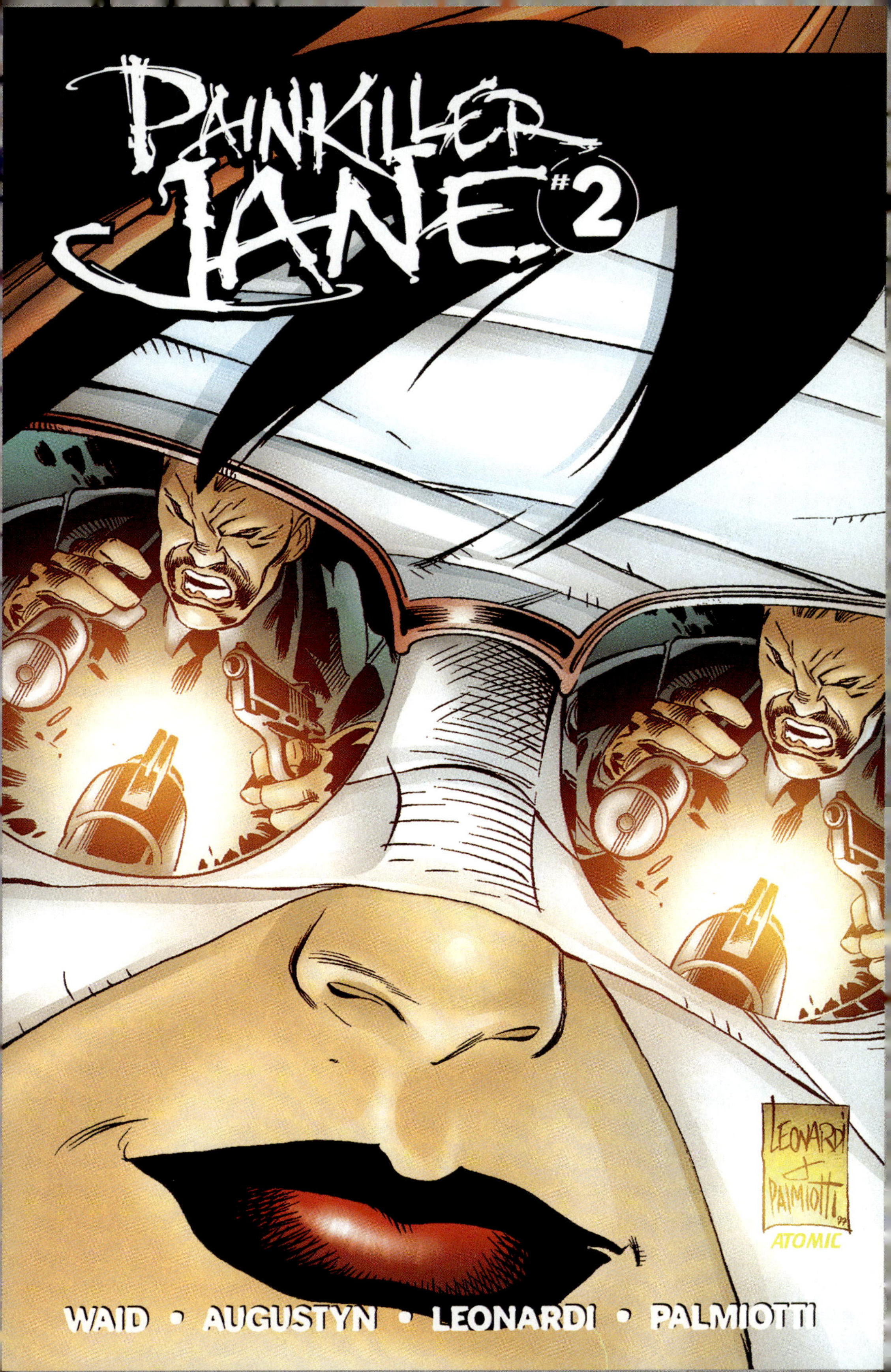
PAINKILLER JANE #2
LEONARDI & PALMIOTTI 99
ATOMIC
WAID • AUGUSTYN • LEONARDI • PALMIOTTI

Cover #2 by Rick Leonardi & Jimmy Palmiotti

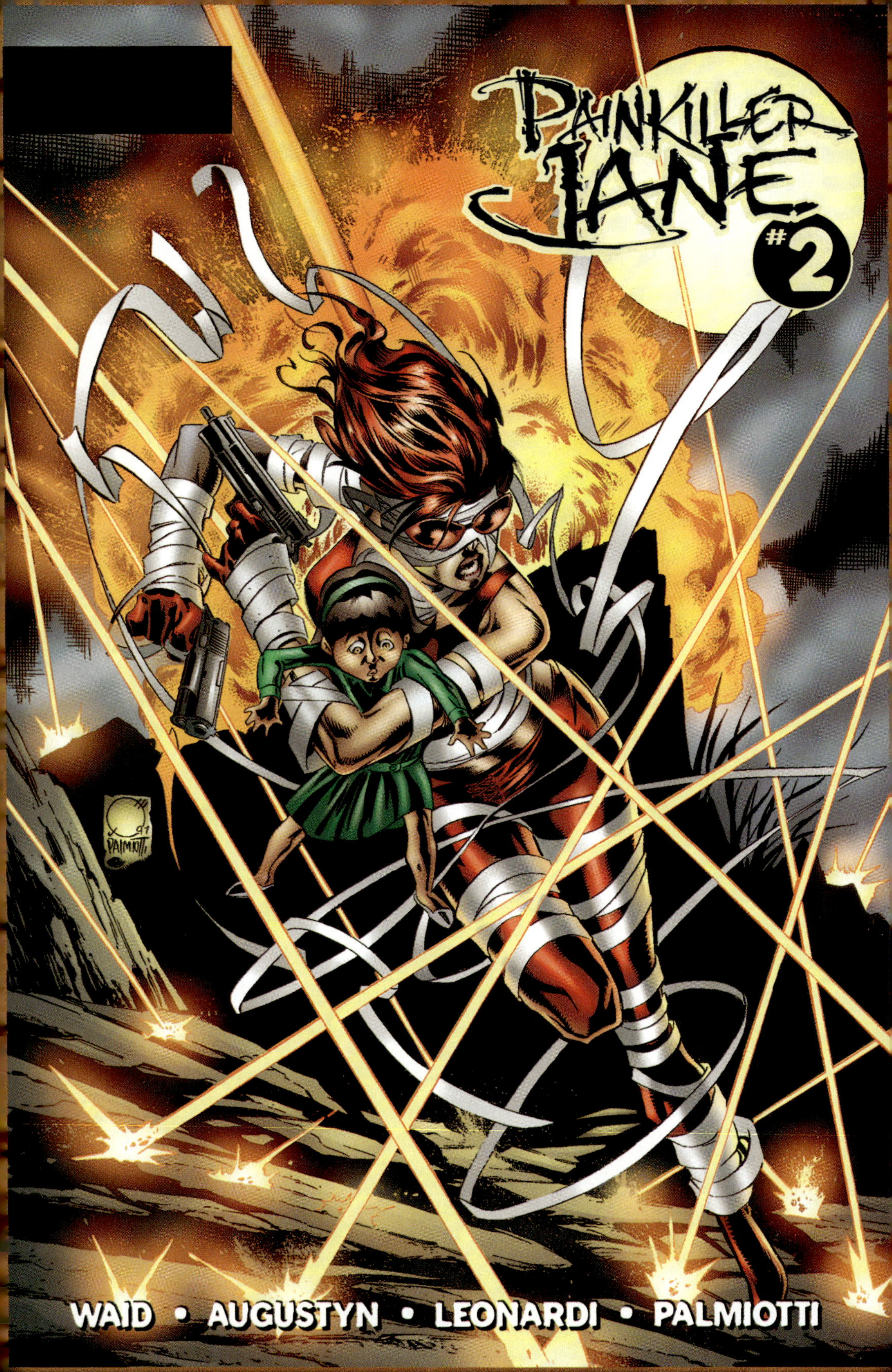
[redacted]
PAINKILLER JANE
#2
WAID • AUGUSTYN • LEONARDI • PALMIOTTI
Cover for #2 by Joe Quesada & Jimmy Palmiotti

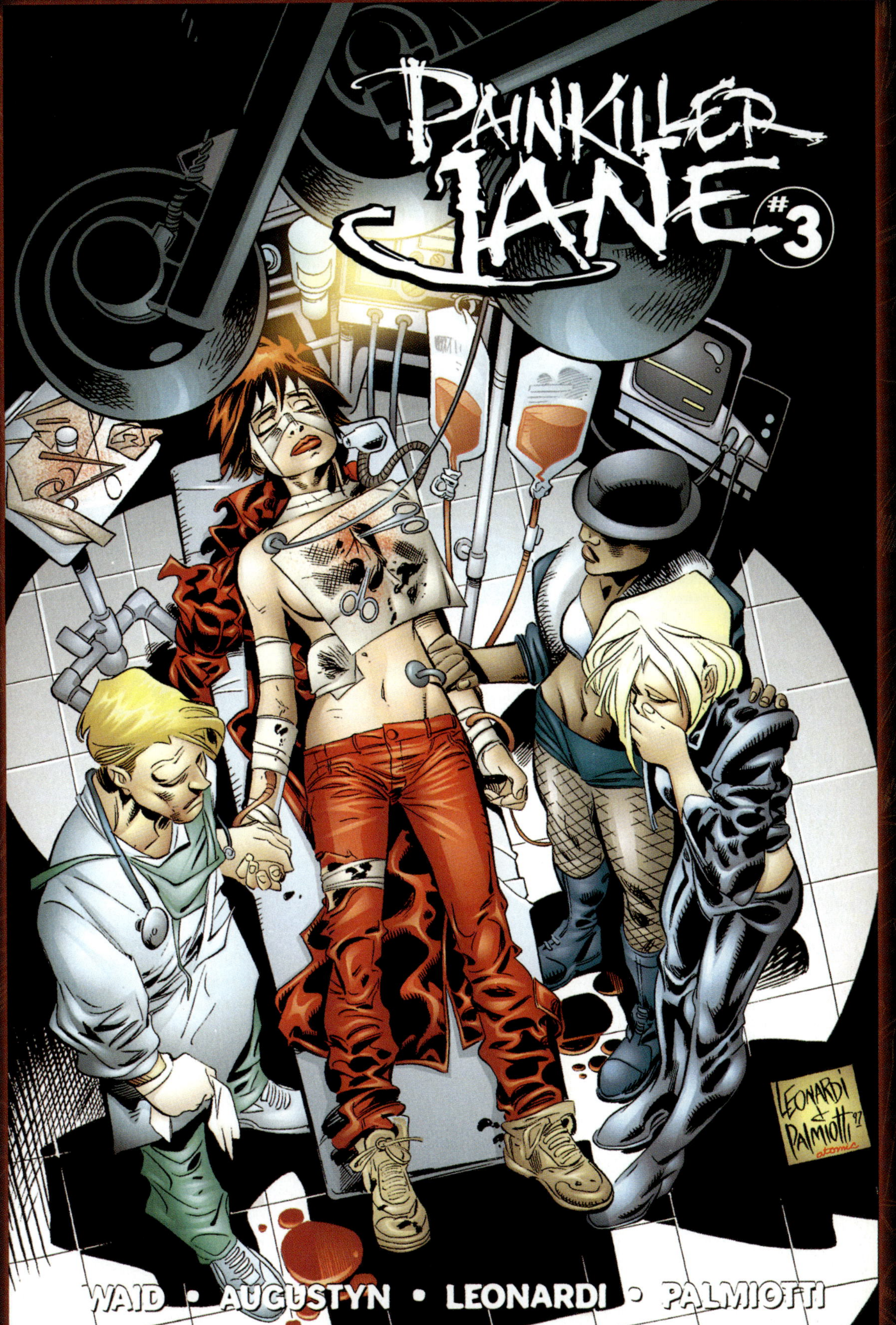
PAINKILLER JANE
#3
LEONARDI & PALMIOTTI '97
WAID • AUGUSTYN • LEONARDI • PALMIOTTI

Cover for #3 by Rick Leonardi & Jimmy Palmiotti

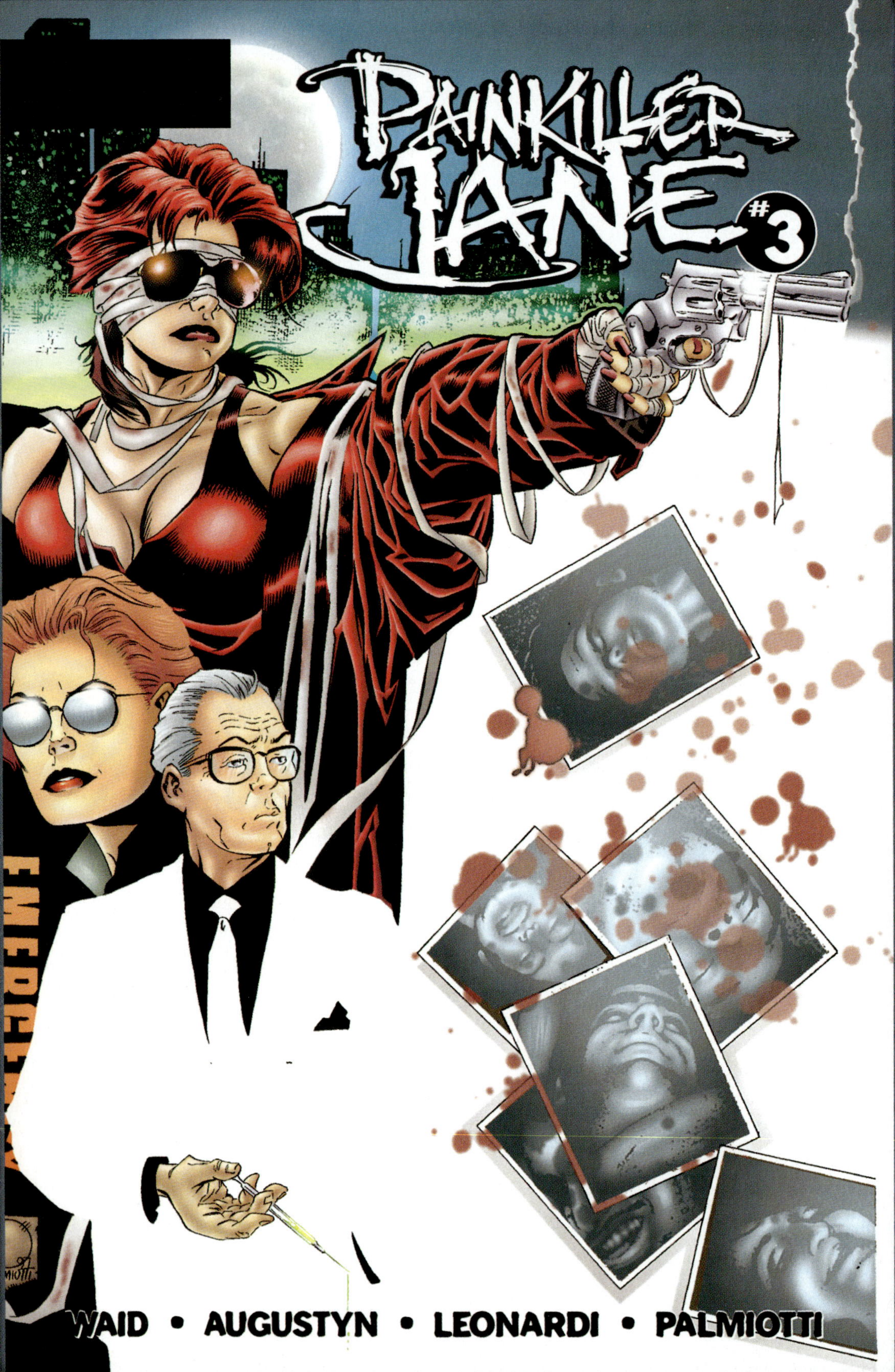
PAINKILLER JANE
#3
WAID • AUGUSTYN • LEONARDI • PALMIOTTI

Cover #3 by Joe Quesada & Jimmy Palmiotti

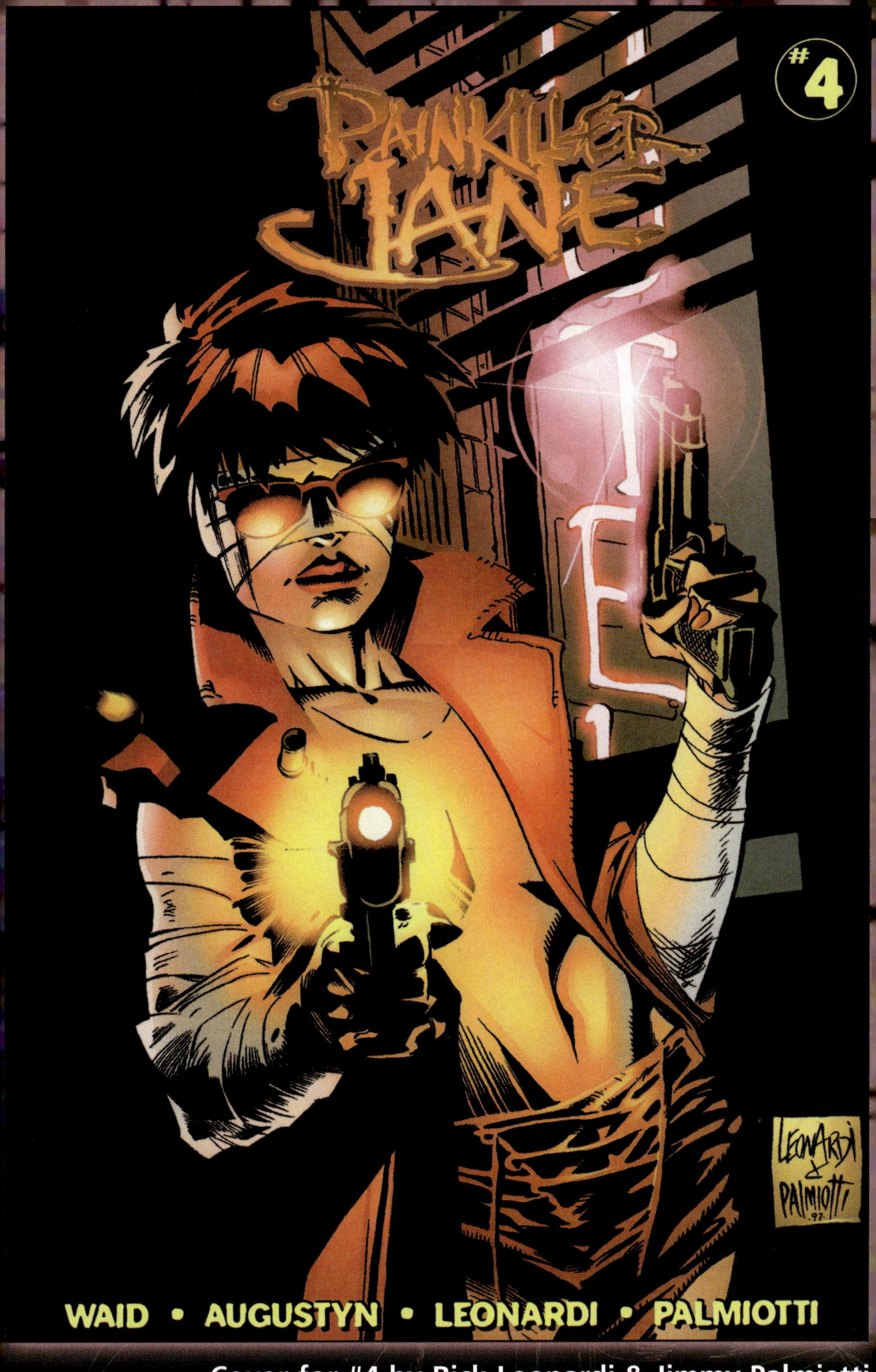
#4
PAINKILLER JANE
LEONARDI & PALMIOTTI '97
WAID • AUGUSTYN • LEONARDI • PALMIOTTI

Cover for #4 by Rick Leonardi & Jimmy Palmiotti

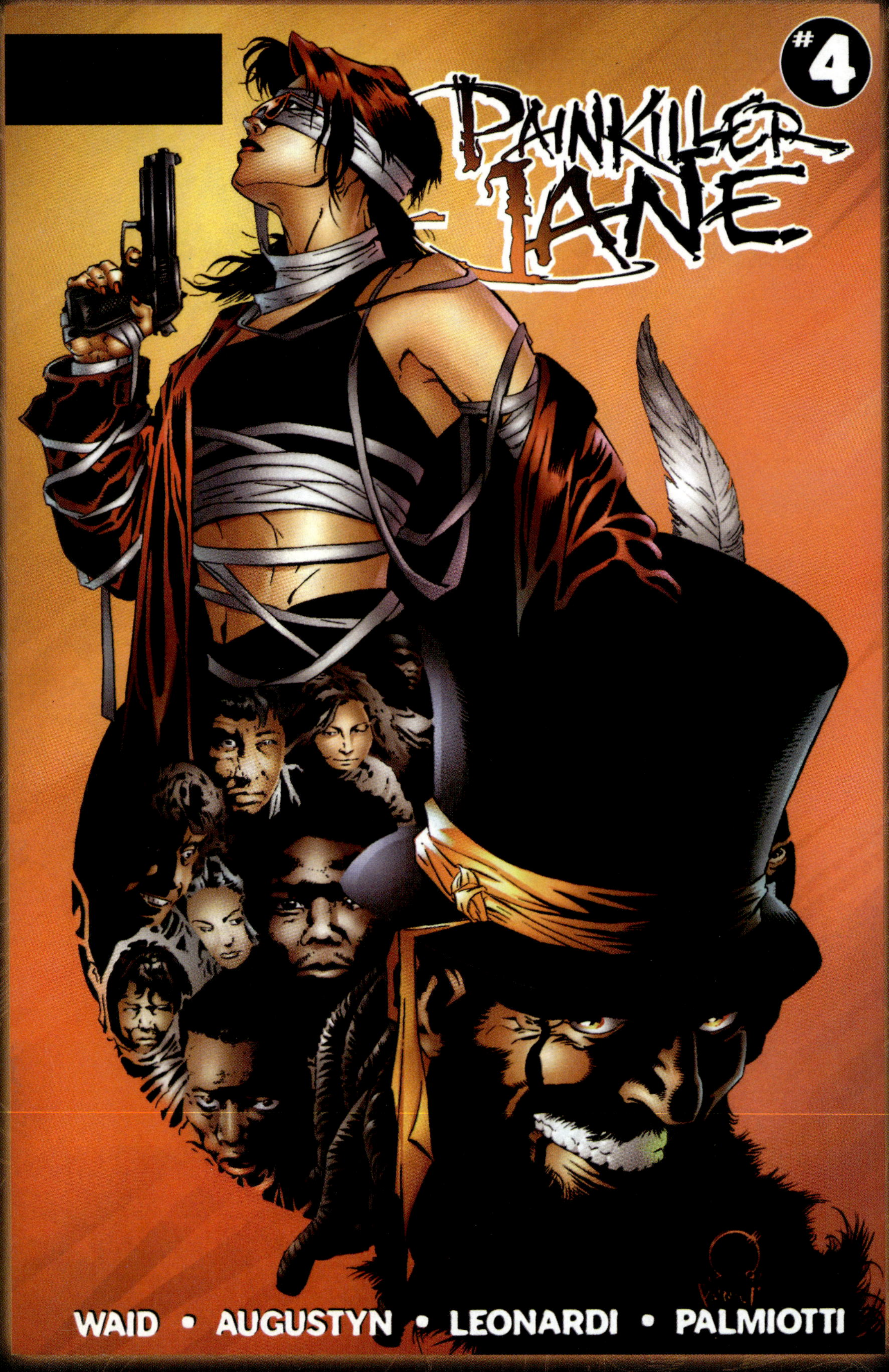
[redacted]
#4
PAINKILLER JANE
WAID • AUGUSTYN • LEONARDI • PALMIOTTI

Cover #4 by Joe Quesada & Jimmy Palmiotti

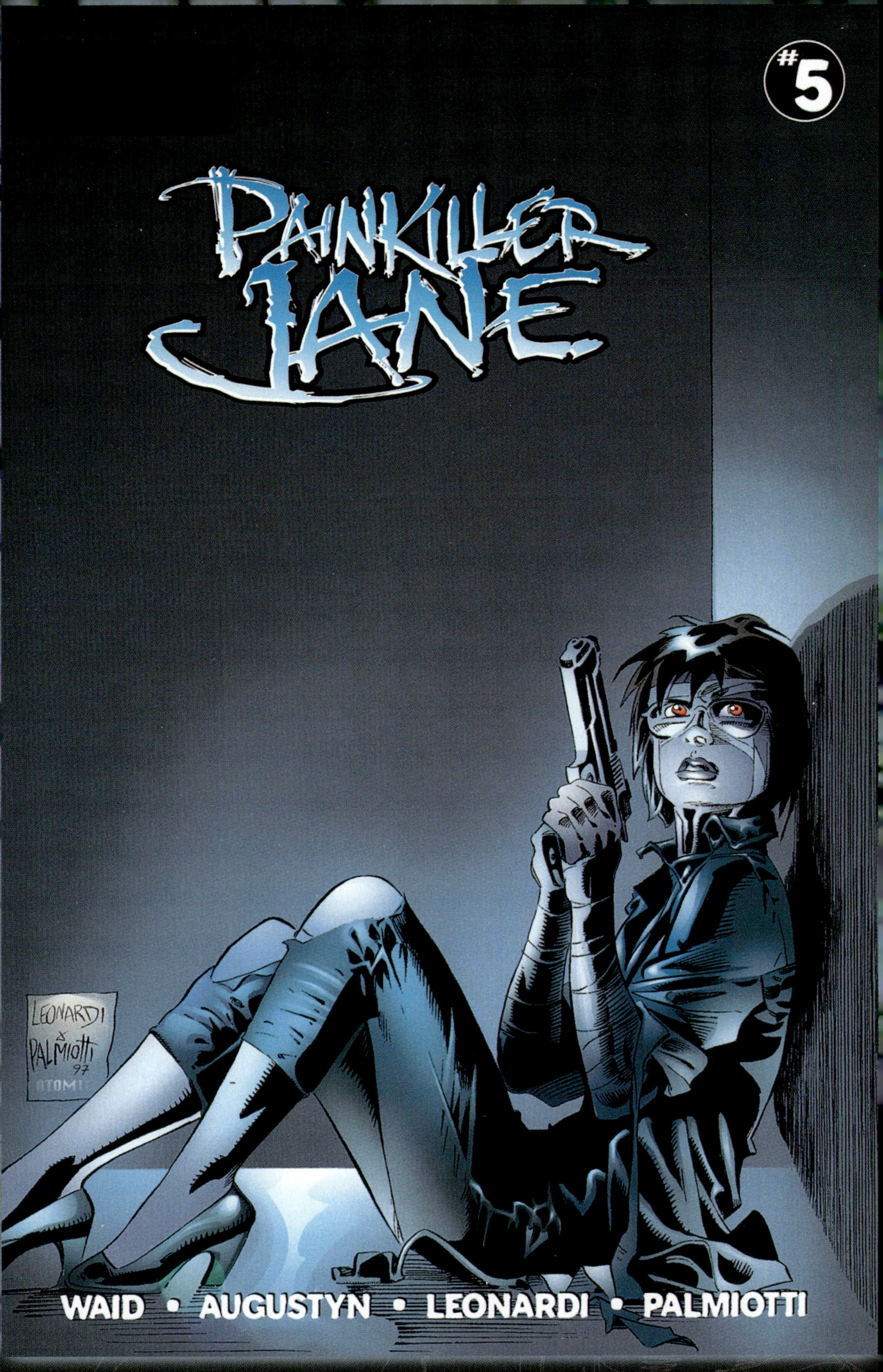
#5
PAINKILLER JANE
WAID • AUGUSTYN • LEONARDI • PALMIOTTI
Cover #5 by Rick Leonardi & Jimmy Palmiotti

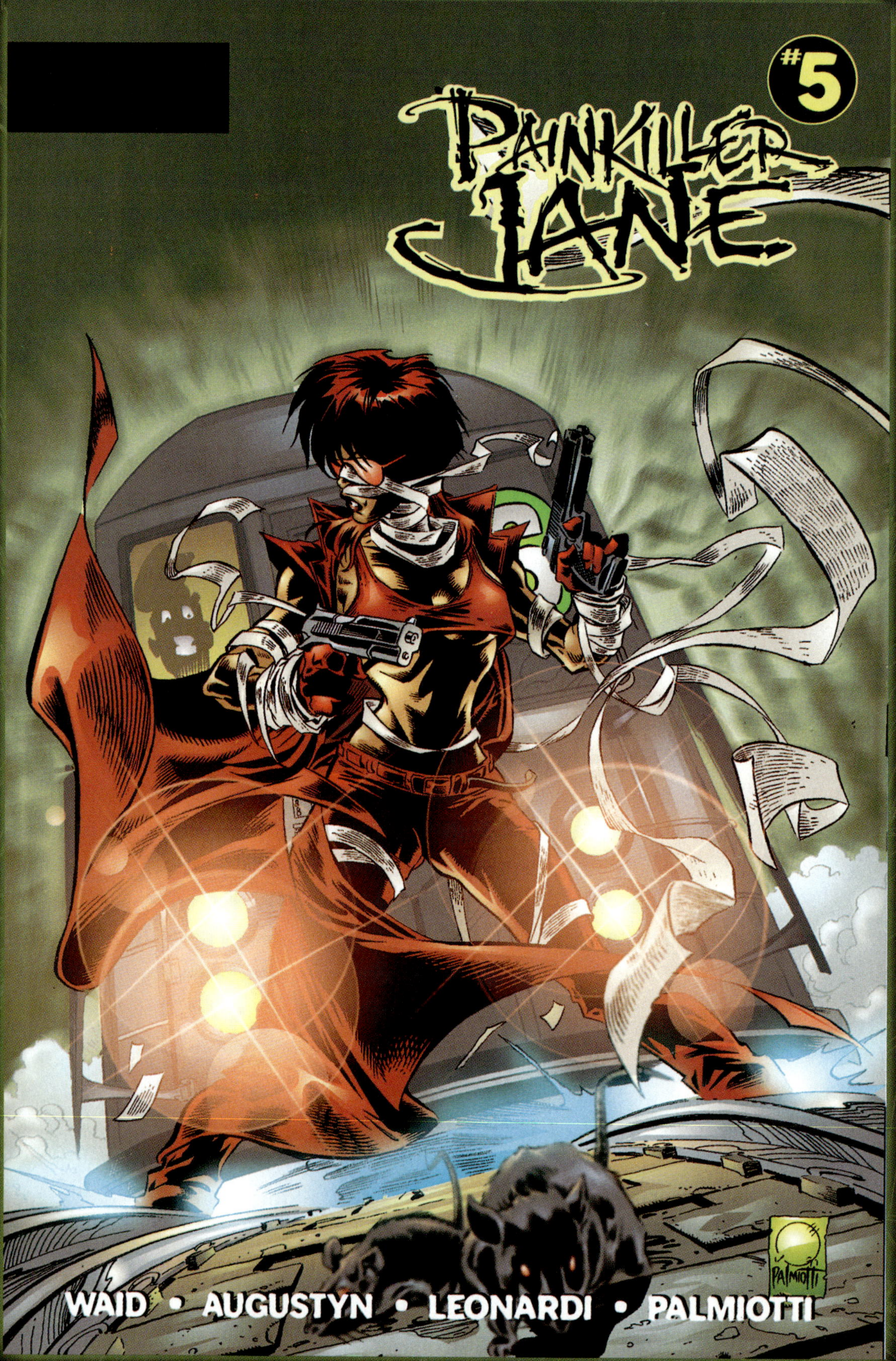
[redacted]
#5
PAINKILLER JANE
PALMIOTTI
WAID • AUGUSTYN • LEONARDI • PALMIOTTI

Cover #5 by Joe Quesada & Jimmy Palmiotti

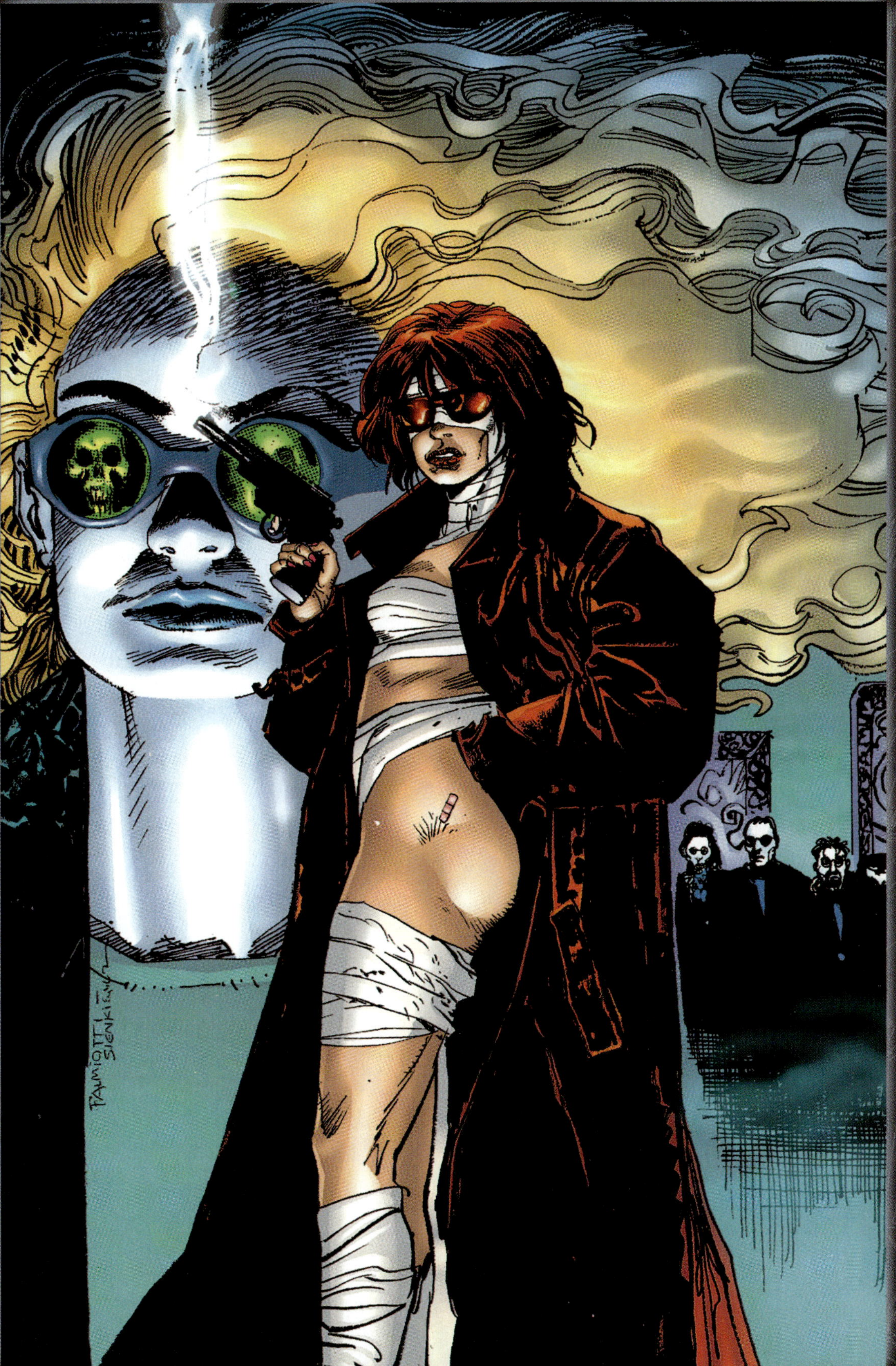
PALMIOTTI
SIENKIEWICZ

Pin-up by Jimmy Palmiotti & Bill Sienkiewicz

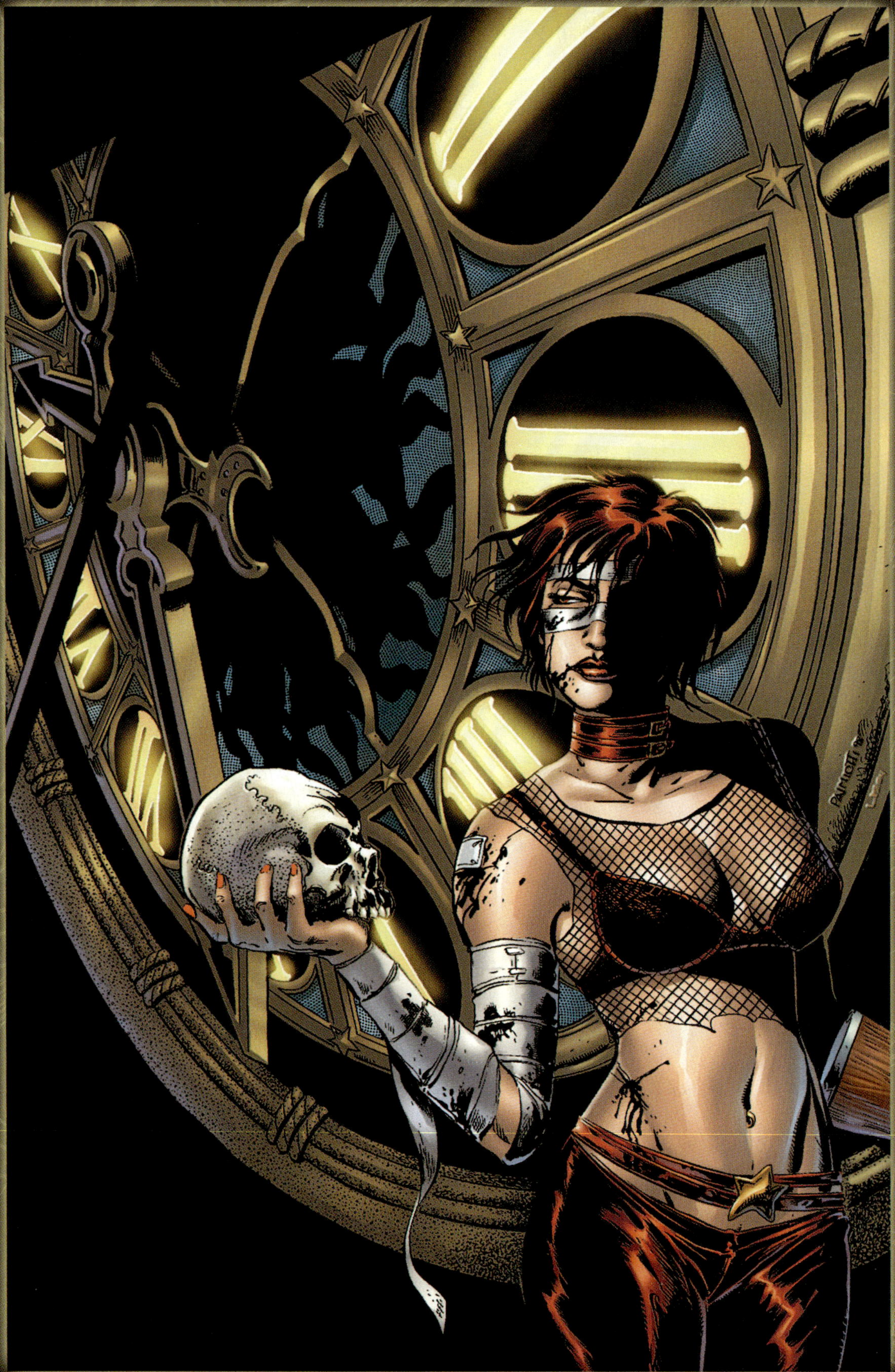

Pin-up by Jimmy Palmiotti

PREVIEW OF DYNAMITE ENTERTAINMENT'S

PAINKILLER JANE™

STORY BY:
JIMMY PALMIOTTI & JOE QUESADA

WRITTEN BY:
JIMMY PALMIOTTI

ART BY:
LEE MODER

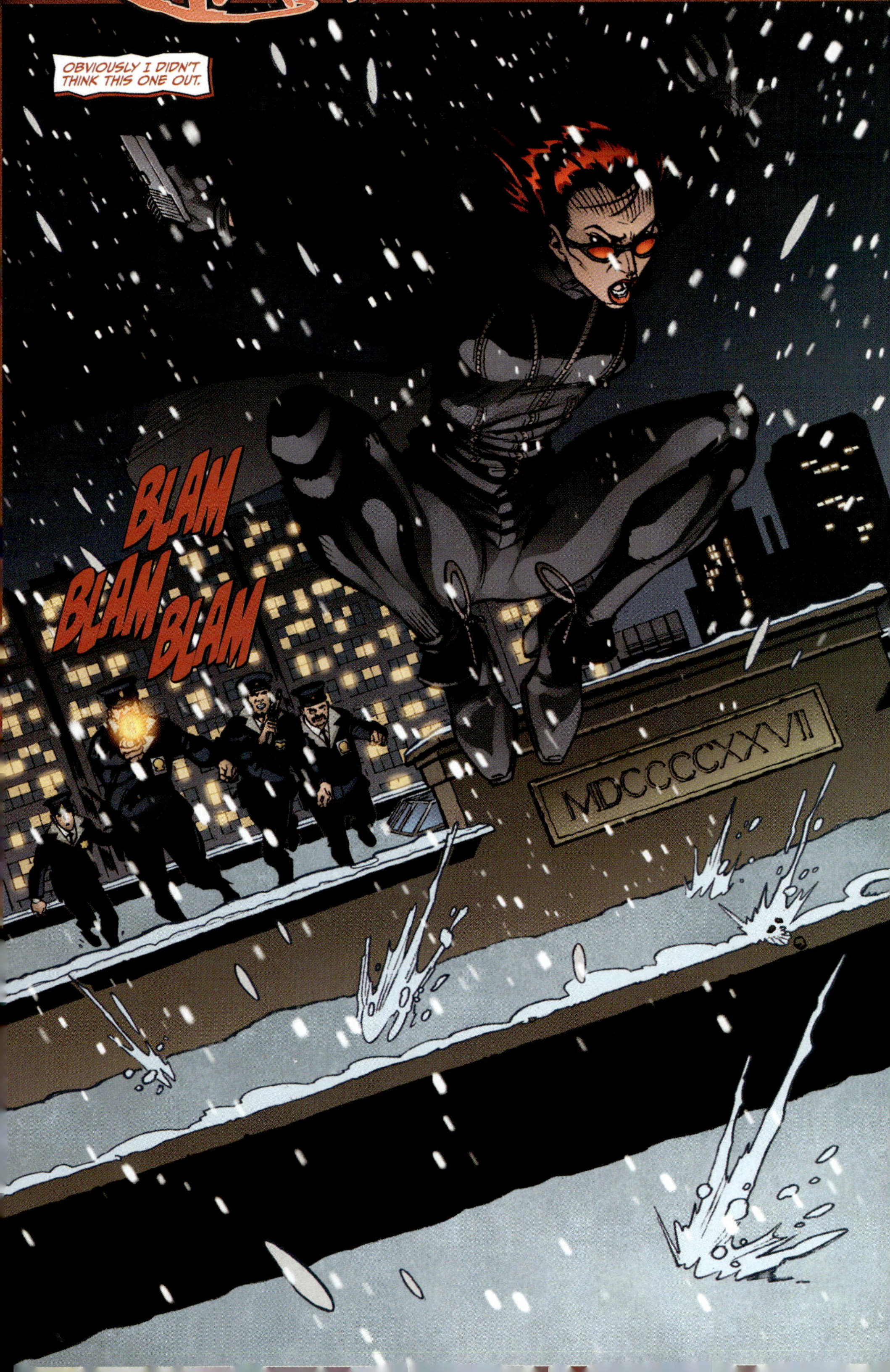
OBVIOUSLY I DIDN'T THINK THIS ONE OUT.
BLAM BLAM BLAM BLAM
MDCCCCCXXVI

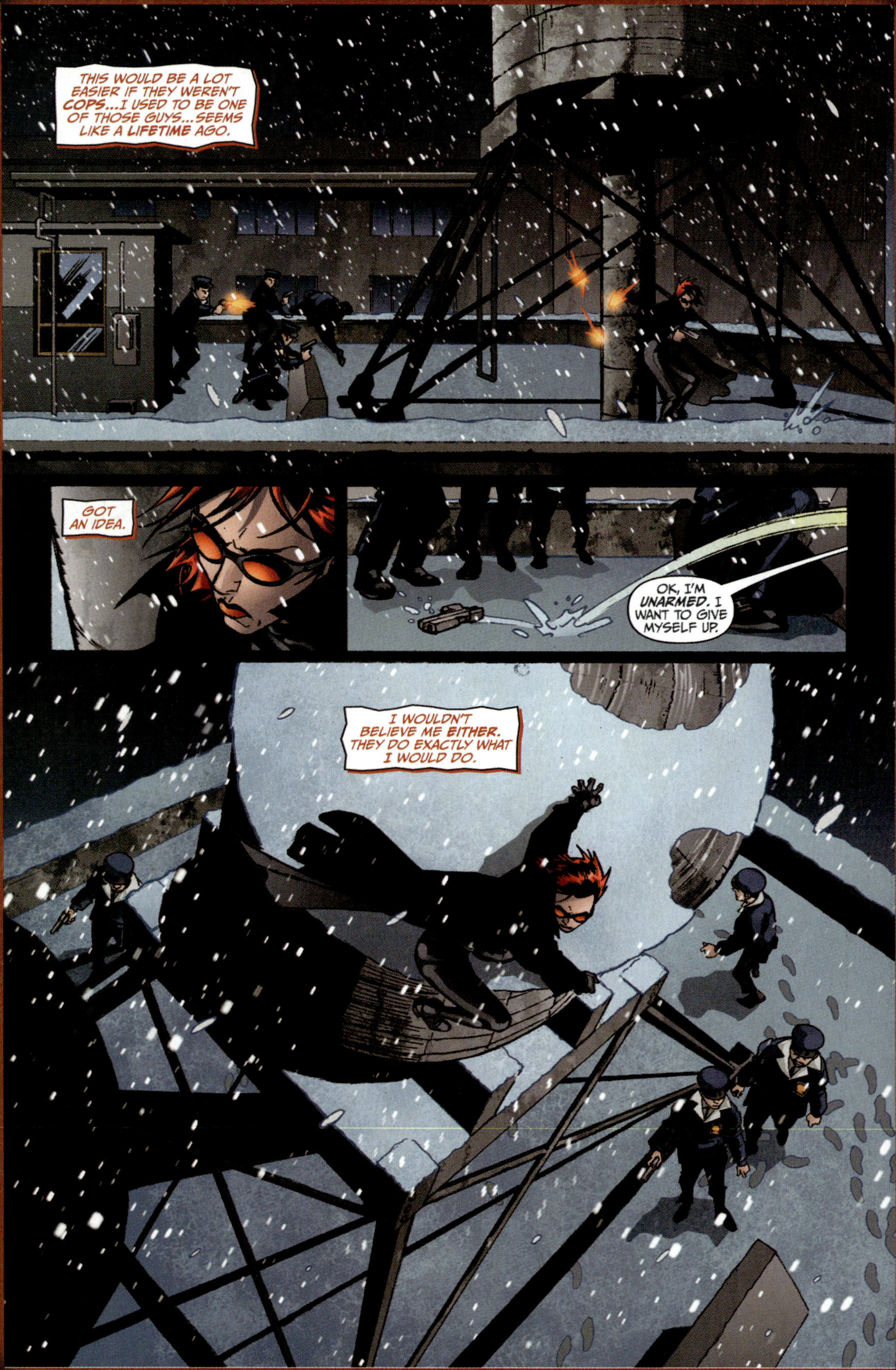
THIS WOULD BE A LOT EASIER IF THEY WEREN'T COPS...I USED TO BE ONE OF THOSE GUYS...SEEMS LIKE A LIFETIME AGO.
GOT AN IDEA.
OK, I'M UNARMED. I WANT TO GIVE MYSELF UP.
I WOULDN'T BELIEVE ME EITHER. THEY DO EXACTLY WHAT I WOULD DO.

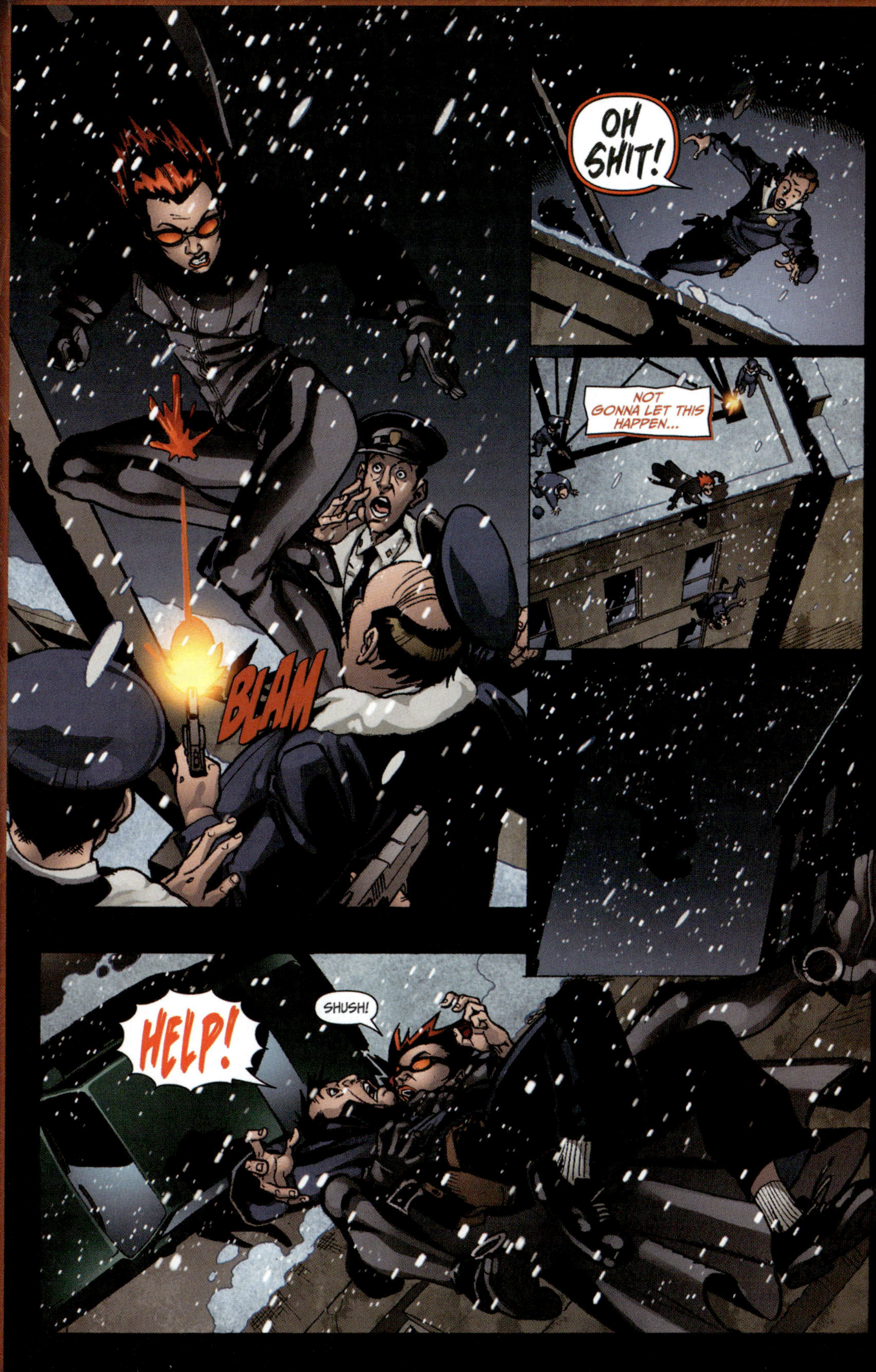
BLAM
OH SHIT!
NOT GONNA LET THIS HAPPEN...
HELP!
SHUSH!

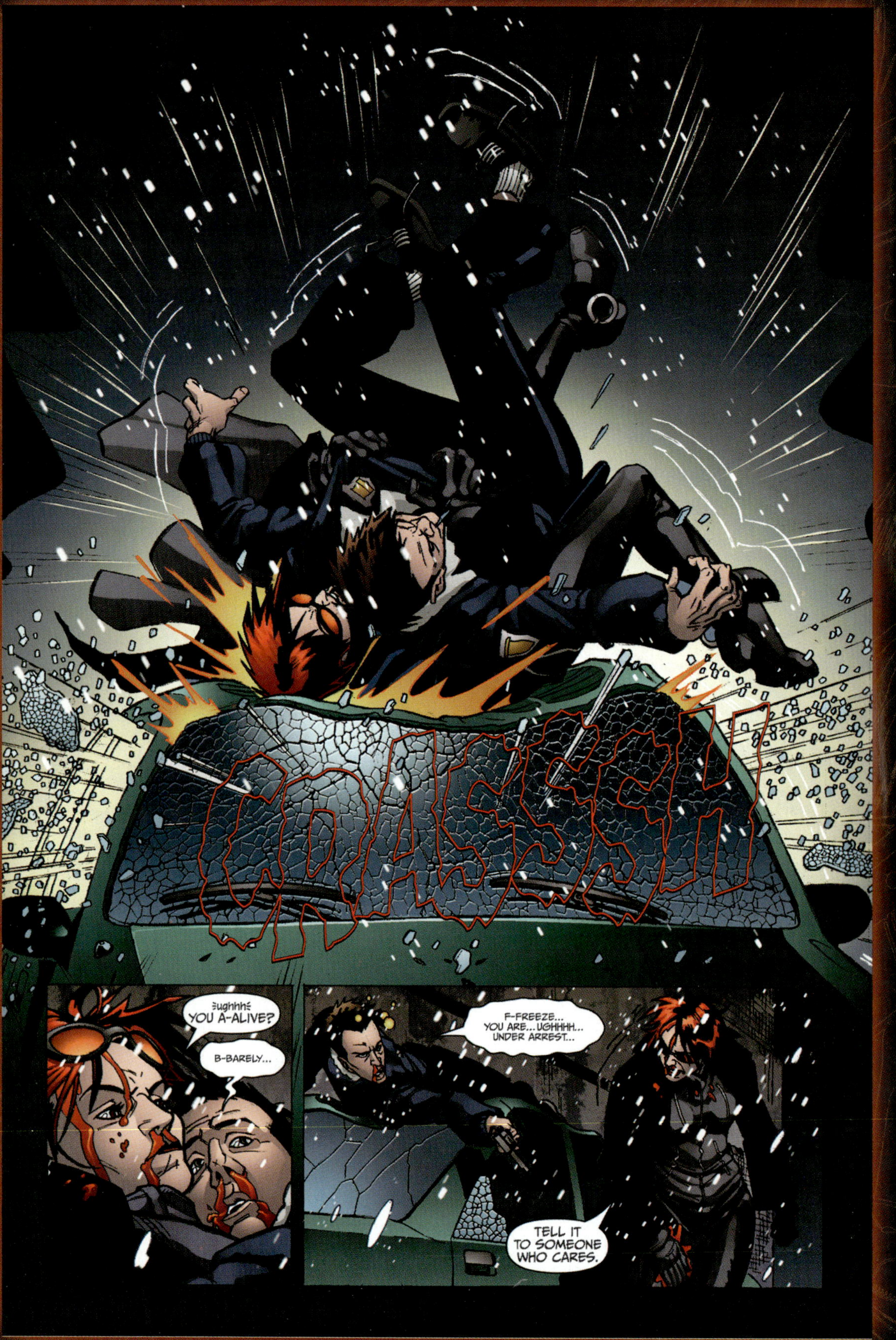
CRASSSH
ughhh
YOU A-ALIVE?
B-BARELY...
F-FREEZE... YOU ARE...UGHHHH... UNDER ARREST...
TELL IT TO SOMEONE WHO CARES.